The Ruler of the Toys

by

Deborah DR Kralich

The Ruler of the Toys
A Lt. Sinclair Plate in Sand Waves Mystery
II

Copyright 2015
TX0008216721

Deborah DR Kralich

First Printing
Published by Ruskras Corner
The United States of America

The Ruler of the Toys, A Lt. Plate in Sand Waves Mystery
ISBN 978-1-942542-05-6
Second in a series
All cover designs, artwork and photography by Deborah D Russo, copyright 2015

Are You Washed in the Blood of the Lamb lyrics by Elisha A Hoffman 1878
Text excerpt from *3748 A.D. The Return of the Cat* copyright 2015 by Carl S. Kralich, used with permission.

The Ruler of the Toys

Cast of Characters

Tamica- Her destiny triggers passions based on love, hate and prejudice. Her innocence haunts those who loved her.

Chief Brecken- Top officer in an exclusive community, Sand Waves, he has to deal with his senior detective being in love with a suspect.

Minyak Tanem- His nickname, Mink Coat, belies his past as a war vet. Now a reserve policeman and private bodyguard, his obsession with a potential future Commander-in-Chief defines his present.

Edward York- A senate candidate, now may be his time, the Presidency his destiny. Cool and smooth like silver, his true passions are few, his memory long but not without mercy.

Regina York- Glamorous, she plans to be a cultured First Lady. To accomplish this, she must survive plots to seduce her away and plots to kill her by likely and unlikely persons unimpressed with her charm.

Grace- Left behind by Edward, she has no desire to see him President, even less to see his new wife First Lady, especially as Regina is one of the few who knows deadly secrets of Grace's past.

Lt. Plate- His love for Grace complicates investigating a murder at her former home behind the gates, where he finds they both must seek shelter. Ultimately divided loyalties must give way to a final choice.

Officer Skaar- Searching for a killer, he is introduced to the world of the rich and famous, and blamed when their antics go wrong.

Dr. JD Apixza- He knows what it means to creatively serve the ultra famous who have enticing vast riches to spend. The rewards are great, the risks are unexpected and the results are sometimes fatal.

Stark Wynter- He has experienced the magic of Hollywood and knows it for what it truly is. A big star turned studio head, he's just a fan when meeting sports heroes, a man when meeting sexy women.

Clip- Over 70, he spends his time reliving his past amid baseball memorabilia. When he feels a present call for action, he's physically ready and stronger than even he realizes. But his mind is less agile.

Chloe- Her suicide many years ago left broken hearts and a trail of sadness that seemingly ends at the feet of the baseball legend.

Ray- A native East Texan, he is a baseball fan with a pickup truck and a rifle, out of place in the rich sophistication behind the guarded gates.

Forrest- An upcoming candidate for African American leadership he is Ray's natural rival, especially since they share tastes in women.

Rev. Frenel- A civil rights leader, he hopes his trip to Sand Waves is personally and professionally productive. He does not foresee murder.

Rev. Skrale- Descended from Scandinavians, established in Sand Waves as a humane and sensitive religious leader, he nevertheless is surprised when an African American legend calls on him for help.

Amelia Mattworks– Needing no doctor at 94, her mind eclipses all a half century younger. But after murder, she is not too proud to call on both pastors and the police for assistance as time grows short.

The Witch- She would claim she had more effect in one action than any doctor can boast of over a lifetime of modern medical treatments.

Corina– Great-granddaughter of the legendary jazz singer, their relationship is anemic. She finds her companion from among the men who slip in and out of the estate at all hours of the day and night.

Burress- Driver to the stars, he nevertheless fits the description of the burglar, a stalker as well. And he is in proximity when terror strikes.

Ken- Rev. Skrale's son, he has not yet had a calling and he is also of the same description as the burglar. And he has a way of showing up in unexpected places at unexpected times with unexpected people.

Daphne- Her unexpected appearance is all about the money and sends shockwaves. Her subsequent actions appear reckless, dangerous and inexplicable to Plate, her mission to serve badly misunderstood.

Roscoe- Still mourned after years, great love of Amelia's life, he would have left the world of jazz, forsook fame and fortune for the sake of his family but cruel fates weighed him down and took his life.

Doreen Darbell- Star of old Hollywood, now aged and frail, mentally incapacitated, she has no idea that deadly actions she took some 30 years ago are still reverberating and may cost more lives.

The Sand Waves burglar- He is getting behind the gates, over fences and up trees, then vanishing with skills of a 1980s Houdini. Is he a lover or a killer or both? Can Plate catch him before anyone else dies?

January 1983

Prologue

Tamica unconsciously ran her fingers over her smooth olive cheeks as she debated which path to take. She had made a mistake. A cancerous folly, which if not cut out at the root would slowly sap the remainder of her life's blood until she became no more than a walking mannequin.

And like the deadliest of tumors, this human error gave out no symptoms until it was too late to eradicate it without risk filled painful consequences. Life altering consequences.

And not just her own life would be affected, also Corina's and that of an unknown. An unknown innocent...

Tamica drew her hand away from her face and held it out before her as though about to seek help from some invisible companion. Instead, she twisted the diamonds adorning her fingers and yellow spurts flashed in the dim light of the hallway.

The back door was just ahead. Beyond it- freedom.

She had the hard antique gold doorknob against the palm of her hand when the sly creaking behind her caused her to stiffen. Though she lived in this huge house, though she had claim to some rights within it, and though it was well protected against those whose claims had to be kept without, the noise chilled her heart and simultaneously her face flushed.

As if ignoring the sound would make it go away, she pulled the door wide without even turning her head a fraction, without even darting her eyes sideways.

She stepped out into the chilled air. It a short time it would be dark. There were interior lights in the mansion she had just exited. Expected interior lights in the cottage that was always lit. They were mere mute glows in the dusk. Only a single outdoor gas yard light, among many that usually lit the huge landscaped back yard, was working tonight. Wondering only briefly why, she decided the lighting failure worked in her favor. She could make her way across the grounds with less fear of being seen and stopped.

The air was crisp and refreshing, unlike the oppressive stale air in the house, and its vibrancy seemed to hold the answer to all of her problems. She picked up her pace as her spirit revived.

The initial sting of the projectile and the sharp sound of the bullet hit her consecutively. She lurched forward. The brisk air now contrasted to the rapid searing inside her. Hot tears filled her eyes clouding her vision and she was conscious of being unable to completely close her mouth, yet also of being instantly rendered beyond uttering a coherent sound.

Like a stubborn marathon runner, she forced her long legs to carry her faster away from the danger behind as if by escaping it she could outrun the damage done inside her. Painful fire erupted in her abdomen and reached her breast she tried to rub herself to put the fire out as she forced on, now panting a sprint runner's breath. Then ahead she spied the cooling waters of the pool.

Now oblivious to the pursuing danger, only dimly alive, aware of just the burning agony inside her, she dove for the water, spreading her arms wide.

She knew nothing of the four repetitive reports that rang out behind her. Neither did she feel them as they hit their target. She felt only relief as the cool refreshing pool water quenched the fire within her as though she were an overdone sunbather plunging in the surf on a hot Sand Waves beach in July.

Then the water engulfed her, evaporated and there was only light all around her.

Provenance I

1907

All gowned in long white robes, the choir dominated the church, facing the congregation, higher than anyone else.

Hand carved wooden décor formed an intricate frame for their presence behind the preacher's podium made of simple wood. A partition behind the pulpit was just the right height to give the impression they were floating in front of the stained glass in the dimly lit sanctuary.

It was evening time but it was summer in East Texas. The air was hot and muggy, the temperature neared 95 degrees. However, this did not deter the members of the congregation from dressing in their Sunday best. The women wore long skirts with tight bodices and pouf sleeves, not just a few of which were also long. The men wore jackets, and if they owned one, a tie.

Wrists moved rhythmically, powering the hand fans possessed by nearly everyone. This rhythm was necessary so that the fans did not slap each other as they were propelled through the thick hot air.

At the front of the church, the preacher stepped aside and the guest vocalist distanced herself from the choir, coming forward to stand alone.

"This be an old song from 30 years ago by Elisha Hoffman. I think y'all will know it."

The soloist then proved she needed no accompaniment, no instrument to help her sing.

All conversation ceased and, as the young girl looked over the congregation, and as she sang, the hand fans slowly became motionless and fell against the chests as if protecting hearts.

Have you been to Jesus for the cleansing power?
Are you washed in the Blood of the Lamb?
Are you fully trusting in His grace this hour?
Are you washed in the Blood of the Lamb?
Are you washed in the Blood,

in the soul cleansing Blood of the Lamb?...
Are your garments spotless, are they white as snow?
Are you washed in the Blood of the Lamb?
Are you walking daily by the Savior's side?
Are you washed in the Blood of the Lamb?
Do you rest each moment in the Crucified?
Are you washed in the Blood of the Lamb?
Are you washed in the Blood,
   in the soul cleansing Blood of the Lamb?...
Are your garments spotless, are they white as snow?
Are you washed in the Blood of the Lamb?
When the Bridegroom cometh, will your robes be white,
   pure and white in the Blood of the Lamb?
Will your soul be ready for the mansions bright?
And be washed in the Blood of the Lamb?...

When she finished, there was silence for a full 30 seconds, then there was crying, applause, some screams and shouts for joy.

The singer blinked back tears.

"Glory Hallelujah," she shouted. "Praise God! Praise God!

Chapter 1

Twilight faded over the land and the sharp edge of night rested upon the branches of the trees. Grace waded through the deep woods to reach the large mansion through its back yard. The woods grew almost completely dark and filled with heart stopping sounds. Unidentifiable sounds.

It became so dark she had to climb a tree to get her bearings. From its branches, she could see the back yard of the York estate. Only dimly lit, it seemed particularly vulnerable to intrusion if the forest was breached.

She climbed back down.

The thick brush scraped and stung, and her hands bled from grasping vines and limbs to clear her way. Edward York grew this forest believing in it more than modern security to keep away intruders. Then, turning her out, he gave shelter to Amelia, Ray and Tamica, with Corina as well. Thinking he could protect them from any type of aggressor.

This was one invader that could not be stopped.

Grace fought the forest until she won. She reached the redwood fence at last. Eight feet high, the smooth board defended the landscaped grounds from the assault of the brush. Remembering all that had gone on before inside its boundary, Grace paused to rest. She had walked those grounds in great joy, then in great despair, and finally had left to start a new life away from the memories, away from the past, outside the patrolled gates that let only the sanctioned few into this world.

And those left in this mansion were once all she had in this life. They had thrown up a barricade to keep her out. They feared her. They had good reason to.

She would not be kept out tonight.

She scaled the fence with the agility of a gymnast and landed on the other side like a cat. She immediately crouched down low and surveyed the yard. All was quiet and now dark, except the interior lights in the one cottage that were always left burning. They contributed too little to the illumination outside. The exterior gas lights were turned off.

Not a lamp was burning inside the house.

Grace wondered why.

Unlike the untamed woods surrounding it, this yard was a model of conformity. Every tree and shrub sat obediently in place on a perfect carpet of weedless grass. The water in the oval pool shimmered in the hazy moonlight.

Grace crept closer. Clouds slipped over the moon causing even less light and a fog like haze. A huge tree limb had fallen into the pool. A blot on this landscape of perfection. Instinctively, Grace bent over the pool for a better look. It had been her pool at one time, designed by her and swam in with joy in bright sunshine.

At that moment, clouds broke beneath the moon. Its light became sharp.

Grace stepped back, frightened for the first time.

There was no limb, but rather a dark haired woman swaying gently with the pool circulation.

Grace clasped her arms close to her chest trying to keep panic down. If she dashed into the pool, she risked exposure. But could she let the woman die?

Her mind seemed to be pulling itself apart. She had come here to destroy, but could she murder by default? She knelt at the edge of the pool for a better look. The panic evaporated. Visible bullet holes clearly indicated the woman was beyond help.

The dead woman floated nearer and nearer to Grace.

Grace grasped the edge of the pool with one hand and leaned over the water. In an agonizing strain, she managed to grab the dead woman's hair and lift her face from the water. She glimpsed it only an instant before having to let go or fall in.

Anger filled her. It was not Regina. The dead girl was Tamica.

Grace collected herself. Only four of them in the main house now. Amelia, Edward, Regina, Ray. Oh yes, Corina, five. It was so easy to forget about Corina. In one of the cottages, small homes located within the huge back grounds, Amelia's doctor lived and, if she knew Edward, he still had Mink Tanem in residence in one of the

11

others.

And Tamica was dead in the pool.

Grace realized she had chosen the wrong night for revenge. She would be accused. How wonderful for Edward and Regina that she should stumble on this scene. She would become Regina's scapegoat, her fool. As she had before.

Grace struck the palm of her hand with her fist. There was nothing to do but go back the way she came. Even then, her coming would be an asset. A trail in the woods for the police to find.

Suddenly there was a noise from the house. A pale light shone behind the back door. A figure holding the light came out onto the lawn. Grace, watching behind the shrub, felt all her resolve entangle and collapse like a house of cards.

A few feet away in the moonlight stood the man who had once been her only ambition. In two years that she had not seen him, he had not changed. Still slim, his silver hair sprinkled with left over blonde strands, he walked like a king. Watching him, Grace felt herself falling into a void all over again. Edward had that effect on people. Magnetism so strong that all the vocabulary from which reason was drawn broke apart into a scramble of letters which jumbled incomprehensibly, then disintegrated into dust.

Grace's head began to pound and the pain caused a cold chill to flash through her. Her head felt full and the pain grew sharper, deeper. She had a suicidal desire to slice open her skull and remove the sharply aching piece of her brain that tormented her. She clutched at her hair and pulled it. Then she pushed the palm of her hand against the pressure. Her scalp was hot as a fever.

A thousand moments they could have shared, did share together, consummated in her mind as one vision, a lovely haunting vision...

A sun kissed day, with warm gusty winds, with happy waves slapping heartily at the shore. Edward laughing as he pulled the kites, two at once, one with bright letters reading 'his', one labeled 'hers'.

Edward. Bringing the wind with him as he crossed the

beach, barefooted, barechested. Falling back before reaching her as the kites soared. His face sobering as he competed with the wind gusts to become the ruler of the toys...

Grace wrenched her mind from the memory, a process so sharp that her eyes burned as though invaded by strong harsh soap.

Then uninvited thoughts flooded her mind as if in retaliation for suppressing any memory of him.

If I could persuade him to take me back, could I stand the pain and torment of loving him again? Of having to milk the moments I spend with him for all the responsiveness I could draw from him? Of always being on edge when he is in the house, looking for clues in his every word and action that he was about to abruptly detach?

Thinking up clever little tricks to keep the other demanding people from intruding?

For everyone was constantly pursuing him as a friend, coworker, relative, father figure, lover, confidant, adviser. And he was not able to distinguish between them, who was important and who was peripheral. He was always giving a little to all, never satisfying anyone. At first, it had been easier for him that way. Attending a little to each hungry relationship. Never having to quite give all.

Then he grew taut, constrained from the constant worry of satisfying a mob. And the burden of those least willing to tolerate a ration of a relationship. Those who abandoned him by not settling for only a piece of him, often were the very important pieces in the structure of his pre-planned life.

From Grace he had demanded total freedom for himself, but for her to always be there waiting and accessible. So when he inevitably snapped and Regina attached herself to him like a leech, he had willingly deserted all for her complete authority and she kept him from the world he felt he had failed.

Grace felt a wave of empathy for Regina and it made her blood run cold. With the constant pressure, what a burden it must be on Regina to keep him surrounded.

Like living with a lover who never ages while you grow older every day.

Relaxing in her memories, plotting in her daydreams, anticipating his voice, Grace let her guard slip a second and leaned into the bush, snapping a twig.

Edward became instantly alert as though he, too, had been on guard. This was so unlike him. Grace watched him with growing confusion.

He stepped in the direction of the noise. Not two feet from her, he halted, listening intently. Grace held her breath. But he decided there was nothing and turned back to his chore.

Grace felt a momentary pang of frustration with him, despite her relief at not being spotted. He always gave up so easily. Always so quick to determine danger nonexistent when it was really there all the time, waiting for an opportunity to strike.

She reached inside her breast and withdrew the gun. But as soon as she touched it, a sensation of helplessness washed over her leaving her weak.

Can I live a life beyond him, without hope of ever holding him again?

She shook, attempting to dispel the moment of doubt before it took hold and grew like a paralyzing virus within her.

She stood up.

"Edward." She spoke both softly and distinctly.

His back to her, some kind of container in his hand, he froze. His shoulder blades sharpened in the pale light from the porch.

"Regina?" he questioned in a small hesitant voice and Grace almost killed him right then.

Nevertheless, she wanted to see his face. She wanted him to see her face.

"Edward." She repeated the name and took a step towards him.

"Grace!" He turned so quickly he almost stumbled. At once, she let the gun drop to her side and slip into her pocket, the immense joy on his face and gladness in his voice rendering it impossible for her to ever harm him in any way.

Made even the mere picture of harm coming to him unbearable.

"Grace!" he said again, setting down his container "Is that you, Grace? Are you real? Or have I gone totally mad at last?"

"It's me."

They ran to each other and as he pressed her to him, she felt such relief from pain and tears came to her eyes and ran down her cheeks although she was not crying.

"Grace, darling," he said, intensely massaging her head so that her physical pain vanished as well. "I can't believe it. I can't believe I'm holding you."

For a long minute she let him caress her in silence, clutching his broad shoulders, her cheek against his bare chest, thinking she had forgotten in such a short time how incredibly strong he was. Then as though remembering that they were not happy lovers reuniting after a long separation beyond their control, he drew back from her in the same slippery way he always used to when he wanted to retreat but not lose any ground.

"Grace," he whispered, with urgency uncharacteristic of him. "Grace, what you doing here? Why did you come here tonight? Of all nights?"

"Did you know what's happened? Are you responsible?"

"I'm responsible for many things, Grace. I swear to God I am. And I never knew it before. But I prayed I might see you one more time before tonight. I thought my prayers were denied. I thought it was too late to ever see you again."

Grace turned away from him. "Then you killed her?"

"Not yet." He drew his breath sharply.

She looked at him puzzled. "But she's-"

"Grace," he said, grabbing her by the shoulders. "You've got to get away from here. You mustn't stay here. You mustn't or I can't- Grace, I must end what I've begun. So you have to leave now."

"I can't leave the way I came," she said, frightened by the strangeness in him. So unnerving to see such strangeness cloaked in familiarity.

"Grace, why tonight? Not tonight! Grace-" The instinct that told him when not to press her, when to let her go, and when she could put her words together, stopped him from continuing.

15

"Edward, don't put me off."

"Come in the house. They are all inside, still asleep. The dogs are loose in the front. I don't know how I will get you out, but somehow I will."

"Edward," she said, still desperate, still stalling. "Who is in the house asleep? Who is here tonight besides you?"

"Grace, seeing you has given me a last moment of joy. And a fraction more courage. I need my courage tonight. But you know how fleeting my courage can be sometimes."

"What do you need courage for?"

Tears came to her eyes. If he saw her cry, the situation would only worsen.

"And, Grace, remember not what a fool I am, but how I once loved you. Promise me that?"

"What's happened?' What were you pouring on the ground?"

Her foot sideswiped the fallen container on the ground. She bent to it. It was tilted over and fumes rose up. She coughed. Foggily, she identified the liquid in her mind. Gasoline.

She turned questioningly to Edward, only to find him once again characteristically rigid, only his eyes, darting from her to the container and back again, revealed uncertainty.

"Trust me, Edward. What is going on? That was gasoline. And it looked like you were pouring it out."

"Yes," he said shakily, trying too hard to be calm. "I was just pouring out this gasoline. In my own yard."

"On the shrubbery?"

"All right." He was defensive now. "I suppose it is obvious to any fool. Especially to you. You're the furthest thing from a fool I know." He sighed. And it took him a few moments before he could speak again. When he did, he had such fierceness on his face that she, for the first time ever, was doubtful of his sanity.

"I'm going to burn this house down. Down," he said. "I want to see it in ashes."

Grace caught her breath. "Because you killed her?"

He ran his hands through his hair in frustration. "Not yet."

"But she is dead." Grace was puzzled. *Why is he insisting he has not killed her yet?*

"I'm going to kill her. I'm going to kill her tonight. Moreover, you can't stop me. It's already too late."

Grace's heart fell.

"She's not worth it. Why didn't you just leave?"

"Don't ask me why. I can't tell you. I can't tell myself. Why I cannot just leave? I don't know. But I want you to go. You must not be involved."

"Edward," whispered Grace, keeping her voice low because she was afraid if she allowed it to rise, it would become hysterical. "What was Tamica to you? Were you having an affair? Why did you kill her?"

Edward stared at Grace as if seeing her for the first time. "Tamica? What? What you talking about?"

"Who is in the house Edward?" Grace persisted.

"No one but those who live here. Amelia, Regina, of course, and Ray and Tamica and Corina." His voice was even with the patience he had always used in their marriage.

She cleared her head, thinking rapidly and speaking even faster. "What about Amelia Mattworks' doctor? And Mink? Is he here?"

"No, they are both gone. Apixza is on a short trip for a study or something. Mink is on vacation, some rest before the campaign season beings. It starts early now you know."

"What happened? Start from the beginning. Tell me everything."

He sat down on the porch steps. She, having learned some patience from him, knelt silently beside him.

"I told you. I'm going to kill Regina. I've got it all planned out. I'm ready."

17

Chapter 2

Edward's voice broke. Grace saw his rigidity for what it was, the hardened mind about to suicidally force itself to snap.

"I'm in the middle of it right now. I've been planning this for months. Now that Amelia Mattworks lives here, and Ray, Tamica, and Corina, I am never alone. So I had to plan their escape as well as Regina's death."

"I don't understand. How can life be so bad for you? I thought you had everything you wanted, except- well- and I thought Regina would soon give you that."

"Regina gives nothing. Mink Tanem drove me hard enough before I married Regina. Together, they are brutal. Every hour of the day is planned. The only reason I am free tonight was because the anti-abortion rally was canceled in Houston. And I am afraid Ray cannot take much more of her either. He's going to snap, if things continue the way they are going."

"How can she run your life? Unless you let her? And what has Ray got to do with it all?"

"Ray's marriage to Tamica is failing. He wants to go on back to East Texas. But Regina will not let Ray go. She keeps him close to her like one of her dolls. People are objects to her, just toys."

"That sounds like the Regina that I know."

"She is not normal. She is a social maniac. She and Mink Tanem aspire daily to extract every ounce of flesh they can from me. I can't take it anymore. I gave her prominence in this life. I'll pay for her death. I'll die with her. I'll pay for my sins. You mustn't be a part of this. You must go and let me be. Let me do what I have to do."

"You can't do this. No one else is going to die."

"Grace, I've already started. I can't stop it now. Tonight I drugged them all. Once I set the fire, I'm going to carry Amelia to safety, then drag Ray and his family clear. Regina and I are going to die in the fire. I still have my social vanity. As you used to call it. It will look like I died heroically trying to save everyone. I don't want the world to know I committed murder and suicide."

"Edward, I came here tonight to do the same thing. I came

here tonight to kill Regina. Seeing you daily in the newspapers, every night on the evening news. You and Regina on the cover of every magazine in the supermarket. I couldn't take it anymore. That should have been me on the cover of the magazines. I was going to kill her. Maybe I was even going to kill you. If that were possible. I don't know. But I am coming to my senses."

"It's too late for me to come to my senses. This was my last can of gasoline."

Grace almost smiled. The recent gasoline shortage still lurked in the back of everyone's mind, no matter what the circumstances.

"You're not going to die. I'm not going to die. If I'm going to murder, I'm going to get away with it. There's no reason to kill more. Let's just go. Let's get away. Leave Regina to account for Tamica."

"What?"

"She is in the pool. She's dead."

"I haven't killed Regina yet. What are you talking about?"

She took his arm and led him poolside. At the sight of the woman in the water, Edward froze. Then he embraced Grace protectively.

"I did not do this, Grace. I swear to God."

"Who would kill Tamica?"

"No one. She was the only one of us that was not hated. Well, the only one besides Corina, a child. Tamica never wronged anyone."

"Tamica was always just a bystander, always in the wrong place," said Grace. "Someone must have mistook her for Regina. There is almost no light out here. What's happened to the lights?"

"I turned them out, so no one would see me setting the fire."

They had walked back toward the back door of the house by then and the strong smell of gasoline took Grace's breath away.

"We need time," she said. "This gasoline must evaporate soon. We need time."

"What are we going to do?"

"Did you kill her, Edward?"

He knelt down on the back porch on one knee, his long arms reaching up to her shoulders.

"As God is my witness, Grace. I did not."

Provenance II

1918

Western Union

DEEPLY REGRET TO INFORM YOU   THAT PVT FRED
MATTWORKS   CANTIGNY
INFANTRY IS OFFICIALLY REPORTED AS KILLED IN
ACTION MAY TWENTY-EIGHTH. HARRIS, THE ADJUTANT
GENERAL
710PM.

"What do they mean Cantigny?" asked Amelia's mother, after
the recipient of the message read it to her.

"I think that is where he was," said Amelia, dry eyed.

"He had no business leaving East Texas, joining up with the
foreigners like that."

"He would have been drafted anyway." She swallowed hard.
"He wanted to go and fight for freedom. He said if Americans didn't
fight, they would come here and take our freedom."

"He might not have been drafted. It might have been over
before he was. Or before he got sent there."

"That does not matter now."

"He was killed at 7:10PM?"

"No, that was the time on the telegram, why we didn't know
till now."

"So I have very little experience with telegrams. I don't read
nearly as well as you. He left a little money, didn't he?" said Amelia's
mother.

"A little. Not enough to keep our house, not enough to raise
our child. I'll have to do some kind of work. I don't know how to do
anything except sing. You know nobody is going to pay me for that

around here. You know the options for uneducated girls and women in East Texas. It's clean houses or pick cotton in the fields."

"Your father and I have six other children. We can't support all of you. If we support one grown child, even you- I know you've always been special, so different, like Carl, but there's no way- "

"I can go to Houston or Dallas. There's a new kind of music. They are looking for singers to try out in the cities."

"And how do you think you're going to make it there with the child in tow? You know we can't keep her and feed her."

"You could if I could send money enough back to feed her, pay some bills. Maybe even something for you."

"How you going to do that?"

"I got to try. I know a salesman that goes to Houston every week. He'll give me a ride. I'll get a job. I'll use the money Fred left to get started. I'll get a little something out of the house when I sell it."

"And if it doesn't work out?"

"When the money runs out, I'll have to come back then. Suppose I leave you with enough money to take care of Oleida for a month. I should know by then if that was the best way to go."

"You don't have to do this. You could get some jobs cleaning. It is not very bad. Many women do it. I did it before I had so many children. You could sing gospel on Sundays and the congregation will take up love offerings for you. They'll know you're a widow with a child. They'll help you out. I've already talked to Reverend Lentes."

"I can imagine how much they'll help me. No, thank you. You can tell the reverend I am not interested. At least for now. I'm going to Houston."

"What will I tell Oleida?"

"Here," Amelia pulled a dark book out of her bureau. The cover was falling apart. Its pages were worn but its print still bright. "Take this for her. It was Fred's family Bible. Tell her- tell her this is her heritage, she must find her nourishment there, not from me. I might as well have been killed, too, as far as she is concerned."

Chapter 3

"Listen, Edward, I believe you didn't kill her. I don't even think you would kill Regina. Never yourself. You are too good a Catholic. That's not going to happen." She knelt beside him, putting her arms around his trim shoulders.

"Maybe. What are we going to do, Grace?"

"First you're going to tell me what happened here tonight as far as you know. Then we'll call the police. Then we proceed with our lives as much as normally possible."

"I don't know. I drugged Tamica along with the others. She should have been in bed asleep. I don't know what happened."

"Maybe someone didn't get drugged tonight? Or they were drugged later. Is that possible?"

"Yes. We eat early because the cook leaves at five. Dinner had been prepared about 4:30 before she left for the day. It was just sitting and waiting for everyone to come and eat. If she does not come down, Amelia rings when she wants someone to bring her a tray. Whoever is around takes it to her. It's not unusual for one or more of us to eat later in the evening. Today, everyone was late. No one was near the kitchen but me. So I had the best opportunity that I've had in a long time."

"Where was everyone when you actually drugged the food?"

"When I checked on Regina she was deeply involved in rearranging her dollhouse and once she starts that, she never quits until it's perfectly finished. Tamica was with Amelia on the third floor. Ray was doing some repairs at Mink's cottage while he was out of town and hadn't finished yet. I don't know where Corina was. She doesn't usually eat in the kitchen anyway, just comes and gets her food and takes it back to her room. While I was alone in the kitchen, I put the drugs in everyone's food and drinks. Everyone except Amelia. No need to drug a 94-year-old. I went outside and ate my food on the porch."

"Didn't you make sure that they all came and ate?"

"They always come and eat. Why should this night be any different? As it started turning really dark, I checked on Regina and Ray. They were both sound asleep. I called Amelia on the house phone. She said she was writing something and was alone. Tamica's door was locked. I assume she was in there, also asleep. I checked Corina. She was asleep. I assumed they had all been affected by the drugs."

"You must say you were never alone in the kitchen. You must say you were out with me at the time."

"What are we going to do, Grace?" He repeated, with a half smile and she was absurdly reminded of the instance he had used those words to her in their marriage. When they were re-papering the kitchen walls and the paper ran out with one side half done.

"What was automatically going to happen tomorrow? What did you have planned, on your calendar, I mean?"

"I have to pay for what I've done. For what I was planning." He dropped his head into his hands.

"Oh, Edward," said Grace. Her practicality fueled the annoyance she felt at his guilt. "You've not done anything. I've not done anything. Just trespassing. And all you've done is poured gasoline on your own flowerbeds. Look." She shook him lightly. "Look, all you have killed are some azaleas."

He raised his head and smiled a little, the desperation in his eyes dulling somewhat.

"So," she said, as much to herself as to him, "we both reached our breaking point the same night. How ironic. But the worst is over. We stopped before it was too late. We're not going to kill anyone."

She looked at him for some support in this last statement but he reserved commitment.

"We are in trouble Edward," she said. "Less trouble than we were in ten minutes ago, thank God. But Tamica is dead. Someone killed her. Who killed her? Edward, who killed her?"

Edward said slowly, "someone else must have been trespassing here tonight besides you."

"What is going on right now? What is on your agenda?"

"Well." Edward had to put his mind in a totally different perspective to try and remember what was going on in his life. "There's been a lot of interest in me lately. I'm getting a lot of pressure to run for President, instead of senator. My time has come, they tell me. They'll find out how true that is after tonight. So what's actually going to be happening in the next week? I hadn't thought about it much because I had planned to be dead."

"That's not going to happen."

"I do recall there's an anti-abortion rally I'm supposed to be speaking at. It should have been tomorrow but it was postponed a week. That was the trigger for my plan. I would have waited one more day but I could not wait one more week. And there is a breakfast meeting concerning the integration problem in Sand Waves. I forget what day. But soon."

"What integration problem in Sand Waves?"

"That there isn't any."

"Okay, go on. What else is happening?"

"Plans and financing for the new movie studio. I think I'm involved in that somehow. I would have to talk to Regina. She has my life totally organized. She knows everywhere I'm supposed to go, everything I am supposed to say. She just hands me a script, a map, and a timetable."

"I can see why you want to kill her."

"She even wrote a speech for me to give at the anti-abortion rally," Edward smiled ironically. "Even though she's pro-abortion herself."

Grace suddenly felt normal again. She slipped her arm around Edward's waist and squeezed tightly.

"It's going to be important that you keep all of those appointments, no matter what happens. You need to go on as normal as possible."

"Nothing has been normal for the past two years."

Grace relaxed her hold on him as he put his arms around her.

"We'd better go in the house and call the police," she said. "You sit down and rest. I'll make the call myself."

Chapter 4

More than one set of eyes saw the top of the police car as it navigated the complicated drive and arrived at the back door of the York mansion. The officer left the lightbar on even after the engine was stilled. The flashing red and blue lights cast striking patterns over the landscape of the back yard. A perfect distraction allowing anyone to come and go any other way.

For as the single officer exited his car, another man was making his a departure from the landscaped grounds. The slim blonde man slipped out of the compound the way he had many times before. Quietly, stealthily.

He did not fear the police officer arriving at the back door. He did not care why a police officer was showing up at this exact moment. It was fortuitous. Distracting the household at the back door was the perfect way for him to get out.

He feared no one. If he got caught, he would justify his actions on the basis of his social position, sure nobody could touch him.

After contacting Sinclair Plate, Edward and Grace decided it was vital they reach two other people.

Easy to reach and eager to serve, Minyak Tanem was shortly speeding back to Sand Waves. Canceling his vacation was no sacrifice. He disliked being away from Edward York under any circumstances. Edward had insisted he take this trip and he had obediently left for an Arizona resort. As far as Edward knew.

Thanks to an expensive car phone, it was not necessary for Edward to know Mink had not gone to the resort like he had promised. The car phone was his lifeline to the York estate and when it rang with a message that he was needed home he felt rejuvenated and appreciated. He was only chagrined that he was far enough away that, even with making a U turn immediately, it would still take several hours to get back.

He sped up. Within minutes, bright lights flashed behind him.

"Oh, hell," he muttered, as he pulled over to the side of the road. If the DPS officer stopping him was educated and politically abreast of the times, Mink should have no trouble getting back on the road, with just a warning maybe, at the mention of his employer. But if the cop was not civic minded, the name Edward York might not register and more time would be lost.

"Did you realize how fast you were going?" asked the stout patrolman as he approached the driver's window.

"I work directly with Edward York."

The police officer stepped back and a look of awe briefly flitted across his face.

Thank goodness, thought Tanem.

"I am also a licensed peace officer and there is an emergency," he capped it off.

"Of course, as soon as I see your identification-"

Tanem relaxed and reached for his wallet.

From the start Dr. JD Apixza had a bad feeling his plans for the weekend were not going to work out. If only money were not so tight, it would be different. Lately it seemed he needed more and more time away from his job. He knew he had the best job in the world for a physician of his status and he should be happy.

He was not.

The lure of the fast life, gambling boats and casinos, sun kissed tropical beaches, and chemical escapism, once only desired with reasonable regularity, had become an everyday obsession. He was aggravated with himself about that. At his age, he should have more self-control and mental discipline. But it seemed the older he got, the lazier he got. There was no thrill in the work anymore. Only in the sensual and alluring companions hired to accompany him to faraway places, where he could release his inhibitions without fear of scandal and retribution.

He had told the Yorks he was only going to be away for a weekend in Dallas. After exiting the York estate, before enduring the long drive, he detoured to a Houston strip joint. It was only after several hours there, he was in a sufficiently relaxed mood to continue his drive to the Big D. But even before that diversion, before he even left the Sand Waves gates, Apixza had turned his phone off.

Provenance III-

Spring 1920

It was dark and smoky in the shack. The jazz musicians were just making it up as they went along, playing to the mood, playing to the beat. The new girl was untried and she would not be the first to be hooted off stage.

These were the best of the white jazz musicians in the Houston area, playing in the least expensive club that boasted an all white patronage. Most of them had played up and down the Gulf Coast with their black jazz musician brothers. And the manager of this club counted such experiences when they were hired. His objective was to provide good jazz music for true jazz fans who needed someplace to take their wives, or their husbands, or whoever their entertainment companions were, without having to explain to those companions why there were dark faces on the stage.

The club manager was spot on about the need and market for such a club. The problem was finding enough good white jazz musicians who were not already working at the high-end nightclubs, which featured jazz as a sideline to big band music, and which paid much more.

Finding a white female jazz singer who was also decent looking and under 30 was a real coup. He had auditioned her privately and hired her on the spot, boasting to the others that she was something special.

He did not want her rehearsing with them, and then see them drive her off, before a real audience got the chance to see her. So she was to come on and do some spontaneous melodies and they were to accompany her as best they could at the peril of losing their jobs if they balked.

They did not really have any choice. But the musicians had heard the best of the best in many of their previous gigs and they were not expecting much.

The nightclub was noisy. People were distracted. Not many noticed when the singer came on stage. She was short, dark haired,

27

dark eyes, a smoky look about her that fit right in with the atmosphere. She had on a strapless moiré satin evening gown with matching gloves coming almost up to her shoulders. A string of fake pearls. And her hair was piled upon her head. Her makeup included rouge and lipstick, and traces of white powder, which caused her face to look blotchy.

She was not an unattractive girl. But most of the women there would not have worried if she sat down next to their husbands. They were better dressed, a number of them even had jewels that were real, and their makeup and hairstyles were done to perfection.

Likewise, most men did not see this girl as anyone worth risking the wrath of their wives or girlfriends. She looked too young, but not virginal, and wore a wedding ring.

That all spelt trouble.

Many of them wondered what was she doing up there on the stage, if she had nothing more to offer than what was overtly visible.

The bandleader consulted with her a moment and then began to play. She started off haltingly and at first no one was paying attention. By the second verse, the air inexplicably changed. It started with the abrogation of the cigarettes held by most everyone in the room.

Strangely they were being pounded into the ashtrays all over the room almost at once. Then the drinks were set down with a universal clinking sound. The few people who had actually been eating food, stopped doing that as well. Conversation faded out and everyone turned to look at the singer.

As her voice continued to overwhelm them, the musicians joined in the odd cessation of movement, causing the music to fade slowly, and then finally stop. Involved in the song, it was not until she reached the last words of the last verse that the singer realized she no longer had a musical accompaniment. She coughed a little, as was her habit when she needed to detach herself from a song too deeply felt. The she saw that the musicians were all staring at her.

Wondering what was wrong, she ended her last words as a question mark instead of the declaration that they were supposed to be.

She looked over at the musicians for an explanation and was still staring in their direction when the overwhelming applause shattered the room. The nightclub patrons were on their feet shouting and yelling at her.

It took a moment before she realized they were happy with her.

Tears came to her eyes when she saw the number of faces before her that had also tears streaming down their cheeks.

And those in that nightclub, that first night the great jazz singer Amelia Mattworks performed in public before a sophisticated city audience, knew they were witnessing something beyond humanity.

A performance that may be repeated in times to come, routinely even. But would never again be done for the first time. And they had seen it, heard it, for free. Or almost.

The manager folded his arms, knowing he had just struck gold. He loved her singing too, but found the idea of making millions of dollars even more exciting. He had a contract.

This girl was young, relatively. She was unencumbered by a husband. The ring on her finger represented a man killed in the Great War. She was fairly attractive, maybe needing to lose little weight.

She was incredibly gifted.

And she was white.

Chapter 5

A fire crackled cheerfully in the dining room fireplace. Edward York stood near it, letting its flames warm his hands. On either side, nestled in floor-to-ceiling shelves, priceless miniature figurines watched over the room, interspersed with small antique bottles in various colors- amber, green, cobalt blue, and some were clear.

Ignoring the gaze of the miniatures and the sparkle of the bottles as firelight sent occasional showers of sparks at him, Edward poked at the fire with a stick. It flared up, then died back. Its glow fell against his head causing the gold and silver of his hair to shine as if it were really the precious metals spun into fine strings.

"Funny," he said, never taking his eyes off the blaze. "How easy it can be to come to the conclusion that the only course of action left is murder."

"Yes," said Grace.

Grace sat, almost buried in a huge velvet chair that seem to mold itself around her, sweetly supporting her aching muscles. "Yes. I can't analyze it anymore now. I'm too tired. But you are right. It's damned easy."

"When did they say they would get here?"

"Any minute."

"How are we going to explain all this?" Edward turned to the figurines picking up the statuette of a Napoleonic era Maréchal.

"We are not. We are not going to explain anything."

"We have to." He twisted the figure in his hands, thinking how it might have resembled his French ancestor who had held such a rank in the Napoleonic army.

"No we don't. We don't know why Ray and Regina were drugged. We just know we can't wake them."

"What about Corina? So we just-? Just what?" The statuette was rough porcelain crudely painted, the face looking like a theatrical character in makeup.

"We were out. Meeting secretly. I came home with you at your invitation."

"Why would I bring you home?"

It was the minor details that made the figure so impressive. One hand wore a white glove, so was unpainted, left white to represent the covered hand.

"Right. Scratch that. Well, you found the body and called me. That's what you must say. Or we met somewhere and then came here. Something. We will work out our story. The important thing is to stick to it, whatever we decide to tell the authorities," said Grace.

"All right. I don't think that will go very far. Why would I call you?" He wondered at the fragility of the sword carried in the hand how easily it could be broken. But it was not.

"Yes it will. You called me because you knew that I know someone in the police department. When I called, I asked them to send him."

"Who do you know?" The other hand that carried the glove was painted a pale flesh color, the glove remaining white.

"A Lieutenant Plate."

"I don't remember knowing a Lieutenant Plate."

"You don't know him. I know him. You must say that you knew of him through me."

"How do you know him?"

"I am seeing him."

"Seeing him?" Although Edward heard the words that he spoke to Grace, the image in his mind remained the statuette. Its eyes were painted blue and its hair, painted a light brown, was slipping out from behind the Napoleonic triangular hat in a ponytail almost reaching past the shoulders.

"Yes, dating him. We are divorced. Remember? For two years. You're remarried. Remember? I haven't taken up the convent, you know." She watched for any reaction to her dig at his religion.

There was none. "On what level could you possibly know an ordinary cop?" In Edward's mind, Grace's constabulary friend took on the image of the Maréchal.

"Don't be such a snob. Besides this cop is a little different."

"What do you actually mean by dating?"

"What do think I mean by it? I am divorced, thanks to you. I see men. This man, Lieutenant Plate, happens to be a man I am seeing right now. Stop playing with that statuette. It's worth several thousand dollars." Grace felt her old role as protector of the family valuables slipping back on her shoulders.

"He must be a great deal to you if you came back here to kill me tonight." Edward sat the figurine back on the shelf where it belonged, picked up an amber bottle and held it so that he could see the light of the fire through it.

Whatever liquid it had originally held when the container was first sold 60 years ago, was almost gone. But a little residue remained.

Grace did not reply.

Chapter 6

Sinclair Plate was a methodical man. He easily followed the complicated directions to the back yard and was now climbing the few steps to the deck. He took steps one at a time when his long legs could easily negotiate two. The tip of his finger pressed the button, the purpose of which was to communicate to those inside that someone desired admission to the mansion of the Honorable Edward York, ostensibly retired, and his wife, Regina.

"His wife Regina," murmured Plate aloud.

That fact that York had a wife pleased the police officer tremendously.

Edward York, himself, opened the door.

"Lieutenant Plate?" Edward blinked, looking outside beyond Plate, as if he did not expect Plate to be so alone.

"My instructions were to come to the house alone to assess the situation with discretion. I understand this is also the home of Amelia Mattworks," said Plate, keeping his voice light and crisp. He thrust his hands into his uniform jacket pockets and, without asking, shouldered his way into the foyer. It was, he knew, a very effective entrance, one in which he could rely on to put him in instant control of the situation. He usually acquired instant superiority on the scene.

"Please, then. Come on in." It was somehow a visual shock to Edward to see Plate dressed in a traditional contemporary police uniform instead of the costume of the Maréchal. Inadvertently, Edward glanced over at the shelf where the little statuette stood as he led Plate into the den.

"County personnel are on their way," Plate said.

"Yes. Miss Mattworks lives here. I hope we can avoid disturbing her. She lives exclusively on the third floor, which has its own private stairwell and elevator off the foyer. She rarely comes down." Edward was mentally assessing Plate's appearance, still comparing him to the French Napoleonic officer. His face was far from theatrical and unlike the clean shaven Maréchal figurine, he had a mustache. A simple black uniform, no epaulets, the white hat with the yellow band, a pale blue slim tie. It was the mustache that showed him to be a member of the small autonomous police force, which could afford lax facial hair standards. And it was the white hat that signified he was something more than just a traffic cop.

"Plate." Grace flinched at the very idea of one room holding the two men in her life, the only two men ever in her life from her point of view, although there had been many others who would have claimed to have been such, had they had been writing her biography from their point of view. Having both of these men in the same room was an implausible situation requiring improbable diplomacy that she did not possess. Nevertheless, there they stood, Edward York and Sinclair Plate, side by side.

"Plate," said Grace again, attempting normalcy for the second time. "You came alone?"

Plate seemed to take offense that Grace minded or questioned his coming alone. What Edward said to him or thought of him mattered far less than the opinion of him held by the newest rookie on the force.

Nevertheless, as for Grace, he was well aware that how he performed, or rather the impression he made in his performance, might have a bearing on the rest of his life. Therefore, he had to choose his words with great care and the words, every word he would speak, would be aimed at Grace, with the idea behind them- what does Grace think?

And how will I fare in her thoughts tonight when she lies down and lets the day's events pass before her mind? How will I fare in her summation of the action, of my actions? Will any of my words come back to her and shed a negative light on me?

Having similar thoughts, Edward closed the door behind Plate, feeling a little bit of an outsider in Grace's life for the first time since he met her. He found himself strangely wishing that Regina was beside him, the first time he had wished that in many months. But at least with Regina there was no competitor. Moreover, with Regina there was never any question of how she felt.

"Grace," said Plate, "I thought if I came in alone first, then later perhaps I might could spare you some of the discomfort, the unpleasantness. Unpleasantness is bound to become the norm after

34

this. Any ostentatious response behind the gates alerts the press."

"Aren't you interested in the dead woman?" asked Edward evenly. He left the thought, *or just Grace,* unspoken.

"Of course," replied Plate. "But I presume there's no hurry. Am I not correct?" Implying dead was dead,

"I don't understand any of this," said Grace.

"My darling," said Edward. "Lieutenant Plate is trying very graciously to tell you that he is going to do his best to see to it that your name is not dragged through the mud on this. After all, we are what passes for celebrities these days."

"Oh," said Grace. "I see." Then she said to Plate, "don't worry. We, Edward and I, were just seeing each other tonight on business, and fortunately I- we discovered the body."

"Which is?" asked Plate. "Where?" He looked around as if expecting to find Tamica's body displayed on the den room floor or beneath the coffee table.

"She's in the pool," said Edward.

"The pool? I understood from what Grace told me on the phone that this is a shooting."

"It is," said Grace. "It was rather, a shooting, that's obvious when you see her. You will see that it is definitely a shooting."

"Let's go outside," said Edward.

Plate showed his confusion at the ambiguity of those words but had nothing to say as they led him back through the foyer to the back door, across the deck, down the steps and across the back yard to the pool.

Just before leaving the den, Plate had glanced around at the fine collectibles- the statuettes remaining as mental pictures all the way through the cold air outside. For some reason, the images of these miniature sculptures filled Plate with an unanticipated loathing, a feeling so deep that it threw him slightly off-balance and he limped just a little as he approached the pool.

The figurines vanished from his mind as soon as he saw Tamica's body.

Chapter 7

Plate followed Grace and Edward to the edge of the pool where everything looked still much the same as it had when Grace had discovered the body. Tamica's body was still much in the same gentle swaying position.

The divorced couple and the policeman only had moments alone with the body. They stared at Tamica silently, each considering how this death might change their own lives.

County personnel began arriving. Soon the back yard was alive with lights and activity. The air became colder.

Grace asked could they please go back inside.

Plate told her and Edward to go ahead, remaining briefly himself to give preliminary instructions to the county officers. Sand Waves depended upon the county for all forensic procedures. Shortly he left them to their work and went to the back door, now unlocked.

Grace and Edward sat before the fire as Plate came back into the den. Grace had once again sank into the velvet chair with fatigue. Her golden hair rested against the back.

"Now," said Plate to Edward. "As for the identity of this unfortunate woman- Grace did not elaborate on the telephone. She simply told me that a murder had been committed. That the victim must have been the victim of a shooting. I presume she was one of your wife's domestic help, Mr. York? I'm sorry. Judge York?"

"I'm afraid that she was not domestic help, Lieutenant. She was my sister-in-law." Edward's attention turned to a statuette of an 18th-century Prussian soldier. It had a mustache.

"I beg your pardon?"

"She was my sister-in-law. The wife of my wife's," and he inadvertently looked at Grace when he said wife, "the wife of my wife's brother."

"But," Plate stopped himself from saying anymore. That he had automatically assumed the woman was a servant embarrassed him. Although her skin was light, it was her hair which indicated her race.

36

"Tamica Cathare was a black woman. You are correct in that observation, Lieutenant Plate." Edward's voice had just a tinge of sarcasm in it. The sarcasm being all the more effective due to its understated delivery.

Plate had made a gaffe in front of Grace and both men were watching for her reaction. Plate staring at her directly, Edward, out of the corner of his eye, as the former judge picked up the Prussian soldier from the shelf.

"I think that is an understandable error," said Grace delicately. "Prejudice and stereotypes run deep in our society. It's no reflection on the lieutenant that he should fall victim to one."

Grace spoke clearly in Plate's defense even if her words were not effective. Loyalty was Grace's strongest virtue.

Edward was suddenly lonely for the security that Grace's loyalty used to provide him. He felt vulnerable to see that loyalty given to another man.

"Yes, well," said Plate, aware of the support but continuing to think it was best to change the subject. "I'd like to know, Judge York, about your sister-in-law. Her name was?"

He pulled out a notebook

"Tamica, Tamica with a 'c'- Tamica Cathare."

If Plate recalled that was also Grace's maiden name, he did not let on. He did write the surname down without needing it spelled.

"She was with you this evening?"

"No, she was not."

"Then you were alone with the victim until Grace arrived?"

"I don't quite understand what you are saying."

"Well," said Plate, "I mean, your wife and her brother are obviously not here."

"They are asleep upstairs," said Edward.

"Asleep! Don't you think you should wake them? I can understand not disturbing Miss Mattworks, but-"

"We tried," said Grace, without thinking. "I'm afraid that they are-" She looked at Edward with a look that made Plate cringe a little. It was a look that said 'help' and Plate wanted those looks coming to him. He watched with great interest Edward's response.

"Yes. I'm afraid," said Edward, "my wife and her brother are sometimes dependent on sleeping pills and they have both, must have, both taken several this evening."

"So much so that they cannot be awoken?"

"Well, they can be roused somewhat," said Edward. "But I'm afraid getting them wide awake enough to understand what is going on will be questionable for at least some time."

"I see. In that case, we need to call medical assistance for them."

Without asking permission, Plate went to the back porch and spoke with officers still busy in the yard. Then he turned back to the two people seated before him to find both of them staring at him with blatant fear on their faces.

Their fear vanished almost the instant he turned, but not quite fast enough. He had seen it.

"And so therefore, besides Miss Mattworks, there are only two other people in the house beside you? Is that right, Judge York?"

"Oh my God," said Grace. "I forgot Corina."

"Who is Corina?" asked Plate.

"She is Tamica's daughter. She is also asleep," Edward said.

"She cannot be awakened either?"

"Corina is in the east corridor. I'm afraid we didn't check on her," Grace said.

"Then we must see to her at once. She is a minor child?"

"Yes and no. She's 16," Grace informed him.

"And neither of you thought to check on her?"

Edward, replacing the Prussian soldier, said, "Corina usually keeps to herself so much that I wasn't too worried about her. To tell you the truth, I also forgot about her."

"Could you please come and show me her room?"

Edward reluctantly started in the direction of the east hall.

The house consisted of a T-shaped first floor. The cross of the T was at the back of the house. It was divided into two wings, referred to as the east and west wings by its inhabitants. If detached from the third section of the mansion, which reached to the front circular drive, the wings would form a one story structure. But between them the third long section had two floors above it and formed the core of the house.

"Corina occupies the east wing and Tamica and Ray live in the west wing. Those wings also contain various collections that belong to members of the household," Edward York explained to Plate, as they walked down a hall the size of a hospital corridor. "The front forward section of the house has the formal dining room and other entertainment areas. My wife and I live on the second floor. Miss Mattworks lives on the third floor."

Plate was trying to recall newspaper stories about Amelia Mattworks moving into Edward York's compound some time ago. He was fuzzy on the details.

"Forgive the intrusion but could you tell me again why Miss Mattworks lives here? I forget. Is she a relative?"

"My wife's brother, Ray, married Tamica French in 1980."

"I don't think the lieutenant understands, Edward," said Grace. "Plate, Tamica was Amelia Mattworks' granddaughter."

Chapter 8

Plate stopped in mid-step. He felt his throat go dry. "The murder victim is Amelia Mattworks' granddaughter?"

"Yes," said Edward. "Tamica and my brother-in-law were married slightly more than two years ago. Up until that point in time Miss Mattworks, Tamica, and Tamica's daughter Corina had been living in a nearby estate, with servants of course, but basically alone. Tamica, marrying my brother-in-law, was going to leave a 90-some-odd-year-old woman living with a teenager, if Corina stayed. Or alone, if Corina came with her mother. So the only human thing to do was for all three of them to live with Ray. Ray was, well, not really equipped to handle such an instant family."

Seeing Plate's questioning look, Edward felt he needed to explain more thoroughly.

"Financially, Miss Mattworks brings in much more than her living expenses. But all her income goes into a trust. She gets a generous allowance but there is the management of her daily life and household affairs, which requires a firm hand with organization and routine."

"So no one lives on this third floor with Miss Mattworks? Has anybody checked on her well-being?" Plate asked.

"The third floor is a virtual fortress. We have extra security features in effect that prohibits access. There is a code to run the elevator. And an emergency code seals the doors and locks the stairwell. No one can get up there when it is activated," Edward said. "Miss Mattworks has a private phone line that connects to our other house phones and direct dials to emergency services if needed."

"I looked in on Amelia right after I called you. She was asleep. She's very eccentric and it causes her stress to be disturbed," said Grace.

"She is a recluse then?" asked Plate, thinking of the famous reclusive billionaire, Howard Hughes.

"Oh no," said Edward. "She interacts with us all the time. She just has to be in the mood. For example, Miss Mattworks likes to bake cookies and have tea parties on demand. It's due to her age that she rarely leaves the house, so all care and companionship must come to her."

Plate and Edward entered Corina's room. It looked like the room of adolescent rather than a 16-year-old. Teddy bears and baby dolls occupied space on shelves, a nightstand, a dresser. A small collection of dolls occupied a little glass case designed to mimic the appearance of a dollhouse.

A glass of milk stood on Corina's nightstand, almost full. The girl was asleep, turned on her side, clasping a stuffed animal that looked to be a cat, her figure eclipsed, her form misshapen by the covers in disarray around her.

Edward woke her. A light sleeper, she was wide awake in an instant. Exaggerated fear took hold of her on seeing the two men in her room. She clutched the toy.

They left her a moment, giving her time to get dressed before bringing her downstairs with them.

All the while she was dressing, she was questioning verbally and mentally what had actually happened, her fear that something was horribly wrong growing stronger and stronger with each step down that she took. Finally, in the living room, the task fell upon Edward to tell her what had happened.

He told her with an extraordinary and seemingly sincere tenderness. For a moment, she sat stunned before blinding tears came. Then like a frightened animal, she gave out a little scream.

Chapter 9

An adjunct county physician, selected for his known discretion, arrived. Edward York had no choice but to let more strangers enter his home. A patrolman entered with the doctor. The officer indicated he needed to speak to Plate privately.

The physician was directed to look after the girl and he took her back upstairs.

"It does look like someone broke into one of the empty cottages and also attempted to break into the cottage occupied by Judge York's security guard," reported Patrol Officer Grant Skaar to Plate. "We can't find any evidence that any attempt was made to get into the main house or the other cottages. But there was gasoline poured onto the shrubbery which indicates plans."

"Plans for what do you think?"

"We can't tell, Lieutenant. To burn the house down, perhaps? Or create some kind of diversion with fire?"

"Any sign of any incendiary devices?"

"No, nothing. Not a match. If you want, we can go ahead and interview neighbors. But the way this compound is laid out, only someone who climbed up in a tree could possibly have seen anything. Unless they were in that weird structure that's next door."

As he considered this information, Plate told Skaar to resume his position on the back porch.

The physician checked on the other two people also asleep upstairs, then reported to Plate downstairs. He pronounced they were indeed in a drug-induced sleep that would naturally wear off as time progressed. They appeared to be in no danger. They were adults who had the right to take powerful sleeping medications if they so desired so there was nothing to do but wait for the drugs to wear off.

Edward swore they were in the habit of taking such drugs and would object to any form of intervention. Everyone knew his power, so they respected his words.

"Dr. JD Apixza would be their prescribing physician. He lives in one of the cottages on the compound. I know for a fact he was away this night. He is due back tomorrow," Edward told Plate.

Plate told him about the break-in at the empty cottage and the unsuccessful attempt to enter the occupied cottage.

"You are sure about Mink's cottage?" said Edward York. "You are sure you're not mistaking the repairs Ray was making on the house as evidence of a break-in? You're sure none of the other cottages were disturbed?"

"One has the lights on inside. But no one answers the door. There is no evidence of a break-in there. The other empty cottage is dark, but again, there's no sign of any try to break in."

"The cottage with its lights on would've been the more likely target. We are always concerned about the doctor's quarters. Dr. Apixza keeps his lights on all the time whether he is home or not," Edward affirmed.

"That might have deterred the burglar. Are drugs kept there?"

"It's actually a full clinic. Not open to the public, of course. But equipped with most modern medical technology. Miss Mattworks being 94- we take all precautions for her safety."

And for your own as well, Plate thought. *Four complete houses and a full-time doctor in your own backyard*. However, he said, "I'm going to need to speak to the doctor as soon as possible."

"Of course."

"Beyond the drugs located in the clinic, what else on the premises might be the target of any burglars? Do you keep a lot of cash here?"

"No. We have no reason to keep cash on the premises. But we do have priceless collections. My figurines. You have already seen those. My wife has a Victorian dollhouse worth thousands of dollars. Ray has a small amount of authentic Western memorabilia. I have a collection of antique tin toys that is quite valuable. Grace collects Barbie dolls. I don't think they're worth much. Oh, I forget. They are not even here any longer. She took them with her when she left. Nor is Corina's collection of teddy bears and fashion dolls worth much. Some individual pieces may be valuable if they have the right provenance, of course."

"Provenance?"

"Yes, provenance is most important to collectors. I'm speaking of the history and documentation that relates as much of the past as possible for any given collectible. Having a provenance can double or triple the worth. I keep all my papers on all of my collectibles in my safe. Now, an amateur thief would not know to search for documents but if a professional targeted our collection, he would be searching for the provenance documentation as well."

"With a house this size, it is hard to tell in a short period of time if there's been any attempt to break in. But so far only the cottages seem to have been targeted."

"Well, I cannot for the world understand why," said Edward York.

Officer Skaar came back in to give Plate one more bit of information. A thin blonde man had been spotted walking in the street near enough to the York estate to warrant the possibility that he could be a suspect. But somehow, he had slipped into the woods in the dark and eluded police.

County personnel, taking pictures as procedures were readying to take the body out of the pool, had set up huge spotlights in the back yard area. Still, it was hard to see exactly how the compound was arranged. It would be easy to get into the back yard, provided the woods could be traversed.

A fence divided the front yard from the back yard. The two driveways pierced the fence to allow access to the four cottages. Both driveways were bordered by more fencing with automatic gates that allowed the occupants of the cottages access. In the dark, that was the best that could be determined.

The cottages were fenced off with their own private yards. The front yard, protected by the dogs, apparently could not have been breached without some bloodshed by canine teeth. So only the area from the back porch to the back fence, and two small areas that reached behind the parts sectioned off for the cottages, were declared the crime scene for now.

The brightest lights shining on the dense woods on the west side of the compound was still not going to make the forest easy to navigate in the darkness. Patience was called for, as there was no substitute for daylight.

After some discussion, and after all that could be done was done, most of the law enforcement officials agreed they might as well soon go home and return in the morning in the daylight.

Plate was informed that Mink Tanem held a Texas peace officer's license in good standing, fulfilling his required hours of service each month with the county law enforcement agency. Residing in the cottage closest to the back fence on the west side, he was in a prime location enabling him to help out.

Exactly the perfect place for him to keep watch on the crime scene from the comfort of his own home. As he was on his way back, a county patrol officer was temporarily stationed in front of Tanem's cottage to be relieved by him as soon as he got there.

Edward York had spoken to the Sand Waves police chief, Robert Brecken. York had been clear that he wanted no special treatment because of his position in society and that he preferred Mink Tanem to any other guard.

Already under orders to take York's requests as seriously as possible, plus considering who the murder victim was and considering her family, the chief felt inclined to cooperate in any way he could.

Robert Brecken liked his job and wanted to keep it.

Chapter 10

There was so much more for Plate to do but it was so late that little could be done. The body had been fished out of the pool. The burglary was being investigated. Patrol cars were scouring the neighborhood for the thin blonde man.

Any pedestrian in this part of Sand Waves was subject to suspicion. The colony maintained green belts for residents to walk on and few streets had sidewalks. This was not a part of the world where anybody ever walked out of necessity. Walking or running for exercise on the green belts, which purposely led nowhere, was the only ambulatory pastime for most residents.

That the thin blonde man had been involved in suspicious activity was taken for granted by everyone. That he was a possible burglar who had killed Tamica Cathare was a comforting thought to all. Except Plate.

He did not believe it.

The preliminaries of his job were initiated, the verdict practically rendered before the investigation got started good, Plate also was beginning to think it was time to leave. But there remained the question of Grace.

He offered her a ride.

"I'm too tired tonight to go anywhere. I think Edward is going to have to allow me the hospitality of his home for the evening."

Edward looked at Grace. "Of course." There was gratitude in his voice. Plate could not help but hear it.

"I hope it won't be an inconvenience, Edward. I'm really too tired to go home. I don't quite know why I'm so tired. I can't ever remember having been this tired before. But I'm just too tired to go home. Surely, Regina will understand."

"I will need to talk to you, Grace," Plate said. "Officially."

"Of course. We could make it tomorrow? I could come by your office."

"Surely that will suffice, Lieutenant?" said Edward. And while his tone of voice indicated that was a question, his expression showed it was really an order.

"It's not even necessary to go that far. I'll be back tomorrow."

So Plate was forced to walk back down the steps he had so methodically climbed earlier in the evening, feeling vaguely dissatisfied. Not with the murder. He knew he could solve the murder.

It was the mystery of Grace's mind that troubled him. The mystery of her mind, wondering how it worked. Wondering how it processed all the action and information that flashed before it.

Plate had an imaginative mental picture of the inner workings of the human mind. A science fiction fan, he saw the mind as a miniature computer with an infinite file capacity. The speed and efficiency with which information was fed and stored for processing, as well as the quantity and quality of knowledge, determined a person's basic intelligence and therefore his or her actions.

He saw the little computer spinning its files endlessly, every so often coming up with decisions. He wondered what decisions would be forming in Grace's mind tonight. Had he been a different type of person, his wondering might have been a little more precise. For the mystery was not in her mind but in her heart.

Mink Tanem arrived at 3:45 AM. He quickly surveyed his premises and confirmed nothing was missing. He agreed to keep watch the rest of the night.

At four in the morning, Plate was the last of the outsiders to leave Edward York's property and go home.

Provenance IV

Late Spring 1921

An amber bottle rested on a backroom shelf in a dusty general store in a part of East Texas very near the Louisiana border. The store offered non-perishable tins of food, a few crude tin toys for little boys, cloth rag dolls, some decorative handmade ceramics. Other odds and ends.

And a few bottles of medicine.

An elderly proprietor, bent and stamped with age, shuffled slowly behind the counter. Reaching up with difficulty, she took the amber bottle from its shelf. As she slowly came into the lobby area of her store, clutching each structure for support as she made her way, a well-proportioned athletically built man met her from the opposite direction.

His companion was a slight, short woman who wore no wedding ring. But a single strand chain around her neck hinted at some type of jewelry tucked into her bosom, invisible behind her clothing. Unconsciously she fingered the chain clasp at the back of her neck.

The proprietor had finished relating a fairly complex methodology and neither of the customers looked like they had understood.

"I did not tell you these instructions because I expect you to understand them. It just be my duty to relay the rules to the ignorant," said the old proprietor, pulling at the wrinkled skin on her arms and squeezing it until some of the lighter sections turned almost pink. "It's cause I know what you face in this world. And you needs a quick way out of it."

"This is not what we came for," said the woman.

"We will never be using this," the man sneered.

But his companion snatched it from the proprietor's hands. "Let me see."

She held the bottle up and gazed at the liquid. Then she lifted the chain from her bosom, revealing a metal cross. She put the bottle where the cross had hidden, letting the Christian symbol hang down almost to her waist.

"All we want is the best for our baby." said the man. "We would do better to get one of those tin toys or a rag doll for our child than this poison."

"That you look white and you be black is what determines everything. You bewitched as a child to make you white, girl? Or are you really white? With a black driving you around? If so, you both better not let the sun set on you in this town. There is a town hereabouts friendly to the mixing of the blacks and white. It not be this one."

"I was bewitched," the expectant mother said. "I am not white."

"So you been passin' and, the father be either, a baby will give you away," the old proprietor concluded.

And she laughed with genuine cruelty.

"Where is that town?" asked the man, sidetracked by the thought of it.

"I don't be telling that. They under the protection. You might be spies. She might be some rich KKK woman and you be her servant and you two here to trick me into betrayal. Wouldn't do no good, they's under the protection."

"You stupid old fool," said the man. "We're not spies. She can get a white man to wed her if she can be sure the baby will look white. I can be there nearby and nobody will know."

"You be more fool than me. And your baby won't be a mix of you. You know what skin color it will have. And girl, you be too white looking to be with him. You and he are too far apart. And no baby going to pull you two together. Go back to passin' and set yourself alone. Have no babies."

"Are you the witch I am seeking?" insisted the mother-to-be angrily. "It is no business of yours how I pass or not. Or if I have babies. Are you the witch whose potions can make my baby look white? Are you trying to give us the wrong potion? We have enough money to pay."

"No, ain't no witch can do that. Somebody sent you here

telling you that? No, they lied. I am a witch. They knew what I can do and figured you would want my potion when you came to your senses. Only one way to take care of your problem and you have it in your hand. Someday you'll see you're getting your money's worth," said the proprietor, glad to be unmasking herself. She could not let many know she was a witch.

"What kind of protection? What do you mean by protection?" asked the man. "How do I find out and get this protection?"

The old witch laughed scornfully. She reached out and grabbed the cross necklace around the pregnant woman's neck. But the clasp held.

"That be the only real protection." And her laugh almost became a cackle as she pulled harder. "Its price is too high."

"Stop it!" The pregnant woman struck the witch's arm, forcing her to let loose of the chain.

The witch raised her other arm.

The man stepped between them before the witch could strike back. "You're crazy!" he snarled at her, as her blow, aimed at the wearer of the necklace, fell on him

But it was a light blow, feeble with age. He barely noticed it.

"None of that," he said to the witch. He was much stronger and taller than the old proprietor. But it was he that was shaking.

"Why you come here if you want the child?" said the witch, nonplussed. "Nonsense is what you are telling me. Both of you liars or spies. Otherwise, you know exactly what I do. Everyone does."

Ignoring the assault, the gall of which was still reverberating with her companion, the expectant mother said, "the only reason I came here was I was told you were the witch that I should come to. You had the means to make the baby be born white. But all you offer is this poison?"

Giving up on getting an answer, the man turned to his companion. "What do you want to do?"

"Let's go home," said the expectant mother. "I'm going to put this whole part of the country behind me. Out of my life."

"Getting out now is none too soon." The old witch turned her back on them.

The man took the woman by the arm and led her towards the door. The witch narrowed her eyes as they moved away from her.

"Who told you about this?" the man whispered to his woman furiously.

"Someone from the band," the woman whispered back. "Said if I got here early enough, the witch could help me."

"Stop your whispering. Pay me or give me the potion back," said the witch.

She had retreated behind her cash register but now there was a shotgun on the counter top.

"Pay her, Roscoe. Just in case. She might can curse us."

"How's you expect anyone to remember all that nonsense you told us at first, anyways," the man said, and he pulled some money from his pocket. "If we have to remember all that to make it work, I might as well pour it down the drain when we gets out of here."

A saleswoman first, a witch second, she bent slowly over a cabinet and extracted an old parchment. The man walked towards her with the money visible in his outstretched hand.

"You be cursed with death if you pour it out. These be the instructions in writing," she said, handling them to him. "I didn't reckon you two could read them. Go on take it, I've got copies. They's all old looking like this."

"Take it, Roscoe," said the woman, no emotion in her voice. "We won't use it. But take it."

The man reluctantly exchanged the cash for the parchment. "I'll never read this," he snarled. "We'll never use your evil potion."

Mollified, the witch took the money and turned her back on them to put it behind a shelf.

The couple started towards the door.

"Remember." The old proprietor turned back around and called after them. "Two drops for sickness, one more the next day and the baby will be gone. No more than four, more than four will kill you."

"I'm having my baby no matter what." The woman pulled away from the man and stepped back inside to face the old lady again.

"I ain't forcing you to take it. I'm just warning you. Giving

51

instructions to you. Sos you know what you got there. There's no taste and it leaves no trace. Best solution that keeps the doctors out of your privacy when you want death, keeps the lawmen out of it…"

Though she already had her money, the old proprietor witch was still making her sales pitch as the man and the woman exited the building and slammed the door behind them.

But her words echoed in their ears.

Just for safety's sake, Roscoe crawled down in between the seats in the car and the woman covered him with a blanket, taking the paper from his hand.

She got in the driver's seat. Slowly she unfolded the parchment with one hand as she started the car with the other.

"The old witch was right. We can't read this," said the woman, as the car shifted into gear. *It doesn't matter,* she thought.

For silently, as the witch had spoken the words aloud, her customer had memorized the instructions.

She pushed the bottle and its accompanying paper into the glove compartment and then gripped the wheel with both hands as she pulled the car onto the highway.

Chapter 11

Alone after all the police had left, after Tamica's body had been taken away, Regina and Ray were still asleep and the child, Corina, was once again asleep upstairs, Edward and Grace felt very much like actors after exacting performances in a difficult play were over. They were utterly exhausted.

"Is it really all right if I stay here?" asked Grace. "I can go home. I really won't mind going home tonight. I just didn't feel like going with Plate."

"No," said Edward, picking up the British soldier figurine again. "I'd rather that you stayed. I don't feel safe anymore. I don't know if I've ever really felt safe in my life but I feel less safe now than ever and I wish you would stay. I was going to say you'd be better protected here. But then again, that appears to be a fallacy."

"Edward, what are you going to do when Regina wakes up?"

"I don't know. Right now I guess I'm going to see you to a guest room and go on up to bed."

"Edward, Edward, listen to me. You must not do anything tonight."

"Don't worry, I won't."

"You must not attempt to harm Regina tonight. Just wait, please."

"I told you I wouldn't do anything."

"I am so worried about you." Grace bit her lip. She had not wanted to quite reveal so much as that one sentence did.

"And I about you," said Edward, with tenderness.

"Oh," she said, "my actions were a momentary madness. It's all forgotten now." She shook her head, glancing down at the floor. "It was just, I don't know. I don't know why I came here tonight. I had some vague notion of revenge. I don't know why. I have a happy life. Well, I have a life that is not unhappy, if you know what I mean. But sometimes I just have moments of madness. Then all I want in the world is what it seems I can't have, and if I can't have it, I cannot go on anymore."

"What is it? What did you want?" he said, easing the figurine down on the coffee table. He placed his hands on her shoulders, speaking as if he were on the verge of dashing to the nearest store for her heart's desire.

"I wanted revenge," she said simply. "Revenge." She nodded her head.

He dropped his arms and backed away from her.

"What will Regina say in the morning when she finds out I'm here?" Grace asked, but there was little concern in her voice.

"I don't know."

"I know she won't be pleased."

"I don't know," he said. There was apathy in his voice again. "I would think she would be more interested in the death of her brother's wife."

"She won't. She'll be more interested in me."

"Half the time the only thing Regina is interested in is that damned doll house she obsesses over. When she is in the mood to play with her collection, nothing else can get her attention."

"We'll get her attention. We have to have a story to tell her."

"We can't tell everyone stories, Grace. We'll do well to keep telling the police our story. And what will we say?"

"Then, what will you say to Regina over breakfast in the morning?"

"Don't worry about it. I get to eat breakfast alone. It's the most decent part of the day."

"Oh, Edward. How did we get into such a mess?"

His eyes sent sharp glances at her. Little quick sharp glances as if to say *you know better than I.* But he said nothing.

"What's going to become of us now?" said Grace.

"We are fools," said Edward. "What's going to become of us is what happens to most fools."

"Go on. I'm waiting," said Grace. "You have our fate in your hands. Go on. What happens to most fools?"

"First, duration. Then oblivion. They take our toys away and give them to the next fool. Grace, you might have lied to the lieutenant about your fatigue but I am truly exhausted. I think I can better face tomorrow if I do get some sleep tonight."

Grace remembered what he had previously said about sleep. "Why can't you sleep well? You never had trouble before."

"Death of an innocent haunts me."

"Oh," she said, with some disappointment, as though suspecting hopefully there were other reasons for his insomnia. She tried to recall someone convicted and executed whose guilt had been in doubt. She could not think of any such person connected with Edward.

"All the innocents," he added.

They walked the rest of the way in silence to the west wing where Edward showed her to a guest bedroom. As she turned to say good night, he said, "I haven't slept a full night sleep in at least a year."

The comment was lost on her. Practicality returned.

"Edward, I have a gun. What shall I do with it?"

"I've got to go back downstairs. I left one of the porcelain figurines on the coffee table. It will get broken. Give me the gun and I will put it away."

Grace obeyed.

"Go on to bed," he said. "We'll talk in the morning." And abruptly he walked towards the stairs.

She watched as he walked away from her, growing smaller and smaller as he went farther and farther down the wide hallway. She faced the door to the guest room, a guest room she once offered as hostess to many important and distinguished visitors.

Now she was the guest.

She knew exactly what the room looked like, tall sturdy dark oak furniture. Bare. No trinkets or knickknacks left in this room. All the counters would be empty, only a couple of paintings securely screwed to the wall. No décor that anyone might be tempted to slip away with. Just a bed and lots of empty space.

She opened the door and entered this room without glancing back.

Chapter 12

Regina York awakened feeling marvelous. Golden sun flashed into her room via huge picture windows overlooking a blooming front yard landscape of judiciously chosen winter flowering plants. She stretched her arms toward the ceiling and imitated the purr of a cat. Then she slipped out of bed and draped a robe over her bare icy shoulders. Ten minutes later, emerging from her dressing room, her naturally lovely face was now perfected by makeup.

She crossed rapidly to her pride and joy, her dollhouse. Smiling with delight, she raised the massive top allowing her to peer into the innermost rooms of the miniature home. Taking up the entire corner of the room, the dollhouse was an exquisite reproduction of a Victorian mansion complete with several sets of rooms and three stories. Furnished with prohibitively expensive detailed reproductions of the age, its occupants were nevertheless modern dolls. Regina allowed a few modern touches. She had a working miniature hanging lamp of glass grapes that highlighted one room. She had fallen in love with the 1970s era style lights and, while they did not fit in with Edward's idea of 1980s décor, she had one in her dollhouse.

Regina liked her dollhouse most of all because she could have exactly what she wanted there, regardless of whatever anyone else said.

She had searched obscure shops for the inhabitants, a dark-haired lady and blonde man. Other visitors came and went at Regina's pleasure and displeasure. But those dolls alone stayed amid the finery. Regina carefully lowered her slender hand down into the center of the house. Penetrating like a giant hand of a graceful monster, the long sculptured nails were careful not to damage anything on their way down. She carefully extracted the miniature Victorian sofa and held it in her palm. Its small but intricately carved legs resting on the tips of her fingers, she took the dark-haired doll and placed her in the middle of the sofa. Balancing the top, she raised them one level, then higher twisting her wrists to examine them from all angles.

She then lowered the sofa to its place in the parlor. The male doll she placed standing at the edge of the couch, regally but subserviently as if the dolls were Queen Victoria with her consort Prince Albert. Regina sighed with pleasure once again. A desire for a companion in admiring the miniature beauty caused her to briefly flicker her eyes around the room and wonder where Edward was. He'd be at breakfast, that irritating habit of his which she could not break.

Regina did not understand for the world why anyone would want to get up early in the morning and have breakfast. She did not understand why Edward imitated the social habits of factory workers and the like. Try as she might, she could not teach Edward to sleep late. Mild annoyance nipped at her pleasure. She finished dressing hurriedly. But she still made sure that everything was in its proper place before she opened her bedroom door and exited into the world.

She thought about yesterday morning when she stepped into the hallway, leaving the pretty dollhouse behind. Her annoyance increased. She frowned, remembering how she had been summoned to the third floor by its haughty inhabitant for a command visit.

Old lady thinks she's a queen, thought Regina. *Demanding I find her entertainment at a moment's notice. Good thing I still had most of those old movie magazines.*

Regina had recently purchased the entire contents of a small antique shop just to get certain pieces for her dollhouse that the owner, needing money for medical bills, spitefully refused to sell her unless she purchased everything. She had quickly disposed of all the superfluous junk but had kept a large stack of old movie magazines just to read for pleasure before she threw them out. They were more entertaining than contemporary 1980s fiction any day.

And somehow the old lady had found out about them and demanded I lend them to her. As if she had any intentions of ever giving them back...

Well, it doesn't matter. Let the old bag have them and maybe it will keep her occupied and there would be fewer obligatory tea parties for a while...

Regina had a wistful wish that it was her honeymoon morning again. Edward would take her dancing again. She had done the right thing by waiting until exactly the right man came along to marry. She had waited a long time but she felt very wise for doing so.

The idea of being First Lady was never far from her mind.

At the top of the stairs to the second floor, one pointed toe shoe about to step down, Regina had the most extraordinary hallucination that Grace York was standing below, abstractedly drumming her nails on the banister, glancing around in seeming boredom. The pointed toe hit the carpet on the second step. And had it not been for the railing beside her, Regina would have lost her balance. For the hallucination looked up and said, "good morning, Regina. I'm afraid you've missed breakfast."

Regina did not reply for she was still in the awkward mental position of attempting to discern if she were dreaming or drunk.

"We've been waiting for you to get up," said Grace. "I know you're wondering why I'm here. I'm afraid something has happened." Grace spoke as though expecting Regina to know what it was.

"Regina," said the familiar voice of her husband. Edward appeared beside Grace. "Regina." Edward stopped himself just in time from formally introducing them. He bit his tongue to keep from saying 'Regina this is Grace York, my ex-wife. Grace, this is Regina York, my present wife.'

He almost smiled. They had known each other much longer than he had known either of them. Instead, he said, "and you see, Grace is here. She spent the night last night."

Regina's stark eyes widened perceptively.

"Regina, I am afraid something has happened," said Edward.

"Apparently." Regina spoke. "Apparently, something indeed has happened." She started down again.

"Tamica is dead," said Edward.

As quickly as she had resumed coming down the stairs, Regina stopped, then started once more, rushing down all at once until she was face-to-face with her husband and his ex-wife.

"Tamica? Tamica is dead? And Grace spends the night? My, what a connection there must be between those two events!"

"You don't seem too surprised your sister-in-law is dead," said Grace.

"I am utterly astounded," said Regina. "I had no idea in the world she was dead. What happened? Did she go out last night? Did she have a car wreck?"

"She was shot," said Edward.

"Shot? She went out last night? Some Houston nightclub, I presume, and got herself shot."

"No, she was shot in the back yard. In the pool."

"Shot in the pool? Underwater? Wouldn't that be rather difficult?"

"She was shot. Then she fell into the pool," said Grace concretely.

"The pool?" Regina commented. "Did you do it, Grace? Is that why you spent the night?"

"It so happens that Edward and I had some business to discuss and we happen to come back here together and we discovered the body."

"Oh, that explains it all perfectly," said Regina sarcastically.

"Yes it does. Grace and I would have hardly come here together if we were trying to hide anything."

"I'm assuming that you two haven't been seeing each other on the sly. After two years you decide you're going to come and see Edward on some kind of business. What kind of business were you discussing with Edward? At his home? On the night my brother's wife is murdered? Or may I ask?"

"Regina, Grace and I were married for eight years. We did have a few business interests during that time. There were some papers here at the house I needed."

"Oh, I see. I see."

"It concerns one of the oil wells. A detail we forgot. You were already asleep early last night. There was no need to disturb you or anyone else. But when we found the body, we had to call the police. It was a very fatiguing experience and I asked Grace to stay, out of consideration for her."

"My what a lovely way to start the day. With a murder in the family and my husband's ex-wife as a houseguest. Has anyone thought to inform my brother?"

"You don't know how fortunate you were that Grace was here," Edward muttered.

"It was a coincidence," said Grace quickly. "If we had not come here, we would not have discovered that a crime had been committed. You are fortunate it was not discovered by any of the hired help."

"This is going to be my lucky week I can tell."

"Regina, I was not seeing Grace behind your back. I would have told you that she came by."

"I suppose I can accept all this at face value. After all, why should you see your ex-wife behind your present wife's back? I mean, now if it were someone strange, someone who didn't know you, someone I didn't know, I might be worried. I'm sure that Grace, however, never makes the same mistake twice." She paused. Then she continued in the tone of voice often heard by secretaries being remonstrated by their bosses for technical errors. "Very well, Grace, I accept your explanation. And if the business you discussed with Edward, if you wish to keep this confidential, far be it for me to pry."

She whirled sharply to Edward who stepped back reflexively. "At least, darling, you had someone to have breakfast with this morning." Then she walked away from him with her little steps that would have enchanted the most meticulous stage director. "I assume my sister-in-law's body has been removed from the swimming pool?"

"Did you intend going for a dip?" asked Grace.

"Score one point for Grace," said Regina petulantly. "I hadn't thought of that. Maybe I will."

"I'm afraid the police have the area sealed off," said Edward. "No one is going to go near the pool area until they have completely finished their investigation. We're fortunate we don't have to move out of the house. However, there seems to be no evidence that the killer was ever in the house. Just in our back yard and the adjacent woods."

"Thank you, Edward. That information is so helpful. May I ask one little question? Would it have been too much trouble to wake me up last night when all of this was going on?"

"We tried," said Edward. "Apparently you dipped a little too far into the barbiturates last night. We could not wake you. I know occasionally you forget and take the sleeping pill twice."

"I didn't think I took two pills," said Regina, trying to

remember. "What about Ray?"

"He was sound asleep like you. We could only wake Corina."

"That's ridiculous! Ray takes nothing."

"A doctor looked in on you both," said Edward. "He said that while you were in no danger, you wouldn't be coherent until morning."

"I am sure I only took one sleeping pill last night. And I know my brother never takes sleeping pills."

"Look," said Edward. "Ray is a grown man. You may not know everything he does. And no one has the foggiest idea of what's going on except that Tamica is dead."

"And Grace is here."

"That has nothing to do with it. Grace obviously did not know that Tamica was dead before she, or rather we, did not know that Tamica was dead before we came in."

"You came to the house and decided to lounge about in the back yard, as cold as it is? In the middle of January you went over to the pool area? Were you admiring my landscaping, Grace? Such an improvement over what you had done when you lived here."

"Now listen," said Edward. "There's no need for us to quarrel among ourselves."

"Among ourselves? Have we all become a team?" Regina lost her sarcasm and became alarmed. "Where is Ray? Where is my brother?"

"I checked on him not too long ago," said Edward. "He just has not woke up yet."

"My brother does not know his wife is dead?"

"No, only Corina has been told. It was such a shock to her the doctor gave her something to sleep and she has not woken again, either."

Regina ran her fingers through her hair. "I'm going to wake Ray up. I'll get him up somehow."

She whirled and raced back up the stairs two at a time.

Chapter 13

Regina was shaking as she reached her brother's room. All she had accomplished was suddenly precariously imperiled. Anyone threatening her position would be seen by the entire world as without fault, while she would be condemned because she was shrewd. A lesser person, lesser in intelligence and beauty, would be easily forgiven the sins for which she would hang.

She beat her knuckles against the door, demanding it to open and reveal some protection. "Ray! Ray! Are you awake?"

Without waiting for his answer, she went in. Ray Cathare was stretched across his bed, sleeping naked, his chest rising and falling with the breath of a peaceful sleep. She pulled the sheet from the bottom of his bed and covered him up. Then she shook him.

"Ray! Ray!" She shook him harder. There was a glass of water on the nightstand. She threw it in his face. "Wake up! Wake up!" Startled, he opened his eyes and rolled on his side.

At once, a piercing pain shot through his head. "I'm awake! Regina! For heaven sakes, stop shouting at me!"

His motions in the bed caused the sheet to fall away. Regina drew back. She was undisturbed by her brother's nudity. She had more important images in her mind. She had to tell him his wife was dead.

"What the hell is going on?" He pulled the sheet over himself. He rubbed his eyes and shook his head gently in a painful attempt to clear it. He wiped his face with the covering. Ray's hairline came to a point in the middle of the forehead. A thatch of thick brown hair tumbled down, blending with his wide eyebrows. He took a comb from the nightstand and flicked his hair first one way and then another, achieving an instantly sexy style with his historic features, dark enough to be considered sophisticated and suave, hinting at an ethnic background.

Ray was a dark white man, with clear skin, perfect brown eyes and features drawn as if from a Hollywood recipe, yet retaining a native East Texas toughness that would have made him irresistible had he wanted to be a great Western Star and he had been granted the fortune to have been the right age in the 1930s. As it was, these qualities made him a prized asset by the modern day country and western dance halls he frequented in Houston when he could escape the gates of Sand Waves. With his brother-in-law's pending political campaign, that was not going to be often if his sister had her way. And she usually did.

Regina was thinking that this morning Ray did not look his best. His face was flushed. He rubbed his head as though the pressure inside it were unbearable.

"Damned if I got a headache."

"You've got more than a hangover on your hands," said Regina. She wanted to be tactful but she knew she was going to get through to her brother she would have to speak his language.

"Regina, hell! What did you wake me up for? Let me go back to bed in peace. I'll not be involved in any of your schemes today."

Regina caught herself before rebuking him. When her rebuke failed to come, he looked at her more seriously. He rose and searched in his drawer for underwear. Then went to the closet for pants.

"It's Tamica."

"Yeah?" Ray was pulling his pants up.

"Tamica, your wife, is, she's- she's passed on."

Ray was thinking that he probably should shave. "Passed on what?" He went into the bathroom and turned on the water.

"She's dead!" Regina called in exasperation.

The water flow stopped immediately. He came back into the bedroom. "What are you saying?"

"Tamica is dead. Hurry up and finish getting dressed. Do whatever you've got to do and then come down. Now Tamica is dead but Grace York is here and apparently the police will be back shortly."

"Tamica is dead?"

"Tamica is dead. Right. You've got it. Now listen to me, Ray. You've got to stick with me on this." She reached and touched his arm. He drew away from her. "You are my brother. I am your sister."

"Hell, Regina! I'm aware of our biological relationship. Stick to the subject." Ray angrily jerked on a shirt. "What the hell are you talking about? Stick with you? Did you kill my wife?"

"No! It is just that this is a very difficult situation and I'm liable to be made the scapegoat. Tamica was murdered."

"Murdered? You mean somebody killed her on purpose?"

"Yes, will you just shut up and listen for a minute? Tamica was murdered. Here. Last night." Regina sat down on the bed.

"Hell, Regina! That is impossible!"

For a moment, panic came over Ray's features and twisted them. But only for a moment. He was handsome again in a second.

"Look, I've just found all this out. Got up this morning feeling absolutely wonderful. Went downstairs and behold, there was Grace."

"Gracie is here?" A softer look came over Ray.

"Yes, she is here." Regina smashed her fist into Ray's pillow. "Dammit, don't you get started on her. Your wife is dead, remember?"

"Now look, I don't have anything against Grace. Whatever's going on between you and Grace, that's your problem. As well as whatever's going on between you and Edward. Tammy was my business."

"Tamica was your wife. And I expect you to go downstairs and act like a proper bereaved husband."

"What makes you think I'm not bereaved? I cared for Tammy."

"Regardless of how you feel, the police are coming. You have to talk to them. So hurry and go on, get dressed."

Ray hesitated. "What about Corina?"

Regina frowned as if she were trying to remember who Corina was. "Oh. Corina. I don't know. I don't remember what they said about her. I think she knows. But they gave her something to sleep. I wish you wouldn't take so much dope. You'd be more coherent."

"I am coherent. The world is going nuts. My wife is dead."

"Just remember what all I've done for you. Just don't forget what I have done for you and what I can continue to do."

Regina went back into the hallway, shaking more than she had when she first knocked on his door.

Ray grabbed a towel and a razor and held them up to his face gazing in the mirror as he said to himself, *believe me, no way I could ever forget what you've done for me.*

And his eyes glittered as they darted up, over, down, and around.

Chapter 14

Grace, unseen, watched Regina leave her brother's room. A few seconds later, she knocked at Ray's door.

"I'm almost ready, Regina. Give me another minute."

"Ray," Grace said softly.

Then the sound of footsteps, somewhat hesitant, then faster, then the knob on the door turned. And the door opened.

"Hey, Gracie!" said Ray, holding out his arms.

In his embrace, Grace found a moment of unfettered delight. "Swell," she said. "You certainly haven't changed."

Ray took both of her hands into his and pulled her into the room. "Neither have you. Only for the better," he said, looking her up and down.

"So," she said gamely. "What have you been up to?"

"Oh, Gracie, just trying to live."

"I'm sorry about Tamica."

Ray said. "I know you are. I can't lie to you, Gracie. My marriage to Tammy wasn't exactly working out. But I was not expecting this either. And you? Regina tells me you were here. What are you doing here, Gracie? Don't you have better sense than to not leave all this alone. Two years. I thought you'd found another man by now to replace my fool brother-in-law, Edward."

"It's not that simple, Ray."

Ray finished buttoning his shirt inside. "Hell, ain't nothing simple anymore. Everything is so damn complicated. Not like when we were kids, Gracie? Me and you and Regina. Just cousins."

"Regina is not my cousin," Grace interrupted.

Ray looked at her with sympathy. "What's happened since we've been grown hasn't changed the way it was back then. She might as well have been your cousin."

"Nevertheless, she's not my blood cousin, like you."

"I could say she's not my full-blooded sister. Just my half-sister. But I was raised with her. She might as well have been my full-blooded sister. My daddy raised her like she was his own, just as if she was his daughter."

"Uncle Dick was too good of a father for her. She always thought she was better than the rest of us because she was a Lancaster."

"Well, I know that. But you know you got to look at Regina in a certain way. It's nothing personal that she thinks she's better than us because her daddy had a long pedigree like a dog. Wolf wolf."

Grace laughed, feeling relaxed.

"But, well in a way, Gracie, she thinks she is better than everybody. You just can't take it too seriously."

"Tell me, Ray. Why did you marry Tamica?"

Ray frowned. "Why does anybody get married? They're drunk, in love or looking for a paycheck. And she was beautiful."

"Yes, oh, it's not that I'm prejudiced, Ray-"

"Oh, hell no! Course not, ain't nobody prejudiced anymore. This is 1983. Even in the South, even at home in East Texas, we're just all brothers and sisters. One big happy family."

"But would Regina have been so understanding if Tamica had not been the granddaughter of the great Amelia Mattworks?"

"What makes you think anybody was understanding?"

"I suppose you did get a lot of flak. From Regina? How did Regina react to your marriage?"

"You know Regina. The fact that Tamica was related to Amelia Mattworks made up for everything. You know that Hollywood guy is supposed to be coming here this week to talk about the new movie studio. Apparently, Amelia is going to put up part of the financing. Regina has been waiting for a chance like this all her life."

"How long has this actually been going on?"

"This is been in the works for two years."

"I haven't seen Regina for the past two years."

"You haven't seen me for the past two years."

"Not seeing you wasn't my decision. Not coming to your wedding was not my decision."

"It wasn't my doing, you know that."

"No, I know it was Edward and Regina. It was their idea to combine estates when you married Tamica. Now Edward has a new political advantage. Related by marriage to an African American

66

legend. That neutralizes his southern roots without deserting them. Now he is married to the sister of a man who is now the stepfather to Amelia Mattworks' great-granddaughter."

"You know," said Ray. "I have thought about that. My romance with Tamica happened so fast. I wonder sometimes if Mink Tanem didn't somehow arrange it."

"Foster it," said Grace. "Foster is what he does, Ray. Anything and everything that can possibly work to Edward's advantage in the polls, Mink Tanem fosters. He fostered this living arrangement, no doubt. The great Edward York, blue blood of the old South, takes 92-year-old Amelia into his home, along with her only living family, a 28-year-old granddaughter and a teenage great-granddaughter. Three vulnerable women. Builds a third floor for Amelia to live. Considerately provides his new wife's brother as a husband for the granddaughter, creating a loving stepfather for the great-granddaughter, who never knew her own. Now a big happy family. It's a press agent's dream. What's not to love?"

"Mink was trying to figure out what to do about the fact that Tamica was going to divorce me. I wonder what is Mink going to do about this?"

"You know, Ray, I have often thought in the past two years, in a way, I have missed you and Regina as much as I felt the loss of Edward. Somehow, I think Regina is paying me back for all the times we ran off and hid from her. She never would let us play with her toys. So we would not play with her."

"Ha, she is still obsessed with toys. She shops for additions to her collection all the time. She wants Edward to buy that toy museum because some of the pieces there she cannot get any other way," said Ray. "And you ought to see the dollhouse she's got in her room. A $50,000 doll house all her very own, doesn't have to share it with no ill bred irritating little brother."

"Nor her ill bred irritating little cousin."

"But that's, yeah, that's right. I think you are right. She's paying us back for the times we made her 'it' when playing hide and go seek." Ray stroked his chin. "And then rode off on our bicycles and laughed. We were cruel to her, I guess. Selfish little brat she was."

"I didn't come back here to discuss my childhood," said Grace, a touch of anguish in her voice. Then she laughed a little. "I went to a psychiatrist for that and paid lots of money."

"Did you?" Ray folded his arms across his chest and cocked his head at her with interest.

"Yes, after Edward, well, I had to have some kind of help."

"And what did he tell you, Gracie?"

"Among other things, that you were the substitute for the brother that I never had and Regina was the substitute for the sister that I never had. Really, any idiot would have seen that. And I had not just lost my husband. I had lost my whole family. I knew that, too. And now you have lost your wife." Grace looked thoughtful. "I might be speaking out of turn, Ray. After all, I haven't been in on anything for two years. That this is Regina's doing isn't it? Isn't it?"

Ray rubbed his chin and walked away. "Regina's doing? I would say it was Edward York that destroyed our family."

"Edward's been the victim of our family," Grace said.

"Then are you asking me if Regina killed my wife?"

"I know Regina, as you just pointed out," said Grace. "I know how she must have felt when you married a woman that was black. I don't care if she was the granddaughter of the longest enduring female jazz singer of all times."

"If she objected to that, Grace, I have got to give her credit, she never showed it."

"Of course she wouldn't show it. But when your mother married your father and he was just a blue-collar worker, didn't her father's parents sue for custody of her? It's in her blood. For you to marry a black woman? Would Regina kill over that?"

"Her paternal grandparents didn't kill anybody when they lost. In fact, they later on treated me as good as they treated Regina even though my father drove a truck and their son had been a professor. Hell, Regina'd probably kill me before she would kill Tammy. She wouldn't kill Tammy just because Tammy was going to divorce me. Ah, I don't know, Grace. I just can't believe Tammy is even dead. Do you have the slightest idea what's going on? What happened last night?"

Grace looked at him hard for a second and almost began telling him when the thought that three people could not keep their lies straight for the police recurred. Too great a margin for error.

"Edward and I- I had something to discuss with Edward."

"That's why you were here?"

"Yes but, it's of a personal nature. It has nothing to do with anything. And then we found your wife."

"What I don't understand, I mean I slept last night, and Regina said she did too, like we've both been taking something. I didn't take nothing last night, Gracie. Somebody must have drugged me. I didn't even drink and I've got the most awful hangover. Somebody had to have drugged me."

Grace bit her lip without replying.

"Regina said the police are coming. And I guess they've taken Tammy away," Ray said sadly.

"Yes. Ray, I think I should tell you this before you find it out in a more painful way. Tamica was shot- not just once-"

"What you mean?"

"She was hit, then- They say the first shot preceded her fall into the pool. She probably never felt the last four."

"Four?" In his eyes, Grace saw a distant haunting gleam. Far away, but it was there. *So he did care some for Tamica*, she thought.

"And Ray. I don't think you knew. Maybe you did. But if you didn't, you have to pretend you did."

"What else?"

"Tamica was pregnant."

"Oh, my God!"

"Don't let on that it was me that told you."

"When? What did she say? Was I-"

"She was three or four months along. She didn't say who. And I don't think she knew. I think I had better go back down. One of the policemen is a friend of mine. Just to let you know. The lieutenant."

Grace left the room, her last words neither acknowledged nor heard by Ray who was mentally picturing five bullets, one by one, hitting the woman that he had turbulently shared his life with for the past 28 months.

Chapter 15

Lieutenant Plate was back at 10 AM.

The York mansion looked amazingly different in the daylight. The huge den occupied most of the back of the house, divided by a closed foyer opening to a wide hallway where the elevator was located. Only a small section of the kitchen, connected to the foyer by a short narrow hall, looked out upon the back yard with a high small window. Most of the kitchen faced the side where a large picture window gave a wide view of the side yard, which was connected to the front yard. The den also had windows too small and high to see the pool area clearly. On the second floor, a few scattered high windows made it impractical for anyone to view the back yard unless they were quite tall. On the third floor, a row of moderately low matching windows overlooked the murder scene. Those were Miss Mattworks' windows in her private quarters.

The first and second floors relied primarily on manual security with a minimum layer of electronic surveillance. Edward York felt that the house, surrounded by the dogs in front, the woods on one side, trusting neighbors in back and on the other side, was protected. The complicated intra-yard network of fences could keep anyone from the outside world out.

The recently added third floor enjoyed an added layer of security, both manual and electronic, which made it almost impossible for anyone to access the famous songstress without going through the proper channels. Amelia Mattworks enjoyed the total peace of mind that only extraordinary inaccessibility and a 1980s state-of-the-art security could bring.

Equally inaccessible due to its own private security system, the doctor's clinic occupied the west cottage close to the dividing fence. More accessible was the house where Mink Tanem lived. As he functioned much as an armed guard, he felt his presence was the best security possible.

The two cottages directly opposite on the east side were empty and comparatively unsecured. They had manual alarm systems designed to make noise if anyone broke in. Like Mink Tanem's dwelling, they had no electronic security. The Yorks used them as guest cottages or temporary quarters for servants who occasionally needed to stay overnight.

The west fence held back dense woods as far as the eye could see. The east fence bordered the neighboring property of the famous ball player, Clip Pointpar, where he lived with his son, Forrest. The back fence bordered another neighbor's property, the estate of Erick Skrale, the well-known evangelist.

The pool was small in comparison to all the structures surrounding it. It was a relatively short distance from the back porch to the pool, a longer distance from the pool to the cottages that shared the back yard space. Each cottage had its own individual fence and fences bordered the driveways that penetrated the back yard with gates for access. Unlike the eight-foot redwood fences, the fences around the cottages, and those bordering the driveways to the cottages, consisted of widely spaced iron bars which offered no privacy or security, mainly just protection from the dogs, if the animals should accidentally get into the back. This layout had allowed Mink Tanem to easily survey the pool area and most of the back yard from his front doorway. Or his front porch, if he desired.

Plate made little sketches of the topography as he walked the grounds. Visible from the yard was a tall structure on the Pointpar estate, which resembled a type of the tower on stilts. The Pointpar mansion was too far into its own land to be seen from York estate. So was the Skrale home. There would be little use to question the neighbors. Unless someone was actually in the tall structure there was no way anybody at either house could see into the York back yard.

Forensics had taken careful note of all tracks in the back yard and daylight in the woods brought out visible signs of human activity there. Plate watched as the forensics team, in tall boots and brier proof suits, went about collecting the evidence in the dense forest. He figured it would not be long before they made their conclusions and he would know a lot more. There were three rifles on the estate and all had been turned in. One belonged to Edward, one to Ray, and one to Amelia, who actually kept it on the third floor.

Plate did not have much hope that one of them would test

positive as the murder weapon. It was too obvious. These people were not stupid.

Plate suspected that everyone in the mansion would be sleeping late this morning. He had made use of all the early part of the day to complete his survey of the grounds and now it was noon. Time to wake them up.

He was surprised to see a servant come to the back door when he knocked. And apparently, this servant was surprised to see him.

"I come in at six o'clock in the morning for routine cleaning," said the tall thin young blonde man to Plate after he identified himself. "Before you ask, my parents own a cleaning service company and I work for them. I make sure our most important clients are serviced properly. The only way to do that these days is to do it myself."

Plate kept his thoughts about what it might be like to have a male maid to himself. "Where do you park your car? I didn't see you come in. But I have been in the back yard most of the morning."

"Judge York does not allow cars parked on the front premises. He provides a shuttle for me from my apartment in Houston. The staff that comes here varies from day-to-day and so do the hours that they work. I get off at three. Everyone has to be gone by six. We just let Mink Tanem know what we need every day and he arranges it."

Judge York's transportation was on call all day long.

This concrete evidence of the amount of money the Yorks possessed caught Plate off guard. It changed his view of them slightly.

When he went back inside, he found they were all awake already and expecting him, he was even more surprised.

The family was all downstairs in the den, except Corina.

Grace and Edward acted as if he was just picking up from where he left off.

Chapter 16

Regina York took one look at Lieutenant Plate and dismissed him as completely inconsequential. She answered his questions methodically, taking care not to volunteer any information.

No, she had not taken any drugs the night before, other than perhaps her usual sleeping pill. And she had only taken one, she was sure.

No, she knew nothing of her sister-in-law's death.

Of course, relations between her sister-in-law and herself were cordial.

Naturally, relations between her sister-in-law and her brother were excellent.

Certainly, Edward York had no cause to harm Tamica.

Heartbreaking was the only word for Corina's situation, never knew who her father was, now no mother.

"I'll take care of my stepdaughter," said Ray, as he came upon the scene.

"Of course you will, darling," said Regina, pleased. "Of course you'll take care of your stepdaughter, just as if she were your own, like your father did for me."

Plate made a mental note of that comment but did not verbally react to it.

"What about the child's real father?" Plate asked.

"That's a good question, Officer," said Ray. "I don't know anything about him at all."

"We will be checking into him, as soon as we ascertain his identity," said Plate. "Can you tell me anything about any other relatives?"

"Amelia Mattworks had a daughter named Chloe from her marriage to the great jazz musician Roscoe Burns. Chloe made headlines all over the country in 1951 when she married a white man, Alon French. Tamica was their daughter, born 2 years later. Chloe Burns French committed suicide in 1967, the year her father, Roscoe Burns, died of cancer. Tamica was only 14. The next year she became pregnant with Corina. Corina's father is unknown." All this precise, detailed information came from Edward York.

Plate wrote this down and read over it for a few moments.

"What about Mrs. Cathare's father? That would be Alon French, according to what you've just told me."

"Oh, yes. He was a few years older than Chloe. He died in 1978, I think. Before that, he had sort of faded out of the picture. He was sick for years and not really much a part of Tamica's life due to that. Cancer, I think. Amelia Mattworks, of course, provided the best of care for him, but his treatment was in Europe. You might want to research his death to get the exact time and cause. I'm sure it made the papers, at least a small article on the obituary page." Again, it was Edward York who supplied this information.

Plate was impressed. *No wonder people said of Judge York, he knows the complete details of every case*, Plate thought.

"So there is no one else to notify except Miss Mattworks?"

"And the press," Regina said.

"Ah yes, the press. I'm sure they are on this by now. However, you are so isolated and protected behind the iron gates that they cannot get here, theoretically," said Plate.

"Mink Tanem will help me deal with the press. Of course, we don't want anything hidden, but we don't want false information leaked either," Edward added.

"Yes. Mr. Tanem. I appreciate his efforts to help out. Just for my records, his real name is Mink? Or is that a nickname."

"Uh, Minyak Tanem. He goes by Mink. Sometimes we jokingly call him Mink Coat. Helluva time for him to have been gone." Edward spoke wistfully, as if having had his assistant on the grounds would have prevented the tragedy.

"And his official title? Mr. Tanem, that is?"

"Well, for now, just assistant, secretary if you like. He will be my campaign manager for the '84 elections," said Edward.

Plate looked up sharply at Edward, then at Grace but he did not ask the obvious question.

"Everything we say here is confidential, I'm sure," said Grace.

"Right. In the meantime, we have confirmed there's been evidence found that someone came through the woods last night. And there was evidence of gasoline poured out on the grounds. Mostly evaporated but enough left to take a sample. It has also been confirmed that attempts to administer prescription sleep medication to some or all of you was made, successfully in the case of Mr. Cathare and Mrs. York."

Grace shifted and looked at Edward who stood with his hands behind his back and a perfect poker face.

"It's highly possible that someone, some intruder from the outside, came in here last night and murdered your sister-in-law, your wife, Mr. Cathare." Plate addressed Ray secondarily. "The perpetrator managed to attempt to administer the drugs, thinking he or she would need to come inside the house to accomplish the crime, then somehow managed to lure Mrs. Cathare outside. Therefore the crime took place there instead. Afterwards, it appears the gasoline was poured on the shrubbery with plans to possibly set the house on fire so there would be no evidence of the drugging. Someone or something interrupted the killer and that task was left unfinished."

"That must have been what happened," said Regina. The others started to verbally agree.

"However," said Plate.

As usual, he was highly satisfied with the effect of that word. When multiple persons began speaking, the word redirected all attention and everyone focused on him.

"The question is why were Mrs. York and Mr. Cathare drugged? Why was Mr. York, Judge York, not drugged?"

"That is simple," said Grace. "He was gone. He was with me."

Plate flinched a little. "It appears the drug was put into the food and drinks, assuming that everyone would consume them later. Why wasn't anything put in Edward York's drink or food?"

No one had an answer.

Plate told them about the man seen climbing over the fence and the man seen loitering in the neighborhood. He put forth both possibilities- it was the same man or it was two different men, both coincidentally thin and blonde.

Everyone contemplated this for a moment.

"I have an idea," said Ray. "Perhaps Tammy herself drugged

us."

Everyone turned to him for an explanation.

"Well," he said, hesitantly, almost as if he were improvising. "Perhaps Tammy had to meet someone that she didn't want us to know about. This was the blonde man. Someone from her past maybe, and she just thought she was going to meet with this person. She made her appointment to meet them in the back yard, knowing she cannot get them by the dogs in the front. She gave us some harmless medication so we wouldn't interfere. She figured the man would be gone by the time Edward got back. You were gone a few hours weren't you, Edward?"

"Yes." Edward narrowed his eyes at Ray.

"Right. Well, anyway, it's just a suggestion. Tammy was up to something. I am sure about that."

"The question is though, why did Mrs. Cathare have such a guest here?" Plate was trying to throw a kink into this budding theory. He did not like it.

"Are you saying, Ray, that Tamica had a rendezvous with some man she didn't want us to know about? Or could it have been a woman? I guess that she didn't want us to know about this person and so she drugged us? Then, did this person actually come to the house?" asked Edward.

"And then unaware she was in any danger, physical danger, she played into the hands of the killer," Regina added. She was pleased with this idea. It sounded like a good movie plot to her.

"Right, maybe she didn't have any choice," said Ray. "Maybe this person insisted on coming here."

"A very interesting possibility," said Plate. "We will certainly be looking into all of it. In the meantime, uh, the best I can say is to you, Mr. Cathare, my regrets on your wife's death. As soon as the autopsy is completed, we will release the body so that you can make funeral arrangements."

"Yes, I'm going to go to the funeral home this afternoon to discuss preliminaries."

Plate rose to leave. "May I speak with you alone, for a minute, Mrs. York?"

Regina frowned, then she realized he was speaking to Grace.

"Yes, of course, Lieutenant. Perhaps we could step into the kitchen," said Grace.

"That will be fine. Excuse us, please."

"Yes, excuse me," said Grace.

Grace and Plate went to the kitchen.

Ray and Edward walked out to the foyer. All its connecting doors were open. Edward, putting his hands in his pockets, began to pace. Inexplicably, he glanced at the staircase. Sitting at the top, her chin in her hands, was Corina, looking like a little lost waif.

"Corina," said Edward. "Why don't you come down? Join us."

Corina just stared at him with her large child eyes. She sat there sizing them all up as if they were prospective employees.

"Corina," said Ray. "I'm going to make the funeral arrangements for your mother this afternoon. Won't you come with me?" Ray started up the stairs. Corina watched each step he made with trepidation. She shrank against the banister when he squatted down beside her.

"If you don't want to come, you don't have to. Tell me if there's anything you'd like to have at your mother's funeral. Anything special at all. Tell me now, before I complete the arrangements."

Corina turned her head. "I have one request. No. It is a demand."

She spoke softly to Ray.

Only he could hear her.

Ray looked astonished at her words, but not disturbed. "I don't see why not. Who do I speak to?"

"Reverend Erick Skrale. I'll get you his number."

"Anything else?"

"No. I'll write my instructions down for you. That way it will all be clear."

Chapter 17

Regina went back to her room. She pulled out her vanity bench and sat down in front of her dollhouse. She pulled out a drawer of accessories still to be placed in the display. A selection of firearms contained several rifles and pistols. She chose one of each to add to the dollhouse décor.

After placing them satisfactorily, she sighed with mild frustration. She had recently investigated how much it might cost to change the dollhouse's interior to more reflect the oval office and other White House rooms. It would have to be custom crafted and she was a little leery of asking for such an expense approval from Mink Tanem.

If only Edward ran his own finances. Ran his own life. Granted, it was useful to have Mink Tanem to work on when trying to manipulate Edward's behavior to maximize his support among those who make the Presidents. She and Mink's ambitions were perfectly coordinated in that respect.

Mink, however, took offense at her dollhouse expenditures.

Regina sometimes felt that Mink compared her unfavorably to Grace. Yet when Grace was still married to Edward, she rarely even gave Mink the time of day. Regina had noted that and made efforts to cultivate the army veteran even before her romance with Edward began.

Still, he was deferential to Grace without embarrassment. Regina fumed to herself about his divided loyalty. Mink may have some soft spot for the ice princess, as so many men seemed to have for Grace, he actually had profited in power, persuasion, and probably income when Edward divorced Grace to marry her.

Mink's influence over Edward has skyrocketed since Grace left, thought Regina. *And he has me to thank. He doesn't appreciate me.*

She wondered how much Edward suspected many of Mink's ideas were her own.

Edward doesn't appreciate me either, she thought, glumly. After contemplating this for several seconds, she became bored.

78

She sighed again and shrugged. Turning from the dollhouse, she picked up a weekly magazine and flipped it open to read. Nothing interesting. Regina wished she had not let Amelia take all the old movie star stories upstairs. Modern day scandal sheets were so fake. The old ones told the truth. She tossed it aside and went back to her dollhouse...

Mink Tanem had no influence over Ray Cathare. Ray refused to let Tanem call a limousine or even go along to make arrangements. Ray drove away alone in his pickup truck as if he had to answer to no one for his movements.

Ray did not have far to go to make arrangements with Reverend Erick Skrale about his wife's funeral. Although Reverend Skrale's evangelical church was located outside the gates, it was as close as physically possible to them. And the reverend kept an office in his compound which backed up to the York property but was only accessible by exiting the York estate at its front and driving through a maze of winding streets to arrive at the front of the Skrale home. A 15 minute car journey that would have been a two minute walk if there had been a gate in the fence that divided the two back yards.

Ray was welcomed warmly by the reverend in a cottage constructed much the same as the ones on the York estate. The Skrale compound was smaller, however. The main house was a third of the size of the York mansion and there were only two extra cottages. The security was simpler, as there were no dogs and only a single fence. Like the York estate, the Skrale home was bordered by woods on the west side but there were no extra fences to keep the cottages separated.

"You don't know what it means to have you come to me to plan Mrs. Cathare's funeral," said Reverend Skrale.

"It was her daughter's wish and since we have no religious affiliation here in Sand Waves, I didn't see why your church would not do as well as any other," said Ray.

"And you and your wife's religious background?" the reverend politely inquired.

"I'm Baptist from East Texas. Attended off and on most of my life there, sort of casually, I guess. I've been here a couple years and never found any church I felt comfortable in. Must confess I didn't look beyond the Baptist church in Sand Waves. I don't know about Tammy. We never discussed it. We were married at the York estate by a JP."

"I see. Well, about how you want the service to-"

"Oh, my stepdaughter wrote it all down," Ray pulled a piece of paper from his pocket. "Just let me know if there's anything that won't work."

Reverend Skrale took the paper from Ray's hand, not concealing his excitement as he opened it.

He'll get some mileage out of this, doing the funeral of Amelia Mattworks' granddaughter, thought Ray, without malice. *He looks like a Scandinavian with that thatch of white hair at his age. Let's see if he's up to what Corina wants.*

Reverend Skrale carefully read what Corina French had written concerning the funeral of her mother.

"I don't see any problem with any of this," he said.

"And the cost? I don't mean to be crude. But my wife was not a wealthy woman, as you might have thought-"

"Oh, there will be no charge," said Reverend Skrale. "We will make all arrangements with musicians as desired."

"Well, now, that's generous," said Ray, thinking, *you won't get THAT much out of it. After all, Amelia's 94. Tammy wasn't close to her. She might not even come. And while Tammy made a little news ten years ago, she's been nobody for the last decade.*

"Oh, it's no problem."

Ray wrestled with his conscience for a short moment.

"I have to tell you, we cannot guarantee Amelia Mattworks will come."

"That does not matter," said Reverend Skrale. "The Lord has put it upon my heart to do this service for free. Now let's finalize the details."

Ray did not protest again and the two men began working together.

Provenance V

Early Summer, 1921

"Your name is in papers all over the country. Scheduled to sing in New York, Boston, Chicago, and Virginia. We might can still swing New York, Boston, and Chicago but Virginia is going to have to be canceled."

"So we cancel Virginia," said Amelia, taking a drink, fingering the charm bracelet that dangled from her wrist.

"It's not just that. Eventually these rumors are going to get all over the country. There's laws in a lot of states we're going to be breaking just by having reservations in certain hotels."

"So we will stay out of those states." Her long nails tapped against a little miniature copper horse, a miniature ivory cupid, and a tiny gold cross all of which the bracelet carried within its links.

"Amelia, you don't understand. There have already been two demonstrations here in New York. Have you no paperwork, no relatives, nobody to attest that the rumors are untrue?"

"They're just jealous. They think because of the way I sing, I have to be a Negro?" She took off the bracelet and dropped it in her crowded jewelry box.

"It's more complicated than that. I don't have time to explain Darwinism to you. We just need a good witness, some paperwork, something reliable to show that you are white, born of white parents."

Amelia took a deep breath. The image of the unused potion competed with imaginings of the invisible child in her womb. "And what if such witnesses, such paperwork, such something reliable, does not exist."

"What the hell do you mean by that?"

"Exactly what I said. Where do I stand if there is no evidence that I am white?"

"There has to be evidence that you're white!"

"We didn't have birth certificates issued, necessarily, in East Texas in the 1890s. I don't think they even issue them now. You have to pay an extra fee. Many people don't have it."

"What about people that can testify for when you were growing up?"

"I don't think you can rely on any testimony that I was white."

"My God, Amelia. What are you saying? Are you trying to tell me you are not white? That you have been passing all this time? If that is true, do you know what they're going to do to you? They are going to tear you apart."

"No, they won't, I know how I'm going to do it. I'm going to fall on my sword. I'm going to confess and repent. I'll be forgiven."

"They'll never let you back in white society again."

"I can do without white society. I don't feel like I belong there anyway."

"How much is this got do with Roscoe Burns?"

"It might have everything to do with Roscoe Burns," said Amelia, smiling. "Can a white jazz singer marry a black musician?"

"Not in America."

"Well, you can't prove I am white. Because I'm not. That's the truth. My mother was white. All her other children were white. They didn't all have the same white father. But they were all blondes or redheads. I was the only darker one. Let me take my makeup off."

Amelia went into the other room and covered her face with cold cream. She came back out with a white cream still covering her face. She took a towel and started wiping. The makeup came off in large white clumps.

Her olive skin exposed, her thick lips still red despite the lack of lipstick, she ran her hands over her smooth wavy hair.

"I straighten it you know," she said. "It's really as scraggly as the blackest woman in Africa."

Her companion mopped his brow and sat down. This was devastating. He had managed Amelia for two years and made her a sensation in the Northeast, well known in the South and Midwest, and was planning to take her to California the next month.

"You can still take me to California," she told him. "What we will do is, I'll leave New York a white woman and arrive in California, black. Meanwhile, during the train ride, we put out the press release. The Lord done showed me the light. I can lie no more to my public. I

82

have Negro blood in my ancestry. I was being raised up passing as white for my protection, never dreaming I would become famous as a singer. Now, I know what I did is wrong, I apologize for it, beg forgiveness of everybody that I've offended and now I want to live as a member of my own race for the rest of my life and let the judgment of the people be on me."

And incredibly, against all odds, it worked. During the long train ride from New York to California the press had been informed about Amelia. Faced with a repentant sinner willing to accept her proper place in society although it meant a significant step down, they handled it all in her favor as much as they possibly could. Some out of decency, but most because they liked her.

Her white manager was quietly paid off. He went quietly back to the small restaurant he still owned, enough money in the bank for the rest of his life, or so he thought.

All those around her that needed to be black, became black. Some of the whites shed a few tears as they moved on, those that had planned to be with her forever. Others were eager to get on with someone who had no ambiguity in their background.

There were, of course, some racist protests. There were a few Amelia Mattworks record smashing parties in a few spots across the nation. A lot of anti-jazz music fans laughed uproariously at their jazz fan friends who had been fooled. Concerts were canceled, refunds were demanded. Enough were given to placate public opinion.

But, singing as a black woman in California, adhering with humility to the restrictions binding her race, with no complaint, Amelia was soon forgiven pretty much by most of America.

And eventually, embraced by the entire world.

In addition, the politics and times of the age almost promised that it might not matter in the long run. It was the dawn of the 1920s. Want and war were of the past. The future held only prosperity and peace. In such an atmosphere, how could intolerance and prejudice survive?

Within weeks, Amelia had married Roscoe Burns and had taken her place in the black music and theatrical community, loved and accepted, as if she had always been there. She no longer had to wear the makeup that lightened her skin. Without it, she was beautiful. Her only vanity, her only reservation from her previous self, was to keep her hair long and silky, the only reminder that while she was part black, she was also part white.

And she continued to sing jazz like no other.

Not even the birth of her child slowed down her career. It seemed that as a jazz singer, she was more popular than ever and the road to her legend never again took a wrong turn.

Chapter 18

Amelia Mattworks had to be told. The living legend whose jazz voice, in live performances and recordings, had thrilled millions for nearly 60 years, had lost two husbands, one to war and one to cancer, a daughter to suicide, and now a granddaughter to murder.

It was universally agreed to wait for the arrival of Dr. Apixza, to be in attendance. Although Amelia enjoyed excellent health, she was 94.

"Usually when the doctor leaves town, as he frequently does for long vacations, a temporary hire physician moves into a vacant guest cottage. Not into the clinic, which Dr. Apixza allows no one to enter inside unless they are a patient," Regina explained to Plate. "The substitute just stays as our guest until Dr. Apixza returns."

"For some reason he did not do that this time. Such a short trip, I suppose," said Edward. "Not far away."

Apixza still had not been reached when Ray came back from conferring with Reverend Skrale.

"He's tired of being at Amelia Mattworks' beck and call and he turned off his car phone," predicted Regina.

She little knew how right she was. Starting his trip the previous day, that had been the physician's first action.

Dr. Apixza had lived in walking distance from Amelia for years, following every time she moved, from New Orleans to California and back, finally settling in Sand Waves in the very early 1970s when the famous songstress became one of the premiere residents of the gleaming new Command Design Colony located south of Houston in a prime location that caused it to face the beaches on one side, yet be close enough to the city to call what it wanted of Houston's rich culture its own.

Like many doctors, Apixza had coped with the changing times poorly at first, then learning to adapt. By the 1960s, as he witnessed the fundamental consequences of the upcoming changes in medical technology and in the way patient care was delivered, he foresaw the decline of the private practice of the independent doctor.

When the opportunity came for a secure job as the personal

physician of the celebrity, it seemed no sacrifice to him at all that he would be required to live within sprinting distance of his client and be perennially on call. The only drawback was her age indicated a finite term of service.

He was delighted with the move to Sand Waves, defined as one of the most perfect places to live in, not only in the United States, but also in the world. But with no apartment facilities behind the gates, he actually had to live with Amelia and try to maintain his other discreet practice at a Sand Waves strip mall outside the gates.

As his recreation, he began taking vacations in more exotic locations, usually with a hired escort to keep him company. The escort was changed every time for security reasons. Likewise, so was the temporary physician who moved in while he was gone. This meant that everyone's needs were satisfied during his vacations but no one got too close for too long.

A key advantage of Amelia's recent relationship by marriage to Edward York, and the move from her own smaller home to the York compound, was the conversion of one of the cottages to a fully functional medical clinic designed to serve the residents and employees of the estate and for him to reside in. Every medical need, short of anything serious enough to require hospitalization, could be met in the clinic. It had all the latest medical technology including the newest in ultrasound and diagnostic testing.

When the York and Mattworks families united there came another unexpected bonus. Apixza became, by proximity, Edward York's personal physician as well, ensuring the doctor's job security beyond when Miss Mattworks inevitably passed on. Having his clinic on site was icing on the cake.

Two years ago, before the weddings of Regina and Edward, Tamica and Ray, it looked like his easy prosperity might die with Amelia. Now there seemed to be no limit to his future.

Edward York had served in Congress, then as a federal judge, making headlines with innovative rulings never successfully appealed. Now being groomed for the U. S. Senate race in 1984, he was frequently talked about as a future presidential candidate.

Judge York did not routinely consult physicians. But as a

President, he would need exams to reassure the public and a personal physician at his side 24 hours a day.

With all this excellent health abounding, Dr. Apixza had no qualms about continuing his trips. Other residents and employees at the estate had a garden variety of complaints but no one had anything serious that required ongoing attention. If there was an emergency, a resident substitute should be able to handle it until he got back.

This time, almost to Dallas, Apixza began questioning the wisdom of breaking his habitual routine. He regretted not arranging for a substitute. He began to feel a little guilty about turning off his car phone and not checking his messages at all. He just knew he risked losing this small amount of time away from the servitude.

He stopped one more time at a Dallas striptease before reluctantly turning on his phone and checking his recorded messages before registering at a hotel.

As soon as he did, he cut his trip short and started home at once. He had a five hour journey.

So for some time after her granddaughter's murder, there was no doctor available to be by the side of the great jazz singer and she could not be told. It soon became apparent that the doctor's absence was a blessing in disguise. It gave everyone extra hours reprieve before the sad duty. There was time to plan exactly how it would be done and who would be with her when she was informed that Tamica, only 30 years old, married only two years, mother to a child who adored her, had been brutally shot to death.

Lieutenant Plate had observed silently as Edward, Regina, Ray, Grace, and Corina came together to talk about the moment. They unanimously decided only Grace and Corina would go in with the doctor to tell Amelia about the death of Tamica. Grace was so concerned as to how Amelia would take the news that she literally sat down and wrote a script for everyone to follow.

As it always does, time passed. Dr. Apixza returned. He was given a copy of the script, then started up the stairs behind Grace and Corina. The others all waited anxiously downstairs.

And then was Amelia was told.

Chapter 19

After the ordeal of telling Amelia about Corina's murder, everyone scattered somewhat throughout the house. Apixza offered Grace, Regina, and Corina sedatives. Only Corina accepted and went to bed. The ordeal of first preparing her mother's funeral instructions and then telling her great-grandmother about Tamica's death had been too much. She just wanted to sleep.

Regina declined, stating she had work to do on her dollhouse. With Plate's permission, Ray resumed remodeling work on Mink Tanem's cottage. Labor was good for him right now, better than any therapy, Ray declared.

Edward York left also, to confer with Mink while Ray worked.

Back in the kitchen, Lieutenant Plate had his arms around Grace's waist. In addition, she had both of her hands pressed against his chest like a kitten resisting being held.

"I didn't sleep last night," he said, "thinking about you here."

Grace applied a little more pressure with her palms. "That wasn't necessary. I am perfectly safe here. In fact I might be staying a little while." She increased the pressure to the point of pushing. Plate, stunned, released her.

"I really don't like that."

"You and Regina both," Grace said, with a little laugh.

"It's not normal for the second wife to host the first wife at her home. Or am I wrong? I'm not acquainted with the etiquette of divorce."

"But this is Edward's house. Not Regina's. It's more mine than it is Regina's. And this morning at breakfast, Edward graciously offered me the use of it for the time being. My residence is relatively accessible to the press, the media. Here, there are the gates. And now, guards to keep people out. This was once my home, you know."

"Yes, I know."

"This was once my kitchen. Regina doesn't cook. They have hired help for that. I did all the cooking when I lived here. I love to cook. But it wasn't enough."

"Grace, I repeat, I don't like this at all."

"Try to understand. It's necessary." She thought of Edward's plan to kill Regina and was glad Plate could not read her mind.

"How well did you know Mrs. Cathare?"

"I, well, I knew her. I had met her. We were acquainted. I had hoped to be better acquainted. After all, she married my cousin. My only blood relative left in the world."

Plate looked down. He knew Grace's parents had been killed in a plane crash in 1971, along with her aunt and uncle. Living in her native East Texas at the time, Grace had decided to move to Houston and live alone. She had never really given him the details of how she could have afforded such a move. He assumed it had to do with some type of legal settlement regarding the plane crash.

Although she was just over 21 years old, Grace had moved to Sand Waves and bought a home. She had opened a design studio and quickly become the darling of Sand Waves' society, almost overnight. In the course of her business dealings, she had met and married one of the country's most eligible bachelors, the Honorable Edward York, several years her senior. She sold her studio to devote her time to being his consort.

Eight years into her marriage, still childless and wanting family, Grace had brought her cousin and his sister from East Texas to Sand Waves to work for her and her husband.

"My generosity to my relatives destroyed my marriage," Grace had told Plate when they first started dating. But she had not elaborated and he had not pressed her for details then. The subject had seemed too painful for her.

Now he needed to know.

"Exactly what are the statuses of these people in your life?"

"I don't know how to answer that question."

"Who are these people to you? You once told me they destroyed your marriage. And how did this situation with them evolve into the present day arrangement?"

"Some of this is personal to me."

"Grace, there's been a murder. I'm not asking for personal reasons. I need a detailed account of who these people are, how they came to be here, and how they and you are entangled with Amelia

Mattworks' granddaughter and possibly the killer."

"Very well, prepare yourself for a long story," said Grace, with weariness. "I brought Regina and Ray to Sand Waves from East Texas in an attempt to improve their lives, which were going nowhere due to the chronically depressed economy there. Regina was working as a waitress at Dairy Queen and Ray was an oil field laborer in the fields. I introduced Regina and Ray into Edward's social and political world, thinking they were attractive and intelligent people and they would find positions in his political organization related to their skills, plus I could have some family in town. I was lonely."

"So your husband was on board with this idea of relocating your relatives?"

"Edward is a generous and tolerant man. Both Ray and Regina have valuable qualities as people. Regina was always a terrific organizer. She can plot and plan any type of event scheme, or activity, with the assurance of success. She supplemented her income as a waitress by working as a wedding planner back home. Unfortunately, not many people have big weddings where we lived. Ray is just a good person, willing and able to do most any reasonable work. I thought they would get jobs and be in our social world on the periphery. It hardly worked out that way. Instead, Regina took my husband. Ray met Tamica French and they married. I might have retained relations with them, but they moved into my former home, living with my ex-husband and his new wife. It was hard to take."

"Your uncle and aunt killed in the plane crash were Ray Cathare's father and mother?" Plate realized.

"Yes," confirmed Grace. "But Ray's sister, Regina Lancaster, was my uncle's stepdaughter, so I am not biologically related to her. Ray and Regina shared a mother. Regina and I just share a husband." Grace laughed with bitterness.

Plate looked down again. "So neither was married previously? Before they came to Sand Waves?"

"No," said Grace. "I think Ray had a casual girlfriend. Otherwise, I don't think either of them had a serious relationship before Tamica and Edward."

"Aren't you letting yourself in for a lot of pain by staying here?"

"Look, I am not staying on the second floor with Edward and Regina. I'm staying in the west wing. Closer to Ray. Remember above all else, Ray is my first cousin whom I grew up with. Right now, Plate, I know this sounds crazy. I have no family. I need to be here."

"Grace, I want to be your family. I want you to look upon me as your family. I have a large family. Parents, siblings."

"You are rushing things between us."

"We have been seeing each other over eight months. You've not even agreed to meet my family."

"Eight months is not a long time. I was married to Edward eight years. I grew up with Ray, and Regina. I may hate her now but I loved her much longer before. I'm sorry. I don't mean to hurt your feelings. Try to understand that there's been a death in this family and I'm part of this family again."

"If that's what you want, I suppose I cannot sway you. But I don't like this case. I don't know, Grace, but it's possible that this outsider theory is a farce. We're going to do some thorough checking on this path left in the woods. It could be the path taken by whoever broke into Mink Tanem's cottage. Or not. It could've been faked. Someone could have deliberately come through the woods, trying to fabricate evidence that there was an intruder. If we can find definite evidence that there was someone else-"

"If you cannot find- prove- there was an intruder-"

"Then it is obvious. Edward or Regina York, or Ray Cathare, killed Mrs. Cathare."

"Or me," said Grace. "Or Corina."

"I didn't want to say Corina. She's just a child."

"Children can kill. How I know. Daughters have killed mothers. And me, I'm not a child."

"Yes, I should consider you a suspect, Grace."

"Yes, if you're going to consider Ray and Edward suspects, then you're going to have to consider me a suspect as well."

"I take it you have no objection to my considering Regina York as a suspect?"

Grace looked down at the tile.

"So you think she is a valid suspect?" said Plate.

"I didn't say that. My opinion of Regina will not stand up in a shoe factory, considering she's married to my ex-husband now."

"You mean because she took your ex-husband away from you?"

"Really? We just had this conversation."

"I'm sorry. I'm sorry. I know it's none of my business. But you know, Grace, you're the woman I want for my wife. And I don't know anything about your cousin. He might be a fine man. But I know a little bit about Edward York. On the bench, he acted more like a movie star than a judge. I'm not much more impressed by his new wife. I just hate to see you here among these people."

"You forget. I am one of them."

Plate was silent.

"Oh yes," Grace declared. "I'm one of the rich everyone so despises or envies. I haven't figured out which is worse. Don't forget that just because I no longer live behind the gates doesn't mean I'm not one of them anymore."

"I haven't forgotten." Plate paused. "Does that mean my marriage proposal doesn't rate a reply?"

"Don't be silly. Of course not," said Grace, in a pitched voice. "Right now is not the time to talk about our future. Until this situation is resolved, nothing can happen. After all, we cannot have our police lieutenants marry suspects can we?"

"No," said Plate abruptly. He was feeling very depressed. "No, we can't."

Plate's pager went off and he went to a rectangular kitchen phone that hung on the wall. Grace walked over to the large picture window as he picked up the receiver. From the kitchen the glass looked out onto one side of the lawn, where two large dogs raced around in play.

Chapter 20

"Do you have a personal chauffeur who always drives you?" Plate addressed Edward York as the latter entered the kitchen after Plate hung up the phone.

"Not exactly per sé," said Edward York, opening his refrigerator. "I have a contract with a limousine service to provide all my transportation needs and they provide drivers. They vary from day to day, sometimes from trip to trip. So I have no personal vehicles on the grounds. There's Ray's pickup truck. No one drives it but him."

"We spotted a man in a chauffeur's uniform making his way over the fence either coming from or heading in the direction of the Pointpar estate."

"Last night?" York pulled an apple from the vegetable bin and polished it with a handkerchief from his coat pocket.

"Just now."

"And you didn't catch him?" Grace asked.

"He seems to have disappeared into thin air. We think he might still be on the premises."

"Are you asking me if you can search the house?" asked Edward.

"We're pretty sure he's not in this house. We would like to get inside the cottages. It's possible he slipped into one of them and is hiding there."

"Well, of course. By all means. Are you thinking this was Tamica's killer coming back to the scene of the crime for some reason?" Edwards asked.

"That doesn't make any sense to me. You, by any chance, have surveillance cameras here?" Plate asked.

"No, I like my privacy, Lieutenant." Edward York took a knife from the kitchen drawer and sliced the apple. "Don't think I could function with cameras watching me all the time."

"Any type of camera surveillance at the cottages?"

"No. Moreover, I cannot give you permission to search the homes of Mink Tanem and Dr. Apixza. You need to get their permission as well as mine. I'm sure they're harboring no criminals."

"How many vehicles are on the property?" Plate asked.

"I told you my family keeps no personal vehicles on the property. The exception is Ray does have the pickup truck. It's kept in a small garage on the north side, out of sight," said Edward.

Plate had seen the garage. It was more the size of a two car garage. It contained nothing but gardening tools, in addition to the pickup, which had a gun rack in the rear view window that held a rifle.

"Dr. Apixza and Mink have private cars, parked behind their cottages. Is one of those three vehicles missing?" Edward asked.

"No. I am just trying to understand how much flexibility in movement there is here. What about phones? How many are there. I know about one in the den and the one in the kitchen." Plate contemplated how expensive extension phones were. "Isn't there a limit on how many lines you can have?"

"Yes, but we have some privileges. I and my wife have private extensions upstairs in our rooms. Ray and his family have an extension in their wing in the hallway. Amelia has a phone upstairs. We do have two lines, although all the phones won't work the second line. Some don't have the button needed. Our second line is for in-house but you can dial nine and get an outside connection from it."

"Corina does not have a phone in her bedroom?"

"Give an extension phone to a 16-year-old? Absolutely not."

"What about the cottages?" Plate asked.

"They have separate phone lines. Dr. Apixza and Mink, that is. There are no phones in the unoccupied cottages."

"Here are the keys, Lieutenant," said Grace. "To the two empty cottages." She had turned from the window and fished the keys out of a different drawer.

"Thank you," said Plate, taking the keys from her at arm's length. "I think it would be a good idea for you to check on both Corina and Miss Mattworks just as a precaution."

"I'll do that right away." Grace glanced at the large window once more before she left the room.

Both Plate and Edward walked over to the picture window and gazed out at the dogs as Edward bit into the apple slice.

"The dogs are not allowed in the back yard. Why?" Plate asked.

"We actually come and go out of the house through the back most of the time. The front door is never opened. It's a facade, really. We come and go via the two drives that come up the side of the house, passing the cottages, into the back yard. The transportation service picks us up and drops us off at either edge of the back porch. The drivers then turn around in the cottage driveways and go back out the way they came in. The canines are a nuisance, so we keep them restrained in front. Since only the front yard is visible from the street, strangers don't know the guard dogs cannot access the back."

Edward finished his apple.

As they watched, the animals disappeared from view, presumably bounding over to the other side of the yard.

As he and Edward York stood together in silence, looking at the empty grounds, Plate could not help but think that the complicated design of the yard and mansion somehow reflected the complicated personalities and relationships of the people living inside.

Chapter 21

Plate found evidence that both vacant cottages had been inhabited just recently. It was subtle evidence. Less dust in some parts of the structures, and more than adequate supply of toilet paper in the bathrooms. Other inconsequential details that would not be there if no one had been in the houses recently.

However, he found no one around. No clues as to who might have been using the places.

"I need to speak to Amelia Mattworks," Plate quietly told Grace when he returned. Grace had met him in the rear foyer. He followed her into the den and watched her pick up the phone.

A call to Amelia found her unwilling to allow anyone into her quarters at that moment. She assured everyone she was fine.

She wanted to be alone.

She was writing her memoirs, she said, for the movie producer that wanted to make a movie of her life.

"I've heard the rumors about a movie featuring the life story of Amelia, to be produced by Stark Wynter's studio," Grace told Plate after hanging up. "Amelia Mattworks Enterprises is in negotiation with him. I rather doubted anything Amelia writes at age 94 would have anything to do with the movie. I do try to encourage her to write down everything."

"Yes, I heard you promise over the phone you would read it all when it was finished and do any editing needed. It seems like you have a relationship with her."

"I will see what I can do about getting you an interview with her as soon as possible. But I cannot promise anything."

Grace turned away. She seemed tired and unhappy. Edward was in the kitchen and Plate did not want to go back in there. The others had all gone to their rooms.

Plate was beginning to get quite discouraged. He debated calling them all back and questioning all of them more about who might be in the cottages but he decided they were not going to tell him anything, at least not yet. If he could get more time alone with Grace, maybe he could convince her that she needed to speak up a little bit about who might have wanted to kill her cousin's wife and why.

Edward York came into the room. He said nothing but his expression clearly indicated he wondered why Plate was still there.

Plate wondered the same thing.

Right now, the ranks were closed.

He was not going to get anywhere.

The day had passed rapidly and dusk was fading. It was unlikely he was going get much of a forensic report until tomorrow.

He went back outside and looked up again at the strange structure visible on the Pointpar estate. It looked closed and deserted. Yet the windows were not boarded up.

Such a structure would be vulnerable to area hurricanes and tornadoes that occasionally arose. The glass was dark on the outside of four double hung windows that faced the York estate in a wall constructed of old clapboard with a sharply pointed gabled roof. Stairs could be seen on the back, but the actual entrance to the structure was not visible.

Plate stood on the trunk of his patrol car, still parked in the east back yard drive, to try to get a better glimpse of the building.

He was going to have to pay the Pointpars a visit. He debated whether he needed permission to do that.

He decided he would play it safe and talk to the chief tomorrow.

He jumped down off the car.

He decided to go home.

After Plate left, Grace began to fret about Corina. Grace wished she had the convenience of just phoning Corina instead of having to go all the way over to the east wing to check on her but the girl's bedroom was too far from the phone in the hall for her to hear it ring.

As Grace walked the long hallway, carrying a cup of tea, the many decorative and collectible toys distracted her.

The festive mariachi dolls holding fans and guitars cheered her and she could almost hear their music as she passed by them. She had to stop and rearrange a nativity display that had belonged in Edward's family for generations. Someone had moved the animals too far off to the side. Too far away from the Holy Family.

Probably one of the day maids dusting, Grace thought, balancing the teacup as she shifted the ceramic figures.

A small collection of colorful transparent glass grapes in various hues was displayed on a table closer to Grace's destination.

Wonder who collects them? Grace thought, not remembering having seen them before. *They were not here when I lived here. They look so bright and futuristic.*

The optimism left her when she reached Corina's door.

Corina was in bed, her arms clasped under the back of her head, her eyes focused on a small flaw in the sheet rock ceiling. She didn't want a nap but all the adults had insisted. So far the drug Dr. Apixza had given her after the stress of telling her great-grandmother about her mother's murder had not put her to sleep, rather it had made her arms and legs heavy as though each muscle cell were waterlogged and swollen twice its size. And she had no strength or energy to do anything, save think in a slow groggy process.

Her mind strayed to a good looking young man who held her in his arms promising to never leave, promising to take care of her always…

A knock on the door disrupted any potential for relaxing. Corina hastily turned over on her side and pulled the covers around her.

Grace had checked on Amelia. Although the elderly lady was not in the mood to talk, Grace had been given two cups of hot tea, one for herself and one to take back to Corina. It was Grace who was knocking at Corina's door.

Not waiting for permission, Grace entered Corina's room, bringing the tea and soft spoken words that did not penetrate. Her first objective was to see Corina drink the tea. That was accomplished at once. After the nominal conversation that obviously left Corina's mind as soon as the words were spoken, Grace left Corina's room strangely ill at ease.

After ingesting the tea, Corina had fallen asleep. Grace had watched her for a short time during which the anxiety slowly permeated. It remained with her as she made her way back to the opposite wing of the house. It was not the same nervousness connected with Tamica's death bothering Grace, but rather that there had been something about the girl that should have been obvious to everyone.

For some reason they all remained blind.

Chapter 22

Back in the guest room, a spacious and plain room with an equally spacious and plain dressing room off to the side, Grace undressed for bed. She donned a robe that was both light and comfortable.

The room was warm. Several books were on a shelf, provided as a distraction for guests. She selected a romance novel to take her mind off the entire situation. She sat in a soft recliner and read, but could not keep her mind on the book.

A new 1980s style love story, the book was full of aggressive love scenes with explicit sexual violence. Grace could not concentrate on it. She kept picturing Corina from when she had earlier checked on her after the report of the intruder.

She drank the other cup of tea provided by Amelia, then leaned the recliner back. Her thoughts blurred a little and Tamica's face as a bride interchanged with her face as a corpse, and the faces of Edward, and Ray and Regina shrank and ballooned and shrank again as though the nightmares were manufactured by Hollywood special effects experts.

Suddenly one face alone loomed before her, ballooning and shrinking, then ominously growing normal. She felt his warm hand running over her stomach, on her breast. The other hand clasped her mouth shut. She nodded her head in agreement that she would remain silent.

All at once, she was naked from the waist down and he was coming at her. She wanted to move her legs to kick him but they were water soaked, heavy as anvils.

He pulled her apart and came down on her, and in her, she whimpered a little, bringing the backs of her hands up to her face, the tears streaming down into her hair as the jerking persisted, the bed bouncing with each strong thrust. Finally, he pulled away from her murmuring in a low voice, "that's all. That's all." Then he looked her straight in the eyes and commanded, "go on and wash up. Put yourself back together." And he laughed.

She had every ambition of obeying his instructions, washing

up, putting her clothes back on. But she was glued to the bed, her arms and legs heavy laden with some type of weight that prevented her from moving. He was going to come back. She knew it. And she could not move. She could not stop him. She could not let go....

Grace jumped up from the recliner, her body covered in sweat, her arms and legs still feeling numb although she had no trouble moving them. It been a long time since that dream had haunted her.

Why now? They had been told there was no sexual assault on Tamica. That had already been determined. Why should she inexplicably have the old nightmare? Corina's demeanor from earlier that day flooded back into her mind.

And her posture in the bed, the covers all bunched around her.

Yes, that was it! Grace stood up and paced a little back and forth across the bedroom. *Yes, that was it.* Corina was a teenager but she dressed like an old woman. And there was a physical maturity about her that was not quite natural.

And the entire scene in her room just a short time previously had been false. Had been staged...

Less than an hour after her last visit to Corina, Grace went back to the east wing. She trotted down the hall to Corina's room. She knocked again. Assuming the girl was asleep and not waiting for a reply, she pushed the door in.

As she walked to the bed, moonlight delineated the girl's form, her legs sprawled open, knees bent in the opposite direction the soles of her feet pressed together the covers thrown back to one side, her gown pulled up under her arms.

Grace switched on the light and stared down into Corina's suddenly awake, terrified eyes.

Grace backed out abruptly, shut the door, and ran to the phone in the hall.

Chapter 23

Lieutenant Plate, roused from much needed sleep by Grace's somewhat frantic call, in which he detected more anger than hysteria, strode briskly into the den where Grace, Regina, Ray, and Edward were sitting. The latter three were half asleep, also having been roused out of fresh sleep. Only Grace was wide awake, flitting around the room like an angry wasp.

"What's going on?" said Plate, recalling bitterly that when Grace's voice chimed hello over the phone at midnight, his first happy thought had been that she had reconsidered his proposal and called to tell him yes. Waking him for that would have been a most forgivable sin. However, when instead she had insisted he had to come immediately to the York house, he came, not exactly thrilled about it.

"Grace, what did you get me back here for?"

"There's been another crime committed."

"What?" Plate looked around the den, much as he had when first summoned about Tamica's death.

Grace proceeded to tell Plate her conclusion about Corina.

"Was there any signs of forced entry into the house?" Plate asked, addressing all the people assembled before him.

"All kinds of people come into this house, Lieutenant," said Regina tiredly. "I think Grace is imagining things."

"Any fool could see she was raped," Grace insisted.

"Very well," said Regina. "Very well, Grace. I'm not saying she wasn't raped. But all kinds of men coming to this house have access. Gardeners, chauffeurs, delivery van drivers, other servants. Granted, we send them home. We don't have overnight servants. That's one of Edward's weird little ideas that I cannot eradicate. They've all got to go home at 6 o'clock, unless there's a special occasion. But nevertheless, nevertheless." Regina waved her fingers in the air. "Excuse me. Nevertheless, any one of them could have gotten back in the house quite easily."

"I like my privacy at home. Especially at night." Edward York fixed himself a drink.

"I don't think any of our servants has done anything to

Corina," Ray said.

"What does the girl herself say about this?"

"My stepdaughter has been more or less hysterical since the stress of telling Amelia about the murder," said Ray. "She just cried and cried and has not actually said anything to anyone as far as I know. She seems terrified of something."

"Not only that," said Grace, "but I am almost positive the girl is pregnant. She's just beginning to show. Not far along. But she is so slight, it is evident."

"I'm confused." It seemed to Plate that Grace was insinuating the pregnancy was also the result of rape. Surely, Grace knew pregnancy was not a crime. Although she often spoke of it in the same terms. She had told Plate she did not want children.

"The girl is pregnant. Nothing confusing about that. Other than who the father is." Grace followed Edward's example and poured herself a drink.

"She must've been fooling around with some teenage boy," Ray said.

"That's likely the case in my experience," said Plate. "However, unless there is a case of statutory rape, her pregnancy, be that as it may, is not a crime. That would depend upon the age of the father. If the girl will not admit to being forcibly raped-"

"I insist that she should be examined," said Grace.

"All right, we'll take her to a hospital and have her examined. But showing intercourse does not prove rape," Plate said.

"She is under age," insisted Grace. "Undoubtedly all the people Regina referred to as having access to the house are over 18."

"So you're looking at statutory rape, which is a tricky crime," said Plate. "The man will say it was consensual. Judges have a way of overlooking those age gaps if there's no sign of violence."

"Plate, the girl was raped," insisted Grace. "I think while she was sedated, not completely out, but incapable of resisting or calling for help."

"On what do you base that assessment?" asked Plate.

"Are you doubting what I'm telling you? I'm basing it on intuition and observation. I am right, I know it."

"Okay, okay we will take her to a hospital. And have an obstetrician examine her." Plate's agreement was halfhearted at best.

Having won the point at last, Grace was now wondering how that could possibly be accomplished with all of the reporters waiting outside the locked gates. How could they keep it a secret?

"Will she have to go to a hospital if it's not rape? If by chance, it's not rape, Dr. Apixza could care for her here on the grounds." Edward York spoke calmly. Plate decided York was the only completely rational person in the room besides himself.

"Would Apixza's findings be legal?" Grace finished her drink while asking that question.

"I take it- the pregnancy was not known?" said Plate to them, as if reading Grace's mind. "You are hoping to keep it from the press?"

"We had no idea she was expecting a baby. Corina keeps to herself a great deal," said Grace.

"You know how teenagers are, Lieutenant," said Ray. "She was always hanging out with the crowd at school and this and that. I guess she was just afraid to admit she was in trouble. She has such a slight build. She can't be very far along."

"I did notice lately she's been wearing such tacky bulky clothes," said Regina. "These teenagers are so faddish."

"Would anyone know if Mrs. Cathare knew of her daughter's condition?" asked Plate.

"I'm sure Tammy didn't know," said Ray. "She'd have told me."

Plate looked at Edward. "What about you, Judge York?"

"I had no idea the girl was pregnant," said Edward abruptly. "Quite frankly I never had much to do with her."

"I see, and of course you've no idea who might have raped her, if she was raped." Plate rubbed his chin thoughtfully.

"None whatsoever." Edward finished his drink.

"Okay, let's go upstairs and talk to the girl. If she's willing to submit to an examination by your resident doctor, that might be the way to go. His findings would be as legal as anybody else's. As admissible in a court of law as any other doctor's."

Chapter 24

"Corina, we need to talk to you. Can we come in?" Grace spoke the words. But it was Plate who knocked at Corina's door.

"Yes, come in." Corina's voice seemed thick with sleep.

Plate frowned. "You'd think the rape would have woke her up," he murmured.

"Not if she was drugged," whispered Grace.

They went inside. Grace first, then Plate, then Edward, Regina and Ray behind.

Corina stretched in bed, appearing for all the world as if she had been sleeping the entire night and had instantaneously been inexplicably awakened.

"Is there something I can do for you?" she said in a pseudo-adult voice.

"We need to talk to you, my dear," said Regina.

"Yes, I know, Mrs. York, Mrs. Grace York was in here earlier and I know she's bound to have seen that I'm going to have a baby." She spoke as if expecting a rebuke from them.

"I also saw what else happened," said Grace.

"What else happened? What are you talking about?"

"I know, my dear, it's nothing to be ashamed of," said Regina. "This is the 1980s. Many girls today have babies before they married. And in these enlightened days there is another choice. Tell us who it was."

"The baby's father was a boy I knew at school. He's no longer even there. His family moved to another state. Contacting him wouldn't do any good. He wouldn't be the least bit interested. I intend to have my baby and have it in peace."

No one in the room doubted that this little speech had been rehearsed. It rang false.

"I'm talking about the man who was here tonight. Who was it, Corina?" Grace asked.

"I don't know what you're talking about. Tonight?"

"We're going to take you to a hospital and have you examined," said Grace.

"I understand your concern. I have worried that by keeping my pregnancy a secret it would keep me from getting adequate prenatal care. So I have been struggling with myself over that. But I presume it could wait until tomorrow morning. Officer, I don't want to go to a hospital. I am perfectly fine." Another rehearsed speech.

"If you were raped, we need to take evidence tonight," Plate said.

"Raped?" The astonishment in Corina's voice and on her face seemed extremely genuine. "Whatever gave you the idea I was raped? I don't know what you're talking about."

"Would you mind coming with me, anyway?" said Plate.

Ray, meanwhile, had opened the door to the bathroom connecting Corina's bedroom. Seeing his interest, Grace followed him into the bathroom.

The bathroom was strewn with wet towels, and the residue of a fresh bath. The air was still hot and steamy.

"Never mind," said Grace, returning to the bedside, staring down at Corina. "I don't think there would be any evidence. Isn't that right, Corina? After I woke you, and left to call the police, you took a bath."

Corina did not reply.

"Well," said Plate. "It looks like you might have been mistaken, Grace."

"Yes," said Ray.

"It's been a hard day for all of us," said Edward.

"I am not going anywhere," Corina announced. "Nobody has raped me. There's been no crime committed except for the murder of my mother. I would think that would be your primary concern, Officer."

"Sometimes when a crime is committed, you get sort of paranoid and start looking for the next one," said Plate to Grace. "You know, like in novels."

"I know what I saw," said Grace. "But if she chooses not to do anything about it, I certainly don't see what I can do about it."

"I don't think I am needed here," said Plate softly to Edward York. "I will be back in the morning sometime, I'm sure, to continue investigating the death of Mrs. Cathare."

He nodded to the others and left.

Grace also abruptly left the room, angry that Corina had such low self esteem that she would cover for her rapist.

This would have never happened if Regina had not usurped my place in this household, Grace thought.

Shortly afterward, with apologies to Corina over her mother's death, and for disturbing her sleep, and after extracting a promise that she would seek prenatal care at once from Dr. Apixza, the others left her alone again.

Corina covered her face with her hands and turned on her side, wondering what to do next.

She slipped down the side of her bed and, on her knees, started to pray.

Chapter 25

"It's an old sports observation station, Lieutenant," explained Forrest Pointpar, as he and Plate walked out the back door of the Pointpar house, into the back yard, passing a near life-size section of a ballfield, towards the towering structure on the Pointpar estate.

The next day, now two days into the investigation, Plate was back early in the morning. Initial forensic evidence had indicated that Tamica was shot once with a .22 and four times with a .44.

Although her position in the pool made it impossible to tell exactly how the shots were fired, in what order, from what distance or in what direction, it was evident to the coroner that the shot from the smaller gun came from the ground whereas the shots from the .44 came from above.

The single shot from the smaller caliber rifle would not have killed her, if she had gotten immediate medical attention. It had struck her in the lower right back and exited through her abdomen, most likely causing intense pain, but not loss of consciousness immediately. Had that been the only attack on her, she should have been able to summon help. However, the other four bullets through her upper back and shoulder areas would have been almost instantly fatal.

Plate was surveying the area. And assuming Tamica was shot not far from the pool, or at the edge of the pool, there were only three possibilities where shots from such a significant height could have come. The third story of the York house or this tower. Or a tree.

A tree in the forest had been climbed recently, evidence indicated. But Plate found the tower much more interesting.

"Any way I can get up there to it? Is it safe?"

"Oh yes, it's quite safe. My father spends a lot of time up there. This is an old-time tower. It came from a small ballpark, not the major leagues. Just a gathering place in a small town. And when my father learned it was going to be torn down, he bought it and had it brought here. You know how these older people are. They need their playthings. This is almost like a tree house for him. He has a lot of fun up here."

Plate did not indicate to Forrest how uninteresting he found baseball. "I was wondering, when viewing it from down below, why the windows face towards the York estate?"

"It has got windows all the way around. But you see the front of it faces the little ball field here. Up until a few years ago, Dad had some neighborhood kids come over and they had games. It got too much for him after he turned 70 and I had to stop it."

"In what way did it get too much for him?"

"He just gets too excited. He's got the high cholesterol they talk about now and some other mild heart trouble. All the medication they gave him nowadays, out in the Texas heat in the summer, sometimes it would all go to his mind a little bit. He would have little heat strokes. He'd think he was back in the major leagues and start yelling and cursing at the kids. This is Sand Waves, you know. The parents complained."

"Yes, I know exactly what you mean," said Plate, with some exasperation. "I can fill up a notebook with parents complaining about anything and everything anybody ever does with their kids in this community. They are never happy."

"You can say that again. As I said, I just had to stop it. We still maintain the field. Dad won't hear of letting me get it landscaped over. He likes to come up sometimes and just sit in that contraption and watch the field."

Plate followed Forrest Pointpar up the gray wooden steps to the lookout building. Inside, he found a rolling desk chair, a battery-powered lamp and scattered papers on the built-in desk that stretched across the structure.

"These old newspapers. Dad buys them in antique shops," said Forrest, picking up a few and causing the dust to fly. "He likes to read the old sports sections. Back from when baseball got more press than football."

"Quite a collection of baseball memorabilia," said Plate, pausing in front of a glass door cabinet that took up most of one corner of the other side of the structure.

"Probably some stuff in there worth some money," said Forrest, nodding with satisfaction.

"Am I to take it this place has no electricity?"

"We're trying to get him to move that collection into the house just because it's got to endure the heat out here in the summer. But he won't do it. Says most of the stuff was made before airconditioning was invented. No, there's no electricity. We couldn't get a permit to bring the electricity out here. It cost a fortune to get the permit to have the structure put here. The only reason we got it was because we hired a lawyer that claimed it was no different than all these expensive dollhouses and treehouses and playhouses that all these people have for their kids. It's just taller. Violates the height restrictions. But we got that problem taken care of by having it declared a historic structure. See, it even has a plaque from the Historical Society."

Forrest pulled the plaque out of a drawer that hung under the built-in desk. He brushed the dust off it and showed it to Plate.

"We just never put it up. Didn't seem to be any reason, since nobody can see it from the road. And the kids that came here didn't care anything about historical buildings."

"From what I have seen, some of the playhouses in this area do have electricity in the back yard," said Plate.

"It cost so much to fight the battle to get the structure here, well we just didn't go any farther. Actually we didn't want them coming out here and inspecting it for fear they would raise an objection to the little ballfield."

Plate looked around the structure for a few minutes more, taking the most time to gaze at the York estate from the back windows, and then started back down the stairs.

An afternoon meeting with the chief loomed.

And he had little more to report.

Chapter 26

"This murder at the York estate is the most inconvenient crime I have ever come across. You know how I hate to have to come in the station on Sundays. Let's get this meeting over with. My wife is waiting. Tell me what you know, Plate."

The chief of police was playing with a small Hallmark statue of a police officer helping a little girl across the road. His wife had given it to him for Christmas.

"Not much," said Plate. "It looks like an intruder might have come in through the woods. The body was in the pool for several hours before it was found. Therefore, there's no way to estimate bullet trajectories at least from a North, East, South, West perspective. I am waiting for autopsy results."

"Let's go with the burglar theory for the moment at least. It will make my life easier, at least in the short run."

Chief Brecken set the statuette down on his desk so hard, Plate feared for a moment it was broken.

"There's more than one possibility of somebody getting in. There's the woods. There's the sports observation tower on the Pointpar estate, although that would be quite a jump. A young healthy man might be able to make it. The man in the chauffeur's uniform might have been coming down from that structure. Then there is the option of simply coming up one of the driveways and circumventing the automatic gates. The automatic gates are designed to keep cars out and are not really that good at keeping people out. The security at that estate looks good on the surface but it is really very weak. Incredibly weak considering who lives there."

"All of that is music to my ears. The more evidence you can find that this was a burglary, the happier I will be. I have to do a press conference. We've got two VIPs landing in Sand Waves. That means two separate press conferences. I'm probably going to be asked about the murder at both of them. The great Amelia Mattworks has ties to both the civil rights and entertainment communities. Reverend Clie Frenel and Stark Wynter are both here for their respective meetings and I'm trying to coordinate security with the city of Houston and the county for both men."

"Surely we're not involved in the reverend's security? Isn't he guarded by the Secret Service?"

"Yes, temporarily at least, due to death threats at the last civil rights rally in the Northeast. It's unofficial still, but it looks like he's going to run for President. There haven't been any threats that I know of in Texas. But we still have to coordinate with them. People threatening him in the Northeast could very well follow him to Texas. And Stark Wynter's chauffeur, his only security, was asking us to provide a man to assist just for general convenience. I was going to send you but I want you to focus completely on this murder at the York estate."

"Even if it is a simple burglary gone wrong?" Plate asked.

"You know as well as I do that no crime is simple if it takes place behind the guarded gates in Sand Waves. That's where the rich, and the rich and famous live. Even a simple burglary gone right is a critical case if it is behind the gates."

"So what are you going to do about Stark Wynter?"

"Well, he's just in town to arrange financing for the new movie studio that is going to be built across the bay. Everyone is all happy and excited about that. Hopefully, no one wants to murder him. We just have to protect him from his middle-aged fans that still remember when he was the biggest male sex symbol star in Hollywood. I will put Officer Skaar on that job."

"Didn't Wynter quit acting and become the studio head ten years ago?"

Plate knew more Hollywood history then he would have liked to let on to the chief.

"Yes, but he still has got a cult following of middle-aged females, some of whom have enough money to follow him around the country wherever he goes. He gets tired of them. After all, he's not an actor anymore. He's trying to be taken seriously here in Texas as a businessman," the chief replied.

Plate laughed.

"I know he doesn't have any oil wells," said the chief. "He doesn't own a ranch. But he's proposing to build the biggest movie set soundstage constructed since before World War II. And it's going to be right across the bay from us and everybody in Sand Waves is seeing themselves in the movies right now. The community theater is in ecstasy and even those residents who haven't been to a movie in years are applying for membership in the Screen Extra's Guild."

"Everybody?" Being an extra in the movies had a certain appeal even Plate could understand.

"Okay, I may be exaggerating. But it is important to a lot of the prominent people in this community that everything goes well, financially speaking, and that movie studio gets built."

"So, Stark Wynter gets the royal welcome here."

"Exactly. Whereas, there's any number of our residents who would like to see the good reverend take a slow boat to China. He is here to discuss desegregation, or the lack thereof, in Sand Waves ISD. Believe me, I am glad the Secret Service is giving him protection. I shall be happy to cooperate with them in any way they want me to."

"So, what are my instructions other than just try to find out who killed Tamica Cathare?"

"Well, there is a little hitch that connects all this and on the day that takes place I'm afraid you're going to have to take the day off." The chief picked the statuette back up and began fondling it again.

"What? A day off?"

"Tomorrow, the good reverend is going to pay a personal call on Amelia Mattworks. The Secret Service is requesting all of our personnel to stand down while he is on the York estate. At the gates, there's going to be photographs taken for the newspapers of Edward York and the reverend. That was already planned before the murder. Not that Edward York exactly supports him, more likely he is going to run against him, but in the name of goodwill, etc. Anyway, after that, the reverend will go up and see the great Amelia as a courtesy call to express his condolences at the death of her granddaughter. No journalists or photographers will be allowed inside the gates. Amelia hasn't allowed her picture to be taken for 30 years. The meeting will be completely private, but publicized, if you know what I mean."

"Okay. I can use a day off. I'm not insulted at all."

"Good. I knew you'd understand. We can just be grateful to God that the reverend does not want to go to Tamica Cathare's funeral. You will be back on duty the next day. The reverend is speaking at several locations in Houston, and there, he won't be our problem. I think they're planning a rally or something. Thank God it won't be in Sand Waves."

"So what did you say he is doing in Sand Waves?"

"Meeting privately with some of the local clergy and political representatives in hopes of working something out about the schools. It's all politics and I don't want to know anything about it if I can help it."

"What if they don't come to some type of agreement?"

"I don't want to think about that. Let's worry about that bridge when we come to it."

The chief walked over to a closed cabinet where office supplies were stashed and put the statuette on the top shelf and shut the door.

"Okay, Chief. I will make myself scarce and I will stay far away from the York estate."

I'll stay in bed all day, thought Plate, exultantly.

Chapter 27

Reverend Clie Frenel did not like the look of Sand Waves.

It was too perfect, the yards all meticulously landscaped even those in the lesser expensive neighborhoods. There were no ditches, only curbs. There were no telephone poles or wires strung through the trees.

Everything was underground. A cleverly disguised manhole graced every street. Fire hydrants were not painted red and silver or yellow and black but rather the primary colors of the home on which lot they were located, so as to be inconspicuous. The roofs were all the same color in the lower echelon colonies.

As he got closer and closer to his destination there was a variation in the roofs. They were not all composite shingles anymore, some were tiled, others wood.

The black limousine carrying the famous civil rights activist had eluded the press that had lain in wait for him at his Houston Hotel. The dark windowed vehicle had endured slow-moving Houston traffic on bumpy freeways with lots of potholes and smog trapped by low hanging clouds. This made the reverend feel right at home since he normally resided in Chicago.

Only the extra muggy air belied his Texas surroundings. However, when he reached Sand Waves, the sun broke out. The humidity lessened, even though they were closer to the ocean, as the air got fresher from the sea breeze.

The change in atmosphere made him uncomfortable.

The reverend gave his sandy haired driver a generous tip upon arrival at his destination. The hired limousine service would not keep the car waiting but would send another limo for him and his Secret Service agent bodyguard when the meeting was over.

The Toy Museum, located in one of the few strip centers in Sand Waves, was deceptively simple on the outside. It boasted its own exclusive restaurant at the back of the establishment.

As he made his way to it, he glanced at the row of antique tin toys from the 1920s that graced that particular aisle. A colorful 10-inch Ferris wheel caught his attention and brought back a childhood memory. He stopped for a second but the Secret Service agent beside him pushed him forward and the memory was lost.

Going through a nondescript door into a little empty foyer, the second set of doors opened up into plush luxury, no expense spared decorations, with comfortable chairs at round tables including those set up in little curtained areas. Frenel was led to one of those and cordially greeted by the small group of men that he had come to meet.

"I appreciate your kind words, gentlemen," he addressed them all. "But I think this is a futile exercise. I don't see how a federal lawsuit can be avoided."

"There must be some practical measures we can take," said Congressman Mark Brown. "I can introduce a bill to construct magnet schools in the Sand Waves area. Schools which are not restricted to area residents."

"That sounds like a reasonable compromise to me," said Reverend Erick Skrale. "Most members of my congregation pay a high price to send their children to a diverse private school. The only one of its kind here in Sand Waves. Competition is keen to get in and as the community continues to grow, if there is no alternative, the public school will also become overcrowded."

"Magnet schools only serve those students gifted in some particular field. The ordinary child is left behind. From my point of view, the only solution is for Sand Waves ISD to be absorbed by the Houston Independent School District and thus integration can be achieved by appropriate busing," Frenel replied.

"Doesn't that always mean our black kids are going to be bussed to the white schools? While the white kids just stay home and go to their schools. It's our people that have to pay the price," said Forrest Pointpar, remembering some of his own schooldays in the Houston area before Sand Waves was even dreamt of.

Forrest already held a minor political position in Sand Waves, assistant to the colony federation president. He was studying law at South Texas.

"It's not going to be that way this time," said Frenel, with an admiring glance at Forrest. *Young men like him are going to be the future,* he thought silently, *and it's my mission in life to make sure there is a future for him and all of those like him.*

"I think you underestimate the amount of objection, the type of trouble the Powers-That-Be here can cause," said Reverend Skrale.

"He's right," said Congressman Brown. "You don't understand these people. You don't understand how rich they are. How much power is behind them. I know most of them are not directly involved in politics, business, or anything. But they are the children, brothers, sisters, and all the other relatives, and non-relatives, if you get my drift, of the really rich and the really rich and famous. Then there is a small percentage which is involved in everything. And they have the contacts like you won't believe."

"I understand a lot more than you think," Frenel said.

The group grew quiet as restaurant staff came in with drinks and hors d'oeuvres. As if they had no cares in the world, the men ordered large lunches. The head of the Federation Council, the school superintendent and two more civil rights activists arrived simultaneously and took their seats at the round table.

The two clergymen at the table flipped a coin to see who would say grace. More orders were taken and the conversation went on...

Chapter 28

Forrest Pointpar trembled a little as he approached the civil rights leader after the discussion about school desegregation had ended, lunch had been consumed and everyone got up to leave.

"Forrest, I hear good things about you," said the reverend graciously. "You're going to be an asset to us in the future."

"Thank you, Reverend. I need to speak with you a moment."

"Of course. I know you're finishing up your law degree. But sometimes the desire to get started just can't wait," Frenel said.

"It's not that." Forrest took a deep breath. "It's about a different issue. I have a message from my father about it."

"How is he doing? I was sorry to hear about your mom's car accident a couple of years ago. I know they were married many years and he must miss her."

"Yes, that is true. Well, he's in his 70s now. He has a certain amount of arthritis. Eyesight still good, hearing a little off. Memory failing a bit. I think he's got a lot more years in him."

Frenel was a little disconcerted by the detailed report of Clip Pointpar's health. But he was glad he was able to react positively to the medical rundown. He was used to hearing much more dire reports on elderly African Americans, many of whom lacked access to the healthcare system that the wealthy former baseball star obviously enjoyed.

"Does he still have that replica of the old field observation post from that old baseball stadium in his back yard?" said Frenel, after having given Forrest positive reinforcement about Clip's longevity prospects. "I read about that in the newspaper. Must've cost a fortune."

"It's not a replica, it's the actual structure moved to the property, Reverend, and it did cost a fortune. More to move it actually than to purchase it. Also a fortune every year to maintain it."

"Well, son." Frenel looked at his watch. "Any message from Clip Pointpar is welcome. What did he want to tell me?"

"This is the exact quote he wanted me to say– 'Abortion is all about killing black babies. You're a fool to support it'." Forrest spoke rapidly and stepped back as he did.

Frenel was stunned into silence, but he recovered quickly. "I wasn't aware of Brother Clip's sentiments on that issue. I do have to respectfully disagree."

The rapidity of Forrest's deliverance of the message and the stilted rehearsed reply took both men aback. They stood silently staring at each other and then looking at the floor for short time.

Forrest wanted to press forward with the argument. Frenel wanted to end the scene and leave, but without animosity. Neither knew how to proceed.

Edward York stepped up at that moment. Had he have heard the conversation's topic, he would have supported Forrest and continued the repartee. He had been conferring with Father Patrick Thomas, head parish priest at the Catholic Church in Sand Waves, about the upcoming scheduled anti-abortion rally in Houston.

Forrest knew York's position and looked to him for support. Instead, Edward York repeated almost the exact same line to the Reverend Frenel that Forrest had begun his words with, "I need to speak with you a moment, Reverend. I have a message from Amelia Mattworks."

Reverend Frenel took the opportunity to patronizingly pat Forrest on the back.

"Reasonable brothers can disagree on these points," said Frenel to Forrest. "Give your father my regards. No one can ever replicate what he has done for our movement."

Forrest had no reply and turned away.

As Frenel turned his back on Forrest and gave his attention to Edward York, he fretted a little in his mind about his dismissal of Forrest. If he was closer to Forrest, if he could be sure Forrest would become part of his movement and never betray his trust, he could have told the younger man that he silently agreed with his statement.

I'm stuck on the other side of that issue, Frenel thought, *and I don't know what to do about it.*

It had been easy to give verbal support to the feminist movement's demand for legalized abortion before it actually happened. He had not believed abortion would ever be legal. In his mind, it had been so obvious who abortion was aimed at, that it was a shock to him when more liberal African Americans combined forces with the feminist movement to support its legalization.

Now it was done. The law of the land.

What was he going to do? Join the other party?

He looked at Edward York, one of the most prominent anti-abortion politicians in the country.

But Edward York was not talking about abortion.

He was talking about drinking tea and eating cookies.

Frenel relaxed.

Sometimes it was easier dealing with the mature practical timbre of the opposition then it was the hotheaded youths of the 1980s, who had only heard stories, and the old men in their 70s, like Clip Pointpar, who thought they knew so much more about the civil rights movement simply because they had lived through it all.

Provenance VI

1927

"A beauty, looks just like her mother. She gone to be white as you," said the proud father, as he held his infant daughter.

Still confined to the birthing bed, still a little groggy from some calming herbs, Amelia rose up on her elbows. "She better turn dark."

Roscoe Burns laughed. "I's just teasing you. Lots of us look really white when we're born. She'll turn dark. Look at her old man's black skin."

He handed the baby back to Amelia and pulled up his shirt sleeve and rubbed his arm. "See, it don't come off neither," he laughed. "Like that make up you used to wear. No more of that."

"No more that ever," agreed Amelia, slurring her speech a little, pulling her breast out for the baby to suckle.

"You know I've been thinking," said Roscoe. "Now that we're safe. Legal and married and we got our babies. I've been on this jazz road for many years now. I am a little tired. What you say we settle down with the young one? Find a nice small town, you know, when we're welcome, one we would be welcome in. Like the one that old witch talked about years ago. The one with protection. We got plenty of money. You can go back to your first love. You can find a church and sing gospel again. I can find some kind of a job so we don't eat it all up. We can have some more these."

He indicated the baby by grabbing her tiny foot for second.

"Have you done lost your mind? We got the world in front of us. I'm not doing no more gospel singing for free. What would you think would happen if we settle down in a little small town? What kind of a life could we give Chloe?" Amelia looked down at her baby. "And Constance. She's going to have everything any white baby ever gets in this society. We're going to have so much money it's not go make any difference what color her skin is."

What could possibly put that idea into my crazy head? Roscoe thought. But he said to Amelia, "The idea of dropping all this life and

121

starting over as regular people just give me some kind of happiness inside. Like it come from the Lord Himself. Maybe we should at least pray about it?"

"You been drinking? We got to think of Chloe and this child. Hollywood will accept them because of who we are. They've got bright futures."

"I don't like Hollywood. Maybe New Orleans or Houston. But I think the country where you come from would be best. East Texas. That way we can take other child."

Amelia tensed. She pushed the child from her breast and immediately the baby began to wail. She forced her finger into the child's mouth temporarily silencing her.

Waking up from a nap, Chloe started yelling in the adjacent room.

"We are never, we are never to mention that, we agreed," she scowled.

"Not even to pray about it?"

"That's mentioning it. Now, isn't it?"

Roscoe stood silently for a moment, contemplating the wisdom of her words and regretting the scenario which he had just painted was a forlorn dream, a mystical vision like a dark stained glass window briefly lit by the sun, its darkness remaining long after the sun had gone.

He grabbed Chloe as she burst into the room. "I guess it is the best way for everybody. I feel sad about it."

"I don't," said Amelia defiantly. "You could say I'm cold. But I have disciplined my mind. Oleida is better off without me in her life."

"I won't ever believe that," said Roscoe, bouncing Chloe on his knee. She stopped crying and smiled happily. "A child is never better off without its mother. Even if it means she can live in the white world as a white person. That doesn't make up for not having her mother. I still hope we're going to be able to go and get her and bring her into our lives. Someday. We'll all be a real family. Find a home."

Amelia looked down at the child at her breast. The herbs were wearing off and she was feeling a mild pain, but thinking more clearly. *I hope this child would not be better off without me in her life as well,* she thought.

But she said, "Roscoe, you would never be happy. You are fantasizing. I don't ever think about it. You should not think about it either. My life began in California. As a black woman. I'm married to a black man. I sing jazz. I don't need to pray about anything. Music is my bible and the stage is my church."

The pain started to worsen and she reached for the bottle of herbs to take another dose.

Chapter 29

Most people would have found it incongruous that one of Amelia Mattworks' most cherished possessions was an easy bake appliance. Granted it was a little more sophisticated than the Easy Bake Oven that only contained a light bulb enabling it to be marketed to the youngest possible of children. Amelia's oven was actually handcrafted copy of the famous toy which had been modified with a mild electric heating element that was just strong enough to complete the baking process for small thin cookies, while the small burner on the top could heat tea, coffee, or cocoa to simmering temperature, but shut itself off before dangerous boiling could begin.

Amelia delighted in serving tea and cookies to guests. Sometimes she made cookie dough from scratch, having ordered the necessary elements to be brought up from the kitchen. Frequently she just used prepared roles of cookie dough easily sliced with a butter knife in just the right thickness for her oven to handle perfectly. She occasionally added a few special spices and sweet oils to these prepackaged unbaked cookies that gave them an additional flavor, so that her guests, if they purchased the exact same cookie dough in the supermarket, never dreamed that it was the source of Amelia's cookies. These specialties she added for unique one-time visitors and infrequent visitors. However, for family and household staff, when they were invited, she usually served the product as it was sold.

She was preparing for a special guest.

Amelia took the amber bottle from its hiding place. In the many years she had possessed it, she had been tempted to use it many times. Most of those times, something intervened. Better judgment, common sense, forgiveness, justice, maybe the hand of the Lord.

She poured a little bit into a teacup. Spices and sweet oils would not be sufficient.

While she waited for her visitor, she pulled out the papers she was working on, found her pen, and began to write a little more.

At about the same time the civil rights activist was breakfasting with the representatives of the Powers-That-Be in Sand

Waves, a long black limousine pulled up in front of the York mansion. Getting out of the car and straightening his tie, its passenger looked up at the third floor. He had heard the story of how Edward York had an entire third floor added to his home to accommodate Amelia Mattworks. He marveled at how the house showed no sign of ever being constructed in any other way.

"I'd like the name of your architect, plus your contractor and construction company," Stark Wynter told Edward York as they greeted each other downstairs.

"I'll get those for you," said Edward. "And have a copy of their references for you to take with you after your business is concluded."

"Thank you! As for the reason I'm here, I understand Miss Mattworks has empowered you to speak for her on this matter."

"Yes, I have power of attorney in respect to this matter alone. Being that I'm an attorney myself, it is only going to take my authorization for the funds to be released. Basically, I don't really understand why it was necessary for you to even come here today. But Miss Mattworks is a woman of discretionary whims. She wants to see you."

"I'm honored. Somewhat surprised that the appointment still stands, considering the tragic death of her granddaughter. But my time is at her disposal."

"I'll show you the way. You can take the stairs or there is a private elevator."

"Oh, either one is fine with me."

Once upstairs, Edward York went as far as Amelia's door, knocked on it and announced Stark Wynter, but did not glance in at the old lady. It moved him too much to look at her, knowing what she had just lost. Yet in his position in life, he understood why she would still want to see the man in whom she was entrusting an investment of several million dollars. Edward frequently had to separate his personal feelings from his public or financial obligations, upon which the employment and or savings of ordinary people frequently depended.

He greatly admired Amelia Mattworks at this moment.

125

Chapter 30

A short time later Stark Wynter came back down the stairwell. A fairly proper host, Edward was waiting.

"Could I get you a drink?" He noticed that Wynter was looking a little peaked. "Would you like to lie down for a little bit?"

"No, um. My limousine has a bar inside. Also a bed. My chauffeur has been unwell and needs to take rests occasionally. He's resting right now, in the car. No. The problem is Miss Mattworks insisted that I eat some cookies. Sweets don't agree with me and especially not when accompanied by any liquor. And I've got to get back to Houston. I've got several other business appointments."

"I received a phone call, as you were on your way down, to go ahead and release the funds, so I assume your interview with Miss Amelia, that is, Miss Mattworks, went okay?"

"Yes, indeed," said Stark, his voice a little unsteady. "She had certain requests, requests that I acceded to. Tell me, is the old lady all there?"

The unexpected casual question so surprised Edward York all he could do was cough for little bit in reaction. "I assure you. Her mind is sharp, just her body is frail due to age, not illness."

"I'm sorry," said Wynter. "No disrespect meant. You know I knew, had a date or two with Tamica French, that is, she was Tamica French when I knew her. She came to Hollywood to try her hand at a singing movie career but it went nowhere. I remember also she tried to be an artist for a while. No success there either. Years ago."

"No, I didn't know," said Edward.

"Well, it was a long time ago. I was still an actor, still hot in Hollywood. She was the granddaughter of a legendary jazz singer and a legendary musician. Our date made some news in its day. You know, my being white. It wasn't just in the movie magazines. It was considered hard news in those days. Well, not a scandal like the hot romance between Clip Pointpar and Doreen Darbell. But still a juicy item."

"Well, I guess it is more understandable she wanted to see you, even though it's been so soon. Will you be staying for the funeral

126

then?"

"Yes I will. At Miss Amelia's request. If the funeral isn't held before I leave Houston, I'll fly back from California."

"I don't want to pry," said Edward. "But you're not telling me she made your attending her granddaughter's funeral a condition of releasing the funds?"

Wynter looked at Edward and smiled wryly. "Yes. And the odd thing is she claimed she didn't remember me. Claimed she only knew about me from what Tamica, I mean Miss French, had told her." Stark coughed nervously, not sure exactly why he felt it important to explain to Edward York.

"Perhaps she felt that if she made a big fuss about your prior relationship, you might not attend the funeral."

"It could be that she is afraid nobody will come?" Stark asked lightly.

Edward laughed. He felt strange laughing but it was a little funny. "I've always heard elderly people get a little paranoid about that type of thing when they get older."

"Indeed," said Wynter. "And she told me she's writing the story of her life for the movie. But I'm not expecting much out of that at her age. If she had only written it years ago before she got so old."

"Is there going to be a movie?" asked Edward, with mild interest.

"Still in negotiations. Maybe we will just use her story as inspiration for a fictional character. I'll know more after I get back to California. Maybe by the time I come back for the funeral, it will be settled."

"I hope it's not too much of an imposition. We can't make the funeral arrangements complete because we don't know the date yet. We don't know when the coroner is going to release the body."

"I know. It's no imposition. I have a private jet always at my disposal. I assured Miss Mattworks that I would have it ready to go and that I would be at her granddaughter's funeral. Gracious old lady, she took my word for it. I know I'll have my hands on that money before they can get a funeral together. But I intend to keep my word."

"She's always been very gracious," said Edward. "It's been a joy to live in the same building with her for the last two years, even though we don't see her often. On occasion when she's in the mood, we all go upstairs for tea and cookies or she comes downstairs for a family meal. I don't suppose that will be happening again anytime soon."

"I say, Judge York, thank you so much for your hospitality." Wynter shook Edward's hand vigorously. "I'm beginning to understand why you have so much support across the country."

Edward smiled. "Undeserved, I can assure you."

"Not at all, not at all," said Wynter.

At this moment, Regina York entered the room.

"Mr. Wynter," she gushed. "I have been a fan of yours all my life."

"My dear, are you trying to compliment or insult Mr. Wynter?"

"Don't be silly," said Regina. She walked over to Wynter and took his arm.

"I could never be insulted by such a lovely lady," said Wynter gallantly.

"See, darling! Mr. Wynter knows exactly what I mean. Now won't you be staying for a good meal? We have a really good cook."

"I cannot stay today. But if it's okay with you, Judge, I would like a rain check."

"I'm not sure how much access we're going to be able to give anyone without clearing it with the police right now," said Edward. "As soon as all this blows over, you're welcome to come at any time."

With his wife now present and busily charming his guest, Edward felt relieved of his duties as a host. He made his excuses to his wife and Stark Wynter and left the room.

"Now." Regina recaptured Stark's attention. "Well then, perhaps we could meet in Houston when you are in town and do lunch," she said.

"Miss Mattworks did request that in addition to attending her granddaughter's funeral that I do return at intervals to visit her," said Wynter, looking somewhat embarrassed at revealing this.

"There's no telling what that silly old lady will come up with," said Regina. "But sometimes she is absolutely on target. We need more visitors at this house. We're all wrapped up in ourselves and company would do us good. I'll talk to that nice young policeman. The one that's in charge, every day except for today, because the Secret Service are coming shortly. But I will talk to him and see to it that you can get past the gates and come and visit us."

"I'm actually thinking of looking to purchase a home inside the gated community of Sand Waves. Assuming the studio deal goes through, once we start construction, I'm going to live here."

"Oh, how wonderful!" said Regina. "We're all so excited about the movie studio. You need to get with a good real estate agent and get your name on a waiting list. There's only a small section of Sand Waves inside the gated part and there's a waiting list to buy in here."

"I never even considered that," said Stark Wynter. "I'll get my people right on it."

"You will be a wonderful asset to the community."

"In addition to requesting that I come to the funeral-

"That tiresome old lady! I do apologize for that."

"No no. No need. In addition to requesting that I come to the funeral, Miss Mattworks is pushing for a film based on her life to be made. I admit the idea is intriguing. After all, *Lady Sings the Blues* won Academy Awards."

"So you would be making a movie about Amelia?" Regina became thoughtful.

"It's a thought. The problem is there's nothing to base a script on. The book seems to have never been written."

"She never would authorize a biography. And from what I'm told, she is so revered and respected that no one has dared write an unauthorized biography. Everyone is afraid of the wrath of her fans."

"Well, I am not afraid," said Stark Wynter. "I just need something to go on. She says she is writing her memoirs."

"Writing at her age? I don't even think she has a typewriter up there."

"She did show me some handwritten pages-"

"I know! I've got a lot of movie magazines from the past. They have articles on her and some on her daughter and granddaughter as well," said Regina, thinking, *I'm going to get them back from that old lady as soon as possible. She must have wanted to read them for reference if she is writing her story.*

"That would be a great help," said Stark, trying to remember if his date with Tamica made the movie magazines ten or twelve years ago, or how his date with her mother made the news decades before that. Amelia had mentioned Chloe. He thought he had known her, too, as a young boy, in the carnal way as they called it now. Neither memory came in clear. It was too long ago.

Also, Amelia had talked about the hot romance between Clip Pointpar and Doreen Darbell, the black ballplayer and the white movie star when both were at the height of their fame.

He wondered how many people in 1983 remembered how scandalous that really was back then. It had apparently stuck in Amelia's mind.

I'll bet Regina York is too young to remember how Doreen Darbell was the most celebrated beauty of her time, Stark thought as he watched Regina with admiration. Back then Regina might have been competition for Doreen.

Glancing at his watch, Stark made his apologies at this point. Other engagements mandated that he had to leave.

Regina expressed her distress and begged him to return as soon as possible, which he promised to do.

Walking out to the limousine where his chauffeur was waiting, he got in the driver's seat.

"I could drive, Mr. Wynter, honestly. Today is one of my good days."

"You just lie back there and rest, Burress," said Wynter genially. "I know how to drive in city traffic."

Doreen Darbell, he thought with amusement, as he pulled out of the York driveway and headed towards the Sand Waves gates. *Haven't thought about her in a while. Doreen 'Doorbell', we young actors used to call her. And for good reason...*

Stark Wynter laughed out loud at memories of sexual exploits of his youth, as he reached the Sand Waves exit while his driver dozed in the bed in the rear of the limousine.

130

Provenance VII

1932

"This is a white's only hospital. We would of never even let her in the emergency room except you told us you were the family chauffeur, Mr. Burns. And Mrs. Burns indicated she was the child's governess." A white cloaked woman twisted her hands nervously.

"We are sending for a private ambulance," said Roscoe Burns to the crisply uniformed nurse.

"If you could just take care of her until it gets here," pleaded Amelia Burns. The nurse was attempting to force Amelia to take the child in her arms. Amelia, feeling the heat from the child's fever, even as she did not touch her daughter's skin, was resisting.

"I am sorry. I'm only following rules and regulations. I don't have any choice. One of our doctors is a fan of that jazz music and he recognized you. He reported the situation to the hospital superintendent. It is out of my hands."

"We have money," Roscoe held up several hundred dollar bills. "You know who my wife is. You know we can make good any bill. Here, something special for you."

"I am truly sorry there is nothing else I can do." The nurse, still holding the squirming feverish child started walking towards the front door of the hospital. Helplessly, Roscoe and Amelia trailed behind.

The nurse briskly exited the front door and stretched the child out on concrete bench nearby. Frantically Amelia ran to the child and scooped her up, clutching her by her light brown hair, trying to still her kicking legs which were scraping against the rough concrete. Roscoe caught up to them and bent over to help.

"Don't worry we'll get her to the other hospital. It will be okay." Roscoe took the child in his arms and started out into the parking lot, with Amelia following behind cumbersomely, for she was four months pregnant. A nanny sat inside the couple's car playing patty cakes with Chloe.

"It was my fault," Amelia sobbed. "I should have sent the two

131

of you in with her. It was me they recognized."

"It wouldn't have done no good. White children don't have black nannies anymore," said Roscoe.

And, as she took Chloe in her arms and made way for Amelia to get into the backseat, the nanny vocally agreed.

The death of the second child of the famous jazz singer Amelia Mattworks made headlines in most city newspapers as much because the child had died before she could reach a hospital that would accept her, as because her mother was famous.

Sympathy came from all over the world with near universal condemnation of the hospital that had turned the Burns family away. There was talk from sympathetic liberal politicians of censure and penalties for the medical facility but nothing ever came of it.

Amelia was so distraught with grief that doctors proclaimed it was heartbreak that caused her miscarriage. The loss of both children took a year out of her life and career. Roscoe Burns kept the family going by continuing his musical endeavors and keeping up all contacts Amelia was going to need when she recovered and started singing again. And there was still Chloe to bring them joy.

Strong as she was, Amelia's physical recovery was still remarkable. Some critics did say there was pathos in her voice that had never been there before. Others argued it had always been there and that's what had made her voice great from the beginning.

Emotional recovery was more complicated. Six months after the miscarriage, she and Roscoe took the unusual move of dismissing all their servants- cook, nanny, chauffeur, gardener and maid- and Amelia took over the care of her household personally while Roscoe began manually keeping the yard. In their social circle, this was viewed as therapy for the couple with sympathy and kindly mild amusement. As their house was 7,000 square feet and its grounds over an acre, this attempt at middle class domesticity did not last long.

But it appeared to do the job and, upon hiring a new staff three months later, Amelia and Roscoe, and Chloe put the tragedies behind them and focused on living the good life that the couple's professional successes warranted.

Chapter 31

Sinclair Plate had not had a day off for six weeks. One thing after another had kept him working, sometimes twelve hours a day. Fortunately, there was going to be no trial concerning the incidents at Luxuries and Innovations for the Season that had happened in early November. The culprit had pleaded guilty.

So he was not going to be tied up in court for days on end. However, there was still a lot of paperwork to do and a lot of procedures and a lot of conferences, plus having to deal with all the routine crime and official duties. The chief took time off for Christmas. But he was the chief.

It did not matter to Plate that the weather was not that good on his day off. In fact, it meant that there would probably be fewer complications when Reverend Frenel went to visit Amelia Mattworks.

Plate sincerely wished the good reverend and the great old lady a wonderful healing visit. That way when he got back to work the next day, Frenel and the Secret Service and everybody else connected to him would be out of the way. Amelia Mattworks would be at peace as much as possible and he could get on with his investigation of her granddaughter's death.

But today he was not going to think about it. He was not going to think about Grace either. Not that he loved her any less. Yet somehow it seemed she had suddenly become part of the job. And a day off was a day off.

He picked up his science fiction book, *3748 A.D. The Return of the Cat,* which he had not hardly had a chance to look at, much less finish since before the great Sand Waves flood. He had missed the humorous action plot which enabled him to relax and take his mind off his work. He particularly enjoyed such books and they were hard to find. In his opinion, most science fiction books were far too serious.

This book was about the adventures of a brother and sister, both humans, thrown in contact with aliens and finding true love.

This was going to be a good day, a day of rest. He opened the book as he stretched out on his couch after a good breakfast and put some snack food on the coffee table. He looked at the telephone and threatened its cord with a large pair of scissors if it dared to ring.

Plate found his place in the book, not far from where he had left off months ago. The brother had fought off his assassins but the sister now found herself a slave on a bounty hunter's ship. Plate began reading:

The human girl had just gone from thinking that the bounty hunter was an obnoxious jerk to actually feeling sorry for him. But his statement that he was a "half-breed" was something that she did not totally understand. "What exactly did you mean by the term half-breed?" she asked, hoping he wouldn't take offense to the question.

"Can't you tell by my metallic copper hair and Terran eyes?" he stated, like it was something really obvious. "Did you grow up in some metal tank out in deep space where you didn't learn how to tell the different races apart?"

"Actually, I did," she answered. "The world I came from was completely isolated and we really didn't learn about the happenings of the rest of the galaxy. And what the people in power did know, they didn't tell the general public. I learned more about the different races on the prison planet than anywhere else."

"Well," he stated, as he pulled out something that looked like mashed potatoes.

"So, now that we know a little bit about each other, what's the deal with the catgirl, the little boy, and the woman that has the silver eyes?"

"B-10 is a gynoid navigation unit from a retired Terran battleship that my stepbrother revived two years ago," he answered, as he pulled out the chocolate syrup. "The catgirl is a member of a genetically engineered race of warriors known as the Lrakians. She fled her pride a year and a half ago and my old man recruited her just before he died. She hasn't ever told me about her past before then." He pulled out something that looked like salsa. "And the boy is my stepbrother, my old man's biological son who decided to join us shortly after the death of his mother." He pulled out some fried rice

134

and mixed it with the syrup...

"By the way, why do you need a cook anyway?" she asked...

Plate skipped several lines as he was snacking as he read. He got the idea the author was trying to convey from the chocolate syrup and fried rice combination.

"What? It all ends up in the same place."

"You're worse than my brother." she said, pushing her food away from her after only taking three bites. "I'm done." She stormed out of the room.

"I'll never understand women," the bounty hunter commented just before he inhaled his food...

I certainly agree with that, was Plate's last thought as he dozed on the couch and the book slipped from his hand.

Chapter 32

Clie Frenel stared at Corina thinking how she only showed traces of being African American. Edward had met Frenel at the gates and obligingly posed for photos as planned. Then he led the reverend back to his house, where it only bothered Frenel slightly being taken to the back door.

He wondered how Corina was treated in this household. He wondered how the world outside regarded her. He wondered if her lighter skin caused her as much problems as his sometimes did.

Since interracial marriage became legal and accepted throughout the land, or at least tolerated in many areas, the old mantra that when black married white the only result was black, was proving to be more complicated than previously believed.

The product of such a union, scorned in the 1920s, but enduring in a small obscure East Texas town to form a family, Clie Frenel was waiting to go up the steps to see Amelia Mattworks when Corina passed by him. She nodded silently to the civil rights leader. Edward York appeared and inquired if she needed anything. Never slowing her pace, she silently shook her head negatively and went on to the wing where she lived.

Frenel looked at his own light brown hands. Having moderately light skin had been a double edge sword in his fight for civil rights. He wondered what kind of a life a truly light skinned black person really endured or enjoyed as the case may be. He wondered how Amelia Mattworks had fared all the years of her celebrity after it became known she was African American.

Certainly, Roscoe Burns had been dark and their daughter Chloe only slightly lighter than her father. Frenel knew well the story of how their second child had died after being discharged from a hospital upon finding out that she was the child of a black couple.

It was a popular anecdote that he used frequently in his work. The story never failed to evoke emotion and not a few tears.

It had all the drama of great civil rights atrocities- the desperation that led Amelia to claim she was the child's governess instead of her mother. And the fatal actions of the white hospital when they found out Amelia had lied. He even sometimes mentioned in his oratory the baby Amelia had miscarried, most likely as a result of the tragedy.

However, nowadays he usually dropped that detail. It seemed like overkill in the modern era.

He had known Roscoe and Chloe in the very early days of the civil rights movement and thought with regret how the father and daughter had not lived to see many of the changes of the modern era. Roscoe had been especially old fashioned, the minister recalled with amusement. The famous jazz musician had acted like an overprotective father when they went out on a few dates when they were both very young. That was before she had married Alon French.

Years later, there had been rumors that her suicide, coming on the heels of her father's death, had been triggered more by an unhappy love affair then Roscoe's passing. However, those rumors had faded quickly. Chloe had never made any type of mark on the entertainment world and she was quickly forgotten.

Now, Chloe's daughter was dead too, and had she not been murdered, would likely have been just as easily forgotten.

The reverend shifted uncomfortably. What was he going to say to this 94-year-old lady who had lost so much?

"Please keep in mind you are the second visitor she has had today and she rarely sees strangers," said Dr. Apixza anxiously. He came downstairs, his short frame blocking anyone from proceeding up. He had conducted a pre-visit examination of the elderly lady.

"Are you sure she is up to this?" asked Edward.

"I think perhaps it may actually be helping her to cope with the great shock, this break in routine." The doctor spoke to Edward, then turned to the preacher. "But please keep in mind she is 94."

"You're welcome to come up with me, Doctor," said Reverend Frenel.

"And whatever you do, don't refuse her tea and cookies," said the doctor, balancing a full teacup on several napkin wrapped cookies, preparing to exit in direction of the kitchen. "She was furious that I would not sit and eat with her. Wouldn't let me leave unless I took these with me and promised to ingest them. I don't think she wants to see me again right now."

The Secret Service agent was blocking that way. Annoyed, Apixza moved awkwardly to one side. Frenel advanced forward. It became a three person impasse.

"No, we were given specific instructions. She wants to speak to you, Reverend Frenel, alone," said Edward York.

There was a short argument about this from the Secret Service agent. In the end, the agent had no choice but to stand aside and let the doctor proceed to the kitchen, where the physician surreptitiously dumped the tea and disposed of the cookies, and to let the reverend to go up the stairs alone.

Even after thoroughly checking out the stairs himself and the balcony that led to the third-floor rooms, the Secret Service agent was not satisfied. However, knowing the status of his host, he dropped his opposition and contented himself with an extraordinarily deep scowl.

"Miss Mattworks has a phone in her room. If you pick it up and punch the second line button, it will ring down here and you can let everybody know that everything's okay up there," said Edward York.

"That's going to have to do," said the reverend to the Secret Service agent.

Taking over the situation, Edward York indicated it was time to go up. And Clie Frenel, a man of great courage, still felt not a little trepidation as he climbed the stairs alone. He hesitated before knocking on the great lady's door, as he had been instructed to do.

She must have heard him approach. *Who says the hearing inevitably goes with age?* he thought, hoping when he was 94 his hearing would be that good.

"Come in, child," Amelia called in a raspy voice that no longer sounded much like the beautiful tones still heard on the radio, jukeboxes, record players and cassettes all over the country.

Frenel smiled. His own parents had been dead for years. He was not called 'child' very often anymore.

He opened the door slowly. The old woman was sitting in a rocker. She was dressed in extremely expensive clothes, had jewels around her neck, around her wrists, and pinned on her lapel. A tray of tea and cookies sat beside her.

"Come in, child, and sit down and have some cookies," she said, smiling, showing lovely white false teeth against extremely wrinkled skin that also framed bright clear eyes and stretched over a sharply pointed nose.

Frenel felt like bowing, as he had done when presented to the British Royal family some three years previously. "Madam," he said. "I've come to offer the sorrow that I feel from my heart."

Amelia Mattworks gave him a shrewd look. "The work of fighting for the rights has worn you down. In a few years you will look as old as me."

He laughed. He could not help but admire the old lady even more. She was not dwelling on her grief. He sat down in the chair obviously meant for him and picked up a cookie and indicated the phone on her nightstand.

"I need to phone them downstairs for a second," he said.

She handed him the receiver and pressed the correct button for him.

"I brought you up here to ask you to come to Tamica's funeral," she said slowly, as she hung up the phone after his curt assurance to the Secret Service agent that he was in no danger. "I recall you dated Chloe many years ago. I know it will cause a lot of trouble for you to be there, because I know you have to be protected, and since there's no cemetery here in Sand Waves, we have to go to Houston. I know all that. But I don't care how much trouble it causes or whose schedule it upsets, I want you there."

Frenel was surprised by this request. He thought about all the problems for several seconds and how his staff and security people were going to gripe and complain. But then again, he did have the Secret Service man who was keeping Edward company downstairs a bit intimidated. It could be arranged.

It could be arranged.

"You do me honor," he said to Amelia.

"I'm pleased, child, sit with me a while. Pour me some tea, would you? There's a clean cup for you. Indulge me a little and discuss the old days with me..."

Chapter 33

Downstairs, Edward York was asking a few questions of the Secret Service agent assigned to accompany Frenel. Edward was anticipating what it would be like to have the Secret Service at his disposal. No one had threatened him yet. But if he announced for President instead of senator, it was certain someone would.

Regina came in during the middle of the conversation and hung on Edward's arm, enraptured. She was already in search of all of the right miniatures to make her dollhouse look as much like the White House as she possibly could.

"If I become First Lady, will I have a Secret Service agent with me wherever I go? What happens when I go to the restroom?"

"Regina, I think it's a little premature to be discussing such intimate details," said Edward.

"Of course, you're right, darling. Ah, Reverend Frenel, I hope you had a pleasant meeting with our famous songstress."

"Yes. Indeed. Mrs. York."

Frenel had exited the stairwell quietly. The reverend surreptitiously motioned to the Secret Service agent that he would like to leave as soon as possible.

"Reverend, for lunch-

"No, Mrs. York, I couldn't possibly. I have previous engagements in Houston. Plus, for some reason, I'm feeling a little queasy. Mart, I'm going to need to stop by a drugstore on the way to the hotel."

"Yes, sir." The Secret Service agent guided Reverend Frenel by the shoulders towards the door of the York mansion where a fresh limousine and driver awaited.

"It's been an honor to have you visit, Reverend. I hope our future encounters are equally friendly," said Edward York, as he shook the reverend's hand on his departure.

"Yes indeed," said the reverend, hastily exiting the York house, his hand inside his coat.

"Well, we have certainly been graced today with some

important visitors," said Regina, enthusiastically contemplating how this was just the beginning of such encounters. "When you run for President-"

"I haven't said I'm running for President."

"Oh darling, everyone knows you're going to run for President. It's already worked into all the polling. Your name's on all their lists. Now as I was saying, when you run for President-"

"Let's stay in the present, shall we? Stark Wynter is coming back?"

"I was going to bring that up. Stark would like use of one of the cottages while he looks for a place to buy within the gates."

"I don't see any problem with that. But I thought he was going back to California."

"Oh, he is, darling. But remember, he's coming back for Tamica's funeral and he's got his own private plane. He can come back any time, if accommodations are readily available."

"Could you just see to that without involving me? I don't feel like I can take on any more responsibilities right now, even if it's just playing host to a movie studio official."

"Oh, he is so much more than a movie studio official. And never mind, darling, I will take complete control of accommodating Mr. Wynter."

"I would appreciate that," said Edward York, thinking Regina's skills of organization, as she so frequently displayed in her toy collections, came in handy in real life as well.

And for once, it seemed she was more interested in real life than her toy world.

Chapter 34

Amelia Mattworks did not exactly feel at peace when Reverend Frenel left. But she did feel a sense of relief. She pulled out her Bible and reached for the telephone at the same time.

"She sent fo me," Clip Pointpar told Edward York upon his admittance to the York estate. "I don't know why. We never been friends. Back in the 1940s and 1950s when I was playing ball, she was a famous singer, she didn't have no use for me. She treated me a lot worse than most white people treated me. Even Roscoe Burns had no use for me. He didn't like it that I dated his daughter. Now just because she's in her 90s and I'm in my 70s and ain't many of us left from those days, she supposed to be my good friend? Why she old enough to be my mama. I tell you, I dated her daughter."

"We understand, Mr. Pointpar," said Regina York. "The whole world is supposed to worship her. But they don't have to live with her or even live nearby like you do."

"That's right, Mrs. York," said Clip. "You done hit the nail on the head."

"I assure you there is no coercion on the part of anyone in this household that you have to accept Miss Mattworks' invitation," said Edward.

"Oh hell. I know I don't have to go see that old woman. But like I just said she's about the only one left from the old times, at least only one that lives anywhere near us." He indicated his son, Forrest, who had driven him to the York estate and was standing obediently at his side. "My son wanted me to come."

"I convinced Dad to go ahead and come see Miss Amelia," said Forrest. "I think it is only right that he pay his respects and convey his sorrow at the death of her granddaughter, Tamica. I would very much like to do so myself if she will see me also."

"I don't know about that," said Edward York.

"I will go up and talk to her. But I don't like that idea, Forrest," said Clip, shaking his head. "I know, boy, you've got a good heart. You don't know her, though."

"Mr. Pointpar, could I ask a great favor?" Regina took Clip's arm and offered him her brightest smile, distracting his thoughts.

"Certainly, Mrs. York, if I can help in anyway."

"Amelia Mattworks had borrowed a collection of old magazines from me. Can you tell her to send them back down? She's had them long enough. I want them back."

Everyone was a little stunned by Regina's request. Magazines seemed so frivolous.

"My wife's collectibles are very important to her," said Edward, coughing, his voice weak and thin.

"She never wants to see me. I wouldn't insist on going up to her myself," insisted Regina. "And she cannot be interested in magazines right now."

"I'll do my best, ma'am. Forrest, you wait right here in the house for me. Don't you go out and sit in the truck," instructed Clip.

So Forrest had to wait with Edward while Clip took advantage of Amelia's elevator, since the days of his athletic prowess were long passed.

Not five minutes passed before the phone rang from Amelia's private line and the elevator descended. Regina immediately embraced him and took her magazines from his arms. She led him into the kitchen at his request for a glass of water.

"She actually asked to see you," said Edward York to Forrest, still in the hall. Forrest started up the stairs as his father returned from the kitchen. Her arms bundling her magazines, Regina carried them off towards her bedroom.

There's got to be a lot about Stark Wynter in these, she thought, now treasuring what she had once planned to destroy.

"My boy gone up to see the old devil?" asked Clip, sipping his ice water, speaking to Edward as he slowly walked.

Edward looked at him askance. He did not know how to reply to that question.

"We never got along," Clip continued. "Never will. She made me drink tea and eat cookies. I hate tea and the cookies tasted nasty. She is an old black bitch."

Edward's astonishment grew and his inability to speak felt like it was going to become permanent. Clip Pointpar looked at him with a cryptic gaze and walked out the back door banging it behind him. He opened the door of the pickup truck, a brand-new 1983 Dodge Ram, and sat in the passenger side with his arms folded and a scowl on his face.

Edward York was even further astounded when Forrest Pointpar descended from the stairs and came into the den some 15 minutes later. Tears were running down his cheeks.

He offered no explanation to his host, but put out his hand and Edward clasped it firmly, halfway embracing him as their arms touched. Then Forrest followed his father out to the truck, revving the engine as he pulled away.

Reverend Frenel was also still feeling the aftereffects of his meeting with Amelia.

The civil rights activist, Secret Service agent in the car with him, was relieved as he left the boundaries of Sand Waves. He did feel at peace as his limousine traveled down the Houston freeways.

He had not yet told anyone else about Amelia's request that he stay for Tamica's funeral. Like Stark Wynter, he was uncertain if he could remain in town or he would have to make plans to make a quick trip back.

He wondered if he had any pull in the local county establishment. Maybe he could get Tamica's autopsy sped up a little. He thought about Congressman Brown and made a note to ask him.

By the time he arrived at the hotel in Houston, Frenel was tired. He began to realize talking with Amelia had been more stressful emotionally than he thought at first. The Secret Service agent was most grateful when the reverend informed him that they would not be going out to a restaurant to eat. Instead, they would order room service.

Waiting for him at the hotel all this time, the people who had served with the reverend, some for many years, some at great sacrifice, would not have also minded room service. But the reverend decided just because he was tired, the group didn't have to suffer. So he gave instructions for all of them to just go on and have dinner at one of the exclusive bistros in Southwest Houston without him. In his absence, security fears would be low. They could all relax and have a good time. The battle ahead in Sand Waves would be brutal. They needed a break ahead of it all.

And he had consumed a large meal at his breakfast meeting, plus the cookies offered by Amelia. So he just wanted a sandwich. The Secret Service agent did not mind. Room service at this hotel included steaks.

Chapter 35

The shrill bell of the telephone woke Plate up with a start. He dropped his science fiction book and lost his place as he jumped up from the couch.

"Damn," he said, recalling his threat to the telephone with the scissors. *Well, that didn't work.*

"Lieutenant Plate," he said to the phone receiver, looking at his pager to see if it had gone off and he had somehow missed it. The pager went off a second after he looked at it.

Even before he got a reply over the phone line, he knew the pager and the phone going off at about the same time meant very bad news.

Moments later, as instructed by the chief, he flipped on the TV. The new 24 hour cable news channel was a godsend as far as Plate was concerned. He kept his TV on that channel by default so that as soon as he turned it on, he heard the news in progress...

"...Moments ago, the body of Reverend Clie Frenel was removed from the Sheraton Park Hotel in Houston Texas where he was found dead in his hotel room. A leading civil rights activist, it was rumored that Frenel was in town as a lead-in to pending, possibly pending, litigation against the Houston area command design colony of Sand Waves and its ISD. While most Houston area schools are integrated..."

Plate turned down the volume and concentrated on looking at the pictures being shown on the television. People were shouting and screaming as police officers kept them back from the entrance of the hotel as Frenel's body was removed and put in a hearse. They were shouting and screaming so loud that Plate could still hear some of the pain in their voices even though the volume was turned all the way down.

"Oh my God," he said, running his fingers through his hair.

He put the telephone back up to his ear. The chief was still there.

"Come in immediately, the Secret Service is going to need to talk to us. You remember? Frenel was at the York estate this afternoon."

Plate remembered.

"What's happened? The TV isn't saying anything about him being shot."

"We don't know what's happened. He wasn't shot. It could have even been a natural death. The man was 61. He led a stressful life. Our best scenario- he had a heart attack."

"Our worst scenario?"

"Well. He's dead. Does not look like suicide." Chief Brecken laughed at that thought, somewhat bitterly. Plate understood the bitterness. The Reverend Clie Frenel had been all over the country, to many parts of the world, had been on dangerous marches, spoken at dangerous rallies, risked his life time after time for his cause.

For the first time ever in his life, he had come to Sand Waves. And on that day, he had died.

"We treat it as murder until otherwise proven that it's not murder," said the chief. "Just the opposite of ordinary people. Let's just hope the county forensics can prove it's not murder."

"If they do, what are the odds of the Frenel family finding some private forensics operation that will say it is?"

"That will not be our problem. If it gets to that. If it's anything inconclusive, the federal government will take it off our hands."

The only worse possible scenario would have been if he had actually died while he was still in Sand Waves before he got back to his Houston hotel room.

But that was the only scenario that could have been any worse.

Unless he did not die of natural causes and his death was somehow traced to Sand Waves.

Chapter 36

"You can't come tonight. They are all really crazy here now. Grace York has really lost it. And you heard about Frenel. He was just here!"

Corina was speaking softly on the phone in the corridor. It was well after 6PM. She had seen no sign of anyone else and felt safe making the call.

"Corina, I think it's more imperative than ever that I come and get you. Frenel's death might be connected with your mother's."

"It is certainly a coincidence. He dies less than four days later. Right after visiting here."

"All the more reason I need to come get you!"

"Not yet. We have to think of the baby."

"There has to be a solution to this. We cannot go on much longer the way we are."

The voice on the other end of the line was indeed the baby's father.

"I am afraid if we do anything right now it will draw attention to us. To you."

"And I am afraid if we don't, something will happen to you!"

"Oh, I know, darling, how frightened you must be. How frightened I am. But we have to trust that the Lord will take care of us." Corina's voice reflected more calm than she actually felt. It had the intended effect of diffusing the mood.

"Let me at least come over for a few minutes. I'll come in the car. It won't be noticed. Meet me outside by the back door."

"Back door? Are you crazy? No! It's too dangerous for you. Stark Wynter is occupying one of the cottages now. And that police officer is staked out on the back porch. I am perfectly safe here."

"The police officer cannot possibly sit up all night watching. Stark Wynter's not going to care anything about what we do. He won't even notice me. He'll think I am hired help."

"But Mink Tanem is going to be watching. He watches everything all night long since my mother died. He's the one that saw you slipping over the fence that night my mother was killed."

"But that was not me! I do often go through the woods. It is easy if you know how. But I couldn't make it over the fence that night. Somebody else was in the woods or so I thought. I got in and out a different way."

"Well, that doesn't matter, Mink saw someone he described to that police officer as a thin blonde man." Doubt crept into her voice.

"Maybe it was that male maidservant Edward York hired. Or maybe somebody else."

"Stark Wynter has a thin blonde driver. But he's looks like an old man. When they were here, he watched me," Corina admitted.

"See, you are not safe!"

"He's gone," said Corina.

"If he was thin, he might've been mistaken for someone young during the dark," her conversation partner continued. "He might have been trying to get to you that way."

"I don't know who it was."

"Don't you see? With a whole bunch of people coming in and out of this place, and you don't know who they all are, it is not safe for you anywhere. And there are so many different ways to get in-"

"How did you get in the night my mother died?"

"Through the patio doors that exit into the front lawn from the dining room."

"But the dogs!"

"I fed them a cat."

"Oh my God!"

"Corina! Corina, I'm just joking! I made friends with the dogs. They know me now. They don't give me any trouble."

"It's as simple as that?"

"I'm a likable guy."

"Oh, I know. Nobody can be more wonderful than you. But you have to give me some time to think. This has all happened so fast. Surely you don't think the person that killed my mother is living here on the estate with us?"

"Darling, I don't know what to think any more than you do. All I want is to take you away from there and keep you safe."

"No. Absolutely there's no way I can go before the funeral."

"No, no, I guess not. But promise me, after it's all over, you'll run away with me."

Corina envisioned wrapping her arms around him and holding him close, her olive skin resting on his white chest. But all she held in her hand was the cold black receiver of the telephone.

"I promise. I'll run so far away, they'll never know what happened to me. We'll be together. All in a fairytale world of our own."

Chapter 37

The death of Reverend Clie Frenel sent shockwaves of grief across the country. Whites felt the poignancy that the only authoritative civil rights leader whom they had emotional connections with- as he had white family members that mourned with his black relatives- was gone. Blacks felt the incalculable loss of one of their own.

Everybody felt like one less layer of security in society that kept the peace had vanished.

The murder of Tamica Cathare, already labeled by the media as a domestic crime of passion, slipped from the headlines.

If there was any possible positive aspect to the death of the civil rights activist, it was in Sand Waves and felt by the surrounding law enforcement community. The relief that the burden of providing him security at Tamica's funeral was alleviated.

Frenel's funeral was going to be in Chicago, far removed from Sand Waves, so not a concern for the Sand Waves Police Department or any other area department.

Pressure from every side on every area policing authority made their only concern the death of Tamica Cathare and the life of Amelia Mattworks. Especially the Sand Waves police.

However, since the lives of millions of area residents continued with the same percentage of crime needing police attention, the ultimate burden of finding Tamica's killer, and providing security for Amelia fell on Sand Waves, where routine crime was said to be nonexistent.

Plate was ordered to move into the York compound. Southwestern Bell workmen were working overtime to run a new phone line to the York compound. Plate was to be given the empty cottage nearest the mansion. From there he would have a good view of the mansion on two sides. Mink Tanem occupied the cottage diagonally opposite, which viewed the other two sides. But it was the cottage occupied by the good doctor that most interested Plate. For that was the cottage adjacent to the woods from which apparently the shot that felled Tamica Cathare was fired.

The plan was that being on the scene, he could observe the daily routines of the compound and point out any weaknesses that had been overlooked, all the while still investigating the killing and providing on-site protection for the family. He wondered if this had not been the chief's plan all along, the chief knowing that he was single, lived in an apartment, and had no obligations to any other human or even a pet.

Plate had no objection to the plan. He was hoping being on the scene would help him clarify the situation. It was frustrating not to have a better handle on this murder case. However, direct from the top, his primary instruction was to focus on the protection of Amelia Mattworks and Corina French. As the case may be, he was of the opinion the best way to protect those two women was to catch the killer.

Powers-That-Be really wanted it to be a burglar caught in the act and reacting with panic. Maybe Tamica saw the burglar in the tree holding both of his rifles. She then turned away and he shot her with the .44. Then jumped down and shot her with the .22. While taking time to pour gasoline on the shrubbery at the house.

That was the official line of inquiry at the moment. All known burglars in the greater Houston-Galveston area who had ever used a weapon were being rounded up and questioned.

The burglar might have happened to have two weapons because he had already robbed someplace else and picked up an extra gun, was the official theory.

The more Plate thought about these official lines of inquiries the more certain he was they were puffy cotton candy, surely to melt at the first sign of moisture.

This was the dilemma Plate was contemplating.

While the position of the body floating in the pool made it impossible to tell exactly what direction the shots came from, the forensics also clearly indicated the shots from the .44 came from a height whereas the shot from the .22 did not.

And the only scenario that appeared possible had been that someone high, maybe in a tree right next to the fence, got off those shots, jumped down into the yard, switched guns and needlessly shot again with a different weapon, perhaps just to confuse the situation.

That was the only scenario that made sense with the forensics if there were only one shooter.

Plate did not like it at all.

As Officer Skaar took over the security so that Plate and Chief Brecken could confer, the solution seemed even further away.

"I think we should assume the first shot came from the .22," Plate had told his chief after reviewing forensics reports. "Otherwise why fire it? The shots from the .44 rifle must've been obviously fatal. Why then shoot her with a .22? That had to have been the first shot."

"To disable her," Chief Brecken had concluded.

Plate went over that scenario in his mind. *Instantly in shock from the first shot from ground level, which would not have been fatal, she reacted instinctively. Disorientated and in pain, she took off running towards the pool. Then the gunman fired from above, directly at her back as she dove into the water.*

"Makes sense," Plate had agreed. "Knock her down. Would get her disoriented at least. But why not just shoot her right out in the first place?"

He definitely preferred his first theory that the .22 shot had come first.

But that theory had consequences.

That alternative hypothesis was disturbing and he was under orders to keep that theory to himself for the time being. It might be possible for someone to shoot the woman from above, then jump down and finish her off. But to make the first shot the .22, the killer would have had to shoot her at ground level, then quickly climbed a tree to continue shooting.

That was practically impossible and insane.

If the first shot was at ground level, there were almost certainly two shooters.

One on the roof or in a tree. The other on the ground. No evidence was found that anyone had been on the roof. It was a ceramic tile roof that was extremely hard to negotiate and would not have made a good perch for a sniper due to its steep gables and slick watershedding flanges.

153

There was some evidence someone had been in a tree. Officials were taking that fact and running with it as evidence of their theory. Neither of the rifles that shot Tamica came from the York estate.

An outsider it had to be.

So unless Plate could find evidence of two shooters, the official line of inquiry remained a lone burglar. This was the least frightening and disturbing sequence of events to the rest of the VIPs that lived behind the gates in Sand Waves.

The cottage occupied by Dr. Apixza was the only building nearby that could have been utilized in the ground attack on Tamica. That is, if the perpetrators utilized a building. They might not have. Maybe the shots came from the forest. That might not be the case either.

Without any such certainties, Plate could not get a court order for any searches except outdoors.

So far, on the basis of patient confidentiality, Apixza was not letting anybody in. He justifiably pointed out there was no evidence that his building had anything to do with Tamica's murder. And Plate could not prove otherwise, yet.

Strings had been pulled, the dead woman's body released, and the funeral set for the next day.

Time was getting short.

Chapter 38

Any worries that attendance at Tamica's funeral would be sparse, were put to rest immediately. Reverend Skrale's church was packed. Stark Wynter kept his word. He was there accompanied by his pale chauffeur.

Hired police officers from Houston kept the press away and maintained traffic order. They directed traffic outside the church and would accompany the funeral procession to the highway and on to the cemetery in the big city.

Sand Waves' developers had deliberately designed the colony without a cemetery. They felt a constant reminder of the inevitable would have a negative influence on property values.

The effect of the preacher's sermon was strong enough that few noticed when Corina quietly slipped out the side door.

Plate noticed. He followed her long enough to ascertain where she was going. Then he returned to his seat just in time to see her come out onto the stage and be embraced by the reverend.

Reverend Skrale handed her the microphone and walked off the stage without a word. The pianist put fingers to the keys at the same moment Corina began to sing.

It was a funeral. It was already quiet. No one had cigarettes, drinks, fans. Nor anything else to abandon. But as attention was directed at the singer with such intense focus, it was almost possible to hear the quick abandonment of all other sensations. There was an almost unanimous shifting in body language that gave off little sounds combining into one audible movement of the crowd. Only the elderly could hear the inner movements of their joints as they uniformly sat up straight and turned their heads to gaze at Corina.

No one heard the sounds louder than Amelia Mattworks. Seated on the front row of the family section, she had as clear a view of her great-granddaughter as anyone there. She saw the fire in Corina's eyes, the joy and tears on her face and heard the clear tones of her voice.

And no one better than she, knew what that all meant.

It was a cold January morning. Everyone would have preferred to end it all in the nice warm church and let the remembrance of Corina's voice stay with them as a comfort for as long as the memory could linger.

Most did.

They left chattering about Corina and her voice and how they were privileged to have been the first to hear her sing in public, practically for free. The only payment had been their time and silence.

The family, and a few select others, could not indulge in that luxury. They had to go on to the grave.

Outside, a blustery winter wind fractured all hope of spring.

The dark glasses Ray wore made him seem much more a movie star than Stark Wynter. He walked behind the funeral home pallbearers who carried the casket. He carried three long white roses, freshly cut from Regina's manicured bushes.

He walked alone, his shoes softly crunching freshly purchased winter grass.

Regina and Edward were close behind. Regina had both hands on Edward's bent elbow. Off to the side, like a little ewe trotting parallel a short distance from the herd, Corina tagged along, temporarily no longer the center of attention.

Grace brought up the rear, also distant a little, but not quite as far to the side as Corina. The casket, pale pink accented with a small bouquet of white lilies, was carried solemnly by the strangers. They perched it on the rack above the grave where it sat as though awaiting the solemn formal goodbyes from those surrounding it before being lowered. Ray sat straight, his back at a Victorian angle.

Regina made a point to lean against Edward who settled back in his chair as though he were at a baseball game. Grace stood with the rest of those behind.

They included Stark Wynter and his driver. And the young man who had come with Reverend Skrale, a most kind and considerate young man, resembling him so much everyone assumed it was the reverend's son. This person took it upon himself to see to the comfort, as best he could, of all the mourners there.

Sitting on the end chair at the front nearest the casket, Corina sobbed and her entire body shook throughout the service. No longer needing the discipline she had exercised preceding and during her vocal performance, Corina felt no need to hold back. The preacher's companion knelt on the dewy grass beside her, recklessly ruining his suit in the damp dirt, and without touching her, braced her chair. The action, while not halting her tears, seemed to comfort her and keep her from giving way to true hysteria.

The rest of the group was silently grateful to him, when they noticed him out of the corners of their eyes, for they were all focused on themselves and did not want to have to attend to Corina. Dr. Apixza was needed at the side of Amelia. She too, after having held up admirably at the crowded funeral, broke down at the sparsely attended graveside service.

At the conclusion, foggy wavy clouds, seeming to reach down from the sky to hold all the stale air down, pressing it to the earth, finally broke forth as ice water droplets fell onto mourners and the white lilies on the pink casket were covered with reflecting raindrops.

Lieutenant Plate was watching in the background with a few photographers and reporters who were kept at bay by other security.

Corina seemed to fully understand that her mother was dead, irrevocably dead. Yet at the end of the service, she refused to leave. She resisted attempts by Dr. Apixza, available as he had already settled Amelia, to pull her away forcibly and put her in the car designated to take all back to the house.

Those in the vehicle were left sitting awkwardly with the door wide open waiting for her to come. Finally the young man who had attended her whispered to the doctor and the older man stepped back.

The young man bent down and spoke quietly to Corina and held out his hand. She took it and rose unsteadily, her pregnancy more visible than ever in her awkward movements, and allowed the young blonde man to escort her to the limousine, holding onto his hand even as the door shut between them. He stood watch until it pulled away, then turned to look at his father.

Still standing by the casket, Reverend Skrale watched with pride, for indeed it was his son who was assisting him today.

Chapter 39

"It's incredible," said Stark Wynter. "Did anyone have any idea the girl could sing like that?"

"I didn't even know she sang at all," said Regina.

Stark Wynter, Reverend Skrale, and both men who were acting as their combination drivers/attendants were present. The pastor's son was the more helpful of the two. Stark Wynter was trying to let his chauffeur, a man who had serious health problems, exert himself no more than necessary. The man had been with him for several years and when they were alone in the car together, the relationship functioned more as old friends. However, they maintained a strict boss-employee relationship as soon as they left the interior of the limousine behind or whenever there were passengers.

It had surprised Stark that his chauffeur friend had actually wept all the way to and from the cemetery. His mind on Regina York, and being somewhat of a sensitive man by instinct, Stark did not question his driver about his emotions.

Funerals remind everybody that they're mortal, he thought. *And poor old Burress doesn't look like he's long for the world. I'm really gonna miss him...*

Stark did not physically feel the lack of his attendant's personal attention. Mink Tanem, routinely managing the needs of the family, noticed the new familiarity with which Mrs. York treated Stark, and took it upon himself to add Stark as one of his concerns. Once Tanem considered anyone his responsibility, their every need was anticipated and taken care of.

Forrest Pointpar, Clip Pointpar, and Congressman Brown were among the first funeral guests to arrive back to the house. Having the crowd invited to the usually family-only gathering was at Amelia's insistence. Many declined the rare opening into the York world, but many did not. Amelia refused to let the doctor take her upstairs for rest, insisting she wanted to remain downstairs with people. Most sat at her feet while she held court.

Plate renewed his acquaintance with Brown only briefly. After a polite amount of time, the congressman made his excuses and apologies. He was needed back in Washington. He left. A few others followed.

Reverend Skrale was the next notable to leave. He first took the time to introduce his son, Ken. Polite handshakes were traded all around. The reverend knelt and spoke to Amelia. Then he once again paid condolences to the family. He also departed.

After enduring admirers for a significant time, Amelia went back to her section of the house, insisting that she wanted to be alone. Grace implored her to come back and eat with the family later that evening.

Food had been sent from all over the country. Grace recalled the traditions she had grown up with where family and friends of the bereaved lovingly cooked and brought the best they had to offer to the home and family of the deceased.

Today those so inclined to offer food merely phoned a local restaurant and arranged for delivery. As it was easy to do this from any part of the country, the family finally had to say no more and refuse deliveries. The kitchen had dishes of various foods covering every counter, more than any of them could possibly eat in a month.

Regina got busy arranging for a local charity to take everything that was not immediately perishable and direct future deliveries to a nursing home. Stark Wynter busied himself helping her with that chore.

Edward York once again admired his wife's organizational skills and breathed a silent prayer of thanks that he had not killed her nearly a week ago as he had planned. The plot to rid himself of her by means other than divorce, simmering since shortly after their marriage and almost culminating in the suicide plan that Grace interrupted, died completely with the stark reality of Tamica's funeral.

In the aftermath, Edward mentally prepared for the upcoming anti-abortion rally on Saturday.

He was glad Sand Waves had no cemetery.

Chapter 40

Bored with the high society and getting nowhere with small talk, Plate decided to go for a walk on the grounds. There was always the possibility that he would see something he missed earlier.

He checked out the designated cottage where he would live until the investigation was finished. It was simple in design and furnishings. He approved. Edward York had already given him a key and also the codes to the security systems, except for the clinic, and the code to the emergency system that protected Amelia.

His luggage was to be delivered any time. When it arrived he would have something to do while all the extra security from the funeral took care of the family's immediate needs.

The pool area was still taped off as a crime scene but there was still ample space to walk.

Few people noticed Plate had left the mansion.

Stark Wynter and Regina York were not among them.

"The next Amelia Mattworks!" Stark Wynter happily chatted with Regina. "Who would have thought it would have been her own great-granddaughter."

Regina was packing the boxes of food to be taken to the gates where a local charity volunteer would pick them up. She felt less like a hostess in her own home than ever before. It did not matter that the deceased was her sister-in-law.

"And my brother is Corina's stepfather," Regina smiled sweetly, thinking she would rather be in the kitchen with Stark than queening over the guests in the den anyway.

"What other legal relatives has she got?" asked Stark, his mind working rapidly. He, too, felt out of place in this enormous mansion. His mansion in Hollywood was big but not nearly as ostentatious.

"Is stepfather a legal relative?"

"Hell, I don't know," said Stark, taken aback by the idea that it might not be.

"It must be," Regina said. "Anyway, her parents are dead, she has no named father. Her grandparents are dead. The only other known relative she has is Amelia Mattworks herself."

"Let's hope any other unknowns stay that way." Stark Wynter recalled the old lady's words to him during his visit. He thought about the tea and cookies and the sweet kind way she had told him what she really wanted in exchange for investing millions in his movie studio.

It was not impossible that he was Corina's father. But he knew it was next to impossible. He had slept with the woman one time, he thought. He wasn't even sure when that might have been. There had been a time when he was having a little drinking problem. Wasn't that the time he dated Tamica French? It was so long ago he could not be sure.

He could make a claim but what if it were refuted. That there were now tests, worried him. Before the funeral, before she sang, the idea that she might be his daughter was going to be nothing but a nuisance. Now, being her father would be an asset.

But what would the tests say? That was the unknown.

"Let's see. Corina is the old lady's great-granddaughter. Three generations removed. The introduction of four sets of nonfamily genes into the gene pool. What are the odds? I remember when Amelia's own daughter tried for singing career and flopped. So did the woman they just buried today. She could not carry a note in a teakettle. Didn't she try to make it as an artist, too? Nothing there either. Yet her daughter sings like an angel. That must mean whoever the girl's father is, he's got to be a singer."

"You sang in some of your early movies didn't you, Stark?"

He looked at Regina. Even dressed in funeral black and somewhat haphazardly packing boxes, she was the epitome of glamour and beauty, dark raven hair, fair skin and blue eyes, long graceful arms that moved the containers of food in one box and out the other and back in the next until she got it all packed in just right.

Father or stepfather.

There was maybe a one in a million chance Stark might be Corina's father. On the other hand, Regina's brother definitely was Corina's stepfather.

It was a question of the bird in the bush.

"That's when they forced all of us under contract to sing at the big movie studios under the old star system. I'm a terrible singer, no talent at all. The musicals I sang in were the only ones of my movies that ever flopped. I was a good actor. I had sense enough to retire before I got too old and ugly to be on the screen. Now, I'm a great studio boss."

"Old and ugly could never describe you, Stark."

He walked over and stood closer to Regina. "Let me help you with some of this, you're just taking too much on yourself." He put his arms around Regina's shoulders and helped support the weight of the box she had just lifted.

She turned in his arms, looked up at his face, and smiled.

Chapter 41

Those who had heard her sing in the past, in secret, had told her what to expect if she ever sang in public. Still, Corina was unprepared for the gushing outpouring of attention that enveloped her at her mother's funeral. She did not welcome it. She felt it was the wrong time. And in the emotional state of a grieving daughter, it was impossible for her to know how she truly felt about it.

At the York estate, the reaction was somewhat more subdued once they got back to the house. Still, after Amelia went to her elevator, Corina felt herself the unwelcome center of attention as guests started to focus on her.

She was praying for some deliverance from it when one of the temporary servants came in and announced that there was a young woman who had official business that could not wait and would Corina see her now?

"Who could this possibly be?" Corina asked the messenger.

The answer to that question caused Corina's eyes to widen and her tears to subside completely. Since the servant, under instructions from the visitor to practice utmost discretion, had whispered the answer to Corina in such a way that no one else heard, everyone was astounded and curious when Corina forcefully stood up and spoke with confidence and strength.

"Tell her I will see her in the foyer, privately."

And then Corina walked, beyond all the stares, into the back foyer and closed the door behind her, also closing the door to the kitchen effectively preventing anyone else from leaving the house without risking the animosity of the dogs guarding the front door or violating her privacy at the back.

She was a little taken aback by the look of the blonde who stood before her. About the same height, appearing to be in her mid to upper 20s, this lovely woman was dressed in a professional suit, consisting of a matching blazer jacket and knee length skirt with a white blouse. In addition, she carried a large black briefcase.

"Please let me express my condolences at the passing of your mother," said the blonde, extending her hand in a formal handshake.

Corina shook hands solemnly and indicated the table under a mirror, for the woman was clearly looking for a place to put her briefcase.

"I did hear correctly? You are from a life insurance agency?"

"That is correct. I am with Finest Southland Life Insurance Company. Your mother was my client. She told me at the time she took out the policy that she was doing so somewhat in secret. This was about two years ago and from your reaction here, I presume she never did tell you anything about it."

"No. I had no idea. Could I please see some identification? I really need to make sure you're not from the press."

"Of course." The blonde haired woman opened her briefcase and extracted a set of papers. Rather than handing Corina identification that concerned herself, she handed her a folded insurance policy with Tamica Cathare's name on the front. Corina took the policy and gazed at it limply.

"Here, let me show you," said the agent, opening the policy up to its inner section where it contained a copy of the application. "You can see here- your mother's signature, various information she gave me when she applied for the policy."

The agent flipped over some more pages. "Here's a binding contract and a copy of the first payment with authorization to draw the monthly premiums from her bank account."

The agent closed the policy. "Mrs. Cathare requested that I keep the policy secure in my possession as her agent. While I had heard of the tragedy concerning your mother through the press, I needed to know that an official death certificate had been issued before I could contact you. Since the funeral cannot be performed without a death certificate, I knew that had been accomplished. But I was unable to obtain access to this house or get through to you in any way until now. I finally had to pull a few strings with some of the people I know in Austin to get them to let me in the gates just now."

"I see," said Corina.

"The policy was for $500,000, with double indemnity which will make the death benefit $1 million."

Chapter 42

The insurance agent looked very self-satisfied as she delivered that news.

Corina's knees buckled a little and the saleswoman reached and caught her just before she knelt on the floor.

"Praise God! Thank you, dear Jesus!" Corina whispered.

Corina's knees briefly touched the floor before the other woman grasped her around the waist and pulled her back upright.

"I did make some notes," said the agent cautiously, as she made sure that Corina was able to stand by herself before letting her go. "At the time your mother took out the policy, as you were the beneficiary but you were under age and, according to my calculations, you are still not yet 18."

"What has that got to do with anything?" The weak feeling in Corina's knees left abruptly and a slight surge of panic displaced her initial joy.

"There are some exceptions, but generally speaking minors cannot directly inherit in the state of Texas. Your mother did appoint your stepfather as your guardian, so the money will be paid to him in trust for you."

"No, I'm sure that under the terms of my mother's will, my great-grandmother is my guardian."

"I'm afraid that the terms of the beneficiary designation supersede the will as far as this money is concerned. Your mother's estate may be under the control of your great-grandmother but this money will be under the control of your stepfather."

"You said there were exceptions. What are the exceptions?"

"Well, Texas law considers minors to be adults under certain exceptions."

Corina listen to this explanation of the legal technicality that stood between her and the money her mother had left.

"Could I count on your discretion about all of this for a short period of time?" ask Corina, thinking rapidly. "I need to speak with you before we talk to my stepfather about this. Could you come back tomorrow?"

"It did take quite a bit of effort for me to get through the gates. I'm not sure I'm going to make it again without-"

"I'll get you through the gates and into the compound without any trouble," said Corina. "Give me your phone number and I'll call you and tell you when to come back. Oh please, I'm not trying to be authoritarian. It's just that in the situation I'm in right now, I have to proceed with caution. My mother was killed..."

"Oh, I understand. Here's my phone number on my business card. Call me when you need me and I'll do my best to get here." The insurance agent put her papers back in her briefcase. "I'll pretend tomorrow that it's my first visit here officially to inform all interested parties about the insurance. Do you want me to keep the insurance policy until it can formally be presented to the company?"

She picked up her briefcase by the handle.

"By all means yes," said Corina, handing the policy back to her. "And please, in God's name, don't lose it."

Rather than open her briefcase again, the agent slipped it inside her jacket pocket.

"The policy itself is just like a bank deposit book. Only a formality. The company has internal records so you need not worry about it getting lost. Lost policies are redeemed all the time. But I will hold onto this for you for your convenience."

"Thank you and there's one more thing. Before you leave, there is one more thing I want to tell you. It may affect the situation. I don't know. I'm not sure. I hadn't even thought about it." Corina looked at the card and read the woman's name.

A simple name, she thought, *easy for everyone to pronounce and remember. How much easier that must make it in life.*

"It will need to be in strictest confidence. Do you have confidentiality privileges like a lawyer or counselor?"

"Of course," said the agent, untruthfully. She was not going to let a technicality get in the way of gathering information about a potential million dollar client. She was wondering at the urgency in Corina's voice, but tempering her wonderment with the remembrance that the girl had just lost her mother in a brutal way.

Corina felt her unspoken compassion. As she spoke the next

words, Corina took the arm of this insurance agent, who now strangely felt like a friend, and started walking with her towards the door. The door popped open.

Sunlight and cold air flooded in.

A small set of luggage was quickly and mistakenly being unloaded in the foyer by a limousine driver. At the same time, Plate, having finished his walk around the grounds, entered from the back porch to correct the error.

"Miss, that needs to be taken to the cottage I will be staying in," he said automatically, as he noticed a new person in the foyer and mistook her for day help.

Then she turned and faced him.

"Destiny?" he said, in disbelief.

Chapter 43

"What?" The agent dropped her briefcase and it fell open. An array of papers fell out in a black cardboard box slid to the forefront.

"I mean Daphne!"

The three people crowded around the briefcase and its spilled contents all at once, working as a team, stuffing the papers back inside. The policeman's hand pushed the box down to the bottom. He barely withdrew his fingers in time before Daphne snapped the briefcase shut and twirled the combination lock to prevent it from popping open again.

This task finished, they all straightened up and Corina stepped back, a little distracted and even slightly amused, leaving the police officer and the insurance agent standing together facing each other.

"Officer Plate!" said Daphne belatedly.

"It is you!" said Plate inadequately. "What are you doing here?"

"I-"

"Some business, Lieutenant. And we are finished for the moment." Corina spoke up in a strong confident voice. "Miss Martin is leaving right now. We will be taking up where we left off, sometime tomorrow. Perhaps I can get your assistance in getting Miss Martin back onto the premises without any problems?"

"Yes, Miss Martin and I are acquainted," said Plate, remembering secondarily Daphne's job included delivering death benefits. "Do you mean to say there is life insurance-?"

"I would prefer not to discuss it today as my mother has just been buried," Corina said, with authority and maturity that Plate had failed to observe in her earlier,

"Of course. I apologize. I am sorry."

"No need to apologize, Officer."

"Perhaps Lieutenant Plate and I can work out the details of the situation upon my return?" suggested Daphne.

"After I speak with you privately when you arrive." Again Corina was speaking with a firmness that had been previously lacking in any of her words before.

"Right. As you wish," said Plate, although her words had not been addressed to him.

"If it is all right with the both of you, I need to return to my guests," said Corina. "Reverend Skrale's son will show you out. Please excuse me."

Neither Plate nor Daphne had noticed the young man had entered the foyer with them. He walked with Plate and Daphne out onto the back porch as if to make sure they left.

Plate and Daphne conferred for a moment before separating. Daphne went to her car.

Plate turned back to Ken Skrale and caught him before he re-entered the house.

"Can I speak with you a moment?" he said.

"Can I get you anything?"

The soft inquiry came from Burress, Stark Wynter's driver. He had quietly entered into the back foyer with Corina and shut the door behind him. He and Corina were alone in the small room with all its redirecting doorways closed off.

Corina stared at the blonde man before her and decided 'emaciated' was the only word to describe him.

"No, thank you, no." Corina glanced up in alarm. The chauffeur took her by the arm, saying, "I've never heard anyone sing like that. I was wondering maybe if I could get a picture to remember you by."

If the man had not been so obviously terminally ill, Corina would have felt afraid and perhaps insulted at this intrusion on her privacy the day her mother was buried. However, the man had tears in his eyes, and a weakness in his face, which foreshadowed little time left for him.

"Yes. Okay. Of course."

She and the servant stood before the almost full length mirror on the left side of the foyer where there was no door. She took a moment to stand still in front of the mirror beside a vase of roses on a narrow table in front of it.

The driver pulled a little cheap 110 camera out of his pocket and held it up and snapped.

"I hope it turns out. Thank you anyway. I had the honor of driving your mother a few years ago when she came out on a visit to Hollywood with Ms. Mattworks and dated Mr. Wynter. It's been an honor to hear you sing."

"Thank you, Mr.-" It crossed Corina's mind that the purpose behind all of this was to have a souvenir of her first performance, albeit at her mother's funeral.

Probably planning to sell it, she thought, without bitterness. *The poor old man probably has a lot of medical bills to pay.*

"Burress."

"Mr. Burress." Corina tried to keep the impatience out of her voice. She was exhausted. The good news about the life insurance had given her only a temporary boost. She wanted very much to go to bed. She had done her good deed in letting this man get a potential valuable collectible at her expense. He might be needy, but she was ready to get rid of him.

She looked at the exit door, hoping Ken Skrale would come back in soon.

"I won't trouble you anymore. But I do want to say one thing to you. The Lord honors those that honor him. Don't ever stop singing for Him."

"Yes, thank you so much for those thoughts," said Corina wearily, too tired to let him know concretely that she agreed with his sentiments.

Burress was weary also and vaguely aware Corina's attitude was changing.

"And I have something for you, if it is okay. It's a gift," he said quickly. He reached in his pocket and pulled what Corina first thought was a small necklace. But when he pressed it into her hand, she realized it was a rosary. "It belonged to my mother, passed down in the family. I've no one to leave it to and would like you to have it."

Unfamiliar with Catholicism, Corina had only a vague idea what a rosary was and recognized it only from seeing them previously in movies and TV shows.

Nevertheless, she spotted the crucifix at the end, elaborately carved and ornate, and decided instantly to keep it.

"Thank you," she said simply. "I will treasure it."

This is what it must be to have fans like Amelia did all those years, she thought.

Satisfied, carefully pocketing his camera, Burress turned wordlessly from Corina and went out the door to go rest in Stark Wynter's limousine.

Ken Skrale passed him on the porch as he came back in. Plate had done nothing but take contact information. Still, Ken was not used to dealing with the police and was a little pale. Corina walked over to the preacher's son, took his arm and he led her back to the others.

Chapter 44

Clip wandered into the kitchen, feeling depressed and hoping for privacy. Regina and Stark were still there.

"Mr. Pointpar. An honor. I saw every one of your games, one way or another. Well, 'saw' maybe isn't the word. I forget those were the days before TV was able to show us everything. I either attended or listened to every game on the radio." Stark Wynter, in his time a famous Hollywood actor, had never quite gotten over his fan worship of great athletes.

Clip Pointpar did not return the sentiment.

"Mm," he grunted, in an unfriendly manner.

Stark Wynter was not deterred.

"I remember that time, the bases were loaded in the eleventh inning-" he began.

"I really don't care much for reminiscing about the old days."

"Oh? No indeed! We have to look to the future. Even those of us getting on a little bit. You certainly don't look your age."

Clip could not help feeling just a little bit flattered. Here was one of the most handsome movie stars of the 1940s and 1950s telling him, a man in his 70s, that he still looked pretty good.

Clip agreed.

"You done aged well yourself," he said to Stark, a little grudgingly, but a little less unfriendly.

"You got to keep fit so the women will still want you," said Stark, with a glance at Regina, now talking with Edward and some of the other funeral guests. "Did you know the deceased well?"

"I gave up women long ago. Health reasons," said Clip. "I knew her mother."

Stark cast his mind back. He recalled the romance that swept the nation. The famous black baseball player and the famous white movie star.

"Her mother? Oh, how stupid of me you were referring to Amelia Mattworks' daughter, Chloe? I don't know why, ha ha, someone else popped into my head."

Clip looked at Stark and read his mind. "You thinking about

the headlines with Doreen Darbell? I knew Chloe about the same time. But she was just a friend. Married she was. Or shortly thereafter. To that fellow with the French name. It was a long time ago. Doreen was between husbands at that time. Doreen was the love of my life. Both of them dead and gone now."

"I know you don't want to reminisce, but I couldn't help remember."

"She was beautiful."

"Oh indeed, Doreen Darbell was acclaimed the most beautiful woman in the world in her time." *Just ring the doorbell*! Stark thought, and suppressed a wicked smile. This was a funeral reception, after all. He wanted to be respectful.

"We did love each other with a passion," Clip admitted. "They said it would ruin her career and mine."

"As far as I could tell, I think it helped her career," said Stark, thoughtfully.

"I got all the bad publicity. Everybody saw her as my innocent victim."

"Yes. I recall those stories now."

"But she wasn't my victim. I was hers."

"The last time I spoke with her, she recalled you with great fondness." Stark lied out of kindness. "It's been a few months. But I believe you are mistaken about Doreen Darbell. She is, I think in her early 80s, not passed on yet." Stark felt proud he could deliver some good news to the old man.

"She still alive? You know her still? I kept up with her for years. But I dropped it a few years ago. I couldn't find no more about her in the movie magazines. You know where she is? You know her?" Clip got so excited he began to shake a little bit. Stark was alarmed at first, but the old man settled down quickly.

"Oh, indeed yes. She's in a nursing home. I spoke with her a few years ago. Not really possible now. Some sort of dementia, they just started talking about on the news, some German name starts with an A."

"I see. You know, I think in all the years I've lived here, I have never met anybody else that actually knew her."

173

"Really? What about the doctor?" Stark asked.

"What doctor?" Clip looked blank.

"I met him not too long ago," said Stark. "He's around here, or was, I think. He lives in one of the cottages on the York compound."

Stark explained his agreement with the Yorks, then added about the man he just mentioned, "A strange sounding name, I don't think that was his name years ago though, when he was practicing in Hollywood. You know, he was the doctor they all went to when they got in trouble. His name he calls himself now is something like pixel, what they call those dots in the pictures now. But his name was much more common back then. I guess what he does is legal now. It's a strange world."

"A strange world indeed." Clip's voice was strangled.

Stark Wynter felt abruptly embarrassed for the old ballplayer when he broke down and cried.

He wanted to put his arms around Clip but the natural constraints of a lifetime of masculinity held him back.

Fortunately, the legendary ballplayer's son was made aware that Clip had been overcome and rushed to his side, holding him tightly and guiding him to the exit and ultimately towards their home next door.

Provenance VIII

1951

Amelia Mattworks looked at her daughter in disgust. Mother and daughter stood on opposite sides of the room, like prizefighters about to go a round.

"So you are in lust for that ignorant baseball player? When you could have the best the Negro race has to offer?"

"You had no right to read my diary."

"I had to tell what was going on with you. The way you've been moping around here like you've lost your best friend."

"I don't know how you can be so carefree and callous when you know that Daddy might not live another year."

"Child, your daddy and me have lived our lives. We've been through many things together. This illness of his is one more. If the Lord sees fit to take him, I can go on."

But I don't know how, Amelia thought silently.

"Chloe, you have the rest of your life ahead. You can't get yourself into a deep dark rut over a man who's not interested in you."

"You don't know that he's not interested in me. He hasn't had a chance to get interested. Daddy won't let him get anywhere near me."

"And your daddy's got the best instincts of any man this side of the Rocky Mountains. If he don't want you to see Clip Pointpar, then you don't need to be seeing him."

"You can't stop me from seeing him."

"That may be true. But from what I see, he isn't interested in seeing you. He's interested in that white movie star that's older, and been married and divorced so many times she doesn't have any-"

"Mother, has it never occurred to you that I can't help how I feel about Clip? I love him and- I just can't help it."

Chloe burst into tears. Amelia walked over to her and embraced her.

"There there, child," said Amelia, stroking her daughter's hair, as if she were still a little girl instead of a woman with more than a quarter century behind her.

"If he doesn't love me, I just want to die! I failed as a singer. I'm a failure at everything."

Amelia simply held her daughter and did not reply, thinking about her husband's illness and the word 'die'.

"All I really want is for Clip to give me a chance. I just know that if he would spend some time with me and get to know me, there would be a possibility that he would come to love me like I love him."

"It don't work that way," said Amelia. "You don't realize how young you are. There is lots of nice men interested in you. What about that man from France?"

"He's not from France, Mother. His name is French."

"Oh. Well, he seems like a nice man, a little older maybe. Try to think ahead, child. In a couple years, you'll be over Pointpar. Your father will be well again. Don't discourage this French fellow."

"Oh, he's a square. The studious type. And he's quiet and he is white."

"All of that sounds good to me. Maybe not the white part." Amelia bit her lip worriedly.

Chloe burst into tears again.

"Okay, maybe that's okay, too. Times are changing."

"Mother, sometimes I think you have your head in the sand." Chloe let her tears fall on a baseball card in her hand, the collectible portraying the face of her beloved surrounded by his statistics.

Amelia thought how if she had spoken that way to her own mother, she would have been slapped. However, she stepped back, feeling lenient, knowing Chloe was upset over her father's illness. Relieved that, at least for now, she had again stopped crying and was distracted some by a set of baseball trading cards that showed off numerous players.

Those alone should tell Chloe there was more than one ballplayer in the world.

"Let's go up to the hospital and visit your dad and try to cheer him up little bit."

"Okay," agreed Chloe, wiping away the last of her tears. Arm in arm, the two women made their way through the house out to their car.

Chapter 45

"Now, I can get you a life insurance policy with an interest-bearing annuity rider. I think you'll find that this is the type of policy you need if you're wanting both an investment vehicle and some protection for your family in case anything happens."

True to her word, Daphne Martin had returned the next day. After talking privately with Corina, as planned, she was now selling Ray Cathare life insurance.

"Is this the type of policy my wife took out?" said Ray.

"Mrs. Cathare was unconcerned about investment opportunities and therefore took out a term policy which maximized cash payout upon her death but had no cash value during her lifetime."

"Well, that's understandable. Tammy had no assets to speak of. But as an heiress to her grandmother's estate, she didn't worry about things like that."

"She must've been an extraordinary woman to consider caring for her daughter by purchasing life insurance in case anything happened." Daphne let admiration creep into her voice deliberately.

"And you say that she named me as Corina's guardian on this policy?"

"Ye- es, you see right here where she clearly wrote your name as the person who would have control of the money if she should die before Corina reached the state of adulthood."

Ray looked over the documents that Daphne indicated without really seeing any of the words on the pages. He was thinking how this bequest tied him to Tamica's family for at least another two years.

"She was a decent and considerate person. Apparently in her will she left me a $200,000 bequest." Ray laughed a little bit. "Unfortunately she did not have $2000 to her name much less $200,000 to leave to anyone. She only had her salary, an allowance really, from her grandmother, which died when she did."

"Well, you understand life insurance proceeds are completely separate from wills and estates and supersede any will under Texas law. I'm afraid you cannot claim any bequest out of life insurance proceeds," Daphne said primly.

"Naw, I would never do that. Tammy wanted Corina to have this money. It's all hers."

"Ray, I'm sure we will be able to work something out."

Neither Corina nor Ray gave any indication to Daphne that they were more strangers than stepfather and stepdaughter. But somehow by their physical posture and gestures, Daphne knew.

"I think you'll find it's best to work out such details in the upcoming months. Meanwhile, it's possible the proceeds from this policy will be delayed until the investigation of Mrs. Cathare's death is concluded."

"There is nothing to stop me from applying for insurance right now? Is there?" Ray asked.

"No indeed. Certainly not, Mr. Cathare. Sign right here. We can fill in the blanks later."

Daphne pulled out her standard application form, and related instructions and details about the policy that Ray was interested in. He had already signed the form and was writing her a check when there was a knock on the door.

When Daphne took the check, he turned back to the unfinished sections of the application.

"Don't make me the beneficiary, Ray," said Corina. "It should be your sister."

"Maybe." Ray hesitated.

"If you're undecided, you can just put your estate," said Daphne. "That way you can make a will that can affect the divestiture of the proceeds any way you want or name a beneficiary later."

Most people had no doubts about who they wanted to be beneficiary, but when they were unsure, having them designate the estate saved the decision for later and did not impede the application.

"Okay. Sounds good," said Ray, and he resumed writing.

"Come on in, Officer," said Corina, responding to the day maid's introduction of the policeman into the room.

Plate walked in just as Ray was handing the completed papers to Daphne. She looked up at him and smiled as she folded the check inside of the application and put it in her briefcase.

"I hate to be rude," Plate began.

"But you need to know what's going on, Officer? I just bought an insurance policy from Miss Martin here," Ray said smoothly.

"I'm considering a policy myself," said Corina. "I have my child to think of."

"Let's just talk about that later," said Daphne. The expression on Plate's face was unrecognizable to the others but she knew the look.

"Will she need something like a cosigner? Since she's a minor?" asked Ray.

"Yes. Maybe. Something like that," said Daphne.

"There's no rush," said Corina. "We can go ahead and talk to this police officer about the situation."

"If I have permission to relate to him the basic details of what your mother did, then we don't really need to trouble you any further at the moment. Right, Lieutenant?"

Before Plate could protest this logic, Corina rapidly agreed.

"Just the basics. You don't mind speaking with Miss Martin, do you, Lieutenant? My stepfather and I are quite tired. Our business with Miss Martin was imperative but now we would like to try to get some rest."

"Okay," said Plate, feeling helpless.

"Why don't you take me to lunch, Lieutenant? And I can give you the basic, just the basic details of what Mrs. Cathare did." Daphne smiled.

Chapter 46

"McDonald's?"

Plate made the suggestion as they got into Daphne's car. They decided to take it to lunch instead of his patrol car.

"I really would prefer The Toy Museum Restaurant, thank you," said Daphne, driving purposefully in that direction.

"Have to be dutch then. I thought you didn't work on Fridays."

"I make exceptions."

Daphne and Plate sat quietly for several minutes in the elegant restaurant, having ordered their food, before Plate started asking questions.

Daphne cut him off.

"She took out a life insurance policy so that if anything happened to her, Corina, her daughter, would have a measure of independence. It is quite common. Happens all the time."

"A million dollars?"

"The face value of the policy was actually $500,000. It had double indemnity."

"Mrs. Cathare could afford such a premium on the allowance Miss Mattworks gave her? You told me last year, such a large amount was a red flag for suicide if the policyholder didn't have a substantial income."

"That's true for the middle class. The upper classes are different. It's not unusual for some of them to have very large dollar amounts on their lives even if they don't have a substantial income. Mrs. Cathare was an heiress, for heaven sakes. She was going to be worth millions someday. The idea was that if anything happened to her before she inherited her grandmother's millions, her daughter would have something to fall back on. Great-grandchildren don't fall into the direct line of inheritance in Texas. They're too far removed in the lineage."

"Are you telling me that if something happens now to Amelia Mattworks, her estate does not automatically go to Corina?"

"Not speaking in specifics, speaking only in generalities, when somebody like that dies without a direct heir or without a will there is often a court battle over who the closest relative really is. You'd be surprised how many relatives can come out of the woodwork. Relatives ignored and abandoned and forgotten about. Mrs. Cathare wanted to make sure her daughter was provided for if something happened to her before Amelia Mattworks died."

"Amelia Mattworks was already 92 when this policy was issued. There was no reason to think she would not survive her great-grandmother. Her autopsy indicated excellent health. Did Tamica Cathare give you any indication that she expected something to happen to her?" Plate asked.

"She was a young healthy woman. But for that amount, the company now verifies health statements. The premium was cheap because she took out term insurance, but still it wasn't free and she did have a limited allowance. Unfortunately, she did not confide in me. If she had, I don't know if ethically I could tell you what she said. But she did not. I was recommended to her. She called me and told me exactly what she wanted. I drew up the papers, visited with her briefly at her home, completed the process in an hour. She paid via monthly automatic withdrawal premiums. She never had a bounced premium so I never had any reason to contact her again. I tried, of course, hoping to get more business. But she was not interested in seeing me again."

"And there you were selling policies to her relatives the day after her funeral."

"It's not at all unusual. In fact, it is a common point of sale, more frequently, on the day of the funeral. At the reception afterwards, discreetly we attempt to turn the small talk to the value of the policy, that is- its social value, and the merits of taking out life insurance. Many policies are sold after the funeral is over. Unfortunately, this funeral was by invitation and I couldn't get one. I had to pull strings to get there before the reception was over at the York house. So I had to wait until the next day to come back and finish the business."

"Instructions were given that no strangers were to be let in."

"People rarely turn down a life insurance agent bringing proceeds. Besides I was not a stranger. I had been there before when I had consulted with Mrs. Cathare. I had legitimate business with the family."

"You didn't bring the proceeds."

"Normally I would've shown up with a check. However, as the beneficiary is under 18, there are complications. In addition, the fact that the victim was murdered, that can be a complication, too. However, I assume Corina is not a suspect?"

"Strictly speaking, I can't discuss that with you."

"My company has a legitimate interest. She's the beneficiary entitled to $1 million. I can make a formal inquiry and you can have more paperwork."

"Strictly speaking, it is within the realm of possibility that Corina could be the perpetrator. However, no. I'm ninety-nine percent sure she didn't do it. "

"That's good enough for me." Daphne reached down and snapped her briefcase open. "I have a general form here attesting to that. Although eventually I'll need a copy of your formal report, this will do for a moment in getting the paperwork red tape going."

Plate took the paper from Daphne's hand. "I don't see where this is going to do you any good. I can sign off on Corina without any real hesitation but I can't sign a similar paper saying that Ray Cathare is not a suspect. I'm not saying that he is a suspect officially, you understand. But I'm not saying that he isn't."

"That's okay. He's merely the trustee. A court can appoint a different trustee if it becomes necessary. All this paper will do is get the process started. Since the trustee is under suspicion, everything will be delayed until your investigation is over and he is cleared."

"You seem pretty certain he'll be cleared."

"I'm just speaking in generalities. Just sign this for me and make my life easier. How about it?"

Plate signed the paper attesting that he did not consider Corina a suspect in the murder of her mother.

"I have a feeling I'm going to regret making your life easier." But he smiled when he said that.

"You have to understand, I'm only trying to serve my client as best I can." She smiled back at him.

"You better not show up at my funeral trying to sell my bereaved relatives life insurance."

"I would be excused from that duty as you are a personal acquaintance, if I so requested. I would then be free to attend in a private capacity."

"You might not be invited," said Plate.

"There are agents who specialize in delivering benefits at funerals and get most of their sales that way. They take up the slack for those that don't care to go to funerals and for those who are emotionally involved with the deceased."

"I want some type of clause in my policy that prevents my bereaved relatives from being given a sales pitch." Plate bit into an appetizer.

"And would your relatives be bereaved?"

"Very funny. You haven't forgotten we have an appointment in February?"

"Certainly not."

I have thought of it most every day this year. And I sincerely hope I don't ever have to attend your funeral, ever under any circumstances, Daphne thought, as the waitress arrived with their entrées.

Chapter 47

With a speech written by Regina in hand, Edward took Mink Tanem with him to the anti-abortion rally Saturday. Grace and Ray decided to go out to an early dinner. Plate was to leave his cottage and stay inside the mansion along with Regina, Corina and Amelia while the others were gone. Dr. Apixza was in his clinic and Stark Wynter, having moved in right after the funeral, was now safely ensconced in his cottage.

Stark was taking advantage of Edward York's transportation network and had sent Burress back to Hollywood for more medical treatment. It was a little aggravating having to call and wait for a driver to show up before he could go anywhere, but it saved money.

Edward had offered him the service for free and, while he still had Burress on the payroll, unable to in good conscience not pay his loyal employee now that he was ill, Stark was spared the expense of gasoline, which was climbing higher in price every day. He was planning to take full advantage of the service and spend most every day enjoying the sights and experiences of the Houston-Galveston area when he didn't have business connected to the future movie studio.

The night of the anti-abortion rally, Stark decided to head to the opposite side of Houston to check out a new nightclub that had just opened. He confided his plans to Regina York.

Regina, uninterested in abortion one way or another, graciously decided to go along with Stark so he wouldn't be alone in a strange city.

They elected to keep their outing a secret from the rest of the household, including Officer Plate. But he saw them leave in the limousine and made a quick call to Officer Skaar, instructing him to stake out the one exit from Sand Waves and follow them if they left the colony.

That left Plate with only Amelia and Corina to worry about.

With a security system on the third floor making it near impossible for anyone to get in and do anything to the old lady without being detected, Plate was more concerned with the security of the young girl.

Virtually ignored before she sang at her mother's funeral, she was now the center of attention from her family, the press, and God knows who else had her in their sights.

After checking with the elderly lady by the in-house phone, Plate went to find Corina, hoping to talk her into letting him spend the evening either with her or at least near the entrance to her room, if she wanted to be alone or sleep.

He walked past countless dolls and antique tin toys that lined the hallway in the wing where Corina lived. He wondered if that wing had been selected for such open display of childhood mementos to somehow try to comfort the child that lived there.

He knocked softly and politely on Corina's door. It was already turning dark. He didn't want to startle the girl.

He only had gotten halfway through his knocking when he heard shots.

He wasn't sure if the shots came from the other side of house or from the outdoors. But he was positive the sound didn't come from inside the room that he was trying to gain entrance to.

He beat on the door frantically but there was no answer and when he tried to kick it in, it remained stubbornly in place, too high quality and strong for a single man to break it down.

He turned around and raced for the nearest phone to summon the patrolmen stationed as guards outside the fence. He quickly dialed their pager numbers from memory and pressed an emergency signal, knowing they would alert others. He figured they must have heard the shots as well and would know what was expected of them.

As he was calculating which way to go, he heard more shots in a different direction.

This time though he was certain they came from the back yard.

Running through the connecting foyer, he nearly collided with Corina who threw herself in his arms.

"Someone shot at me," she said, more coherently and with less hysteria than he would have thought possible for someone her age and condition. "I was outside and the bullet went right by me before I even heard the shot. I turned and ran. It just happened. He has to still be out there."

"Where exactly were you?"

"Near Mink Coat's cottage."

"The safest place for you right now is up on the third floor with your great-grandmother."

"I can't disturb her without her permission."

"No, but I can activate emergency security and you can get in the elevator. Just go up there. You don't have to disturb her. I'll send one of the others or an officer up after you when it's safe."

Plate was already summoning the elevator, using the security code Edward York had taught him, and he waited until Corina was safely inside before he turned back on the path to the back door.

As he reached the door, he was aware that Ray and Grace were coming up behind him, obviously just returning from their dinner, with take home food containers in hand. But he could not stay to talk to them and simply barked at them to stay inside.

Crossing the porch into the back yard, he saw the patrolmen were just making it through the iron fences.

"Near Mink Coat- Tanem's cottage!" Plate yelled at the other officers who turned and started in that direction at his command.

And they ran toward the sound of the bullets.

Chapter 48

At that moment another shot rang out. The sound did not come from the direction of Mink Tanem's cottage, rather the cottages on the opposite side of the yard. And there was a clear yell for help.

The officers all sprinted in the direction of that shot, weapons drawn. They encountered Stark Wynter midway between his cottage and the pool.

Officer Skaar also appeared, breathless, and whispered to Plate quickly. "They turned around on the highway and came right back here to the cottage. The woman is inside."

"Someone is shooting at me," Stark yelled.

"I saw a blonde man go over the fence." This shout came from Dr. Apixza, who had come up behind the police officers, unnoticed.

"Did the shots come from above or from down on the ground?" Plate directed Skaar to make a quick search.

"I'm sure from above," said Wynter. "I saw him!"

"No, they were from the ground," declared Apixza.

"They were on my side of the yard," said Stark Wynter. "How could you possibly know what direction they came from?"

"No, they were on my side of the yard," said Apixza.

"It appears multiple shots were fired," said Plate. He then directed the other patrolmen to start searching the grounds. He shone his light up at the sports observation deck on the Pointpar estate. It was dark and deserted.

"They must've gotten away through the woods," said Apixza.

"Describe the man you saw going over the fence."

"He didn't go towards the woods. He went towards the front yard. He was slim and blonde, just like the burglar you said was seen the night Tamica Cathare was killed," said Wynter.

"Then, the dogs would have gotten him." Dr. Apixza twisted his hands nervously. "I insisted I wasn't going to live here if those dogs were allowed anywhere in the back yard, anywhere near me or my clinic. They would tear anybody to pieces that they did not know well. Even if you do know them, well, they are hostile and aggressive. No one could've gotten by the dogs."

"I know what I saw," said Wynter. Stubbornly, he pointed towards the Pointpar structure. "I think the shots came from there."

Officer Skaar returned. He was adamant. "No sign of anyone. Not unless they are inside a building. What exactly happened? Do I have probable cause to go in?"

"I want no one in my residence," said Apixza.

"Someone shot at Corina near Mink Tanem's cottage. Grant, take these men in the larger house. If you gentlemen will go inside the mansion with Officer Skaar. Grace York and Ray Cathare are inside the house. Corina has gone up to the third floor to be with Amelia. I think you will all be safer if you'll go inside to be with them. Doctor, no one will violate your wishes."

At that moment, Regina York emerged from Stark Wynter's cottage.

"Good evening, Officer," she said evenly, walking toward Stark. "I didn't see a thing. Come along, Stark."

She took Stark Wynter's arm and they took off for the back door immediately.

But Apixza declined. "I need to get back to my clinic. It's more important that my clinic not be left alone. My personal safety is secondary. I have a security system with an audible alarm that will sound if it is violated."

Plate wanted to argue with the doctor but he did not have time. He sent Skaar to the mansion with instructions to reach Edward York at the anti-abortion rally one way or another. He did not care about the ramifications of not having probable cause. He wanted to get straight to Mink Tanem's cottage and see if anyone was hiding there.

Chapter 49

Two hours later, after a thorough search of the grounds, it was succinctly established that whoever had fired the shots had gotten clean away.

Plate checked with the Pointpars. Forrest and Clip had both attended the anti-abortion rally but had returned home early. They had been watching westerns on TV and had seen nothing. Any shots they heard blended in with the westerns. They watched television in an almost soundproof modern home theatre room. They would have only witnessed the shooting if one of them had been on the sports tower. But it was western movie night and they were inside the whole time, they both asserted.

It seemed that only Mink Tanem's cottage had been broken into. He had been contacted at the anti-abortion rally, had turned over Edward York's security to Houston police and was on his way back to the mansion. But there was a wreck on Loop 610 and almost immediately he had gotten caught in stop-and-go traffic.

Corina had been banished to the third floor foyer. She had spoken to her great-grandmother through the door but had been told to wait out in the hallway the entire time. Amelia did not want any company at that moment and would not let her in the room.

Corina came back down and complained to Plate about discomfort. Amelia told Plate over the house phone she was working on her memoirs and Corina's safety was his problem.

Plate sent her back upstairs anyway and told her to wait on the third floor until it was safe. Other bedrooms on the third floor were closed up and inaccessible. They had been furnished and readied when the upper floor was first built, originally anticipating caregivers would be needed for Amelia Mattworks in her decline. When that need failed to materialize, the rooms were utilized to store excess items and locked.

No one was hiding at Tanem's cottage. Apixza searched his own quarters, still refusing to let anyone else in. But the doctor was willing to let the police observe on the cottage's porch, through the open doorway, as he went through the structure. It seemed obvious no one was there.

Skaar was sent back out into the field with the rest of the searchers. Plate suggested to everyone inside the mansion that they freshen up and get a bite to eat while the search proceeded. Once everyone felt better and more secure, they could meet as a group.

Shortly after Officer Skaar reported a second sweep of the grounds yielded no results. Feeling the crisis was over, Plate allowed Corina to return downstairs. He wanted her present for a discussion about what everyone had seen and heard.

An hour later in the York living room, Ray, Grace, Corina, Regina, Stark Wynter, Dr. Apixza, and Officer Plate sat in the various chairs and sofas. The tension was gone from the group for a moment. In its place was resigned exhaustion on the part of everyone.

"I'm going to need to speak with all of you individually about what happened this evening. But I'd like to try to establish a timeline, with those of you involved filling in the pieces for me as best you can. Now, I was actually knocking at Miss French's bedroom door when I first heard the shots. I was under the impression, Miss French, that you were in your room. But you were not? Where were you?"

"Plate, I think you need to take into account the trauma this girl has been through," said Grace snappily.

"It's okay," said Corina. "I am all right. Please call me Corina, Officer. Grace, I can answer the officer's question. To get a breath of fresh air. I wandered over to the cottage just, I guess, not paying attention."

"Why would you go to that particular cottage?"

"I don't know. I didn't want to go back to the pool area."

"I think that's enough," said Grace, standing up.

"I need for you to tell me exactly what happened while you were outdoors," said Plate to Corina. He stood up immediately after Grace, blocking Grace from going to the girl.

"I was merely walking, probably rather slowly, but I heard a noise that sounded like branches rustling. The next thing I knew, something had whizzed by me and my first thought was that it was a wasp. But then I heard the shot and I knew it was a bullet. I ran. I

190

probably screamed. I don't remember that. And the next thing I remember, I was in your arms."

"Thank you, Miss French. Corina. That corresponds with my recollection. From the time I heard the shot until you got to me, probably was just enough time for both of us to make it to that exact spot," Plate said.

"Now, I think that was about 7:45," said Corina.

Plate was surprised that Corina would know the exact time. He had not been sure of the time himself, failing to look at his watch while he was knocking at her bedroom door.

"That's extremely helpful. Can any of the rest of you tell me if you heard a shot about that time and where you were, and where you think the shot came from?"

"Corina just told you. It was over by Mink's cottage," Grace said.

"Grace," said Ray, speaking for the first time. "Bullets can travel long distances. Someone may have shot at her from way across the yard, from the woods, from the house or any number of other places and the bullets still fly by her while she was near that cottage."

"Exactly," said Plate. "That puts it very succinctly, Mr. Cathare."

"The shots came from above," insisted Stark Wynter.

"Let's not get ahead," said Plate. "Again each of you needs to tell me what, if anything, you heard at approximately 7:45PM and where you were."

"Ray and I were in the kitchen," said Grace. "We had just returned."

"If we heard anything, I don't think we had noticed it. Wasn't the den TV on in the background, Grace?"

"Yes it was. I think it was a western."

"I thought there was a shot on my side of the yard," said Dr. Apixza. "Of course, I'm a much older man and I'm sure my hearing is not as good as Corina's."

"I heard the first shot at about that time," said Stark Wynter. "We had just gotten back. We- er- Mrs. York was going to show me Houston. But then we returned because I was not feeling well."

191

"Dr. Apixza, did you did get a good look at the man going over the fence?" Plate asked.

"No, I did not. But then, I wasn't really looking at his face."

"There wasn't any man going over the fence," said Corina.

"Yes, there was," insisted Wynter. "Regina and I had returned home early from our outing in Houston. And I saw him on my side of the yard."

"I did not see anything," said Regina.

"I would have seen anybody on the grounds. I had been out there a while. If there had been anybody, I would have seen them," said Corina, with surprising determination.

"Okay, we're beyond the point where Corina has run into the house after someone fired a shot at her. Undetermined where it came from. Was it before or after that when you saw the blonde man, Mr. Wynter?"

"It was after. It had to have been him. He must've scaled the fence and climbed a tree and then shot it me."

Plate tried not to give away the stress he felt at the idea of another shooting which started on the ground and ended in a tree. "This assumes that it is someone who wishes to harm both Miss French and Mr. Wynter here."

Corina and Stark gazed at each other, both of them thinking how they were totally complete strangers. It ran through Stark's mind that there was a million to one chance the girl was his daughter biologically. The more he looked at her, the more he thought it was really a ten million to one chance or actually impossible. He had seen a depiction of himself and her mother in an old movie magazine recently, and the more he thought about it, the best he could recall was that he took her out one time and had never slept with her at all. He did drink a bit back then...

Maybe it was Chloe I slept with, he thought with confusion.

Corina was thinking, *there is no way this man and I have anything in common.*

Plate was sharing that thought. "It seems to me there's a possibility that both Miss French and Mr. Wynter have seen or heard something that has caused Mrs. Cathare's killer to come back and possibly attempt to kill the both of them."

"But I wasn't even here when Mrs. Cathare was killed," said Wynter.

"I know, I know," said Plate wearily.

"This doesn't seem to be getting us anywhere," said Grace.

"I do think since you and Mr. Cathare did not see anything or hear anything, there's no use in my detaining the two of you any further," Plate said.

Ray stood up and started towards the door.

"Gracie," he said, looking back at his cousin still seated on a sofa. "I think he means we need to leave."

"I don't have to go anywhere. This is my–" Grace stopped herself before she said 'this is my house'.

Regina snickered.

"Actually, I don't think I need to detain any of you any longer." Plate added, "except I need another word with Miss French."

Dr. Apixza and Stark Wynter returned to their respective cottages quickly whereas Grace and Ray took more time just to go to a different section of the mansion. Stark Wynter agreed to allow a police officer to spend the rest of the night with him. But Apixza refused and there was no way Plate could force him.

"I refuse also," said Corina to Plate, after they were alone in the living room.

"You're a minor. You don't have any say."

"My great-grandmother is my guardian and you don't have access to her," said Corina.

This was true. Although he had spoken to Amelia Mattworks on the in-house phone, so far she had declined to see him in person. She had assured him it was not a permanent refusal. She just was not ready yet. And Plate was under strict orders not to insist on disturbing her until she was ready.

It was a *Catch-22* situation.

"Could I at least ask you to go and stay again with your great-grandmother, taking advantage of the extra security on the third floor until the Edward York or Mink Tanem gets back?" Plate asked, gritting his teeth. He was not used to having to ask 16-year-olds for cooperation or favors.

"If she will let me," said Corina.

Amelia refused, so Plate spent the rest of the night on a chair outside Corina's bedroom door. He did not even leave the post to brief Edward York when he returned to his home. Plate left that to the other police officers who were guarding the back door.

Although Edward stayed for the full length of the rally, he actually arrived back in Sand Waves before Mink Tanem, who had left when it was less than a quarter over. Mink had sat most of the night in the stopped lanes of the loop while an emergency accident had been serviced by Life Flight. Edward, knowing of the traffic jam, had come home a circuitous route through old Houston neighborhoods and arrived faster.

Skaar had sent Tanem inside to be briefed by Plate. Speaking in low tones in front of Corina's bedroom door, there was little Plate could tell him. Tanem went back to his cottage. He reported once again nothing was missing. Skaar brought the message to Plate.

It was morning before Plate felt the situation was safe enough for him to leave the post and go to his cottage to get a couple of hours sleep. Corina had opened the door and stepped out to tell him that her great-grandmother had summoned her.

Plate accompanied Corina to the elevator, waited until its doors closed, then went out to his cottage leaving Officer Skaar in charge of security for the day.

He had to get some rest.

He had not had a complete night's sleep for several days and he had to at least get a nap.

Chapter 50

"I just wanted to see you, after what all happened, to give you a little advice."

"Yes, Great-grandmother."

Early Sunday morning, Corina had come to Amelia as asked.

"I know I've never developed a relationship with you. I guess I thought I was so old when you were born, I needn't bother. I figured I wouldn't be around long enough to see you grow up. And, when you looked back on your family ancestry, I didn't want you to remember the shriveled up old woman I've become. I wanted you to investigate and find the beautiful young woman I once was."

Corina was silent.

"Well, that was stupid." Amelia picked up one of the antique baby dolls with cracked porcelain skin that graced her bed.

Corina's eyes darted all around the room. Several baby dolls with glass eyes stared back. They were not comforting vinyl dolls with cheerful painted expressions like those in her own collection.

These dolls looked more like they were dead with open staring eyes. Their skin was crazed with tiny lines and they were dressed in such frills that babies never wore, except for Christening or coffin.

When prone, their eyes are closed and they really look dead then, Corina thought.

For the life of her, Corina could not think of a thing to say. All she could mentally focus on was how the skin on the dolls compared to Amelia's neck, face, and hands. Like the dolls, her visible skin was lined with thousands of tiny hairline cracks. But while the dolls had taut skin, hers was loose, not flabby, more like a crinkled silk garment which enveloped Amelia's thin neck and shoulders, a soft satin mask stretched on her face and comfortable velvet gloves covering her hands.

"Today, I see you are grown," Amelia continued. "Despite your teenage years, you have a maturity about you that neither your mother nor your grandmother ever achieved in their lifetimes. Therefore, I will be brief and not insult your intelligence.

"When you're young and strong-minded and mature like I was

at your age, and your life is laid out for you and you are happy with it, like I was at your age, it is easy to follow the path. My advice is- in the Revelations the Lord chides those for forsaking their first love. I also made that mistake many years ago. I forsook my first love. Do not repeat my mistake."

Corina sat down and braced herself for a long lecture.

"As I said, it easy in the beginning when it appears to be all set out for you. You know who you are. You know what you got to do in life. The problem is when the plan is interrupted. I was all set until the Great War. If there had been no Great War. Well, there's no sense in saying if- what I am trying to say is, it be easy to keep going when the road is marked, but when the guiding signs are torn down-"

Amelia interrupted herself.

"You believe? Know the Lord?"

"Yes I do," Corina began, elated, yet feeling unprepared for this unexpected opportunity to discuss and share her faith.

The chance to speak about her beliefs with a relative, especially her great-grandmother, heretofore so aloof, was a dream come true. So far-fetched that she had never even considered it could become a reality. She was at once afraid she was unprepared.

"Then let me tell you, if your path is broken," said Amelia, turning away, remembering the day years ago Roscoe Burns had offered to give up his life, as he had known it, and return with her back to the world she had known in East Texas.

Remembering how she had rejected that suggestion without even any serious thought, as she had cradled her child in her arms. How sure she had been that there was no going back to that path...

Tears came to her eyes.

After all these years she had now realized that path had been Constance's only chance...

Until Constance died I always believed the Lord gave everyone a chance in life, she thought. *For years I felt like He never gave her none. But He did. He spoke to Roscoe. If I had listened to Roscoe, if we had gone back to East Texas...*

In empathy, not knowing why, tears welled up in Corina's eyes also.

Both women were silent.

Corina was at a loss again. Amelia was staring into space as if in a trance.

"If my path is broken? Great-grandmother? You were saying?"

Amelia turned back to Corina. *It was my fault, He spoke to Roscoe because He knew I wouldn't listen to Him,* she thought, seeing Corina but not yet comprehending her words. *It was my fault...*

"What was your fault?" Corina asked.

Amelia had not known she had spoken aloud.

"Are you all right?" Corina stepped towards her.

Amelia coughed, then took a deep breath as she had done so many times when she had lost herself in a song.

"What I'm saying is, if as you go forward in life, your paths are broken, don't go the other way, stay on the path to cross over those breaks. Navigate your way around, but stay on the road. Do you understand what I'm saying?"

"Yes, I think so, Great-grandmother," said Corina, swallowing hard, as she prepared to start telling her own story.

"Good. That is all. You may go." Amelia rose abruptly and turned away.

Corina stood up, confused.

"I thought I was going to get tea and cookies," she said, unable to think of anything else, feeling a little cheated.

She knew her own mother's relationship with Amelia had been contentious. She knew Amelia was domineering and desired to control the lives of others. She had been relieved years ago when she realized that Amelia ignoring her was the best possible familial outcome she could hope for with the old lady. But now, looking at her, knowing they were flesh and blood, Corina felt a new affection and a desire for the beginning of a relationship, no matter how short-lived it was fated to be.

"Not today. Perhaps another time. I'm a little tired now."

"Okay, thank you for seeing me, Great-grandmother," she said, as she reached to kiss the old lady's cheek. She had expected a discussion of her pregnancy, her singing at her mother's funeral, lectures on race, sexuality, morality, and lifestyle.

Instead, she had received curt cryptic wisdom so generic and ambiguous she could not see how it applied to her life at all. Yet it was refreshing that her great-grandmother had asked about her faith.

No family member had ever done so before.

"Is there something else you need, child?"

Corina's thoughts turned from religion to less comforting concerns. "Yes," she said, taking a deep breath. *I owe this to my mother,* she thought. "There is one more thing. I need to ask you about."

"Go on then." Amelia gave permission for her to continue.

"Years ago my mother had a boyfriend. Before I was born. Her first real boyfriend. Do you remember him?" Corina spoke rapidly and her heart pounded as she awaited Amelia's response.

Amelia put her index finger to her lips and cupped her chin. Her eyes darted around the room. "No-o. I don't think so. Wait. Was he a blonde boy? Worked for us? No- that's not right-"

"I don't know anything about him. I was under the impression she knew him at school."

"That was so long ago, child."

"She was about 14. You objected. She was taken out of the school to get her away from him-"

"Well, I would have objected to any boyfriend at 14. Her mother had just killed herself. Her father was sick with the cancer. My husband had just died. I had to make all the decisions. Seems like it. But I simply cannot remember. Is it important? Certainly it was before your time-" Amelia broke off awkwardly, remembering Corina did not know who her own father was.

"I know. No. I'm not asking about someone who might have been my father. It was before. Mother just mentioned it. Once. That's all."

"I'm sorry, child. I just cannot remember." Amelia frowned as faces from the past came before her.

Was that one Chloe's? Or Tamica's? I am getting them mixed up. Was there somebody that dated both of them? Too young for Chloe and too old for Tamica. I just saw him recently, or did I? I gave him the medicine? Or did I?

Amelia was telling Corina the truth about being tired.

"Are you okay?" Corina was noticing that Amelia was staring blankly into space.

"I just cannot remember," Amelia repeated. Nevertheless, she came to herself and smiled at Corina. "I will try later."

"That's okay." Corina backed away, still facing her great-grandmother.

"Anything else you need? If so, could you please take it up with the Yorks? I am quite tired."

"Ah, no, Great-grandmother. Nothing. Other than thank you for the advice."

Corina turned and left the room, placing her hand over the child in her womb protectively as she walked through the door.

As soon as Corina had shut the door, against her will Amelia saw more faces from the past come before her eyes. Too many faces.

Amelia Mattworks placed her hands over her face and wept.

Chapter 51

Corina knew what she had to do. There was only one person she could trust to remove her from the house who also could get in. She picked up the phone.

"I just got a few hours of sleep," Plate complained to Skaar. "I couldn't have been asleep more than four or five hours at the most. After not having had any sleep for days. And you couldn't keep the girl secure for that short period of time?"

"You were asleep for eight hours, Lieutenant. My shift had ended. I had practically spent the entire time with the girl. The only time I wasn't with her was when that insurance agent came by and she only stayed about ten minutes. She needed a signature or something. They're trying to get the life insurance proceeds straightened out."

"Did you see her again after Daphne Martin left?"

"Corina French passed me on the way back to her room and said 'I'll wait right in my room. Would you please go and get Lieutenant Plate? I have something important to tell him'. You didn't answer and she insisted I go get you. She had to have vanished while I was walking over here to your cottage to get you. You didn't answer your pager or your phone. Your phone was busy after that."

Plate had already turned the pager back on and hung up the phone before Officer Skaar got there. He did not respond to the last comment.

"I know Daphne Martin," Plate said, instead. "There's no way she's involved with Corina's disappearance. That's one reason why she was on the list of people to be allowed into the estate. I know when I talk to her, she will confirm that it was absolutely necessary to get Corina's signature. Or was it Ray Cathare's signature that she was after? Where is Cathare? Have you accounted for him?"

"I'm not sure. They asked for privacy. The insurance agent didn't ask to see anybody else," Skaar said.

"There's always the possibility that somebody got in at the same time Daphne was let in. Even the possibility that there was someone hiding in her backseat or in the trunk of her car," Plate speculated out loud.

The thought that Daphne might have been used to traffic in a killer chilled him to the bone.

"And it's apparent how the kidnapper got the girl out."

Plate looked at Skaar in surprise. "Don't tell me he climbed a tree?"

"One of servants was dropped off at almost exactly the same time and we have determined that the limousine that picked the servant up and brought her to work was not from the regular service that Edward York uses. The shuttle that was supposed to have brought this servant in showed up at her apartment complex just about five minutes after the fraudulent limousine had picked her up. Apparently this limousine took Corina out of the compound, probably in its trunk."

"Oh my God," said Plate "and the girl is pregnant. If she's harmed– " Plate failed to continue verbalizing the thoughts coming to his head. "Has the rest of the house been told?"

"No, Lieutenant, I haven't contacted anybody, or done anything, other than issuing an alert for the limousine. I did that immediately of course. First thing."

"Which by now, it's probably too late."

"The household knows something has happened but I have not told them what. I wanted to leave that to you."

"Thanks a lot."

After conferring with the chief, it was decided that the disappearance of Corina was not yet going to be officially treated as a crime. The APB put out on the limousine was a generic one for a fabricated fender bender in Sand Waves. The chief did not want any other law enforcement agencies involved, at least until the 24 hour waiting period, standard search time for runaways, had expired.

Only Edward York and Corina's guardian, Amelia Mattworks, were informed of what really happened. Communication with Miss Mattworks was still being conducted through Edward. He reported that she was taking this new development well and agreed that as few people should know about it as was possible. All agreed that was the best course of action to pursue.

"We need to treat this as a kidnapping, therefore we will need to tap your phone lines and wait for a ransom call."

"How might we stop anyone else from answering the phone and thus intercepting the ransom demands?"

"We will put a van outside the house and an operative will answer the phone 'York residence, please state your business'. When a suspicious call comes in, we will have it directed to you specifically."

Plate also put in a call to the Hollywood police to have them check on Stark Wynter's driver, Burress, and make sure he really was still in Hollywood.

After receiving and transmitting these instructions, Plate drove to Daphne Martin's house. She had called and left him a message that was cataloged urgent and private, requesting he stop by her house in person.

She lived in a one story 2100 square feet tract home in one of Sands Waves' lower priced colonies. Not the lowest price, however. And her neighborhood was designed with homes with eclectic fronts and a wide choice of floor plans.

Populated by self styled young urban professionals, it was considered a stepping stone to the next level of flexible floor plans with custom features.

Plate had put off responding until he got everything else as much under control as possible. But now there was nothing else to do.

Plate was beginning to wonder if the key to it all was not the thin blonde burglar.

He is apparently getting behind the gates, over the fences, climbing up and down trees, then vanishing with the skill of a 1980s Houdini, thought Plate.

But was he the killer?

Chapter 52

"I might just kill you right here and now." Plate folded his arms across his chest and glared as they exited the guest room where Corina had gone to bed.

"Now, there's no reason to get all steamed and huffy," said Daphne, closing the bedroom door behind her.

"No jury would convict me."

"Do I need to show you Miss Mattworks' handwritten permission? Again?"

Daphne led Plate down the hall back into her spacious den. Nothing like the den at the York mansion, it nevertheless was open and inviting, just off a slightly raised tiled foyer, partially open, and adjacent to a rectangular kitchen and dinette. It had a comfortable sofa and a nice TV.

"You would look beautiful in a coffin."

"I called you right away to tell you what was happening as soon as we safely got her away from that place."

"Blonde hair spread out on a satin pillow. Your arms folded over your chest. All laid out in your nice business suit. Have you got a pink one? That would go with your hair, better than that beige you normally wear."

"It's not my fault that you didn't answer the phone or respond to my message. Your phone line was busy. Did they give you an old party line at the York mansion?"

"I'm envisioning the coffin lid closing on you right now."

"This is the safest place for her."

"I am in the hearse with your casket, traveling towards the cemetery." Plate closed his eyes and put his forefingers to his temples, elbows extended.

"Nobody will dream to look for her here. I left the York estate in my car. She was seen by your officer colleague after I left, so nobody can think she went with me."

"I presume you have plenty of life insurance that will console your bereaved relatives after your burial." Plate opened his eyes, looking for family photos, but he saw none.

"It's perfectly legal and she is within her rights to leave that place, especially with the express permission of her legal guardian. Miss Mattworks agreed to let on that she knew nothing to lessen the risk that others would find out."

"And what about the limousine driver? That was the weakness in your plan. If you had consulted the police before this daring operation, we could've at least had a police officer driving."

"The chauffeur driver in the limousine is somebody we can absolutely trust completely."

"You have to tell me who it was. And how he got the limousine. There isn't anybody in the world you can absolutely trust completely."

"The man's name, I don't know. Corina French assured me—"

"Corina French is a 16-year-old child!" Plate snapped.

"She's more mature than you think she is. Anyway, tell me the truth. Assume, just for a minute, that the limousine driver is trustworthy or didn't really understand what was going on, whatever makes you feel better, we've got her here. She is safe. And, knowing for sure the driver is not the killer, but again you have to take my word for it- Can you think of any better place for her to be? You could put a patrolman right outside the door. You can put a policewoman in here with us. I have a gun myself. And you can come over anytime you want to, without arousing suspicion. We can pretend we're dating."

Plate looked at Daphne and felt his hostility towards the situation evaporating against his will.

"If I can believe the limousine driver is trustworthy, you may have a point or two, and I may not kill you."

"Thank you for small favors. I will cancel the grave digging." She smiled at him.

"Uniformed officers in this neighborhood would be too conspicuous. I'm going to ask the county to put your house under surveillance with plainclothes detectives. I will tell them you have received death threats from a client or something. Do you think it's possible you could back me up on that? If the situation should necessitate it?"

"Of course. I'm sure there's a few times some of my clients want to kill me, especially when their premiums come due."

Plate became serious and thoughtful.

"For now, I'm not even going to tell the chief about this. Or at least, I'm going to tell him I have Corina French in a safe place in an undisclosed location. I'm going to need that authorization from Miss Mattworks."

Daphne handed the paper over to him. The flowery handwriting looked almost like calligraphy.

My great-granddaughter Corina French has my authorization to reside with Ms. Daphne Martin for the duration of time necessary to resolve any threats to her life or other dangers she may face. It is my express wish that she remained in Ms. Martin's care and that her whereabouts remain cloaked in utmost secrecy. This permission is valid through the remainder of January 1983,
Amelia Mattworks.

"I'm trusting you," said Plate to Daphne, "with Miss French's life and my career."

"I know," Daphne said solemnly.

Plate was touched that tears came to her eyes.

"I'll do my best not to betray that trust, either one of them," she added.

Chapter 53

"Then there's no question that the .22 rifle is the right gun?" asked the chief. "And the drugs found in his possession were traced to Dr. Apixza?"

"Confirmation. He uses drugs from a compound pharmacy in Humble. Even the labeling had his name on it," Plate said.

He and Chief Brecken were conferring in the chief's office the next morning.

All the routine police work by the county and HPD had paid off and a serial burglar had been found in possession of the .22 rifle that had fired the nonfatal shot the night Tamica Cathare died. It was an unregistered firearm but a paper trail suggested it belonged to Dr. JD Apixza. And drugs that belonged to Dr. Apixza's clinic were confiscated from the burglar's apartment.

"Apixza claims the drugs must've been stolen the night Mink Tanem's cottage was broken into. Although at the time he claimed nobody had gotten into his clinic," Plate said.

"What do you make of that?"

"Somebody got into the clinic and he didn't want us to know it. Probably made off with some drugs."

"The suspect is a known drug dealer. So he was after drugs the night he killed Tamica Cathare? And came back later for more? Then came back a third time?" Chief Brecken analyzed.

"So it appears," Plate said, without conviction.

"There was another trail coming from the woods, different from the one found the night Tamica was murdered. He's a tall thin blonde. And he has worked as a chauffeur for the limousine service that Edward York keeps on call."

"What is he saying?"

"He's not talking right now. He's lawyered up. But I think when we mention the possibility of charging him for Tamica Cathare's murder, he might open up."

"Do you think it's safe to say that he was the burglar on the premises the night Tamica was killed?"

"I think it's a strong possibility," Chief Brecken asserted.

"Where do we actually stand right now, Plate? What do we literally know?"

"Corina is safe in an undisclosed location."

"Thank God for that! What else?"

"Not much. Let's assume this burglar did shoot Tamica with the .22. That doesn't explain the other shots that killed her. No other gun was found in this guy's possession. Why get rid of one gun and keep the other?"

"The other was more incriminating."

"No, that doesn't make sense," Plate said.

"It also doesn't make sense why Apixza would cover up the theft of the drugs."

"Apixza is also saying he might never have received delivery of the drugs. That they were intercepted before they got to him. That would make more sense in a way. This guy gained access to the York compound. Observed the clinic, maybe even made an appointment. He would qualify as a patient, working for a transportation service Edward York employs. Apixza is checking his records. That's the only cooperation we're getting from him. Anyway, the burglar either conspires with the delivery service to intercept the drugs or he's figured out the delivery schedule."

"What kind of drugs are we talking about?" Chief Brecken asked.

"Anesthetics mostly. Locals. Ingredients for spinal shots, given to women having babies or-"

"Or what?"

"Or abortions."

"This is an abortion clinic? On private property? On Edward York's property?" Brecken was incredulous.

"That is what the drugs would indicate. Right under York's nose, on his own property. But the quantity Apixza ordered is small, so he has few patients, if that is what he is doing. Now that it's legal, abortion is mainly profitable in big numbers. Unless he's ordering more drugs elsewhere from different pharmacies that don't know about each other."

"Maybe it's something different? Someone at the house with a strange addiction to anesthetic drugs? Is that possible?"

"Unusual. But not unheard of. Some of the drugs could be used as a high. But they would require a doctor's supervision or they could be fatal," Plate said.

"What is Apixza's explanation for all this?"

"Patient confidentiality."

"Patient confi- Hellfire and damnation, Plate. We've got to get into that clinic."

"We're not getting anywhere without a warrant. And we're being blocked. I'm living a few feet away from it and I cannot set foot on the front porch. Someone powerful is blocking any warrant requests."

"Why? Who?"

"I don't know for sure, but I can guess. Edward York."

The chief leaned back in his chair, dumbfounded. Both he and Plate knew if Edward York had put the word out to quash any warrants letting them into Apixza's clinic, no fellow judge would defy him.

"If that is what is going on, Plate, you get back there and don't leave no matter what. Before they decide to kick you out if you come too close to the truth."

"Yes, sir."

Chapter 54

"I can't let you leave," said Daphne. "I'm responsible for you to Lieutenant Plate." She and Corina stood in the den.

"I appreciate what the lieutenant and you have done for me," said Corina. "I just want to be with my baby's father. I'll be perfectly safe with him. Please let me go to him."

"If I let you go, the lieutenant could lose his job. And I think I may have a long term interest in seeing that he keeps it."

"I just have to see him." Corina broke down in tears.

"Was he the limousine driver? You swore to me that the driver would be somebody you could completely trust."

"Yes, that was him. And he was taking a terrible risk."

"Won't it be more of a risk if you show yourself and go to him? What if he came here?"

"I'm not sure that would be possible."

"Why not? No one knows you are here," said Daphne. "Worse case scenario, I'll say he came over to see me to buy insurance. I don't see clients at my home but who knows that? A few agents do. As long as he keeps quiet, there'd be no harm done. You tell me you trust him absolutely. I've got a feeling you're right."

"You don't understand. It is hard for him to be able to get away without attracting attention. He took all kinds of risks, driving that limousine. If he had been recognized, it would have been a disaster."

"He's a celebrity? I didn't recognize him." Daphne didn't mention that she didn't follow contemporary celebrities religiously, unless they were clients, and might not have known him even if he was quite famous.

"Not exactly. His father is a celebrity," said Corina, wringing her hands.

She looked in Daphne's soft brown eyes. She was trusting this woman with her life, with her baby's life. She might as well trust him her with the life of the man she loved. It was an all or nothing game.

"You can trust me. I have some celebrity clients. That one of them might want to come see me at home, well, that is not too farfetched these days," said Daphne, as if reading Corina's mind.

Corina took a deep breath. "Before I tell you about the man I love. I want to tell you about the man my mother loved. When she was a young girl about my age. I think her story will help you understand mine."

Daphne was used to listening to therapeutic stories from her clients. They frequently saw in her someone they could confide in. Someone who would be neutral and nonjudgmental. Sometimes they even told her stories from the past like Corina wanted to do now.

"Okay. Tell me." Daphne tried to look relaxed and casual. She was hoping to put the girl at ease so the story would flow and not take on elements of a marathon. She was fairly successful at this most of the time with needy clients, but sometimes she got caught up in an all night soap opera session.

"For all practical purposes," said Corina, "with the assistance of servants, my mother was raised by Amelia Mattworks. Her own mother was somewhat flighty and took drugs at times. The she committed suicide and my grandfather had one of those long slow cancers that takes over 25 years to kill you. After my grandmother's suicide, Amelia shipped him off to Europe for treatment and took over. When my mother was in junior high school she fell in love. I don't know who with. I think it was just a boy she went to school with. But Amelia did not approve and forbade the relationship. She took my mother out of the school. It's not true that such relationships are always frivolous when you're young. My mother never got over the denial of her right to love this boy. She rebelled against Amelia and part of her rebellion was to become- it's hard to say the word- promiscuous. That's where I came from."

"And when you fell in love at a young age, you were determined you are not going to be separated from the boy you loved," Daphne concluded.

"Pretty much," said Corina, feeling calmer.

It's going to be easier to get her to understand than I thought it would be, she thought.

"In a strange way, I have more curiosity about the boy my mother first loved then my own biological dad. It would break my heart if I ever found my real father and he turned out to be a criminal.

210

Or dead. Or didn't want me. So I think it is best I never know. After all, why would he have not come forward after all these years? No one cares now."

"Corina, you know what happened to your mother is in the past," said Daphne, feeling the more than ten year age difference between the two of them at the moment. "Right now we have to think about the future. If you think your future is with this boy, now's your chance to convince me."

"Okay, let me tell you about him."

Daphne and Corina held both hands together. Corina backed up a little and Daphne moved forward. Still holding hands, they sat together on the den sofa as Corina told Daphne about her romance.

Chapter 55

"I told Clip Pointpar my granddaughter, Tamica, was pregnant. I think you need to consider him a suspect."

Plate regarded Amelia with alarm. He had been told so much about how sharp she was at age 94, that he had taken for granted that she had something important to tell him.

Possibly something she had seen from her third floor windows the night of the murder, or some other past secret that she knew about some member of the family. Or just anything that could help him out.

He was elated when she had finally summoned him ten days after the murder of her granddaughter. He had rushed to the main house, rapidly ascended the stairs to the third floor and the coveted interview had begun.

But here she was trying to point the finger of suspicion at an elderly man who could not possibly have anything to do with the young beautiful victim. And she was insinuating he wanted to murder the victim because she was pregnant.

"It went like this. He was making jokes about Tamica being pregnant. Joking about how white the baby was going to be with a white father."

Plates shifted uncomfortably.

"You listen to me. I told him the marriage was in trouble and that Tamica did not intend to have the baby. He is so anti-abortion. This absolutely enraged him."

"Did Mrs. Cathare confide this to you? Do you know if her husband knew of her plans to terminate the pregnancy?"

"I don't know anything about her husband. I'm telling you Clip Pointpar killed my granddaughter. He went to that anti-abortion rally. I saw him talking on the TV."

"Most pro-life advocates do not believe violence is the answer or contributes to their cause in any way."

"He is an old devil," Amelia warned. "He killed Tamica. And if you don't bring him to justice, well, I've meted out some justice in my time. The old days may be gone. But I can do it again."

"Why would Mr. Pointpar want to harm your granddaughter?"

212

"I have just told you. He's big on anti-abortion. I wasn't thinking when I told him Tamica was considering an abortion."

"Just because Mr. Pointpar is active in the pro-life movement, is not enough for me to consider him a suspect in your granddaughter's death. Even the most violent anti-abortionists don't usually kill the mother-to-be. That sort of defeats the purpose. They go after the abortion doctors."

"Clip is not playing with a full deck anymore," Amelia insisted. "All I'm asking from you, young man, is that you take my word seriously and realize Clip is guilty."

Amelia indicated to Plate that she expected him to sit down at her little table. Feeling he was wasting his time, but out of politeness and respect for the elderly great jazz singer, he followed her suggestive gesture and sat down.

"Now. Let us join forces over a cup of tea. I insist you eat some cookies."

"Yes, ma'am." Plate obediently bit into a chocolate chip.

"I done told this to Forrest a long time ago. I did say I was not sure then. I am sure now. I thought he would find out for sure and would take care of it. But apparently he's going to stick up for the old bastard. Well, I know you won't let him get away with it."

Plate closed his eyes as he enjoyed the chocolate chip cookies, which were quite good. Despite getting sleep relatively recently, he felt himself doze as Amelia continued her diatribe against Clip Pointpar.

Pointpar is not the only one not playing with a full deck anymore, was Plate's last complete thought before falling asleep.

Chapter 56

A more dramatic meeting was occurring as Corina confided in Daphne, and Amelia spoke with Plate.

Forrest Pointpar had death in his heart.

He had always looked at Ray Cathare as his enemy and rival. Now the two men stood face to face, like two gunmen in the wild wild west.

Forrest had insisted on the meeting between the two men. Ray had reluctantly agreed.

They decided to meet in the baseball tower. Although it was on the Pointpar estate, Ray felt like its historic atmosphere made it neutral ground.

Plus he had always wanted to get in it somehow.

Ray had been a serious baseball fan in his youth, had played on amateur home teams in East Texas before Grace had brought him to Sand Waves, where his interest had died out with inactivity.

He looked around the structure at all the collectibles with great interest, despite the circumstances of the meeting. As he waited for Pointpar to open some of the windows to let in some fresh air, he surreptitiously pulled open a long drawer in a built-in desk. It held a plaque, an antique rifle and dozens of old baseball cards.

"You sell this stuff?" Ray asked.

Finishing with the windows, Forrest noticed Ray's action and quickly pushed him away and shut the drawer.

"Valuable antiques and our historical plaque," Forrest said brusquely. "Not for sale or display or public viewing. I'd think you'd not be interested in toys right now considering what has happened to Tamica. She was your wife. You should have protected her."

"I don't want any trouble, Forrest. Tammy's dead so what are we doing here? Why don't we just let it go?"

"We can't let it go. The police are not going to do anything. Your brother-in-law is too powerful and too important. Tamica was nobody next to him."

"Apparently she was nobody to Amelia Mattworks as well."

"That is not really accurate. But in a way it's not far from the truth either."

"I did not kill Tammy. I swear that to you, Forrest. I didn't even know you were having an affair with her."

"I know you didn't kill her. I didn't either. If you don't blame me for Tamica's death, then I don't blame you."

"Both of us," said Ray. "We're both to blame, or not to blame, in equal measure."

"There's only one bastard to blame," said Forrest. "I know who killed Tamica."

"You know who killed her?" Ray felt his blood pressure rise.

"Yes, and the Powers-That-Be will never let him be brought to justice. I'm going to tell you all this in confidence. Then if you repeat it all, I'll deny I ever said any of it. On the surface it seems like you'd be the last person I would trust, but I think you want justice for Tamica."

And then Forrest told Ray all that he had told Lieutenant Plate and all that he had not told him.

"So you see why I say there's really only one bastard to blame," Forrest concluded.

"I do think we can agree on that," said Ray. He held out his hand to Forrest. Forrest hesitated only a moment and raised his arm.

"I say we flip for it," said Forrest. "Loser provides an alibi."

"Sounds fair," said Ray. He pulled a quarter from his pocket.

The two men clasped their hands in a firm handshake that lasted a lot longer than normal.

Then Forrest pitched the coin high in the air.

Chapter 57

"Lieutenant Plate?"

Plate woke up with a start to find Grace York bending over him.

He looked over at Amelia Mattworks. She was in repose on her bed, her eyes closed peacefully.

Plate jumped up in alarm.

Grace took hold of his arms.

Reading the expression on his face, she quickly said, "don't be alarmed. She's okay. Just sleeping. She called me up here and said I needed to come get you, then dozed off when I got here. Good thing she called me. I needed rather badly to find you."

"What time is it?" he asked, whispering.

"After five," she replied.

Plate and Grace quietly left the room and stood in the small third floor foyer. An old fashioned chair with an attached side table was its only furnishing.

Plate realized that is what he had condemned Corina to sit on for several hours. He felt stronger emotions about this injustice to the pregnant girl than any current feelings towards Grace York, once the woman he thought was his own.

"Oh," Plate said, "I'm embarrassed. I fell asleep talking to her. What must she think?"

"She probably thinks the herbs she puts in her cookies worked really good on you," said Grace, smiling.

"They tasted good," said Plate.

"Never eat more than one. If she puts the herbs in, and she doesn't always, they are mild and one won't affect you."

"Now you tell me." He smiled back at Grace, seeing her as a warm, nurturing person no longer, but not a completely cold one either.

"I didn't know she was going to call for you. She rarely sees a stranger up here."

"She claimed Clip Pointpar killed Tamica and she was expecting Forrest Pointpar to exact revenge," said Plate wonderingly.

"That failing, she has nominated me to get justice for her granddaughter by nailing Clip Pointpar for the crime."

"She is 94. I know she is supposed to be sharp but age gets us all in the end. Certainly it is ridiculous that Clip would hurt anybody, much less Tamica," Grace said. "I've always like the old guy. He is crusty, but always sweet to me."

"Anyway. I suppose nothing has happened to Clip Pointpar while I was napping up here?"

Plate smiled at his weak joke.

Then the expression on his face changed as the look Grace gave him caused his blood pressure to soar.

"Not Clip Pointpar," she said.

Chapter 58

As he flew down the stairs, Grace watched after Plate for a moment.

She had a pang of regret.

Returning to Amelia's room, she found the elderly lady had become refreshed from her catnap and was sitting up, brewing tea again.

"What did you give that nice policeman?" Grace said, smiling at Amelia with love.

"Nothing, Gracie, nothing." Amelia assumed an entirely innocent look.

In a pink crinoline long sleeved dress with lace trim, a wide two inch belt outlining her slim waist, giving her an attractive figure even at her age, she looked a picture of healthy wholesome grandmotherly womanhood.

Then she caught Grace's eye and the two of the burst out laughing.

"Shall I sit with you awhile?" Grace asked, when the laughter had subsided.

"Oh yes! I would like that a lot. I wish we could have known each other better," said Amelia. "Such different worlds we have lived in. Still do."

"There's still plenty of time," said Grace lightly.

"Now, don't treat me like a fool, and I won't return the favor."

Amelia pulled out some cookie dough. "That nice boy ate all my cookies." She giggled impulsively. "I like him!"

"I liked him, too," said Grace wistfully.

Amelia lapsed into thought for a short time, then looked more coherent and spoke more concisely than ever. She cast a shrewd glance at Grace.

"Ain't nobody for you except that silver haired fox."

"Now, how many of those cookies did you eat?"

"Not so many that I cannot see what's right in front of me. Accept the wisdom of my 90 plus years. Don't run away from the truth."

Grace sighed. "I might wind up alone then."

Amelia recalled the images of both her husbands.

"It was always said there wasn't nobody for me except Roscoe Burns," she said, looking at Grace. "Except-"

"Yes," said Grace, understanding her completely. "Except- the exceptions! What men there are in this world!"

Grace was thinking not of Edward, but of Plate.

"I'm seeing a lot of things more clearly now," said Amelia.

"Oh."

Grace pulled her mind from the previous subject, ready to follow Amelia's lead. But apparently her comment was not a topic changer.

Amelia placed the cookies in the oven and turned it on.

"It's those exceptions that will bring you down. More chocolate chip or shall I go for oatmeal?"

Chapter 59

A quick call to Daphne confirmed Corina was safe.

Everyone had alibis for the latest attack.

Edward and Grace had been together in the mansion along with Stark Wynter and Regina. Ray Cathare and Forrest Pointpar were having a drink together at the Pointpar estate, where they were transacting a deal that concluded with Ray buying some of the Pointpar sports memorabilia.

Edward York had loaned Mink Tanem to Clip Pointpar and the bodyguard had taken the old ballplayer to Houston for an exam with a new doctor. Forrest, overcoming his animosity for Ray, had taken advantage of his father's absence to surreptitiously sell a few obscure pieces of the collection to help with ongoing expenses.

Officer Skaar and other officers on guard duty had seen no one come or go.

The dogs had been silent all afternoon.

There was no fresh trail in the woods. Trees appeared unclimbed.

No one had even seen a blonde man jump over a fence.

"Well, we're finally inside the doctor's office," said Plate to the chief as they stood on the front porch of Dr. Apixza's cottage.

The front door was wide open as were all windows. The county forensic team was inside. Bright lights were being set up in anticipation of dusk.

"From the looks of it, it's going to be a long slow process," said the chief, also addressing the team members who could easily hear.

No one disagreed. Trying to stay out of forensics' way, Plate and the chief peered through the doorway.

Dr. Apixza's clinic appeared as if someone had taken a baseball bat and smashed every item individually. That included the doctor himself who lay sprawled amidst the debris, his hands up near his head as if he were surrendering.

But it was not a baseball bat that crossed the doctor's body like at a 45 degree angle. It was a .44 rifle.

"How did the alarms get turned off? Did it have to be somebody from inside the house? Why don't the dogs ever bark? Why didn't the police guards outside the house see anything? It's a waste of time to guard the front door, it seems," the chief commented.

Plate did not reply.

"All these questions have to be answered," continued the chief, his voice pitched in the direction of the team members. But Plate knew the comments was really directed at him.

The two men walked to the side of the cottage porch as the body was being carried away by the county team, through the front door, down the porch steps to a waiting county vehicle. Following, a technician carefully carried the rifle, now wrapped in a white cloth.

"We might get faster answers if we had our own forensics department in Sand Waves," Plate murmured, as they watched the vehicle drive away.

"The Powers-That-Be don't support that. And you know it," said the chief. "Find out what is going on here, Plate."

"Yes, sir."

Plate went back into the clinic. "Any files on any of the members of the York compound, I want them in my hands personally," he said.

"Here is an old set of files marked inactive," said Skaar, who was cataloging everything the forensics team removed. "Also there are files on all the York family, the Cathares, Pointpars, and others."

Stepping back in also, the chief took the older files from a team member.

"Looks like they're from the 1940s and 1950s. I don't think these need to be cataloged."

He handed them to Plate.

"They don't need to be logged in?" Plate flipped through the files, mostly handwritten in fading ink.

"Just take them. Better go to your quarters and look over them in private before someone objects," said the chief. "I'll handle the social scene for awhile. I'll work out permissions from the others for the current files that are pertinent and send them to you."

Chapter 60

Back in his guest cottage, Plate looked over the old files. Notations on most of them indicated the subjects were deceased. Plate looked at the science fiction novel propped open, face down on his coffee table.

He started to pick it up but then put it back down.

Temptation resisted, he opened up the dormant files to look for any familiar names.

By the time the contemporary files had arrived with necessary permissions for him to view them, he had learned more than he had ever dreamed he would from the older documents.

He thanked the patrolman who had brought over the new documents and began flipping through them. Only one had the bright blue sealing tape that he was not permitted to peel off.

He had permission to look at Edward York's file, Regina York's file, Ray Cathare's file, Corina French's file, and even Amelia Mattworks herself gave permission.

Grace York had refused. The chief had spoken to her personally and failed to sway her. She refused to see Plate. The chief instructed Plate to phone her. Plate had kept his relationship with Grace on a very low-key level but it had never been clandestine.

In her own quiet way, she played on her relationship with Plate to deny him access to her medical records

"As our relationship goes forward, I feel like you having access to my prior medical records would be like you're reading my diary," Grace said softly to him, over the phone. "It's not that I don't trust you. However, I feel like my medical records are very private to me."

Without waiting for his argument, she had hung up the phone.

It was prudent to keep the files intact as a unit. So the file labeled Grace York had a piece of supposedly tamper proof blue tape on it. And Plate was going to need a court order, which he knew no judge would issue under the circumstances, to open the file.

The chief was not pleased.

If Grace had presumed upon their relationship to convince

herself that Plate would ignore her refusal, putting it down to romantic anxiety, and accept her statement that there was nothing in her medical file that could possibly have a bearing on the case, she did not know him at all.

A knock on the cottage door was timed perfectly to stop Plate from cutting the tape himself and risking dismissal from his job.

Plate rose slowly, walked the three steps to the door and turned the knob without his usual customary caution of looking out the peephole.

"Grace told me you had called. She doesn't know that I am here. And I want to find out. What do you think you know? I don't know why you think Grace's medical records would be important," said Edward York, as he ducked slightly to come through the doorway. "But I also don't understand why she would refuse to let you see the file, considering what's going on. And I do know we have to find out what's happening here. We cannot go on this way."

"Are you suggesting we look at the files anyway?" Both men glanced down at the large pair scissors in Plate's hand.

"I have legal permission to view my ex-wife's medical records."

Plate slowly dropped the scissors down on the coffee table next to the folder.

"Grace and I gave each other durable power of attorney many years ago, and we signed living wills, and gave each other permission to view medical records under all circumstances."

"Your divorce did not change that?"

"I would have received notification of the revocation of power of attorney. I have never revoked those papers and neither has she. I seriously doubt she even remembers signing the medical records information permission. But that would not negate the signature."

"Considering you're a lawyer and a former judge, I'm willing to risk allowing you to open the envelope without her permission," said Plate, thinking *what really matters is that you are Edward York. Nobody will do anything to you whether what you say is true or not.* "I have a strong suspicion that there is something relative or she would not have said no. Grounds for blackmail possibly?"

"I couldn't agree with you more," said Edward York. "If it is a question of blackmail, whoever is doing it, is going to stop right now."

"If it was the doctor, it's already stopped," said Plate.

"I can't imagine how she could be blackmailed. I know what she did. It was legal. Apixza did it. She does not know that I know. The only thing I can think of is that she does not want you to know."

Both men were silent for a moment.

"Maybe she plans to marry you?" Edward asked.

"She has not shared that intention with me."

Edward sat down on the couch and carefully removed the tamperproof tape. It left a scar on the envelope without a doubt.

"What she does not want you to know. What she does not understand that I know is- the year of our divorce she aborted our child. Without my permission or knowledge."

"I truly did not know that," said Plate softly, as he took the envelope.

Edward York was silent as Plate thumbed through the medical file. His browsing stopped at a report dated 1980. He was no medical expert. But it was easy to see the results of the sonogram labeled as taken during the fourth month of Grace's pregnancy.

"I don't want to see the records myself," said Edward York, rising and turning to leave.

"You are making a mistake. I think you should see this," said Plate, putting his hand on Edward's shoulder. "You need to see it. It is important that you see it. To you and to Grace."

Chapter 61

Reluctantly, Edward took the sonogram x-ray from Plate's hand. If it was possible for him to turn whiter, he turned even whiter as he gazed at it. His hands trembled and the x-ray shook making an audible noise.

"She didn't tell me this," he gasped, as tears slid down his cheeks. "She didn't tell me. She was too proud."

The sonogram showed a distinctly abnormal baby, even to the eyes of a medical layman, and the notation in the file beside it read *genetic malformation hereditary, maternal side*.

Edward York resembled a man haunted. "She never told me. I found out about the abortion quite by accident. She knew I wanted children very much. I divorced her, planning to eventually annul the marriage through the church. I haven't been able to bring myself to do that. She sacrificed the child for me?"

"Yes, I think she did. Unnecessarily."

Edward looked at Plate in confusion.

Plate opened the file on Tamica and positioned the two side by side. "Yes, perhaps she sacrificed her unborn child, in her mind, so that you might not bear the stigma of fathering a deformed baby," Plate concluded. "I don't know. I do know I was expecting to see that sonogram x-ray with that notation in her file."

"You were expecting to see that?"

"Here is why."

Plate opened Apixza's file folder on Tamica and arranged the x-ray from her sonogram next to the one labeled Grace York. There was a file on Corina also, incomplete and sporadic, but also with a sonogram result.

They were identical. More than identical

They were the same x-ray.

"Take a good look at that sonogram," said Plate. "I don't believe it belongs to either Grace or Tamica. Most likely, it's a sample from a textbook case. Possibly not even real. Years ago, abortionists would use these types of ruses when they were caught, as a sort of moral defense. Rarely were they legitimate medical reports. The same ones would surface again and again, passed around from abortionist to abortionist. He just updated the racket with the sonogram."

"Then, Grace was led to believe that our child was deformed when-"

"When quite possibly, quite probably, it was not."

"And he had the same file made up for Tamica?"

"Undoubtedly he did. Probably Tamica became suspicious. Especially if she knew anything about Grace's pregnancy? Is there any reason to suspect they would've talked to each other? It seems like when her brother married Tamica, about the same time Grace practically left the family."

"They might have talked, Lieutenant."

"As cousins-in-law? See, that is where I'm confused. As I just said, I thought Grace became estranged from the family just at the same time, or even before Ray married Tamica."

Edward York stood up abruptly. "You'll need to ask Grace. I think you might find she knew Tamica prior to her having married Ray. Perhaps even prior to Ray and Regina moving to Sand Waves."

"Are you saying you knew the murder victim before her marriage?"

"I don't see why you find that idea so astonishing. We moved in the same social circles, more or less. We all lived behind the gates of Sand Waves."

"Judge York, I need to know the entire extent of all these relationships. If you hold back-"

"Lieutenant, I don't think you fully understand the situation. I now handle Ms. Mattworks business affairs. It is necessary that fact remains confidential. I am a conservative politician and she is– well, she is Amelia Mattworks. Miss Mattworks is an institution in her own right, not to mention Amelia Mattworks Enterprises. Her recordings still bring in a phenomenal amount of money. She has in her employ several hundred people-"

"Several hundred people? What do they do?" Plate felt like Edward York was deliberately distracting him. But if he didn't follow the politician's lead, he might miss out on learning something.

"Well, most of them are involved in promoting her music and

memorabilia. There are reenactments of her concerts with new and upcoming young jazz singers. Thousands request autographed photos monthly and she endorses a line of clothing and cosmetics marketed for African American women," said Edward.

"So most of these people are not directly employed by Miss Mattworks?"

"No. In fact, none are directly employed by Miss Mattworks," said Edward, contradicting what he had just maintained. "Only a handful is directly employed by her corporation, Amelia Mattworks Enterprises."

"Exactly who are those people?" Plate noted the discrepancy. But Edward York had just experienced a shock. He let the conversation continue without challenge.

"There's myself, my wife, Dr. Apixza, Mink Tanem, and Ray Cathare."

"What position does Ray Cathare hold?"

"He doesn't have a specific title. He's just available to do whatever is needed."

"Did Mrs. Cathare draw a salary also?"

"Yes, she did."

"And Grace?"

"No, Grace did not draw a salary from Miss Mattworks."

"Why leave her out?"

"Lieutenant, I don't appreciate the sarcasm at this point."

Plate did not reply further to Edward York. He could think of nothing else to say to him. That Edward York perceived his investigation as threatening Amelia Mattworks Enterprises baffled him. But he didn't want that bafflement to show. He wanted to leave Edward York thinking about what Grace may have confided during their relationship. Or let slip.

He did not want Edward to realize how little Grace had ever said. How little he had really ever known about her.

Chapter 62

Plate was alone in his cottage and on the phone with Chief Brecken. By now, he had thoroughly studied all of the dead doctor's files.

"I think I know the motive for all of this."

"And that is?" Chief Brecken asked.

"Trust me, you don't want to know. If it never comes out it will be by the grace of God. But you only want to know if it does, if there's any testifying about it in court, well —"

"Okay. I'll trust you on that one. Motive established. But who is the perpetrator?"

"That's trickier. If abortion were still a crime we could arrest several people."

Grace included, thought Plate.

"But it's not. Who shot the girl? Do we think one person is behind all of this?"

"Amelia Mattworks claims it is Clip Pointpar," Plate said wryly.

The chief laughed. "Seriously?"

"Seriously. Truth is, I just don't know yet."

"You're going at it backwards. Finding the motive before the killer? You're forgetting Detective Class 101. When will I see the proper order of evidence?"

"I don't know. First, I need to summarize these medical files from ages ago. Then I need to connect them concretely with the current file. To do that, I have asked Regina York for access to her collection of old movie magazines."

"Movie magazines?"

"Yes, she collects them, I think. You know *Movie Mirror, Photoplay*, that type. Not the scandal sheets of today, but the more fictionalized, no- sanitized movie stories- sometimes true, but romanticized truth."

"And you're getting those when?"

"Oh, any minute, Mink Tanem's bringing them over. He's sorting through the years I am interested in. Narrowing them down for the sake of time. There are hundreds of magazines in this collection, maybe even thousands."

"Isn't he a suspect? How do you trust his sorting?"

"If Mink is the killer, then I'm barking up the wrong tree. He's a Vietnam vet ex-army guy, anti-theatrics, hardly ever been to a movie in his life. And any mention of a celebrity gets a blank look from him. Edward York is the only celebrity in the world as far as he is concerned. Nobody else is important unless York designates them important."

"Okay-"

"Chief, let me go. He's here with them right now."

Chapter 63

Grace woke up with a start.

Her illuminated alarm clock proclaimed it was Tuesday morning but still very dark. The man with the flashlight in her room was not Edward as she had first hoped, or even Sinclair Plate as she briefly fantasized. But she reached out her arms to him and embraced him anyway.

"Ray," she said, noting on the periphery of her mind that he had something made of a bulky material under his arm. "What on earth are you doing?"

"Gracie," he said, grasping her with one arm as he deposited the largest piece of his load on the bed beside her. "You are coming with me tonight whether you want to or not. It's not safe for you to be here. It's not safe for me. It's time to go home."

"Ray, get ahold of yourself. I know you've been under a great deal of stress these last few weeks. It's the middle of the night. Lieutenant Plate is on guard out there somewhere. We couldn't get through the gates of Sand Waves if we wanted to. And I don't want to leave Edward right now."

"Edward will be all right. His position in this has been secure all along. I have figured out the motive for all this. It is only the women who have been in danger. It's still the women who are in danger and you are the woman in the most danger of all. Trust me. I'm just going to take you back home."

Grace quickly realized exactly what Ray had under his arm. She wanted to scream as he quickly wrapped her sheet around her, binding her arms to her side and her legs together. But she could only stare at him in mute terror.

Too late, she realized the smaller cloth was meant to be a gag, not a blindfold. And the larger bulky material beside her was a sleeping bag.

"Don't struggle, Gracie, and you won't be hurt. I know what I'm doing. I think all this is because of the secret. The real secret. And you are the best evidence. In the long run to keep that secret safe, they'll have to kill you as well. So I'm taking you home."

He shoved her into the bag as if she was a rag doll in his hands. It was hard for her to resist the one man in the world she loved like a brother and her struggle against him was minimal.

He carried her gently down the stairs, through the house and out on the driveway, placing her carefully in the back seat of his pickup truck.

As soon as Ray got the truck off the grounds and through the gates, he pulled over and stopped to make sure Grace was not too uncomfortable.

He pulled the gag from her and she whimpered a little as he gave her a sip of water from a plastic bottle.

"When we get further away, I plan to let you out of this and sit you up right. Meanwhile, when we're on the highway, I'm going to explain…"

He got back into the driver's seat and the pickup roared down the road.

Chapter 64

It was not long before they were on US 59. And when they had passed Cleveland, Ray pulled over to the side of the road, as he had promised.

In a few moments, Grace was riding in the front seat with him. The further they got towards their hometown, the more she relaxed in a way that was not possible to relax in the city.

Dawn came. A dark dawn with dense clouds.

She watched the trees and the grass go by, observed the small towns at a slower speed as Ray complied with their speed limits, enjoying it as the vehicle sped up again in open spaces.

The area's growth in the middle 1970s as the price of oil had increased healthily and slowly for the region, enriching and bolstering the lifestyle of the people there.

Prosperity was now just a remnant. When the Arab oil embargo hit America in at the sunset of the turbulent decade of the 1970s, it had caused a frantic boom in Houston, the center of the energy industry. But the extended oil industry, always less stable, had suffered. The shock was too great, the change too quick, and the income of the area population too low to easily absorb the dramatic price increase in gasoline and the runaway inflation in many commodities the area depended upon for its economic regularity.

While most Houstonians adapted to credit card use and temporary loans to bridge the financial gaps until their personal economics could catch up to the macro environment, most rural East Texans clung to paying in cash, eschewing any type of credit. These attitudes impeded their economic flexibility and caused them to fall further and further behind as the oil and gas industry struggled to adapt to the new era.

Grace could not help but feel a tug at her heartstrings as they left the outskirts of the big city and started passing small dilapidated buildings and towns with structures that were no longer being maintained.

If only there could be some balance between the excessive prosperity we have in Sand Waves and the conditions in the rural areas, Grace thought. *Maybe if Edward does become President...*

Every blip in the price of oil, which was a roller coaster of dips and pinnacles these days, sent another layer of businesses into bankruptcy. Property values soared, then plummeted. Strong and steady in their faith, patriotism, and stability, East Texans could do little but pray and hang on.

But her thoughts faded as the truck sped faster.

The further she got in East Texas, the more she wondered if prosperity was really the answer to the area's problems. The abundance of nature and sporadic carefully maintained gardens at old turn-of-the-century houses made her wonder if the solution was more intangible.

As traffic lights grew fewer and fewer, roads narrowed and curved and wound, Grace became more confused.

The air became pure and fresher. Clouds dissipated. The sun seemed brighter and the winter less bleak.

For the first time Grace considered that her memories of life in East Texas, plain and simple they might be, were more comforting to her than all the memories of the glamour and excitement she had experienced in her life after moving to Sand Waves.

She had once thought the plain and simple life was so boring. Now she longed to go back to it.

Chapter 65

Grace had left the country behind her when she had moved to Sand Waves and then married Edward York. Many others in the area had seen migration to Houston or another large city as the answer to their financial quandary.

However, a significant number of people clung to the area, convinced that being poor in East Texas was superior to being rich in the big city in every possible way.

Maybe they were right, Grace thought.

"I think I'm going to come back here to live," said Ray, as if reading Grace's thoughts.

"I can't ever come back," said Grace sadly.

"I can get a job in the oilfields," said Ray. "And get me a little white clapboard house on a hill somewhere. You can come visit."

And I will find a wife, too, he thought. *A country girl.*

Grace smiled at the image of returning to her childhood home, maintaining ties with the old life as she carved out her profile in the new. Tears filled her eyes at the hopelessness of ever fulfilling such a dream.

"You would have to come get me and kidnap me again," she said lightly. "I'm afraid that's the only way I'll ever come back after I do what I have to do now. What is the real reason you're bringing me home, Ray?"

"I think you can guess."

"You think it's time the whole truth comes out?"

"I think that's the only way you're ever going to be safe. The only way Corina is ever going to be safe. Maintaining the fiction is not worth living the rest of your life in fear. Somebody killed Tamica because she had become interested in the family history."

"Maybe. You always did have a lot of common sense."

"If I have had any common sense, I'd have stayed in East Texas and just let you take Regina to Houston and make her rich."

"Do you remember the bank where the safety deposit box is?" Grace leaned her seat back.

"I'm taking you there first," said Ray, with confidence. "You

234

know I'm right about this."

"I expect you are. It's going to take me a while to gather up all my courage. You're going to have to cover for me. You realize that if the entire truth comes out, the consequences could be financially detrimental to everybody even remotely connected," Ray said.

"Somehow Edward York will stop that from happening."

And the image of Edward York came before her, running and splashing on the Galveston beaches, his hair shining silver and gold in the sun. For the rest of the drive thoughts of her ex-husband and how he would react to what she was about to do, and what he was about to learn, obliterated any thoughts of the land and lifestyle surrounding her as the truck sped deeper into East Texas.

She leaned her seat back and dozed.

When she awoke they had arrived. It was after 9 AM and the bank was open. Ray pulled into the parking lot in a small bank in Jacksonville.

The bank manager personally assisted Grace in obtaining access to her safety deposit box, partly because he recognized her, partly because he was one of only three employees there and the others were busy.

Alone in a small locked room, Grace opened the tin box, a medium size container, big enough to easily hold large manuscript size envelopes.

Grace removed the fashion dolls of her childhood from the box. She had a small collection of modern dolls in Sand Waves but she had always kept the old one, the one she loved, safely hidden in the vault.

She picked up the blonde ponytail Barbie. The oldest one, it had metal rods in its legs and pure white skin. It was wearing a pale pink dress.

There was no color in the doll's eyes.

I wonder if this is worth anything, she thought. Then after a moment, *it's worth something to me, this is the one I loved.*

She slipped it in her purse.

She looked at the blonde male doll that accompanied it. It

looked genuine but she knew it was not. Her parents had only been able to afford one genuine doll. This one was a thin plastic that caved in a little at her touch. *What was this one's name?*

She could not remember. Strangely, the imitation had not lost its skin color with age, and his face was painted bright colors. The fragile male had especially blue eyes and scandalously red lips.

He must be an anomaly, an interesting addition to any collection, she mused. *But still a fake.*

She pulled the envelopes out from under him. She left him in the box.

She opened the envelopes and fingered the papers, leaving most of them behind, taking only one envelope labeled 'Family History'.

Chapter 66

After Grace had procured what she needed, she and Ray went down a two lane dirt road that led to an old weathered church on a hill.

At the church's cemetery where both sets of their parents were buried, Grace and Ray finalized their intentions to travel separate roads.

No more than he could persuade her to stay, could she persuade him to come back with her to live in Sand Waves.

"Like I said earlier, Gracie, I'm not going back."

"What will I ever do without you, Ray? You're my only contact with the old days. My only link to my home."

Grace looked at the gravestone that bore the names of her father and mother, uncle and aunt, and the notation of how they were killed.

"I'll get one of those unlimited long distance call plans," said Ray half jokingly, removing his hat. "And I'll be calling you all the time. They'll charge you but not me."

Impulsively, Grace grabbed him and held him in her embrace. His cowboy hat was still in his hand, it covered her entire back as she held him.

"And if ever you and Edward York need anything you just call me. I'll get to Houston as soon as possible. Or do you really intend to take up with that arrogant cop? I suppose you do know he is the better man of the two. Even if he is a bit young for you."

"Ray, you are the dearest most wonderful man that I know."

"Naw, I'm just a country boy. A remnant of the past like the old Western movies they show on afternoon TV. Even photographs of me look better in black and white."

"Regina doesn't appreciate the brother she has," said Grace.

"Oh, she's offered me a chance to go to the White House," he laughed.

"Actually, if I have my way, I might be the one able to give you the chance to go to Washington DC.," said Grace, with hopeless persistence. She knew that had no lure for him.

"Gracie, I say to you- call me if you ever really need me. I'll be there to help you for as long as any problem takes to clear up. But then I'm coming back here. And I'm sure that when it does come time that you need help, I'll be pretty far down on the list of knights in shining armor. There'll be many waiting to serve Edward York."

"I know," Grace sighed. "I guess I'm going back to Sand Waves to serve him myself, one way or another. He wants to get out from under Regina. At least that is what he has told me. But I just cannot believe she is going to let him go without a fight. She wants to be First Lady in the worst way. It will be a disaster. And I don't know if he can withstand the threat to his career. He will capitulate and stay with her. I am sure."

Ray moved to embrace her without replying.

She clung to him.

"Stall for me, Ray, would you? Now is the time that I need you. Now is the time for you to go to Sand Waves and help me. Go on back and stall for me," she pleaded. "I need just a little more time."

Chapter 67

"And you don't have any idea where Grace is right now?"

Edward York had reported Grace missing Tuesday morning when she did not come to breakfast.

Engrossed in the movie magazines, which were numerous and full of stories, Plate had left mansion security in Tanem's and Skaar's hands the rest of the night. All the time someone needed to abscond with Grace.

Tanem was full of apologies. His only explanation was being unused to her presence.

Skaar pointed out his primary concern was Amelia Mattworks. Tanem looked after the Yorks.

Regina indicated she had no idea and did not care where Grace was.

By afternoon it was evident Ray Cathare was gone also.

An examination of Grace's room indicated she might not have left of her own free will. Results were uncertain.

They were adults. If they had both left voluntarily, no crime had been committed. There were restrictions on what could be done.

By Tuesday night, efforts to pinpoint the movements of all members of the household since Grace was last seen had succeeded with the exception of Ray Cathare.

With all the forces of the police and all modern technology of the 1980s, they could not find either person.

Early Wednesday morning Plate had been out on the York grounds when Ray's pickup truck had unexpectedly sped down one of the side drives into the back yard. He was now asking Ray this question as they sat at the kitchen table.

"And you don't have any idea where Grace is right now?" Plate repeated, staring at Ray.

Ray was looking out the window, watching the dogs run around the side to the front yard and back again.

"You know where she is?" Plate asked, with more force.

"No. No idea," said Ray, a little too nonchalantly.

Plate wanted to conduct this interview with Ray Cathare at the station but feared taking him outside the gates would cause too much attention from the press who already had wind of Corina's disappearance and would surely figure out Grace had vanished if given half a chance.

And he was mindful of the chief's fear that he might not get back inside if he violated the unspoken rules.

"Gracie is an adult woman. She is free to come and go as she pleases," Ray declared.

"I don't believe your cousin would have left the grounds of her own free will without informing me," said Plate brusquely. He stabbed a pencil into his notebook.

"I think you overestimate your influence with Gracie," Ray said arrogantly.

"I can assure you I do not overestimate my influence with Mrs. York." Plate put pressure on his pencil almost to the point of breaking it into two pieces.

"Well, I really wouldn't know about that. Gracie does not confide details of her romantic life to me. But I do know she's a grown woman and she had places to go that she might not have told anybody."

Plate had to resist grabbing Ray by the shirt and slamming him through the picture window.

"What kind of places?" he said, in a tone of voice that figuratively conveyed his thoughts of action to Ray. The pencil broke.

Ray flinched a little bit. "Think you need to be talking to her husband, not her cousin. That is, her ex-husband."

"That, I intend to do. Go on." Plate dismissed Ray, but did not follow through on the assertion. He did not want to interrogate Edward York just yet.

He had other people in mind to interrogate first. Especially if they showed any signs of not wanting to meet with him.

Chapter 68

Wednesday afternoon, Stark Wynter voluntarily met with Plate at The Toy Museum Restaurant.

"I wanted to meet with you in sort of a neutral territory," said Plate, thinking, *and I had to get out of the York estate, if only for lunch.*

"Oh, I understand, Officer. The set is crucial to honest dialogue. How can I help you? For reasons of my own, I'm anxious to resolve the situation at the York estate. I admit, ever since I arrived there I felt like I was in somewhat of a maze, and I'm still not sure what type of an exit I'm going to find."

"You may find this surprising. I need to talk to you about something that happened in Hollywood many years ago."

"Oh. How so? Something I was involved in?"

"Something I think you might have been on the periphery of. It involved an actress that you were starring with in a movie, who was injured on the set in an accidental shooting. She survived the accident and went on to even greater fame and fortune. She's mostly been forgotten in modern times. Her name was Doreen Darbell."

"Oh yes. I remember Doreen quite well. We dated a while. Everybody dated everybody back then. And I was on set the day of the accident. In fact I was a witness."

"What exactly happened?"

"It was in the script for Doreen's character to get shot. It was the old story of somehow real bullets getting mixed up with the blanks. One of the prop men was fired. Doreen was wounded in the abdomen and rushed to the hospital. Actually, fortunately, a doctor was on the scene, a guest of somebody, and he was able to give her immediate medical attention and actually rode with her in the ambulance to the hospital and ultimately performed surgery on her."

"I have heard rumors that all of that was subterfuge for a covered up abortion."

"Nasty rumors in Hollywood are dime a dozen. I've heard that rumor, too. Times were different back then. I can't say one hundred percent for sure what went on half of the time."

"Just tell me what you literally saw that you can remember."

"Okay. We were about to shoot the scene. Doreen's character was a mobster's moll. It was one of those love-death scenes where he shoots her in the middle of an embrace. I was the hero, who was to burst in, shortly after she was shot, kill the villain, then get to her so she could die in my arms. The shot was my cue to enter the scene. Well, I heard the shot and ran in just like I was supposed to. The poor actor who was supposed to have shot Doreen was still holding her. He was in a state of shock, while she was pretty calm saying she thought she'd really been hit with a real bullet. Everybody else was running around screaming. This young doctor came running up to her and took her out of the other guy's arms. In an incredibly quick time frame, an ambulance showed up and she and the doctor were whisked away. It got a lot of publicity, she recovered, and we finished the movie and made an awful lot of money."

"There's no doubt that she was really shot."

"Absolutely no doubt whatsoever. I saw the blood. Her hand was on the barrel of the gun. She was gripping her abdomen with one hand and the gun with the other."

"She had her hand on the gun?"

"Yes. I think that's what caused the rumors. The other actor later told the police that, as he was embracing her, she grabbed the gun and pointed it differently than it was supposed to be."

"As if she was directing the direction of the shot?"

"But there wasn't supposed to be a shot. It should've just been a blank, a noise, a small discharge that went to the side if anything. Frequently in close-up fake shootings like that there's not even a blank. The noise is put in later."

"I see. In your opinion, what really happened?"

"I hate to say it. One of two things, either a really stupid dangerous publicity stunt or-"

"Did this actress have any romantic relationships going on at the time? Was she married? Were there rumors she was pregnant?"

"I think she'd already been married and divorced twice. We all had something going on all the time. There were always rumors that every actress was pregnant except for the few that didn't engage in the common entertainment."

"And this actress did engage?"

"You had to understand the time, Lieutenant. It had not been that many years since the war. People our age, all we wanted was to get in a bit of life before the Russians attacked and we had to do World War III."

"Can you confirm that the photographs in these magazines are genuine? And that the different events actually occurred? Or were photographs faked in some cases?"

"Oh, of course they were. But even if they doctored the photographs, see, it's easy to tell. Any attempt to falsify who went out with who by doctoring the photographs, sticks out like a sore thumb. The days that a photograph was truly worth a thousand words, those days have passed. Trick photography was a gimmick, an anomaly years ago. Now it's becoming more and more the norm. I fear someday it will be virtually impossible to tell whether a photograph is real or fake unless you have some type of special picture analysis type equipment. Like the spies use."

After this pessimistic forecast about the future of photography, Stark flipped through the magazines Plate had brought and pointed out the few photos that were obviously faked. Once the false lines of the composite pictures were highlighted by the movie producer, Plate soon learned to pick out tampered images easily.

Stark Wynter and Plate finished their meal and spent some time at The Toy Museum exhibitions, particularly studying the display of toy soldiers on the battlefield. It was a rare relaxing moment for both men.

"Been in the service, Lieutenant?" Stark asked.

"Yes, but I didn't see any action. They kept me here."

"You are lucky."

"Yes, I was a little aggravated by it at the time. I see now what a blessing it really was."

Plate rose, terminating the lunch abruptly as his pager went off. As Wynter left, having other places to go, Plate stopped at a pay phone in the lobby and then immediately returned to the York estate.

Chapter 69

Less than an hour later, Plate had Ray Cathare at the police station in Sand Waves.

Outside the gates.

The phone call had told him that all forensic evidence clearly indicated it was Ray who had forcibly taken Grace from her bed.

The press, now used to seeing patrol cars entering and leaving the gates of Sand Waves, paid no attention when a police car went inside. It escaped their notice that the same car exited a couple hours later with two people in the front seat instead of one. The passenger's police hat was removed as soon as the patrol car passed through the gate and left the stalking press behind.

The lieutenant placed Ray in a small cell with a one-way mirror on the wall and the chief observing on the other side. With no gates keeping out reality, Plate almost felt like a real police officer again.

Except, despite all the forensic evidence, he had a sinking feeling this was the wrong man.

"You and everyone at the York compound were under express orders not to leave Sand Waves," said Plate, with hostility. "There's ample evidence you forced Grace York to leave with you against her will."

"Grace is okay. She will be back soon. I needed to get her away for her own safety. You seem like a nice guy, Officer. But I don't know you from Adam and I don't want you to take offense, but I felt like Gracie's life is in danger and I wanted to remove her from the scene and there was no way I was going to tell you about it or anybody else. I didn't even tell Edward York."

Plate sat across from Ray, thinking how much like a Western movie star the widower looked in his jeans and cowboy shirt, his cowboy hat sitting to the side on the table between them. Grace's image intruded into the thoughts unexpectedly. Just a few weeks ago, well, maybe more than a month ago, Grace York practically did not leave home without him knowing it. He had been a daily part of her life, and her comings and goings had become intertwined with his

244

own. Now she was sneaking away, voluntarily or involuntarily, and remaining in an undisclosed location, apparently of her own free will, without even telling him anything. Without contacting him at all.

"I'm going to need contact with Grace York confirming her safety or I am going to lock you up right now."

"I can give you a number to call," said Ray reluctantly. "She may already be on her way back. But these people are family and will confirm she is okay."

"And this number is to whom? What other family does she have?"

"A relative on my father's side of the family. Everybody has two sides to their families, remember? These people are related to both Grace and myself. And Regina York, of course. My sister."

Plate did not need reminding that he was sitting across the table from Edward York's brother-in-law. But they were outside the gates of Sand Waves, in the part of Sand Waves open to all people, theoretically. And Plate considered all people equal outside the gates.

Plate motioned for another officer to enter and handed him the number with instructions to call and see if Grace York was there. "If you can't get confirmation Grace York was there, then contact the local police department in- I can't read the name of the town-"

"Tyler," said Ray helpfully. "It's near where we grew up."

"Tyler. I am familiar with that area," said Plate to Skaar. The patrolman took the paper and left the room.

"We are really from a place called Wilding Falls, closer to Jacksonville. Originally," said Ray.

"I know that area very well. Family relations matter there."

Ray did not reply.

Plate sat silently, twirling a pencil. He was unsure what to ask next. But the expression on Ray's face indicated there had to be more to this.

"You could have taken Grace away to any hotel in Houston and it would've taken us days to track her down. What was so imperative about having to go back to East Texas right now?"

Ray shifted uncomfortably. "I don't have the right to tell you."

In a second brushed by lightning, Plate was on his feet, had grabbed Ray by both shoulders, pulled him up from the chair and flattened him against the wall.

"You don't have the right not to tell me. What is the killer after? You know, don't you? What is this all about? Who killed your wife? Why? You know something. I can tell. If you don't tell me and there's another murder, then you're going to be just as guilty as the killer."

Ray had his hands up in defense, and to his surprise, the policeman let him push back a little. This minor conciliatory action struck a note of trust in Ray. Grace had trusted this man enough to date him.

He thought of his wife and the violence done against her.

A picture of her came to his mind, one of the last times he had seen her, getting dressed. He had knocked on her dressing room and she had called for him to enter and, as he did, she had stood there in her blue jeans, snapping her bra around her waist, then pulling it up over her breasts. He had noticed the little protrusion and had teased her slightly about gaining weight.

She had laughed with a sparkle in her eyes. And she brought her shirt around her shoulders and began to button it...

"Family secrets. I think this is all about family secrets." Tears came to Ray's eyes.

"Sit back down. And talk. What secrets?" Plate stepped away from Ray. Ray took his seat. Plate sat back down in front of him. Hostility evaporated in the eye contact made between the two men. Ray cleared his throat before he spoke.

"Tammy and Grace were first cousins. Like Tamica was, Grace is also Amelia Mattworks' granddaughter."

Chapter 70

"You are telling me Grace York is biologically related to Amelia Mattworks?" Grace's pure unflawed white skin belied such a statement. In the mental portrait in Plate's mind at the moment, her skin was white as snow. "Or adopted? Somehow?"

"She is biologically just as much Amelia's granddaughter as was my wife, Tamica."

"They were sisters?" His mind went from the disconnect between Grace's appearance and such a genealogy, to how this could possibly connect to Tamica's death.

"First cousins. Grace was descended from Amelia's first marriage. Tamica was descended from Amelia's second marriage."

"So Grace, being your first cousin on her father's side, was also first cousin to your wife on her mother's side?"

"That is accurate," said Ray Cathare, in response to Lieutenant Plate's summation of his position between Grace and Tamica. "Secretly. Few people knew."

Ray maintained the eye contact with the policeman as he made that statement.

Plate processed the words, broke the eye contact abruptly and stood up again. He turned his back to Ray, not wanting the detainee to see the expression on his face.

Plate keenly felt the absurdity of the situation. At every step of the way since Tamica Cathare's death, whenever he felt as if he were truly conducting police work which should bring an ordered solution to the crime, it had boomeranged into a soap opera style twisting of the truth which pushed the basic question of who killed the woman even further away.

"You realize what you're saying can be easily proved or disproved? Grace is quite a fair skinned person."

"Maybe. I don't know how easy. It's complicated. It was said Amelia was just part black. Grace is the daughter of Amelia's daughter by her first husband who was killed in World War I. He was a white man."

"So you are telling me Grace York has African American

antecedents? So the idea was that if Grace had a child, despite her being fair and blue-eyed, that child might look African American?"

"I don't see why anybody would care," said Ray. "Her relationship with Amelia is a secret because Amelia wanted it kept secret. It was a Hollywood thing. I always thought, you know back in the 1930s, 1940s and 1950s, the stars had certain images. And many things in their backgrounds was suppressed. That was the story I was told. Why Grace kept her relationship to Amelia secret."

"How many people knew this?" Plate asked.

"Well, years ago I expect a lot of people really knew it. But they're all dead. In the present day- Regina. Me. I don't know what Gracie told Edward. I think he knows. And I suspect what Edward knows, Mink Coat knows. But that's just speculation on my part. Amelia knows, of course. Tammy knew. I don't think Corina has been told yet. She's too young. She'll be told when she is older."

"And what are the consequences if this information does get out?" Plate asked, but he suspected Ray Cathare was not the one who could answer that question.

"I don't know," said Ray. "You need to ask Edward York that question. He's the one that wants to be President."

"Is that why he divorced Grace?"

"I have no idea why he divorced Grace. Didn't Gracie ever tell you?" Ray smiled cryptically at Plate.

Plate was not amused.

The chief interrupted with new information at that moment. Edward York had contacted him to let him know Grace had called from East Texas and requested a limousine be sent to bring her home to the York estate. She would arrive back the next morning.

Ray Cathare was released. He went back to Sand Waves.

Plate went to his own apartment and spent the night, not knowing if his breach of protocol in taking Ray Cathare outside the gates meant expulsion from the cottage on the estate. He had taken few possessions to the cottage and if they wanted him out they could just send his belongings to him.

Skaar was instructed to stand guard at the York compound all night long. And for once, Plate slept in his own bed.

Chapter 71

Thursday morning Plate was back inside the York compound. Fears of his being barred were groundless.

It was Edward York himself who had requested Plate to return with the promise of another meeting. A meeting with Edward, Plate, and Grace, as soon as she arrived back from East Texas.

First, though, Stark Wynter was asking permission to leave for California. His employee was taking a turn for the worse. The studio had business for him there that could wait no longer.

Plate was not enthusiastic about the idea, but really had no concrete reason to stop him. Wynter had been cooperative all along the way. With the caveat that he remain accessible at all times by phone, Plate gave Stark official sanction to leave.

"Thank you, Officer. You saved your department and myself a lot of legal bills," said Stark politely.

"We do try to be accommodating whenever we can," said Plate.

"I hope you maintain that attitude when I tell you Regina York is coming with me," said Wynter with a big smile.

Regina leaving town took Plate a little bit longer to accept. But still, in the end, he had no real reason to stop her either.

"Hollywood! I'm going to Hollywood. I'm going to be a movie star! It's like a dream come true!" Regina's face lit up with a smile.

Stark Wynter laughed. "You're going to find it a lot less glamorous than you think. Still, it has its perks!"

"I'm going to make the most of every minute. I don't care if you don't make me a big star. I don't want to be one of those people who pretends they can act and get the part just because they happen to be married to somebody important. I just want to look beautiful on the screen while I'm still young. Darling, put me in a classic, that way I will live forever. Just a small part will suffice. A walk-on, with a long close-up, of course."

Stark Wynter laughed again. He was greatly enjoying Regina's happiness. Greatly enjoying being the source of it and hoping he would be able to sustain this momentum for some time in the future. At least as long as it took for her to divorce Edward York and marry him.

It had been a disappointment to him to find out that Regina, despite being the sister of Corina's stepfather, seem to have no relationship at all with the girl and a somewhat ambivalent relationship with her half brother.

Not that he had high hopes, but the relationships could be nurtured a little bit. Access to Hollywood tended to bring families closer together, at least in the beginning.

"Dearest, most beautiful, we don't know which ones are the classics before we make them."

"Oh. Well then, you have to put me in every movie your studio makes. Like Alfred Hitchcock. If I show up in every one, one of them is bound to become a classic. Like *Gone with the Wind*. So my immortality will be assured."

"That my love, I have the power to do. That is, if we do make a classic within the next, ah, 20 years."

"Oh, Stark. I don't want to fool you. I know I look much younger, but I am 34. You, of all people, know my looks won't last another 20 years. You are going to have to come up with a classic in five years at the most."

"It's not going to bother you, Regina, that I've got almost 25 years on you?"

"Don't be silly. Love is ageless. Edward was almost eleven years older than me."

"There's a lot of difference between an eleven year span and our age gap. More than twice the difference in fact."

"Oh, but darling! You're immortal! With all the pictures you have made over the years, you will never die! You live on in the movies forever."

"I wish I could find that as comforting now as I did 30 years ago," said Stark Wynter, with a wry smile.

Regina came to him with her arms outstretched. "I will love you forever," she declared, and gave him a hug.

She started to pack, arranging only immediate necessities in her suitcase. Movers would come for the rest of her items later. She was having her collection professionally removed from the York estate, costing more than moving her personal belongings. Stark still planned on having a house in Sand Waves, but the waiting list for behind the gates was long and Regina did not like the idea of her beloved toys being in storage.

The movie magazines she did not care about. She could get them back from the police officer when she and Stark returned to supervise the construction of the movie studio.

Stark Wynter carefully slipped around the dollhouse to get to Regina's private bath.

I'm going to have to set up a museum if she keeps on collecting all this junk, he thought wryly. Then he had a second thought. *Maybe I can get people to pay to see this stuff if I market it just right. Add a restaurant or tea shop like that one that is so popular here in Sand Waves. If I mix in some Hollywood movie memorabilia, get some stars to eat there regularly, it could be a gold mine!* He smiled happily at that idea.

And although neither could read each other's thoughts, Stark and Regina's mental images were in total agreement as to how good each was going to be for the other in Hollywood.

Chapter 72

Grace knew the East Texas dream was over the minute her limousine was enveloped in Houston pollution as it traveled into town Thursday afternoon. She had no second thoughts about having contacted Edward asking him to send a limousine for her. There was no direct train route anymore from Tyler to Houston, and riding the bus was a long circuitous route with many stops.

She wanted to go straight to Sand Waves. Straight to Edward, even if he still belonged to Regina.

But Edward was not in the house when she arrived. He had left a message that he would be back later that evening. She had checked in with Mink Tanem, as he was sitting on the porch of his cottage watching the back yard.

Ray was not still being detained at the Sand Waves Police Department but he had not yet returned either.

She had just spent a lot of time with Ray. She wanted to be with someone else.

Grace went into the house.

Grieved that Tamica was dead and they would never speak again, Grace thought of going up to see Amelia. She phoned. But Amelia had her phone off the hook, which meant she did not want be disturbed.

Corina was still in hiding, not on the premises.

Grace could have gone to her room or stayed downstairs. But she felt such an odd inclination to talk to somebody. Somebody on her level. Family.

That left only Regina, the person she so recently planned to kill. But that seemed like ages ago.

She approached Regina's bedroom door, which was open, and was surprised at the activity going on inside.

"Going somewhere, Regina?"

"Grace! The whole country is hunting for you. You had better contact that police officer, the one who's got the hots for you, immediately. He's still living on the premises."

"He expects me. I contacted him before leaving East Texas.

Edward knows I'm coming back also. He sent a limousine for me."

"So that's where you've been? Home?" Regina sounded slightly jealous.

"Are you and Edward planning a trip?"

Grace eyed a large number of suitcases strewn around the room. Regina had an armload of clothing folded across her chest with coat hangers dropping down and clacking against each other.

"No."

At that moment, Stark Wynter exited Regina's bathroom. Grace gasped.

"Grace, dear. Be a good sport. Edward doesn't know yet. I haven't had the heart to tell him. It's going to kill me to break his heart. He was so counting on me to be First Lady when he is elected President. Maybe being his ex-wife, you can fill in some as White House hostess. I know you will be a great comfort to him. Let me go ahead and leave with Stark without alarming Edward. We don't need any ugly scenes. I intend to have my lawyer contact his lawyer and everything will be handled in the most civilized way possible with the least amount of publicity. Ronald Reagan has been divorced. So there is a precedent. I feel great relief that I won't be doing Edward any harm by divorcing him. We'll all always be friends. If I get the divorce without any trouble, I'll even vote for him."

Never before in her life, not during her childhood, not even when Edward had first proposed to her or she had walked down the aisle in her thousand dollar wedding gown and became his wife, had Grace ever felt the hand of God upon her life.

Regina was voluntarily relinquishing Edward with the least amount of scandal possible.

And they had almost killed her.

Grace was so overwhelmed, tears came to her eyes. Her extreme self-discipline kicked in and she was able to nod briefly to both Regina and Stark before backing out of the room and shutting the door behind her.

Breaking with discipline for one of the few times in her life, she ran down the wide hall, rushing into the room she had been occupying as a guest for the last few days, and collapsed on the bed in tears.

Then she slid from the bed down on her knees and wept an incoherent prayer of gratitude to the God that she had heretofore doubted existed.

The tears of joy seem to turn into a kaleidoscope of her past, all she had done. She had always connected repentance with confession, but now she felt a wave of guilt wash over her and she realized repentance was truly grief for actions previously unrealized as instruments of sorrow.

She sat down on the floor and screamed.

Chapter 73

Unaware she was back, Edward and Plate were in the latter's cottage, both having missed Grace when she came in and went upstairs to Regina's room.

"A question remains. I admit I'm beginning to see a little light here. But you are telling me your employee, Mink Tanem, is the person that conspired with Dr. Apixza to delude Grace into believing she was carrying a deformed child so she would consent to an abortion. What possible motive could they have had?'

"I'm sure the doctor's motive was money."

"And your employee? Assistant? Whatever he is?"

"I don't know," said Edward York. "And I want very much to know. There has to be a reason. He's been devoted to me years. I want to know why he conspired to murder my son."

"And you feel that suppressing all of this information right now is the only way you're going to find the truth?"

"I'm confident that is the only way, Lieutenant. I'm begging you not to talk to Mink about this or otherwise let on that it has been found out yet. Please."

Plate looked at Edward York one more time.

This is the man who is going to lead the nation?

He shook his head. He really had no choice. He knew what defying Edward York's wishes could possibly mean, not just for him but also for the department.

Many residents in Sand Waves considered the police department unnecessary. After all, they had the county to take care of them. They did not like being stopped for speeding tickets. They wanted patrols, but those that had any real power also had enough money to hire private patrols, if they desired.

"I can give you some time to look into this on your own. Apparently, the only possible crime attributable to this would be medical fraud. I'm not quite sure about that even. And that would depend upon Mrs. York's admittance that she was deceived."

"She will never admit that publicly. I can assure you of that, Lieutenant."

By now, Plate no longer really thought of Grace as his girlfriend. Even the remembrance of that thought brought a wry smile, in his imagination, if not on his face. Edward York's confident assertion of Grace's behavior in the future pulled Grace further away in Plate's mind. The line he had mentally drawn to separate his relationship with Grace from the facts of the case, and the pursuit of its resolution, had dissipated.

When he had first drawn that line, he envisioned it disappearing towards the end of the case as the relationship eclipsed professional duty. Instead, it was the reverse. When Grace's face came before his eyes now, when he heard her name, the connotation was no longer instantly pleasant, hopeful, or even personal.

The name Grace now meant a suspect, a victim, a conspirator, or even possibly a perpetrator.

Irrevocably, the relationship was lost.

"And well, can I at least get a stipulation from you that you will share any results that you find with me?" Plate said to Edward York.

"So long as I can be assured of confidentiality."

"I think I can assure you of that without much trouble," said Plate resignedly.

Tanem interrupted their discussion with news that Grace was back. Both men walked quickly to the mansion and had just stepped inside when they heard Grace's scream.

Chapter 74

It was Edward who answered Grace's scream, breaking off his conversation with Plate, indicating to Plate that it was a personal matter that was none of his affair.

Plate did not disagree.

Both men had been unaware Grace was back. Both men recognized her voice in the shrill vocalization.

But Edward recognized the scream of repentance for exactly what it was. And to him it was a sound of hope.

Plate was confused when Edward assured him there was no cause for alarm and forbade him to follow as he rushed to her room.

Edward took the evidence concerning Grace's abortion with him. He had taken the folder with him when he had left Plate's cottage that day he had first seen it. And kept it all the time he had been gone.

When Grace looked at the folder, her fingers went numb as she held it in her hands.

"You knew I had an abortion? That was why you divorced me? It was not Regina?"

"Why did you scream?"

"I murdered our child," Grace sobbed in Edward's arms "Our child was healthy and I killed it."

"Him. The hidden records the police found show it would've been a boy, a healthy boy. But you didn't know that until after you screamed." Edward's face was tense as he clasped Grace in his arms He realized that it was odd for him to be speaking so calmly and matter-of-factly to her. His demeanor, which appeared detached, actually masked his deep feelings, while calming her down at the same time.

The opportunity to discuss what happened was something that both of them had dreamed of, but never expected to realize. It was a therapy more effective than any medication or counseling could ever be.

It was nothing like either of them had imagined. The past two and one half years became irrelevant.

"I felt guilt. I don't know why. Why would anybody do this to us? Why Dr. Apixza?"

"The question for me, Grace, is why kill the child even if you did think he was deformed? We have money. We could have afforded the best of care."

"Mink Tanem said it would ruin your career," said Grace, tears still streaming down her face.

"Mink! I should kill him."

"He guessed I was pregnant before I had a chance to tell you. You know how he knows everything that goes on in your life. He suggested I go see Apixza before I told you about the pregnancy just to be sure there was nothing wrong. After all I was somewhat older for a first pregnancy. 'Have one of those new sonograms,' he said. 'They can even make a picture of the unborn baby for you.' I was going to surprise you with a picture of the baby in the womb when I told you about the pregnancy. Instead, Apixza showed me the sonogram of the deformed baby. He said it would ruin your career. I did not want to bring a child like that into the world."

"You knew my religious beliefs," said Edward softly, almost without emotion. "To deny a child baptism, a funeral- What actually became of the baby?"

"I don't know. I didn't ask. Your beliefs are not my beliefs. Never have been," said Grace, coming somewhat back to herself after the emotional repentance she had just experienced. The pull to be true to herself on some level was strong. "You know I was unsure about having children. The pregnancy was an accident. I was the one who would have had to go through the ordeal physically, not you."

"Would you have done the same thing if abortion had still been illegal?"

"No, of course not. I would never have risked your career by committing a crime. No matter how much I didn't want a deformed child." *That really is true,* she thought, with some surprise.

So if we had only been a few years in the past, my child would have been born, Edward thought.

"And of course, Grace," he said, "if you were worried about your antecedents- if the race of the child had- well, if the African-American side of your family had been visible in the child, we would've handled it."

"Oh, Edward, I'm so sorry. I've ruined our lives. At least my life. You can go on with Regina and have children and have your career and have everything you're supposed to have in this world." Grace let a little bit of guilt creep into her coy statement, but her tone of voice betrayed the lightness in her heart.

"I don't think so." Edward York cast his eyes down, a little coy himself. "I'm not supposed to know yet. Regina has left me for Hollywood."

Grace raised her eyebrows, looking for his reaction.

Edward smiled genuinely for the first time in several days. "She and Stark Wynter have gone. She will file for divorce, I'm sure. Fortunately, I never married her in the church. I had grounds to annul our marriage in the church but I had not yet done so."

Grace recalled the night they had met in desperation, the night Tamica had been killed.

It was the end of Tamica's life but the beginning of a second chance for us, she thought.

Edward was recalling the same night. And thinking much the same thing.

They looked at each other. As they relaxed, they both became extremely tired.

"Maybe I do know why I screamed even before I knew the child would've been normal," said Grace. "I screamed because I knew Regina is leaving you. I knew I had been granted a second chance by the grace of God. And I knew I didn't deserve it."

Edward said nothing. They held each other, each going over in their own mind what all had just been said and what all had changed.

"What did you say about race?" Grace asked warily, after a few moments when she had absorbed that part of the conversation.

"When?"

"Earlier. Just now. But earlier."

"I said that if your African American antecedents had come through. Well, look how white Corina looks, and Roscoe Burns was her great-grandfather-"

She stood up and clutched both her shoulders.

"You thought that was why?"

This aspect of the situation had never occurred to her before because in her mind it had been so irrelevant. The lightness left her heart. Now she understood.

"Oh my God, Edward, that was why!" Grace began to sob again. "That was why! Mink wasn't afraid our child would be deformed. Dr. Apixza wasn't some crazy man wanting to murder by abortion. They thought our child might be African American. That's what they were afraid might ruin your career!"

"Well. I had already surmised that. That does make sense. Had Amelia's heritage surfaced in the child, the public would have an automatic assumption that such a child was the result of an illicit relationship on your part. Of course, we could have provided documentation showing you are Amelia Mattworks' granddaughter. However, there would be a certain amount of doubt, no matter what."

Grace cried for a few more moments, then wiped the tears from her eyes.

Edward thought her soft angled features had never looked more beautiful.

"One of the reasons I love you so, Edward, is because when I told you I was Amelia Mattworks' granddaughter, it didn't matter to you that my grandmother might be African American. You never questioned that it needed to be kept secret and you wanted to marry me anyway."

"I was in love with you. Your racial makeup didn't matter to me. And it was certainly none of my business why Amelia Mattworks wanted to keep knowledge of your relationship secret from the world."

"That's just it. Secrets. Secrets are evil."

"Grace, we're both tired. We've both been through emotional wringers. I have some hope that from now on-"

"Oh, there's one more shock you don't know about. Because I kept it a secret. Out of old loyalties and misguided promises. I kept the secret when it did not need to be a secret from you. A lie that I perpetrated because it made me proud, because it proved to me that you loved me."

"Now I'm totally confused. What are you saying?"

"I'm saying that our child would not have been African American. Would not have had any African American features and would never have been mistaken for anything but white."

"How could you be so sure? Because Amelia's first husband- your grandfather- was white?"

"Because the deep secret in the family is not that I am descended from an African American grandmother, it is that I have no African American bloodline in my history."

"Amelia Mattworks is not really your grandmother?"

"No. You don't understand what I'm saying. My mother Oleida, was Amelia's daughter."

"Then what are you saying? You were adopted?"

"No, no. I was not adopted."

"I don't understand what you're trying to tell me."

"I'm telling you- my supposed black grandmother, the great African American jazz singer, Amelia Mattworks- she is not black. She is white."

Chapter 75

"It's all here, all the family secrets," said Grace York, as she handed Lieutenant Plate a large manila folder full of newspaper clippings, old photographs, military records, and birth certificates.

Grace had brought all the paperwork to Plate's cottage. They were sitting on the sofa with it spread out in front of them on the coffee table, much as he had perused the doctor's records a few hours ago with Edward. Edward had sent Grace to Plate's cottage alone with the genealogy paperwork she had brought back from East Texas. It included numerous old parchments, fragile newspapers, yellowed tablets and a well-worn Bible. A few 19th century photographs were paper-clipped to some of the documents.

"What am I supposed to be looking for?"

"I don't know how any of this connects to Tamica's death. But I will tell you the secret if you cannot figure it out first. The ultimate secret. And then you will have to decide. Here, these are the papers that prove what I'm about to say."

Plate took from Grace's hand service records from the Confederate States of America Army of 1862.

'Killed in action– Major Foresight Mattworks borned February 15, 1842. Died April 16, 1862. Bravely fought, felled by musket ball, age 20. Survivors wife, Sybil, children Simon, Zachariah, Rebecca, Danielle.'

"The first child listed was the parent of Amelia's father-in-law," said Grace.

"So we knew Amelia Mattworks had a white mother. And she was from Texas. It's not a stretch that she, also, might have an ancestor that fought on the Confederate side in the Civil War. I imagine that would not go over well with the jazz world of the 1940s and 50s. It is 30 years later. Why would anybody care?"

"There's more. You need to see everything in context. You need to see the whole picture. Remember Mattworks was my grandfather's name. My grandmother had a maiden name. It's here in the Bible. The poor didn't get birth certificates back then. They kept the records in the family Bible."

Plate carefully opened the old Bible. The family records section was in front. He read it from the bottom up. " 'Born to Fred and Amelia Mattworks- a daughter, Oleida, May 14, 1916'."

"That was my mother," said Grace. "By the time I was born of course we had birth certificates. So I'm not listed here. But you see their names on my birth certificate. My mother was Oleida Mattworks and my father was George Cathare. Ray's father Dick was my father's brother. But that is irrelevant."

"It is?"

"Yes. Look at the Bible again. It a family Bible belonging to Amelia's in-laws, later to my mother."

" 'Born to Simon and Lucia Mattworks- a son, Fred, born February 27, 1893.' So what? I'm still confused."

"Now flip over to the marriage page."

"Shouldn't it be in front of the birth page?"

"Don't be facetious. Just read it."

"Why can't you just tell me?"

"I suppose because if you can't figure it out from this maybe I'm wrong. Maybe Ray is wrong about the motive behind all this. Maybe nobody figured it out. Just read."

" 'Fred Mattworks married Amelia Rosa, April 15, 1910'."

"Keep going."

" 'Simon Mattworks married Lucia Raymond, June 07, 1888. Foresight Mattworks married Sybil Pennington, January 1, 1861'."

Plate thought about all this for a moment. It still was not clear.

"You don't know your Hollywood history well enough," said Grace. "The story put out was that Amelia's father was unknown. It was the custom in the old days to make an addendum to the family Bible when the family was expanded by marriage. Turn over one more page. These are the records of the in-laws brought into the family by their son's marriage to Amelia."

" 'Sybil Pennington- born September 20, 1843 to Jak and Catherine. Lucia Raymond Sanchez- born February 25, 1865 to Jose and Maria'."

Plate stopped a moment before reading the next line. He read it but did not absorb it fully for several seconds.

" 'Amelia Rosa- born Jan 1, 1889 to Carlos and Hildegard'."

This was only one of many children listed born to that couple. Although all Amelia's siblings had died at least 20 years ago, someone had dutifully noted the dates of their deaths next to the dates of their births. The others had been long forgotten. Only she had become rich and famous, and had no date of death.

"You see what it means," said Grace. "And furthermore, here is the father's military record. Not just the record, but also a picture. He was a major."

Plate looked at the photo. Its sharp high quality black and white tones printed more than 100 years ago were as good as anything produced in the 1980s by contemporary photography. There was just no color.

In detailed cursive, the inscription on the back of the photo read 'Major Carl Rosa, CFA, 1862. He served with honor.'

"He lived to be 89," said Grace wryly. "I actually remember him, vaguely. As a small child. He was Amelia's father. He was not African American. She was not illegitimate. As a young woman, she even looked like him. See?"

Grace held a picture of a young Amelia in a 1920s formal strapless gown next to that of her father in his Confederate uniform.

"The dark skin, that got her accused of being African American, came from him, blended with the Mexican lines on the other side of the family. Her mother, my great-grandmother, Hildegard, was a blonde German immigrant. Most of their other children took after her for some strange reason. Somehow, she had the stronger genes. My mother was very fair. I took after them also. Grandmother took after the Hispanic side. It wasn't until the vicious racism rose up in the cities in the mid-1920s that anybody questioned my grandmother's skin color. There was a great deal of intermarrying with the old established Spanish and Mexican American families in Texas before the Civil War."

"I'm aware of that," said Plate, wanting her to know he had some knowledge of Texas history.

264

"Amelia's first husband died in the 1918 war. She was in love with Roscoe Burns. It was actually illegal for her to marry him in most of the states in the country, unless she, too, was black. So she fed into the rumors. I don't think she realized even then what a legend she would become. The movie that Stark Wynter is about to make about her is going to employ thousands of people. And make money possibly for tens of thousands of people. All based on her legend as a great black jazz singer."

"Who knew all this?"

"That's just it. Nobody knew. Well, Ray and I knew. Ray kept the family records all these years safe in a Wilding Falls bank safety deposit box after our parents were killed in the plane crash and I married Edward. We were both on the box and the agreement stated we both had to be present to open it unless one of the other was deceased. Not standard but we set it up that way for a reason. We wanted to make good and sure nobody could force the other to get the records."

"And after Ray came to Sand Waves and married Tamica?"

"We feared our relationship would attract the attention of the press. We took the records and moved them to a different safety deposit box in a small town in East Texas called Jacksonville, setting up the same arrangement. We had no other connection to the town so we didn't think anybody would trace the records there."

"Edward York did not know this?"

"Edward only knew that I was Amelia's granddaughter. I have connections to Mattworks enterprises that I could not hide from my husband. We also kept Regina in the dark about Amelia's race. Ray and I didn't really trust her. If we had, things might have been different."

"So Mink Tanem-"

"Knew that I was Amelia's granddaughter. Regina told him what she knew after she and Edward were married. So he, as well, did not know the whole story," said Grace. "Tragically."

Plate bowed his head.

"Mink conspired with Dr. Apixza to convince me to have an abortion because he knew I was Amelia's granddaughter and was afraid I would give birth to an African American baby. He thought such a scandal would damage Edward's political career."

"No one knew Amelia was not black? Are you sure?"

"No one still alive, except me and Ray. And you know Ray is not the killer. He did not kill Tamica. Please tell me you don't think that."

"I agree. Your cousin did not kill his wife," Plate conceded. "He was convinced that he, and not Forrest Pointpar, was the father of Tamica's baby."

"Who was the father?" Grace asked.

"It doesn't matter who the father actually was, it's who the killer thought the father was."

"Somebody else must know about Amelia," said Grace, trying to envision who that could be. "Somebody who did not want Tamica to have a child. We have to find out who that was. Apixza is certainly not going to tell us who conspired with him. The only way anybody would find out would be if they did a family tree and somehow put all the pieces together. Without these papers, how could they?"

"That is indeed a good question. The papers were undisturbed when you and Ray Cathare retrieved them?" Plate asked.

"The papers were untouched in the safety deposit box just like Ray and I left them years ago. The box was even dusty. But somebody had to have known."

"Somebody had to know. Somebody still knows," said Plate. "And if they find out these records are available, somebody else might die."

Chapter 76

Erick Skrale had heard Amelia Mattworks was strong.

Surprised when she sent for him Thursday evening, Skrale tried to keep an open mind about what Amelia would be like. But stereotypes loomed large. Her age had impressed a false vision on his mind- A frail old lady bedridden behind curtains in a canopy bed.

This image was dispelled the minute he saw her.

Far from being bedridden, Amelia greeted him on her feet. She was petite, but unbowed. Crisply dressed in well fitting clothes. Bejeweled.

Her spacious room contained a dinette type setting in one corner with the couch and coffee table in another. The enormous bed in the center of the room was completely made and might not have been slept in for weeks.

"Sit here, Reverend," Amelia commanded, indicating the table on which there was a tea set and some cookies.

"I'm honored you want to speak to me," said Erick. Then he thought, *why am I saying that?*

Even the most dedicated ministers were susceptible to the macro-culture.

It creeps in and catches people off guard, he thought.

"You seem a little nervous. Don't be nervous, Pastor. I've talked to many preachers in my day. I understand where you're coming from. Hopefully I can get you to understand where I'm coming from."

"I'll do my best."

"I'm going to assume confidentiality attaches to our words in the same manner as if you were a Catholic priest and I was doing confession."

"We can proceed on that basis yes. I am actually a licensed counselor with the state of Texas."

"I'm so pleased to hear that. Excellent. I shall pay you a consultancy fee, if that's necessary."

"No, of course not. I will need a record, that you have become my client, of some kind."

"As long as there's no record of our conversation. No notes, no tape recorder. I have the right to write my own story."

"Granted, no problem."

"I'm going to tell you a story of young woman who became a very lonely woman and then a much loved woman. It sounds like a pretty story but unfortunately it is built on a lie, on evil..."

Chapter 77

Grace York had said nothing to anyone about how she had been taken by force from Sand Waves by Ray Cathare. His subsequent behavior and explanation of motive had caused her to put his method of operation aside as long as they were both in East Texas.

In the old days, taking a relative forcibly away from a situation where he feared she might come to harm was a respectable course of action for any decent man. Brothers had authoritative positions over sisters.

And Ray was like a brother to Grace. If the old ways still prevailed, he would be the male head of the family.

However, the old ways were gone. This was 1983 and Grace knew Ray could be prosecuted for what he did.

It was time for him to leave Sand Waves.

That was what he wanted, he had told her. Now she knew that had to be.

Some type of arrangement was going to have to be worked out over the fact that he was trustee for Corina's life insurance proceeds. He would somehow have to resign that position, Grace decided. There must be a legal way to do it. She resolved to bring it to Edward's attention.

Edward would know how to handle it.

The night she had come through the woods, now a world ago, Grace had brought little with her to the mansion. Since her impromptu stay had turned into a much longer visit than originally anticipated, she had arranged to have some of her things brought from her house outside the gates into the York estate. But she had not brought her doll collection, so the Barbie that traveled with her from East Texas had no company in the small dresser drawer it now occupied.

Grace pulled the drawer open. The doll looked lonely.

Grace moved it from the dresser to the bed and slipped it under her pillow.

At the same time Grace was worrying about her cousin, Daphne Martin was debating on whether she needed to call Plate about Ray Cathare's persistent phone calls. He claimed the reason behind the repeated contacts was that he wanted everything settled.

He really wanted the money, she suspected. Politely putting him off was not working.

He was threatening to get a lawyer and find out what was going on, he was now telling her.

He was not really being nasty about it, just continually pressing, with messages continuously left on her answering machine, after she had stopped taking his calls.

And Daphne, as an insurance agent, had learned persistence was the most prevailing quality of all.

She was worried.

But she felt Plate was already somewhat exasperated with her and she did not want to antagonize him further. It was getting late and she knew he was busy.

She did have a gun.

She decided not to call.

Chapter 78

Their meeting continued well into the evening, longer than either had anticipated.

Erick Skrale knew the right words to counsel Amelia but he was not sure his words would bring her any comfort. He liked to feel that his counseling degree gave him great insight into the way people's minds worked.

Yet, in practice, as profound as that insight frequently was, it did no good to many clients seeking his help.

Clients like Amelia.

He reached for the Bible.

"I cannot condone or counsel away the guilt you feel," he told Amelia, after hearing what she wanted to confess.

"The law will bring me no retribution," Amelia said defiantly. "I've broken no law."

"That is not exactly true, but my consideration is God's law. Man's law and God's law frequently conflict."

"And by what consideration do you put me in the same category as criminals? I'm no common ordinary person. Look at the talent God gave me. Have you never heard me sing?"

"Do you honestly think there's a difference between you and ordinary people, as you call them, because you can sing? Because you have money?"

"I'm the head of an empire. Thousands of people depend on Amelia Mattworks Enterprises. Albums, tapes, concert reenactments, books about me. Stark Wynter is going to make a movie of my life."

"You say you have repented. You say you take responsibility for your sins. But you are still defiant. Still looking for excuses."

"I know I was wrong. I admit that. I've written it all down. Here it is."

Skrale reluctantly took the papers she handed him. "You are using this to avoid directly addressing your Creator. Writing it down may be well and good but your next step is to pray directly for forgiveness."

"I'm entrusting this to you. Don't read it until after I am dead if you don't want to read it now. I wrote it down to help clarify it in my mind."

"You are looking for absolution. I do not give absolution. Look to your Savior. Speak your words to Him."

Erick Skrale rose, towering over the frail elderly woman whose penetrating defiant stare suddenly got through to him. Without another word, he took the Bible, opened it to the New Testament, and underlined Matthew 18:10-11., and placed it in her hands.

Amelia was still staring at him when he turned and walked out the door. She stared at the closed door for a long time after he left.

She looked at the modern-day portraits hanging on the wall. Snappy slick photography. There was Tamica and Ray at their wedding. A golden portrait of Grace alone. A blown up school picture of Corina. A smaller more professional looking photograph of Edward York.

Amelia went to her bureau and pulled out a small wooden box. She opened it, took out other worn and faded photographs, and displayed them on her bed. There was a young man in a World War I uniform. There was her wedding picture with Roscoe Burns. There was a small thin blonde child, wearing a straight white dress too short for her for the time, standing in front of an old shack. There was a healthy husky African American baby girl laughing, blurring the picture a little, as movement did in those days.

There was another light brown haired girl with a sweet smile and happy eyes. Amelia picked up this picture and slowly ran her hands over the girl's face.

Tears trickled down her cheeks. "I'm sorry, Constance," she said to the picture. "I'm sorry I could not save you. I'm sorry I could not tell them you were white."

She thought about the child that was never born. That there were no pictures of. That she had never known for sure was boy or girl, black or white.

It might have been a girl that looked like Grace York, like Oleida. Constance might have grown up to look like Gracie... What would I have done then? The other might have been a boy that looked like- like who? I can't even remember. And another white child, that would have broke Roscoe's heart. Or would it have been a black boy like Roscoe? A son like Roscoe? No, I'll never know...

She put all the pictures back in the box and closed the lid. Amelia slowly walked over to the little oven where she kept her cookies. She opened the small cabinet hanging above it and took out the amber bottle.

Many years ago, after the witch had given it to her, Amelia had taken the liquid to a pharmacist be analyzed. A harmless mixture of herbs, the report had come back, unlikely to do anyone ill. Maybe a few side effects of nausea and/or delirium for a short time.

She had not forgotten the verbal directions the old woman had spoken. She had never had the written version translated. Yet deep in her heart, she knew they said the same.

She opened the bottle and smelled the liquid. She had forgotten what it tasted like after all these years. She poured some into her teacup and prepared to heat the tea.

It was all inadequate, she was sure.

There is only one thing to do now, she thought.

Then she got down on her knees and prayed as the minister had instructed.

Chapter 79

The next day, at the police department, Dr. Apixza's murder was the topic of discussion between Plate and Chief Brecken. The burglar suspected of being there the night two weeks ago that Tamica Cathare was killed could not have been the killer of the doctor.

He was still being held in jail.

Nevertheless, Plate was convinced the two murders were connected.

"We need to get the burglar to talk. The break-in was too smooth. There was too little evidence left behind. Hell, if he hadn't been seen, we wouldn't be one hundred percent sure there was a burglar. He had help from the inside. We need to know who it was. Chances are that was our shooter," Chief Brecken insisted.

Plate was contemplative. "I don't think the burglar is the answer. Not to the murders. As I said, I think it's much more complicated than that. There's more evidence out there, I'm sure of it."

"I do have a bit of news from California."

"Yes?" Plate perked up.

"Stark Wynter's chauffeur Burress has died out there. Of natural causes. Apparently the end of a long stretch of cancer, that originally showed up when he was in high school. He was only 30 years old."

"He was never a real suspect," said Plate, losing interest. "I don't think he was able to climb a fence or tree or even make it up steps to the ballpark tower, even before he took a turn for the worse."

"They said they found some interesting things in his apartment. Hollywood PD went to search there since they knew he was of interest to us here. They did take one of those videocassette recorders and filmed the place for you."

"Well, that was nice of them."

"It is Hollywood. They are into taking pictures of everything out there, from what I hear. I guess that's the way it's going to be here, once they build the movie studio."

"Are they sending a copy?"

"Yes, should get here in a few days. You know how slow the

mail is."

"No, I won't hold my breath. Still might be worth taking a look at when it does arrive."

"Plate, you look exhausted. Take the afternoon off at least."

"I'm beginning to get superstitious about taking any time off. Something else will happen."

"Don't be ridiculous. Go home. To your real home. Officer Skaar has everything in hand at the York estate. Nothing is going on there except Edward York reported that Amelia Mattworks had requested to see Clip Pointpar again. And they were expecting the nice old man to come by in the afternoon. You take the afternoon off. Read a science fiction book. Or better yet, go to bed. That is an order."

"I just wish we could still make arrests for abortion."

"Well, you can't. So just forget it."

Chapter 80

Mink Tanem never quite understood how lucky he was to escape with his life.

He only felt betrayed by the man he had idolized for so long.

Edward's desire for revenge concerning the death of his child increased exponentially as he walked towards Mink's cottage.

By the time he kicked open the front door, Edward wanted to murder Mink in the worst possible way.

He had the means. The small caliber gun Grace had given him the night Tamica Cathare died was in his pocket.

However, the image in his mind was strangulation. A slow deprivation of breath much as he envisioned his son had suffered at the hands of the abortionist in the conspiracy with Tanem.

But Edward's instinct, self-discipline, and self-preservation activated almost immediately at the sight of Mink's surprised and confused expression and pushed the fantasy of strangling his employee out of Edward's mind.

Deep down inside, Mink Tanem would have preferred being killed to being fired. He was a man of little emotion but in that instance he feared Edward York terribly. He was ashamed of the fear simultaneously as he experienced it.

Repentant initially, Tanem vocally resigned, thinking to dilute Edward's rage, as the men confronted each other verbally.

As he faced Mink Tanem, serving him formal notice of eviction and termination of employment, Grace's image kept coming before Edward, imposing a restraint of joy, like the boundaries of honor which prevent an officer and a gentleman from harming a lesser man.

At first.

When Mink Tanem began to hesitantly protest the treatment he was receiving, Edward felt like he was losing focus. Mink claimed his actions were justified but if Edward wanted him out, he would not make trouble.

Silently, Mink was swearing revenge, politically speaking, and made mental plans to join the opposition as a formidable opponent as soon as possible.

Seeing Mink's demeanor change from defensiveness to justification, Edward pulled the gun.

Tanem grew quiet and held his hands up. He backed up as far as he could against a wall.

While Grace's image was not strong enough to stop him from using the gun, Edward's eyes somehow connected with a crucifix positioned on the cottage wall, where it served as part of the décor of the furnished dwelling, hanging just above where Mink was cornered

Ultimately the cross made the difference.

Each time the hand holding the gun flinched, Edward's throat would thicken at the visual symbol of his faith and the cross would repeatedly save Mink Tanem's life.

A long time passed as Edward held the gun firmly. Mink never moved or spoke again. Eventually the gun dropped slowly. Edward could not kill Tanem in the shadow of the crucifix.

He pocketed the gun and backed away from the man who had served him for so long that his service had evolved into fanaticism.

"Get out," Edward managed to say before opening the door and stepping onto the porch. "When I come back to my property, if you are not gone, I will kill you then, so help me God."

And Edward walked out of Mink's cottage just in time to hear Clip Pointpar scream as he fell to his death from the baseball tower.

Chapter 81

Officer Skaar was already on scene at the estates behind the gates. Plate was still with Chief Brecken when the call came about Clip Pointpar.

His afternoon off was canceled before it began.

Plate rushed over to Daphne's house. Seeing that Corina and Daphne were safe was his highest priority. Making sure they were okay was going to take more than just a phone call. He knew he had the house well guarded and Daphne was armed.

But now, knowing what he knew, he feared more than ever that Corina would be killed before the wheels of justice could begin to grind.

Normally when he surprised Daphne, he felt the effect was usually pleasant. But this time she seemed a little angry when she opened the door.

"May I come in? Or do I need a search warrant?" He half smiled at his attempt at humor, expecting her bubbling laugh in return.

Instead, her lips pinched together, she silently opened the door and stepped back and let him enter. As he stepped off Daphne's raised foyer and into her den, he was relieved to see Corina sitting calmly on the couch, petting Daphne's cat.

Everything was okay.

"Honey, we still have to make the arrangements to-"

The masculine voice halted as its owner became visible, emerging from Daphne's hallway.

Ken Skrale was as shocked to see Plate as Plate was to see him.

Both men stopped in mid-stride, for to have continued moving they would have hit each other at a 90 degree angle.

Plate felt the impact of the collision even though it did not occur.

"What is he doing here?" Plate turned angrily to Daphne, the thought crossing his mind for a moment that the preacher's son was Daphne's secret lover. This crazy notion spun into his head an almost complete conversation about why she would have such a young lover, why she had not told about him, and most of all, why she would have him present, compromising Corina's security.

He almost followed up his question about Ken's presence with an admonishment that the least he would have expected from Daphne, if she had a secret private life, was to have put it secondary to the situation he had entrusted her with.

All this was a fleeting brainwave that caused him to stand totally still, even though Ken, after his initial halt, was now moving swiftly.

To Corina's side.

The next scenario in Plate's mind that replaced his imaginings about Daphne should have made him even angrier but instead, despite his better judgment, actually gave him some relief.

And it was closer to the truth.

"Mr. Skrale, am I correct in assuming you have a relationship with Corina French?"

Without waiting for reply, he turned to Daphne, fury on his face that she would accommodate illicit young lovers in her home, knowing full well that Corina French's minor age would cause any carnal relationship she had with the preacher's 22-year-old son to constitute statutory rape.

"I take it, this was the limousine driver that you two trusted so much?" Plate yelled angrily.

He practically had the arrest of Ken Skrale for kidnapping and statutory rape completed in his mind. Reaching to his utility belt for his handcuffs, he took a step forward.

Then again, he was halted, this time by Daphne inserting herself between him and the young couple.

He scowled at her. If he charged Skrale with kidnapping he might have to charge Daphne also. He felt like a little cold water had been splashed on his face.

"Will you calm down?" Daphne folded her arms, on tiptoes in front of Plate, and despite being several inches shorter than the men in the room, completely dominated the area by her action.

"Calm is not a word in my vocabulary right now," he said,

clenching his teeth, yet registering the depth of concern in her eyes somewhere in his heart.

"Plate," she said, in a voice that reflected noteworthy patience. "Just step back and take a deep breath."

Inadvertently, against all his training, better judgment, and free will, Plate did just that. He was unsure if it was shock or relief that sent adrenaline through his veins at Daphne's next words.

"He is her husband."

Chapter 82

"I wasn't really trying to deceive anyone," said Corina, then added, "well, maybe that's not true."

"We were married just before that massive flood last year," said Ken Skrale. "My father married us and it was our intention to tell everyone that weekend. We were supposed to leave that Saturday afternoon and go on a honeymoon to San Marcos. My father was going to announce the marriage while we were gone and handle all the repercussions. The idea was that when we got back, things would've settled down and we could begin our married life together."

"But the flood changed everything. We could not get out of Sand Waves. Amelia sent Mink Tanem out looking for me. They had thought I was shopping with some girlfriends. But the police located my girlfriends at the boutique and took them home and their parents alerted Edward York that I wasn't with them," said Corina.

"A church member who had recognized Corina when she had attended some of our more private Bible studies, and generally knew what was going on with us, risked driving through the high water to locate my father and tell him Mink Tanem and the police were looking for her and she was going to officially be reported missing, if she didn't turn up soon. We didn't even get to finish our cake," Ken recalled.

"So I went with my mother back to the York estate. I told them I had just gotten separated from my girlfriend, who had gone to a different store, in the strip mall. And then, they had left without me and I had called my mother before the phones went out. We hadn't realized how bad it was and were just shopping. Stupid story. But nobody questioned it. After all, my mother was backing me up. Funny they had not cared that she was gone. But I was a minor. The flood was getting so bad. And there I was trapped at the York estate for its duration," Corina finished the narration.

"You had no phone service?"

Plate was remembering his own experience during the flood. It had risen suddenly from a normal storm warning to quickly cutting off Sand Waves from the highway, then restricting movement within the colony, finally trapping everyone in place for several days. Many were stranded in strange locations. Others caught at home with no means of exit. The impasse had lasted for several days until the waters receded.

"No. I had no way to communicate with Ken. By the time the flood was over, it had been three days since the wedding ceremony and we had both had some time to think over the situation. In a way, it seemed like the marriage had never happened," said Corina.

"It was my fault. I should've come and got you right then."

"No. It was my fault. I was afraid. My mother said don't rush it. Stay at the estate a while longer. Keep the marriage a secret. By this time, I knew my mother was pregnant. I was confused. No, conflicted is the word. I knew my mother had been seeing Forrest and she confided that she was not sure whether Forrest or Ray was her baby's father. She felt very alone and I didn't want to leave her."

"At this time no one else knew about the marriage except your mother and your parents?" Plate asked.

"My parents did understand the Corina was very young. I am an adult, Lieutenant. The decisions I made were my own," said Ken.

"Ken was very understanding. My mother arranged for Ken and I to start meeting and spending time together. She covered for me many nights. It became sort of a game. It was exciting and romantic and we didn't have any reason to feel guilty because we were married. Ken found several ways in, through the fence, sometimes through the Pointpar estate. I don't know how all he got in. At first, he just came to my room. Then we decided it was too dangerous. Regina York was snooping around and almost caught us one time. My mother had a duplicate key made to one of the vacant cottages. And after that, we spent the nights in the cottage. We were there the night she was killed."

Chapter 83

"Corina was asleep when her mother was shot. I heard the shots but I had no idea what had happened. So I got Corina back into the house, back into her room as quick as possible, telling her somebody was trying to break into the house," Ken declared.

"I remember jumping into bed, taking a drink of the milk on my night stand, so it would look like I had been there all the time. And the next thing I knew, I was being told my mother was dead."

"I left through the front, as all the commotion was in the back yard," said Ken.

"So Ken coming forward would not have shed any light on who killed my mother. Ken and I had no reason to kill her. My mother gave us permission to marry. In fact, she was at the ceremony. She didn't mind the marriage as much as she minded my leaving the house for good. But Ken could hardly move here. I thought she was reconciled to my going away. But then she used the flood as an excuse, or opportunity, to convince me to cover the marriage up. I think, really, she did not want me to leave home because she did not want to be alone. And I think now, she sensed danger. She warned us several times not to tell anyone and facilitated our romantic games. I didn't understand why. Now, I think maybe I do."

"So do I," said Plate. "Are you sure no one else knows you are married?"

"No. Ken's father married us and our mothers acted as the two required witnesses," said Corina.

"My parents did not want to intervene but they advised me not to take Corina away from her family until she was ready to go. As long as we could be together whenever we wanted, there didn't seem to be any detriment to keeping it a secret."

"Didn't you consider the risk of being mistaken for a burglar and harmed?" Plate asked.

"I never thought of that at all," admitted Ken. "I just thought if I got caught, we would reveal the marriage and it would be a-"

"A fun end to the game? Shocking everybody?" Plate folded his arms across his chest.

"Yes, foolish, we realized soon enough. I should have taken my wife with me from the beginning," Ken said.

"Then after my mother was killed, we could not figure out how I could go. I was afraid Ken would become a suspect in her death. We were planning to have a fancy wedding later and we didn't take any pictures of the ceremony. It might have been questioned whether she truly gave permission for me to marry Ken. I wasn't sure a signature on a piece of paper was enough proof."

"By that time, we had reconsidered telling anyone," said Ken. "Corina was not quite 16 yet and we felt it might be wise to wait until after her birthday. There is such prejudice against young marriage these days."

"More prejudice against marrying young than getting pregnant without marrying," said Corina cryptically.

"I am 22. No relationship with Corina was possible, from my point of view, without marriage. Fortunately, as soon as we met, we knew…" said Ken.

"My mother fell in love when she was my age and my great-grandmother used her money and power to stop her from ever again seeing the guy she loved."

"How was that done?" asked Plate.

"She took her out of the school they attended together. Sent her elsewhere. Monitored her phone calls and letters until the romance faded from lack of contact. And I think my mother never knew why."

"Tamica was very bitter when she told Corina about it," said Ken.

"Yes, she never forgave Amelia," confirmed Corina. "After all, my great-grandmother had married her first husband as a teenager. At least that's what the family always heard. You know, the one that was lost in the war, not Roscoe Burns. Anyway, my mother did not want what happened to her to happen to me. She and the boy she loved- she told me their love had been pure. And their love was denied. I do know my mother ached for that innocent love all her life. She immediately started sleeping around when my grandmother removed her from the school and got pregnant with me. I don't think she really knew who my father was."

Ken Skrale put his arms around Corina protectively.

"When Corina realized she was pregnant, we didn't know what to do. My father wanted to announce the marriage openly, but someone pointed out to us if she was married to me, she would no longer be covered under the group insurance carried by the Amelia Mattworks Enterprises for her pregnancy. And because I had not enrolled her in our church's group insurance before her pregnancy, it would not be covered as a pre-existing condition."

Plate looked at Daphne. "Is that right?"

"Fraid so," said Daphne. "Corina's coverage eligibility under the Mattworks company policy actually ceased on the day of her marriage. She was only a dependent and had no coverage in her own right."

"What do you mean by that?" asked Plate.

"She was her mother's dependent. Her mother was the employee at Mattworks Enterprises. Corina's coverage ceased the day she stopped being her mother's dependent. That is, the day she married. She then was eligible to be covered on her husband's policy as his dependent."

"That is where we screwed up," said Ken.

"In trying to keep the marriage a secret, Ken did not enroll her on his group policy, as the wife of a church employee. During the time she was not covered by either policy she became pregnant. So her pregnancy falls in a gap. Ken can still enroll her as his wife and she will be covered. But the pregnancy is a pre-existing condition and will not be covered at all. Likewise, the terms of this policy, which Reverend Skrale has let me examine, states that the newborn, if not a product of a covered pregnancy, does not qualify as a dependent on the church's insurance for the first 24 hours of its life. Therefore if it is born with a pre-existing condition, that condition will never be covered under this particular group insurance."

"And we did have some indications from the beginning the baby may have some health problems," said Corina, biting her lip.

"We're really not criminals. We didn't want to commit fraud. But Corina really needs to deliver her baby in a hospital," Ken said.

Plate looked bewildered.

"Why couldn't she go to a hospital and just pay the bill? Hospitals have to let sick people in."

"Not pregnant women. Pregnancy is not an illness. The only hospital she could go to without any insurance is the county welfare hospital," said Daphne.

"And I know for a fact they don't give anesthesia for pregnancies," said Ken. "Several members of our congregation have had to go there to deliver their babies since this economic downturn caused them to lose their health insurance. My mother has gone with them and sat with them through their labor."

"The pregnant woman has to be in advanced labor before they will admit her. They keep her until she gives birth, like he said, with no anesthetic. And in 24 to 36 hours, she and the baby are sent home. It's practically assembly-line delivery." said Daphne. "It is a major selling point with young couples when I point out if they don't buy insurance first-"

"Daphne," Plate cut her off. "Let's focus on this situation. You can sell later."

Daphne stopped speaking but she smiled at him.

"And if there are problems?" he asked her, a little conciliatory. "Medical conditions suffered by the baby or mother, I mean."

"For poor mothers, Medicaid kicks in if there any complications. Barring anything serious, the mother and child are actually lucky if there's minor complications. Then they get some free healthcare. However, without complications, pregnancies are not considered disease needing medical treatment."

"So if you already know there are going to be complications-"

"That doesn't apply in this case. The Skrales would not qualify for Medicaid under any circumstances. Just owning a nice car can disqualify you. You have to be destitute. As a married couple, they have far too many assets. Because the hospital would know in advance she could never qualify for Medicaid, they would refuse to admit her because complications from pregnancy could run into hundreds of thousands."

"But if she agreed to pay the bills or put up collateral-"

"I know how you feel, Officer. I thought we could put up her doll and bear collection if nothing else," said Ken, smiling slightly.

Corina elbowed him in the side.

"Doesn't work that way," said Daphne. "Hospitals cannot refuse admittance, legally, to ill or injured people, but they can refuse expectant mothers about to give birth. In reality, they do both. And they do not accept collateral."

Plate looked bewildered.

"Can't you do anything?" Plate asked Daphne.

Daphne laughed.

"I'm just the agent that writes the policies. All I can do is pick the best that will cover each situation. And that's not necessarily the one that pays the highest commission so all agents don't put that as their criteria. Even for those of us who do put the client first, there's no policy that's any good that picks up a pre-existing pregnancy. If an individual or small group makes that claim, they are lying. Now she could get a job at Exxon or maybe the federal government, places like that have major medical group policies that cover everything."

"I'm too young to get hired by companies like that," said Corina.

"Small to medium companies like churches, or an entity such as the Mattworks Enterprises that has only a limited number of qualifying employees, don't actually get true major medical coverage," said Daphne.

"But if they make millions-" Plate started to argue.

"Doesn't matter how much money they bring in," said Daphne. "What matters is the number of employees the company has. Those policies for companies with less than 50 employees have dozens of loopholes, the biggest of which is lack of coverage for any type of pre-existing condition.

"Most private hospitals will not even consider admitting a pregnant mother without insurance unless there's a huge deposit, upfront. There's always the possibility something can go wrong. In that case, once admitted, a patient cannot be turned out, so if there are expensive treatments needed for either mother or child, the hospital gets stuck. In those situations most people walk away from the bills. They declare bankruptcy."

"I don't even see how that could be legal," said Plate.

"You are used to your civil servant benefits. I have fabulous coverage at my company," said Daphne. "Insurance wise, compared to Ken and Corina, you and I, Officer Plate, live in another world, despite they're being, no offense intended- upper-class."

"Our only hope was a small private hospital," said Ken. "Willing to accept a several hundred thousand dollar deposit in advance. There are still a few of those left."

"Our only hope was Jesus," said Corina. "And He delivered-"

"Yes," said Ken, interrupting. "The life insurance left by Corina's, mother, God bless her soul, is going to assure Corina can give birth at a good hospital. We can afford such a deposit. I've already made arrangements for Corina to deliver the baby at a small private hospital."

"Is she registered there as Corina French or Corina Skrale?"

"Corina French," Ken responded. "We have not taken any chances the marriage will be detected. Somebody would have to go to the trouble to get the courthouse records. And then, they would have to know what to look for."

"I am afraid the marriage cannot stay secret much longer," said Plate to Corina.

"I know. I was so afraid after my mother was murdered. I didn't know what to do. Who to turn to. All I could do was pray for guidance. My mother had told me nothing about the insurance. When Miss Martin showed up it was like an angel sent from heaven."

"Where was the policy?"

"I had it," said Daphne. "Some clients entrust me with their policies for safekeeping."

Plate's mind went from medical to money.

"So you know the terms of Tamica French's life insurance policy?" Plate asked Daphne.

"Of course. I wrote it."

"What about the will?" Plate asked.

"Life insurance proceeds, unless left to the estate, go directly to the beneficiary," said Daphne. "Life insurance supersedes a will. Proceeds go to the beneficiary named specifically in the policy, unless said beneficiary is a minor, and then it goes to the named guardian as trustee. I told you all this."

"Forgive me for not memorizing everything you say," said Plate to Daphne.

Then he looked at Ken. "But she is not 18. Ray Cathare is her guardian."

"That no longer applies," Daphne responded. "She is married. And legal status of a husband blows everything else away. Any question of her stepfather being involved was negated."

"Ray Cathare does not know?" Plate asked, wondering how much trouble Ray would give them before they could get their money.

"He does not," Daphne declared. "He has been pestering me about the benefit and I've been trying to stall. But of course, the company has already paid."

Daphne waved her hands as if she were a skilled magician showing off a successful trick, her theatrical gesture indicating Ken and Corina with triumph. With a huge smile at Plate, she announced, "Mr. and Mrs. Skrale already have the money."

Chapter 84

"The life insurance benefit has already been paid?" Plate asked incredulously.

Ken and Corina Skrale were smiling also.

"Of course it was paid," said Daphne. "The company had no legal grounds to hold the policy money. You, yourself, signed off that Corina was not a suspect."

Plate recalled the notation that Daphne had insisted he sign about Corina's status in the investigation, and the double talk she gave him when she had pestered him about it.

"Don't get angry with me," she said, reading his expression. "I was only doing my job."

"And you didn't think you could tell me any of this?"

"Not without their permission!" *Really! You should understand that,* thought Daphne, exasperated. But she did not want to berate the policeman in front of her clients.

Almost simultaneously, Plate and Daphne looked away from each other and at the couple.

"And she did not have our permission," said Ken Skrale.

"I am sorry, Officer Plate. I was not sure I could trust you," said Corina. "Please don't blame Miss Martin."

"I wasn't going to trust anyone without Corina's permission. After all, it really is her money," said Ken Skrale. "I'm afraid I didn't trust you either. I'm not going to apologize. As a professional, you should understand. But I hope there's no hard feelings."

"Fortunately, I trust you," said Daphne brightly.

Plate glared at her without replying.

"After the attempt on Corina's life, I decided we were going to get her out of there one way or another."

"We conspired with Miss Martin to stage my disappearance. I felt like she was the only person I could trust. She was an outsider. She was a friend."

"I only felt I could trust you when you approved, after the fact, that I came here to stay with Miss Martin. Then I knew you were on my side. After all the attention I received at the funeral, I was still feeling unsure about letting the world know I was married. Please don't blame Ken."

"No hard feelings, of course," said Plate sincerely to Ken and Corina Skrale, thinking how much they had been through so quickly.

"There is one more thing," said Corina. "I told you my mother sensed danger. There is a little more to that."

"Really?"

"Tell him everything," urged Daphne.

Corina looked at Ken. He nodded.

"My mother told me a few strange things. I didn't take them too seriously at the time. I was wrapped up in my plans with Ken. And, you know, she sometimes, well, drank and used drugs." Corina swallowed hard. "Anyway, she talked about how much trouble it was going to cause her to have another child. One time she said, 'he's going to kill me for having this baby'. I thought she meant Ray, if he thought it was not his child. I knew she was not faithful to him. I really don't know him. But what time he's been around, he's been rather sweet to me. I thought maybe he might divorce her. I didn't take it seriously."

"Was that all?"

"No, one time when she was rather, well quite not herself, she said something else strange. She said Great-grandmother was going to disinherit her. That is, if the baby was the wrong color. That made no sense. We are rather light skinned for our heritage but I cannot imagine Great-grandmother minding if my mother's baby had been darker skinned. Like, maybe, like Forrest Pointpar. I mean, even if she was embarrassed that my mother's baby might be Forrest's, any skin color could easily be explained by the family history, if their affair was to be hushed up."

"Did my mother in-law's autopsy show- anything definite about her child?" Ken asked Plate.

"I know she was considering an abortion," Corina continued. "Reluctantly. She knew my feelings about abortion being murder. She was hoping Apixza could run some tests that might indicate who the father was. She said he was giving her some kind of trouble over it. Wanted a lot of money or something. That was at the same time she insinuated Ray might kill her over the baby."

"And Amelia Mattworks would disinherit her?" Plate asked.

"No, that was another time. I'm not sure that was not just a joke. To the best of my knowledge, Great-grandmother has no will. She is too superstitious to make one."

"About the tests, Lieutenant?" asked Ken, again.

"Yes, I would want to know," said Corina.

"I don't know," said Plate.

There was an awkward silence. Everyone felt the conversation had worn itself out.

Ken Skrale spoke up. "I repeat, Officer, no hard feelings? We do appreciate your efforts."

"No, indeed, of course not," Plate said, then added to make small talk, "are you a minister like your father?"

"No," said Ken, hesitantly. "I received a degree in electrical engineering last spring. I do work fulltime at the church, servicing the electronic needs. I know I will receive a calling one day. Not sure exactly where it will lead me."

"I am just hoping to get all this cleared up as soon as possible so everyone can get on with their lives," said Plate.

He glanced at Daphne and, unexpectedly, Grace entered his mind.

He dismissed the image.

He did not have time for any hard feelings, soft feelings, any type of feelings at all.

He needed to quickly reassess the entire situation and figure out how to move on, while best protecting this young couple, expectant parents, hated enough by somebody who would destroy theirs and their unborn child's future.

Chapter 85

"The question is, was Tamica killed because someone thought she was going to give birth to a dark skinned child or a light skinned baby?" asked Daphne.

Ken and Corina had gone to bed. Daphne and Plate were alone in her den. It was still Friday, barely. Reports concerning Pointpar's death would probably not be ready until Monday.

"I shouldn't be talking to you about this," said Plate.

"They told you all about it right in front of me!"

"Well, what I told Corina was true. This fetus was very small and significantly- damaged. And as I said to, well, to somebody else, it doesn't matter what dominant race the child would have been. What matters is- what the killer thought. If that was the motive."

"I can tell you what the killer must've thought," said Daphne.

"Oh, you can?"

"Think about it for a few minutes. Do you think the same person that tried to kill Corina, also killed Tamica?"

"I don't know."

"Isn't it the most reasonable assumption? That it is the same person?"

"There's nothing reasonable about any of this. But I'll go with that assumption just to hear what you have to say."

"Suppose somebody, namely the killer, knows about Corina's relationship with Ken Skrale. Suspects he's the father of her baby. May not know the whole truth but doesn't care, doesn't want Corina to give birth to the child of a father who is blonde haired and blue-eyed third-generation Scandinavian immigrant."

"You've got a point, maybe. But-"

"Doesn't that narrow down the suspects? Somebody doesn't want the bloodline showing through, not showing through as the case may be."

"I can't believe anybody cares about all of this in the 1980s."

"You know, for a veteran police officer you can be naive at times."

"It's my naiveté that makes me attractive, wouldn't you say?"

Daphne reached up and kissed him.

He fell down into her arms.

"No," said Plate abruptly pushing Daphne away from him.

"Why not? Is it Grace York?"

"No, of course not. She didn't kill anybody," Plate replied, misunderstanding Daphne's question. "Well, yes, in a way, she did."

Then he told Daphne about Grace York's abortion. Told her in such a way that indicated he felt sorrow and pity for Grace. But there was no other emotion in his voice that indicated a truly personal interest in her. It was all professional now.

"How evil," said Daphne. "To trick someone into an abortion for any reason. It's sadistic, if you ask me. Why else?" Daphne pushed herself up on the couch. She tried to ignore the flood of relief she felt about the way he spoke of Grace.

The feeling that he could trust her came back. *Her insight is worth the risk of telling her everything*, he thought.

So Plate told Daphne about Tanem's fears about Grace's child and why they were unfounded.

"Wow," said Daphne, as she took it all in. "Wow! Does Corina know all this?" She lowered her voice and glanced down the hallway at the closed bedroom door behind which the couple was sleeping.

"I don't know and I don't want to ask her right now. Can you fish around without letting anything slip?"

"I can try. I am pretty good at getting information. It just usually has to do with health problems and medical history."

"You see how complex all this is? It all depends on what everybody thought they knew at any given time. And what they did know," Plate said.

"Maybe you're making it too intricate. Maybe there is a simpler explanation," Daphne suggested.

Plate thought about that for a moment. "I think you may be right. We are making it too complicated. Let's forget what everybody thought for a moment. Let's concentrate on what they actually did."

"It all seems to center around abortion," said Daphne.

"That's right. We know about three abortions concerned in this case. Think about them for a second. What is different about them?"

"Well," she said. "The first abortion of Clip Pointpar and Doreen Darbell's child was in the 1950s. The second, of Grace and Edward York's child was in 1980 or so, you said-"

"The third didn't happen," said Plate. "It would have been this year, Tamica's child and Ray's, or Forrest Pointpar's."

"If she had gone through with it."

"Right, and compare the circumstances. Doreen was deliberately wounded in a movie set 'accident' so she could be rushed to Dr. Apixza, or whatever he called himself then, so he could perform an abortion."

"What a great publicity stunt for that day and age. Female lead in the next big movie wounded in shooting accident on the set. It must've caused a sensation." Daphne let her mind dwell on the silver age of Hollywood for a moment.

"It was an open secret in Hollywood apparently, according to Stark Wynter. Many knew how and why the incident was staged."

"But the general public never knew?" Daphne asked.

"I read the official story in the old movie magazines Regina York lent me. Doreen got reams and reams of publicity for the upcoming movie and lots of sympathy. Becoming even more famous."

"I wonder if in the long run, she felt it was worth it."

"Worth it for the publicity? Or worth it because she took care of a problem pregnancy?" Plate asked.

"The pregnancy, of course. It shows you the desperation involved back then with abortion both illegal and socially intolerable. Despite the physical danger and pain, Doreen Darbell took the risk because she didn't want the child. She wouldn't have done that just for the publicity. They would have come up with something that held no risk, like a fake kidnapping or something."

"So, looking at the motivations of the mothers, Doreen Darbell didn't want to bear a black man's child. It would have ruined her, not only her career but also her whole life at that time," Plate said.

"Right. And Grace York also cooperated in her abortion. Also did not want to bear a child, which she thought would be deformed,"

Daphne concluded.

"One possibility. Grace may have had multiple motives."

"Oh?"

"She told me she did not want children," Plate said, thinking suddenly- *But I guess I thought I was the one to talk her into it...*

Daphne was silent. She firmly forced herself to stay focused on the subject at hand.

"I suppose the diagnosis was the deciding factor," Plate added, without conviction.

"Maybe. But, remember, for the purposes of our comparison, that is irrelevant," Daphne pointed out.

"How so? Oh, I see what you mean. She sought and received a legal abortion."

"Right. The difference was, in 1980 abortion is legal and no accident had to be staged. All Grace had to do was go to the clinic and submit herself to his care. The abortion was performed. She was given proper postoperative treatment. No worry about jail. Fines. Or any of that. She used Apixza for purposes of discretion, not legality."

"And of course, Tamica was pretty much in the same situation. If she really wanted an abortion, all that was needed was for her to go to the clinic, now right there on the property where she lived. So, if she was not planning to have an abortion- " Plate broke off.

"Right again. Looking at it from this point of view, the evidence suggests Tamica had decided against an abortion. But somebody decided she was not going to have the child. But how could they be certain that the fetus would die if she were only wounded?"

"They could not. Not unless-" Plate paused. "Not unless the doctor was in on it. In fact, let's assume he was more than in on it. After all the .22 was his gun. He would have known just where to shoot. All this smokescreen about a young blonde man on the premises was just that- a smokescreen."

"He would have never trusted anyone else to fire the shot that would disabled Tamica and get her into his emergency care. He shot her himself," Daphne concluded. "So then, who fired the four fatal shots? Apixza did not want her killed. That's obvious. So he did not know that was going to happen."

"Let's continue on with the most likely scenario. Who is most likely to be in the sports observation station?" Plate asked.

"One of the Pointpars," said Daphne.

"Right and we know Forrest was on his way to meet Tamica. He was on the York grounds. And he wanted the child."

"So that leaves Clip. But that's ridiculous. What would he have against Tamica? I could see him killing Apixza."

"I know it doesn't make sense. Let's say he was in the tower. He saw Apixza shoot Tamica. Why would he shoot at the injured woman?" Plate wondered. "Could he have mistaken the two in the dark? Thought he was shooting at Apixza, but hit Tamica instead?"

"And Clip Pointpar's death? Suicide? Because he made a mistake? Was it suicide?" Daphne asked.

"Straight case of suicide, or at least he jumped, perhaps not knowing what he was doing. No drugs or alcohol involved. Apparently his latest doctor's visit in Houston confirmed a diagnosis of Alzheimer's. You know, what they call the severe dementia now. Last person to talk to him was Amelia Mattworks. He went up to see her again and had some tea and cookies. Then walked back over to his side of the fence, climbed up on the tower and dove off. If it was murder, we can't figure out how it could possibly have happened or who could have possibly done it."

The phone rang and Plate's pager went off at the same time.

"Oh no! They know I am to be here. I gave them your number," he said, reaching for the phone.

As Daphne watched, his face turned pale. He repeated his words into the receiver. "Oh, no!" Watching his demeanor, she did not hear what other words he spoke to the other party on the line. His mannerisms told her the whole story. Somehow, she knew exactly what he was going to say to her when he got off the phone and turned to face her.

"Amelia Mattworks has died in her sleep."

Chapter 86

She told me it was Clip Pointpar who killed her granddaughter, thought Plate, as he searched Amelia's room Saturday morning. *I thought it was her age catching up with her at last. But I didn't consider it from every angle.*

The small black book had the word 'Diary' engraved on the front in gold letters. Plate thumbed through it. The entries were all the same, a variation on one simple theme.

I love Clip. He's the only one for me. Clip is the dream. He is the only boy in the world and I know someday he's going to look at me and see that I'm the one for him. If only he knew how much I love him. I think he's afraid that Daddy might not want us to date. I can convince Daddy just as soon as I know that Clip wants me as much as I want him.

And so it read on and on. It was Chloe Burns' diary, page after page of declaration of love for Clip Pointpar.

A minor notation when she married Alon French.

Another minor notation when she gave birth to her daughter. Then all the pages were blank.

Plate picked up the small Ziploc bag containing cookies and labeled 'Clip'. He would send those to county forensics. He was not sure why. He had no idea what he was going to tell the county. Nevertheless, he was going to have the cookies analyzed.

A small amber bottle sat near the cookies. It was almost empty. Plate bagged that for analysis as well.

In a small notebook, Amelia had a list of her visitors in reverse order. It appeared she had been keeping records ever since moving to the third floor enclave in the York estate.

Plate started reading the names:

Clip Pointpar.

He had known about the second and final visit of the ballplayer but the next name had slipped by him.

Reverend Erick Skrale.

Then he used Amelia's private phone to contact the minister, telling him it was imperative they talk right away.

"Lieutenant, since all the parties involved in what I'm about to tell you are now deceased, I don't feel like I'm betraying any confidences so long as I can count on your discretion, as it pertains to dealing with the press and other official agencies."

"Law enforcement is not in business to prosecute the dead." Plate was back in his cottage. Reverend Erick Skrale had come to him.

"Exactly. I thought you would feel that way. I wanted to tell you about the confession, I don't call it that, but that's what Ms. Mattworks referred to it as."

"Yes, she attempted to confess to me to what she thought was her crimes but, based on the analysis of the substance she gave me, and the autopsy results on her suppose it victims, she didn't commit any crime. There was no law broke."

"You understand my motive in discussing this with you is to make sure that no one gets blamed for crimes they didn't commit."

"I appreciate that," Plate said.

"She wrote it all down for me. Most succinctly."

"You understand, under the circumstances, although addressed to you, her letter may be evidence in a crime. If so, I will have to confiscate it. You will be able to claim possession of it after everything is settled. Considering everything, it's likely to be worth a great deal of money."

"It will never be sold in my lifetime. And read what it says before you decide it is evidence."

"Okay, I'll reserve judgment," said Plate.

Skrale paused a moment, remembering how Amelia slowly had stirred her cup of tea and fingered the cookie crumbs in front of her before handing him the document she had painstakingly written in short stocky printed letters. Then he handed the paper to Plate.

"I warn you, it is long and somewhat repetitious but very coherent and clearly written in depth. I think she must have been working on this a long time."

Chapter 87

Plate read Amelia's story silently as Skrale watched him.

'I fell in love with Roscoe Burns.

I had become known as a singer in church, for singing the gospel songs in churches throughout the area where I lived. And there would be love offerings taken for me.

My life was good. I married a good man. Had a little girl.

But then came The Great War. And my man decided he had to go fight. He had to go fight for our freedom to live and worship as we please, he said.

And he was killed.

He left me with a girl to raise, no money to speak of, no work for a woman like me, save cleaning houses or working in the fields.

I could sing. And there was the city, not very far away. So I went to try my luck, learned the jazz and made it big.

You know most of the rest. At least the public part but there was the private part. Before I committed finally with Roscoe, I went back home.

I knew that life ahead would be hard. I was already expecting Chloe. I went to a shop where I knew I could get the medicine if I changed my mind.

I told Roscoe a story about how there was a witch who had a potion that could make my baby look white, with the idea that if I took the potion, I could marry some white man for a short time. Then raise the baby as a divorcee', with Roscoe nearby.

Fantasy, of course, but Roscoe would never have gone with me if he had known the truth, and I was afraid to go alone. So he went with me. The old witch gave us the potion and we paid for it.

I resisted temptation that time. I didn't use it. Instead, I renounced my race, gambled everything. But I won. Got to marry Roscoe and have the baby.

Kept the potion, though, just in case. I thought when my life settled down and everything was smooth going, I'd pour it all down the drain.

But you see, it didn't happen that way. Life never got smooth. It never settled down. I was beautiful in my 30s and 40s in a way that I wasn't in my 20s and before. Some people just go that way in the looks department. There were men. I had my man that loved me...

But there was a white man who liked me. He reminded me of my first husband who was killed in the war...

You've undoubtedly heard of the story of how my second daughter died at age five because she was refused treatment at a white hospital. How I brought her there in an emergency knowing they wouldn't take her. So I said I was her governess and Roscoe was some kind of household servant and the parents were away.

They took her. Then turned her out a few hours later when they found out the truth. And she died before we could get her anywhere else.

She wasn't Roscoe's child, but the child of that white man whose name I cannot even remember anymore.

I told Roscoe I took the potion to make her white. And if Roscoe ever knew better, he never said. But there was another child on the way and somehow I could see it in his eyes that he could believe one child might look white, the potion might work once, but the next child- well, I couldn't take the chance. I loved Roscoe, you see. That blonde man was just so good-looking, so like my first husband whom I had loved also, well, the flesh is weak....

I had sinned. But they were small sins in the world I lived in. Everyone lied about their background. Everyone slept around. Many babies claimed fathers that looked nothing like them.

Then there was the sin concerning the child I had left behind when I had said I wasn't white so I could marry Roscoe. She was taken in by relatives and cared for and it was better that way. There was no reason for her not to grow up as a white woman. I put her out of my heart on purpose.

I did not understand I had placed her in safety and my other daughters in peril.

The small sins gave birth to my great sin.

I turned from the Lord after Constance died and it is not until now that I have turned back to Him.

Between those times I have done evil.

My first evil act after Constance died was I took out the potion. And I took it.

I was afraid of another white child. I was afraid Roscoe didn't really believe the potion could turn a baby white. Sure enough, I lost the baby I carried. And I lost the slender white man as I didn't want him anymore anyway. So I sent him away, back to his white life.

I had Roscoe and I had Chloe and I had my career. The three children I lost, one a stranger, one dead, one unborn, I put their memories away. I didn't repent for my sins.

I blamed the Lord for Constance's death.

I had turned from the Lord and He took his hand from me.

Chloe never grew up really.

I knew she had wanted Clip Pointpar. He was ten years older. He didn't want her. He wanted that white movie star that aborted his child. They staged an accidental shooting on the movie set, saying the blanks were mixed up with the real bullets by mistake. The woman would rather risk getting shot- she did get shot- than have a black man's child. Everybody knew what had happened.

I don't know if that mattered. Chloe tried to use my lie to get Clip. Pointpar kept her hanging on for years, even though she got married and had a child, he never told her no.

Then at age 45 he gets married and has a baby. Suddenly he is a family man.

Ten years passed by. I thought she was over him.

I lost Roscoe. The cruelest blow of all.

Then I lost Chloe. It was when Roscoe died- somehow her daddy's death finally caused Chloe to see Clip did not, and would not ever, want her. It was the timing.

Bad timing. Just like the war in 1918. Just like Constance being born the wrong color...

Many times over the years as I became richer and more famous and more involved in the African American community I had cause to think, what if Constance had lived, a testament to my real race? Like my other daughter, Oleida and my granddaughter, Grace were. But they were safely secret in East Texas. Only I could not have kept Constance secret.

So somewhere deep within me, the evil within me did not mourn her death, nor the death of the unknown unborn...

When I found out Tamica was pregnant, again the fear of a baby being born the wrong color brought out the evil in me. I knew there were papers and a Bible somewhere in East Texas that told my whole story. If they ever came to light, Tamica's child by a white man would be one more piece of evidence that they were true. I knew Grace York would never reveal anything, but Tamica was talking about genealogy and tracing her ancestry and other dangerous things.

I told her to have an abortion and I would give her a lot of money.

After all, it's legal now.

I guess, in a way I was thinking that made it not wrong anymore.

She would not agree.

So I offered Apixza $1 million, not much money to me, to persuade Tamica.

I swear I never dreamed he would harm her.

I repeat, I didn't know he was the same doctor involved in staging the accident with Clip's girlfriend so many years ago until too late. The very afternoon I was reading some old movie magazines and I saw him in the background of a picture that had Doreen Darbell in it. I puzzled over that photo.

When I saw the shooting, it hit me then. I knew why.

Yes, I was watching that night and I saw the doctor shoot Tamica. It was dusk but I could still see in that direction, the sun not being completely down.

After seeing the doctor shoot her, I thought it was all arranged that help would be coming for Tamica just like it did for Doreen Darbell.

I thought there would be a crew of people there to help her.

Then I saw the shots coming from the old ballpark tower. In that direction it was darker and the shots were sparks against the night. I could not see who fired them but I thought, well, Clip has got his revenge.

He was watching too. *He has shot that doctor,* I thought. He knew what Apixza was up to.

I turned away from the window then. I was tired.

I assumed help would come for Tamica. I thought it was all arranged like the movie set accident.

That Clip had shot Apixza made no difference. There was no need for me to get involved.

I didn't know Tamica was the target of those shots from the tower until they all came up and told me she was dead the next day.

Later, I realized I could not be sure it was Clip just because I saw the flashes from the gun coming from the stadium tower.

I heard about a thin blonde man who had come over the fence.

I decided it couldn't be Clip since he had no reason to kill Tamica. He didn't know her.

But I hated him for the past and now his tower had been used to kill my granddaughter.

I sent for him to give him the potion. I figured if he knew the Lord, it wouldn't hurt him.

I didn't know about Tamica's affair with Forrest Pointpar until the boy came up to see me after his father had come with his fake sympathy. The old bastard didn't make any sense that day so I held off giving him the medicine and sent for the boy to try to get the truth.

I never in a million years dreamed that Chloe's child and Clip's boy were in love. Tamica had just got married two years ago. She was five years older than Forrest.

I didn't even think of them in the same age group.

I was two years older than Roscoe. That was a lot back then for a woman to be older than a man. Five years would have been a scandal.

I told Forrest what I had seen when Tamica died. I wanted him to know the shots came from the tower. I told Forrest that Tamica was going to meet Apixza to have an abortion and he had shot her first to make it look good.

But someone else had fired from the tower and killed her.

Forrest told me then about their affair. That she didn't know who the father was but she had decided against an abortion. She was going to meet him and he was going to take Tamica away. The baby might have been black. Or maybe it was her husband's. She was going to have it regardless.

Abortion was legal now, there was no reason to shoot her to cover it up, Forrest said.

I had not thought of that.

Maybe I was wrong, I told Forrest. Maybe I had been dreaming.

I don't know what conclusion he came too. He started crying and left.

Before all that I had tried to give the potion to Apixza and to that movie actor that dated Chloe when he was real young and then dated Tamica later. But I got the teacups mixed up, I guess.

Because that day it was the Reverend Frenel that died and not the movie actor or the doctor.

Or maybe it was because I was afraid to read the instructions. Maybe I didn't remember them right.

The old witch had told me but that was more than 60 years ago...

I know the policeman says the potion was harmless but I think he is wrong. If he is dead now, you know he was wrong. I am sorry if he is. I sincerely hope the Lord protected him.'

Plate shifted a little at this stage in the story. He looked at his hands and moved all his fingers. No words passed between him and Reverend Skrale before he resumed reading. Skrale could not know where Plate was in the narrative. The minister sat with his eyes closed, as if in prayer.

Plate resumed reading.

'I'm telling you this because I want to repent. Oleida had a good life with my family. I made it up to Grace by settling a fortune on her after her father and Oleida were killed in the plane crash.

But I can't make it up to Constance, nor to the other child that never was. There's nothing I can do for them. I can't make it up to Tamica what part I played in her death and the death of her unborn

305

child.

My heart was cold towards the Lord who was innocent of what I accused Him.

He did give Constance a chance.

He had prompted Roscoe to ask me to go back home to give up the celebrity life, go back home to East Texas, find a place where our family could be together.

Only God could have directed Roscoe to say such a thing. God had to have put that in his head. So there must have been such a place.

And I casually dismissed it.

Never giving it a serious thought, much less a prayer.

So Constance died and true evil entered my heart.

I want forgiveness. That is why I am writing this now.'

"So she was an eyewitness to the shooting," said Plate, thoughtfully, as he lowered the paper down. "And she didn't completely understand what she saw. Not unusual for eyewitnesses. And are these the instructions she wrote about?"

Skrale opened his eyes as Plate pulled out another type of paper from his pocket.

"I found this in her room. Do you speak Spanish?" he asked the preacher.

Skrale took the parchment from Plate's hand and skimmed it lightly. He paled a little.

"I would not trust myself to translate this. It appears to be an old literature quality Spanish."

"It's probably not that pertinent." Plate took the parchment back and casually put it inside his notebook.

"You had better read that somehow," said Skrale, in all seriousness. "I think it may be important."

Chapter 88

With the death of Amelia Mattworks, there was no reason for Plate to remain in the cottage on the York estate. He rapidly moved back to his apartment on Sunday.

Grace York had decided not to publicly come forward as Amelia's granddaughter. Corina took full responsibility as the only surviving relative of the great lady.

Corina's marriage to Ken Skrale was revealed to the press, which promptly hailed it as a fairytale romance and busily started writing stories for their newspapers and preparing segments for their TV stations.

They much appreciated this fresh angle to the story of Amelia's death. Living legend she may have been but she had lived to be 94 and her highest days had passed.

Corina and Ken were fresh faces, their romance, marriage, and upcoming baby would be hot.

Executives at Amelia Mattworks Enterprises were also thrilled. The happy story would be a boon to sales.

The real secret would be still kept.

Grace was not the only person immensely relieved by this decision.

No one outside the family noticed that Amelia's grandson-in-law, widower of her granddaughter, whose passing from the earth was still backpage news only because of the manner of her death, would not be at the funeral.

Ray Cathare left for East Texas in his pickup truck. He was glad the burden of being trustee for Tamica's life insurance benefit was taken off his shoulders. He refused Corina's offer of financial settlement, took only the small savings and checking accounts he had shared with his wife. He renounced his position on her credit cards and packed his clothing and his collection of western memorabilia, his newly acquired baseball collectibles, and his wedding photographs.

And Grace York's genealogy records...

During the planned Tuesday funeral service at which Corina

intended to sing, and the reception at the York mansion, all her belongings would be discreetly removed from latter estate. They would be placed, along with a few items she had left at Daphne's house, in a cottage on the Skrale estate where the newlyweds were going to reside.

The chief agreed it was prudent to keep Corina and Ken at Daphne's residence until after the funeral. This would give the couple one more day of privacy at Daphne's house before they took their places behind the gates in Sand Waves' upper society echelon once more.

Ken Skrale did leave Corina's side for a brief time that Monday to confer with his father and Edward York on planning a stirring final farewell to Amelia Mattworks. He had Corina's express instructions concerning the service written down. All area resources were marshaled to make the funeral exactly what Corina wanted.

Amelia's funeral was a celebration of her life, attended by thousands of people. The church set up chairs, loudspeakers, and floodlights in the parking lot for the overflow crowd and held most of the ceremony outside.

Not many 94-year-olds could boast of such a turnout.

And at dawn.

Her family arranged the sunrise service for the famous singer. As the sun rose, the floodlights were dimmed and the formalities began with Corina's fresh voice-

> *Have you been to Jesus for the cleansing power?*
> *Are you washed in the Blood of the Lamb?*
> *Are you fully trusting in His grace this hour?*
> *Are you washed in the Blood of the Lamb?*
> *Are you washed in the Blood,*
>   *in the soul cleansing Blood of the Lamb?...*
> *Are your garments spotless, are they white as snow?*
> *Are you washed in the Blood of the Lamb?*
> *Are you walking daily by the Savior's side?*
> *Are you washed in the Blood of the Lamb?*

Do you rest each moment in the Crucified?
Are you washed in the Blood of the Lamb?
Are you washed in the Blood,
   in the soul cleansing Blood of the Lamb?...
Are your garments spotless, are they white as snow?
Are you washed in the Blood of the Lamb?
When the Bridegroom cometh, will your robes be white,
   pure and white in the Blood of the Lamb?
Will your soul be ready for the mansions bright?
And be washed in the Blood of the Lamb?...

Corina sang for a half hour and her voice hushed the entire crowd, several times as large as at Tamica's funeral.

Still, only the family went to the cemetery outside of Sand Waves for the short graveside service. Others went to the York Estate or just went home.

Plate was excused from working security unlike several dozen of his fellow law enforcement colleagues. He and Daphne were honored guests with seats near the family at Corina Skrale's insistence.

Due to the crowd, carpooling was encouraged whenever possible.

"You're not going to sell anybody anything," said Plate, as they traveled together back to the York estate to wait for Corina and her family to return from the cemetery for the brunch reception.

Everyone who came to the service did not attend the reception. Onsite security was grateful. Even the huge York estate was not large enough to accommodate all the attendees at the funeral service.

Chief Brecken, along with most of the security forces no longer needed, went straight home. Most civil rights celebrities did the same as did political supporters of Edward York.

At The Toy Museum Restaurant, Forrest Pointpar hosted an informal get together with old friends of his father's from the sports world who were in town for Clip's funeral the next day in Houston. Some of them had attended Amelia's service with Forrest as a courtesy although they had not really known her.

Regina and Stark Wynter flew back to California in their private plane, also having stayed only for the service, also declining to attend the reception at the house.

Ordinary fans had been forced to settle for the periphery of the outdoor service. Most were grateful for that. The press was also kept outside. They were not grateful.

So Edward York hosted the funeral reception at his mansion and Grace acted as hostess for the remaining family, Daphne and Plate, and several hundred celebrities and non-celebrities from the jazz world.

"After the baby's born we're going to have a formal wedding renewal of vows near our first anniversary. Next November. I hope you will both be able to come." Ken shouted at Plate and Daphne.

"Yes indeed. You will both be honored guests," Corina yelled.

Corina and Ken Skrale had offered the invitation to Daphne and Plate as the latter couple attempted to offer their condolences above all the impromptu loud music in the York den that made talking difficult.

Not trying to reply above the music, Daphne and Plate simply embraced the couple and indicated their willingness to come with positive gestures.

Ken and Corina did not stay long but graciously greeted and thanked everyone at the reception before they left for their new home at Erick Skrale's compound. No one criticized them for leaving early.

"I hope that you are going to a happier home, at last," said Ken to his wife, as the quiet Skrale limousine took the Skrale family around the corner slowly, as traffic was still thick.

This limousine actually belonged to the church and Reverend Erick Skrale was driving it himself.

"You will find our family is warm and loving, I hope. We attempt to put Christ first in every way. I know you and Ken are going to be happy, very happy," said Mrs. Skrale to the daughter-in-law she could now publicly acknowledge.

"And I am hoping now that we don't have to keep you a secret, you will sing in Dad's church," said Ken. "And take your place in public as a member of our family."

"Under one condition," said Corina solemnly.

The Skrales were slightly surprised. They had not expected conditions.

"While you were gone yesterday, Ken, helping with the funeral arrangements, Daphne and I slipped out for a short shopping expedition," Corina continued speaking. "We happened by the Sand Waves Pet Store. And the short story is, I won't be the only one moving in. I will be bringing a pet. I will be getting it next week. It will be weaned by then."

"A pet?" Ken looked at her in surprise. Sand Waves only allowed one pet per home, except service or outside guard dogs, and he had thought he would be the one to pick out a puppy.

"Yes, and you will be taking care of it until after our baby is born," said Corina, with firmness. "I got a low price. The pet shop owner said the mother was a stray that was brought in pregnant."

"Of course," said Ken, as an image of his child frolicking happily with the puppy gave him a warm and cozy feeling inside.

"I've already named her," said Corina, with some defiance in her voice.

"Fine," said Ken, thinking he wasn't particular about a name and a female would be all right, too. "What's her name?"

"Tigress," said Corina, emphatically, then added with equal firmness,

"And there will be no more cat jokes."

Chapter 89

"Corina is to be a great gospel singer," said Daphne confidently. After the funeral reception brunch was over, she and Plate rode together in her car. Leaving the exclusive gated area of Sand Waves, going back to the other side which remained without visible barricades, they both relaxed.

They had met at her home while it was still dark that morning and left his car in her drive, so as to have one less vehicle crowding inside the gates.

"I agree. And I think her music will go farther and live longer than Amelia Mattworks," said Plate, resting his eyes in the passenger seat. His head hurt from all the loud music he had just endured. But the food had really been good.

"Your job is done behind the gates," said Daphne, as she drove the car passed the shade of the forest out into the sunlight.

"What makes you say that? You know we still don't have an official verdict as to who fired the four shots at Tamica that killed her," said Plate, keeping his eyes closed.

"Now really, don't you know that I know that you are smarter than that?"

"I don't know what you mean," said Plate, with an air of innocence.

"As far as I can tell there are only two possibilities who could have fired those four fatal shots. The only ones not accounted for who had access to a height the shots came from. And the most likely was A-"

"Don't say it. It could still all come out. We could still wind up in court," warned Plate, opening his eyes and sitting up as she turned into her neighborhood.

"Was it Amelia Mattworks?" Daphne persisted.

"She's dead. We just went to her funeral at the crack of dawn this morning," Plate noted.

"That doesn't negate it, if she did it. And millions would be heartbroken. Lawsuits galore filed claiming fraud. Millions of dollars could be lost. So it's true. So it will never come out. Well, you can keep it all to yourself."

"Okay. I will."

"Was it her? You have to tell me."

"I do?"

"You do. You have to live with it." Daphne paused. "Come on. You know I'm the only one you can trust. I can always claim client confidentiality, too."

"I don't think so."

"I can try. Come on, what did Amelia Mattworks tell you? She told you she was responsible for Tamica's death?"

"Yes, but not in the way you are thinking. She was not physically capable. Listen, nothing she said would be taken seriously at her age."

"That's a terrible attitude. People don't become less human as they grow older."

"That's just the way it is. People feel guilty a lot when they have committed no crime. They want to confess."

"I get that in my job as well, you know. I understand the difference."

"Amelia Mattworks confessed to asking the doctor to persuade Tamica to have an abortion. And she was convinced she was responsible for the deaths of Reverend Frenel and Clip Pointpar. I had to dissuade her from making a legal confession, so she made a moral one to Erick Skrale. I told her she had done nothing wrong."

"Doesn't giving absolution go against your job description?"

"If you're going to get sarcastic, I am not going to tell you any more. If it all comes out, the paperwork will be horrendous."

"Okay, okay. I'll shut up. I really need to know that Corina is set to stay safe. I became attached to her when she was staying with me," Daphne said.

"She is. The person that made the attempt on her life is dead. The person that killed her mother is dead. They were one and the same."

"It was really Amelia Mattworks?" Plate heard real fear in Daphne's voice as she asked that question. The idea that Amelia's legacy might be impaired frightened even those who had no remote connection with it.

"No, it was not Amelia Mattworks. I just explained that to you. She was a strong 94-year-old but she was unable to fire a rifle four times and accurately hit a target that far away in the back yard from her third story window."

Daphne relaxed, as they turned into her driveway. There was only one other conclusion. The car came to a stop.

"It was Clip Pointpar."

"Yes," said Plate. "It was."

Chapter 90

"It's the questions we fail to ask that impede the answers we need," said Plate.

He was sitting on Daphne's den sofa while she was in the adjacent room that she used as an office, looking for a notepad for him to use. The small room was on the other side of the foyer wall, so when seated in the den Plate could see both the interior of Daphne's office and her front door.

Her raised foyer had no wall on the other side, which was open to her formal dining and living room combination.

"Um, right." Daphne shifted papers around audibly, found what she wanted and stepped back into the den.

"We were thinking about white people who knew Amelia was really white," Plate said, as she handed him the notepad and sat down beside him on the couch.

"That's right," Daphne said, her eyes widening at the pronoun he was using.

"But there must have been black people who had to have known also," said Plate. "We let our attention be focused elsewhere."

He really is saying 'we', thought Daphne, with delight.

"Roscoe Burns, of course."

But does he mean me and him, or does 'we' refer to the police department? Daphne thought, with new trepidation that doused her delight.

"And they would have told their daughter."

Daphne ventured, "And it was she who told?"

"Yes. They told Chloe the truth. It was a minor notation in her diary. She didn't care at first. Chloe's diary revealed Chloe had been in love with Clip Pointpar, who preferred Doreen Darbell. Even after Doreen aborted his child, Clip was uninterested in Chloe, marrying Forrest's mother instead."

"So all these years Clip knew that Amelia was not African American?" Daphne joined Plate on the couch, handing him a spiral notebook.

"Chloe told him, hoping that would make her more attractive

315

to him. She wrote about that in her diary, also." Plate opened the notebook and pulled a pen out of his shirt pocket and started writing.

The night of the murder Edward York and his ex-wife, Grace York, arrived at the estate, having met outside the gates for some type of business. (Note- Normal routine entry at this establishment is through an elaborate fencing system in the back yard.) They found Mrs. Cathare's body in the back yard pool and called the police.

"Do you think that is accurate?" Daphne asked, with skepticism.

"No- I don't know. Sort of," said Plate. "Unfortunately I do not have access to any diaries of the Yorks. I have to rely on their statements."

"What else was in Chloe's diary? Did Amelia Mattworks have a diary?" Daphne asked.

"No, she did make lists in notebooks. So you have to look at the lists and put together what they're trying to tell you. And there was a little, maybe unofficial, blackmail going on. She kept copies of the canceled checks and made notations. And there were some irregular payments here and there. To Clip."

"So Clip Pointpar and Amelia Mattworks moving to Sand Waves about the same time was not entirely a coincidence."

"Looks like he followed her here. But they didn't live that close together until after she moved to the York estate," Plate said.

"Tamica was probably handling the situation for her and, in the course of dealing with Clip, she met Forrest and fell in love with him," Daphne concluded. "Did you want some coffee?"

"The real irony was that Amelia brought Apixza from Hollywood to Texas with her, not knowing his history. He had changed his name, planning to start a new career as a personal physician." Plate started writing in the notebook again. "No, thanks. Maybe in a little while. Let me start this over."

Synopsis of the events on the estate of Edward York that resulted in the death of Tamica Cathare. Dr. JD Apixza ran a private medical clinic that served a private clientèle of the estate. This clinic was located on the estate.

"Apixza set up an abortion clinic in Sand Waves?" Daphne relaxed. *So he's going to stay a while,* she thought.

"Yes, near Amelia. Abortion is legal but his clinic violates the colony federation restrictions so it had to be kept secret."

"He must have lost most of his potential market when abortion was made legal."

"Right, so he was dependent upon Amelia Mattworks for income and she was not going to live forever. But when she moved to Sand Waves, a new clientèle opened up. Women, who because of their social position, still needed their abortions kept secret. Women such as Grace York."

Plate's mention of Grace's name brought about an awkward silence. He wrote more in the notebook.

Dr. Apixza was for unknown reasons engaged in medical fraud.

Reading his words, Daphne arched her eyebrows. "Unknown reasons?"

"If you're going to make comments, I'll go home and do this."

"You know you need me to help you edit it," she said confidently.

He kept in his office a set of records that indicated a pregnancy would result in the birth of a deformed child that would not live too much longer after birth. If paid by an interested third party, he then would show these records to the expectant mother and convince her to have an abortion.

"How could he do that? I don't mean how he could do that as in how could any decent man do that. I mean why did the women not question him at all?"

"Do you have a doctor you trust?" Plate asked.

"Pretty much." Daphne shrugged her shoulders.

"Suppose your doctor took you into one of those little examining rooms, closed the door and pulled out a file, opened it up and showed it to you? All the while he has his hand on your shoulder telling you it's bad news and an operation is in order."

"I see what you mean. I probably wouldn't even pay any attention to the x-rays or the records," Daphne said.

"Grace said she barely glanced at the sonogram."

Daphne fell silent at the casual way he referred to Grace. She wanted to ask but felt like it was too soon.

On the night Tamica French was killed, Dr. Apixza, who had pretended to leave the York estate for the weekend, instead returned secretly. He had entered into an agreement with one of the limousine drivers employed by the agency Edward York used to manage the household transportation. This driver, who moonlighted as a burglar, returned with Apixza with the intention of accessing a different cottage where Dr. Apixza left drugs for him to take. This burglar, who was later caught and confessed, said that Apixza told him to take the drugs, sell them, and then return a portion of the proceeds on his next legitimate visit to the doctor.

"That's all pretty accurate," said Plate.

"When Tamica went to see Apixza, she must have known he was the doctor who did Grace's abortion," said Daphne, moving closer to him on the pretext of better seeing what he was writing.

"No. Grace had told her the details of Apixza's diagnosis, not his identity. He had not yet moved his clinic to the York estate when Grace had her abortion. Grace was keeping Apixza's secrets for her own reasons."

"So when Tamica consulted him-"

"She was after the identity of the baby's father. Knowing Tamica was pregnant, thinking she was just seeking prenatal care from Apixza, Amelia approached Apixza about persuading her to abort the child."

"Amelia was sure it was Ray's baby?" Daphne speculated.

"Clip knew about the relationship between Forrest and Tamica but Amelia did not. Tamica knew that Amelia hated Clip and feared her reaction, especially after she got pregnant."

"How did you know that?"

"Forrest told me that. But Tamica told Amelia about the pregnancy and that she was considering an abortion because her marriage had gone bad. Amelia told me that," Plate said.

"Why would Amelia tell Clip that Tamica was pregnant and planning an abortion?"

"Who knows? She didn't give me a reason. Just for meanness, perhaps. Probably she knew about the abortion in Hollywood years ago and just wanted to bring up the subject. Because she knew it haunted him. And he had taken a political stand against abortion."

Actually, the doctor was using the driver as a decoy and planned to throw suspicion on him as an intruder if anything went wrong. Events did go wrong and the doctor followed through on his plan.

Apixza was apparently expecting Tamica Cathare to exit the York back door and proceed to his cottage in order to consult him. He had been promised a monetary reward if Mrs. Cathare would consent to an abortion. He and Mrs. Cathare had an appointment to meet and discuss the results of recent tests he had conducted on the victim.

"Is that right? Are you sure about that?" Daphne asked.

"Actually that is the one thing we are not sure of. Apixza, and possibly Tamica, only really knew why he was outside that specific night. My opinion- he was watching her. But I could be wrong. This is simpler to explain."

"It's not fair to Tamica, though. It insinuates she was going through with the abortion."

"Okay, I'll scratch it out."

Plate scratched out that part and wrote instead-

Mrs. Cathare had undergone tests to see who the father of her child was and was originally to meet with the doctor clandestinely to obtain the result, and let him know if she would go through with an abortion.

Apixza was intending to make sure she did. If she decided against an abortion, he planned to wound her in such a way that, with his immediate care, she would survive but the pregnancy would not. He had been the perpetrator in a similar situation many years ago which had been successfully executed.

"How do you feel about abortion?" Daphne asked Plate.

He reflected only a moment. "The science is pretty clear. From what I have read and the pictures I have seen, it's obvious. Babies are formed at conception. Regardless of your religious beliefs, they are human from the beginning. It's murder."

"Hmm," said Daphne. "I hadn't thought of it that way. Murder."

"A lot of deaths are really murder. You just can't tell always."

"Well, you are probably right," she said, in a matter-of-fact tone of voice. "But it is really easy for men to be anti-abortion. It is easy for married women and postmenopausal women and other people who can't have children. But for people like me, it is harder. I may have children someday, but I certainly don't want any now. I don't plan to get pregnant outside of marriage."

"There's one sure way not to." Plate smiled. "No offense. I'm not being suggestive."

"I know how not to," said Daphne, not at all offended. "I know the 100 percent effective method. But I am human. Suppose I slip up? Suppose I am raped?"

Plate felt ambiguous about the subject for the first time.

"I don't know what the answer is, truly. But I think it- the actual act of abortion- is murder," he said.

"You are probably right," Daphne conceded, thinking- *talking to him is as comfortable as talking to a girlfriend at times.* "Until they made it legal, I never thought about it. No matter what, I would never have risked an illegal operation. No. I don't know the answer either."

Chapter 91

Mrs. Cathare, already having deciding against an abortion, had changed her plans. Now instinctively fearing Apixza, she was planning to flee the York estate with her lover, Forrest Pointpar. Fearing negative consequences of not keeping her appointment with the doctor, she called Forrest Pointpar that evening to come and get her.

"Accurate?" asked Daphne.

"Simplified," Plate replied. "Covers everything, I think."

"Maybe. So you said Forrest Pointpar made a statement. Learn anything else?"

"His statement filled in many of the gaps. In Forrest's mind, Clip did nothing wrong. He was provoked into a reaction. Several people see it that way. Probably Edward York himself. Which is why it will never come out."

"What do YOU see? What is your point of view?" asked Daphne, as if Plate's were the only interpretation of the events that mattered.

"You see, from my point of view there really four murderers. More than that, if you are going into the past. Years ago, during his scandalous, at the time, affair with Doreen Darbell, Pointpar found out she aborted his child. He was determined that was not going to happen to his son. But with abortion now legal, he had no way to stop it. Amelia, believing Ray was the father of Tamica's child and fearing that another illustration of how white the family really was would start rumors about her own origins, tried to influence Tamica."

"So from the beginning, Amelia was pushing, and Tamica was resisting, the idea of an abortion?"

"I think so. Corina said her mother was nervous and afraid. Tamica probably did not fear actual violence."

"You think she feared Amelia's pressure?"

"Yes. She was trying to escape before it got too much and she capitulated to an abortion. That's why she wanted to run away with Forrest the evening she died. They were adults. They didn't have to run away."

"It was a symbolic escape. A psychological break," said Daphne.

"Forrest was playing Romeo. He was going to rescue his girl. He told his father something like that and Clip went up into the balcony to watch, like watching a play."

"Only it went wrong."

"Yes. It should have been simple. But it all went wrong. The miscommunication between Amelia and Clip, then incomplete communication between Forrest and Clip, was one key to the tragedy. The other was what effect Apixza's appearance on the scene had on Forrest Pointpar."

"Explain what you mean."

"Remember when Corina said Tamica feared someone?" asked Plate. "Corina thought it was Ray, but that was obviously wrong."

"It was Apixza?"

"Maybe. We don't know exactly when Amelia approached Apixza. Amelia told Clip that Tamica was considering abortion because the father was the 'wrong race'. Clip must have thought Amelia knew about the affair between Forrest and Tamica and was gloating to him. He and Amelia were old enemies. They never liked each other and that didn't change with age."

"Do you think Tamica really said that?" Daphne asked.

"Maybe. People have conflicting thoughts all the time."

"Especially pregnant women," she said, adding hastily, "so I'm told. Did y'all work out what actually happened that evening?"

"That evening, before Forrest could get there, Clip, in the tower, saw Tamica come out the back door and saw Apixza emerge from his cottage. He saw Apixza fire the disabling shot, same as had been done years ago with Miss Darbell. Clip thought this was a plot to abort Forrest's child. He shot at Tamica from the tower with the .44. When Apixza heard those shots, he grabbed his rifle and ran."

Apixza had been watching for her and when he saw she was going towards an exit rather than towards his clinic, he put his backup plan in action. He shot Tamica Cathare with a .22, hoping to fell her and then run to her side, carry her to his clinic, and fulfill his plan.

After he shot her, four shots from a significant height struck the victim and fatally wounded her.

As only the third floor of the estate, the tower on the next-door Pointpar estate or a tree could be the source of these shots, the assailant remains unknown. The two former locations were ruled out. A tree, showing evidence of recently having been climbed, must have been the scene from which the fatal shots were fired.

"Was there evidence of a tree having been climbed? Did the burglar climb the tree?" Daphne asked.

"Yes. No, we don't think it was the burglar."

"Who climbed the tree? It was on the wrong side of the yard for it to have been Ken Skrale."

Plate failed to answer her and resumed writing.

Apixza fled the scene at once, embarking on a previously announced weekend trip. Later, upon returning, before he could be fully implicated, he was killed during a burglary of his clinic.

Daphne tried another tactic. "What would the report say if Clip were not dead?"

"Let's just say it would be different. How, I must admit, I'm not sure."

"The dementia would have been blamed, I suppose," said Daphne, thoughtfully.

"Maybe. What Clip did not understand was that with the new law legalizing abortion, there didn't have to be a pretext for getting the pregnant woman to a doctor. If Tamica had been cooperating with Apixza then it would not have been necessary to wound her. One theory- when Clip concluded that Tamica intended to abort Forrest's baby, it pushed him over the mental edge. Clip was mentally back in the 1950s- into a rage directed irrationally at Tamica. Maybe in his mind, she was more than the woman about to abort his grandchild.

She became the movie star who had aborted his own child."

"Where was Forrest? What about the burglar?" Daphne asked.

"Forrest was coming and maybe Apixza saw him. Already certain Tamica was not going to abort the child, seeing Forrest coming cinched it. If Forrest got to her, she would be gone from the compound for good. The payoff lost. So Apixza fired. Unlike all the other actions, which were acts of passion, Apixza's plan was wholly premeditated. He would 'save' Tamica. Abortion accomplished and Amelia would pay. The burglary was a set up to cover for Apixza if anything went wrong."

"And the burglar? Apixza would claim he was the target and Tamica got in the way?" Daphne asked.

"Yes, exactly. The thief knew nothing about the plan to wound Tamica. Apixza set him up. The thief thought it was all about the drugs. So he said in his confession."

Forrest Pointpar came upon the scene, saw Mrs. Cathare was beyond help and also fled. The hired burglar took the drugs and also fled over the fence, without realizing Mrs. Cathare was dead in the pool.

"And the other murderers?"

"They would not be murderers under the law as it stands."

"Murderers in your sight? But guilty of no crime."

"If abortion is murder, Apixza is guilty, so are Mink Tanem and Grace York."

"As well as the movie star, Doreen Darbell, from 30 years ago, that took the child of Clip Pointpar?" Daphne asked doubtfully.

"That is all beyond the reach of the law now."

"Just as Mink paid Apixza money to persuade Grace York to have an abortion, Amelia offered the doctor money to persuade Tamica to have an abortion. There has to be a crime in there somewhere," Daphne said.

"Maybe something like conspiracy to commit medical fraud. Amelia is dead and Judge York does not want to prosecute Mink Tanem. There was no violence connected with Grace's abortion."

"So Mink just offered Apixza money and did not conspire to have Grace shot if she didn't cooperate? That's what you're telling me?" Daphne asked.

"That's the story. I don't necessarily believe it. Tanem says he never dreamed Apixza would resort to any type of violence. He just wanted JD to use his influence as a doctor. No doubt, Apixza would have harmed Grace some way if she had not gone through with the abortion. But Mink Tanem apparently did not know Apixza had used violence in a conspiracy to make sure Doreen Darbell's abortion was completely covered up. He claims he never heard of Doreen before going through all those old movie magazines."

"And Grace York doesn't want to prosecute him?"

"I've had no communication with her. She knows the situation. She knows how to contact me if she wants a different outcome than what Edward York desires."

"Why did Apixza succeed with Grace and fail with Tamica?" Daphne felt a happy glow at Plate's statement that he no longer had communications with Grace. But she was trying to hide her joy. The subject they were speaking about was so serious.

"When Apixza tried to persuade Tamica to have an abortion, he told her the child was deformed just as he had done with Grace. But Grace had told Tamica about her abortion. After all, they were first cousins, closer than anyone realized. At that point, Grace still believed Apixza had been telling her the truth. Tamica probably was a shoulder for Grace to cry on. She could tell Tamica her secret, since her relationship was Tamica was a secret itself. Then when Apixza told Tamica her own child was deformed and abortion was indicated, Tamica became suspicious. It sounded too much like what he had told Grace."

"Apixza would have had no idea Grace and Tamica were close."

"Edward York knew."

"Is that how he found out about Grace's abortion?"

"He never said. Apixza could have told him, trying for blackmail. From the interactions I have had with York during all this, I don't believe he will ever tell anyone."

"Tamica really didn't know who the father of her child was ever, did she?"

"We think Apixza may have already told her the father was Ray and she was vacillating about abortion. But finding out that Apixza was Grace's abortionist killed Tamica's trust in him."

"Then she didn't know what to do," Daphne concluded. "Ray would want the child if it was his. But Forrest might not."

"No, she knew better than to believe Apixza by then. Forrest finally told her if the father turned out to be Ray, she could divorce Ray, give him custody rights, act like most divorced people. Then she and Forrest could start their own family. At some undetermined point in time, before the night she died, she made her decision to have the child. And then she became afraid."

"She felt like she had to slip away."

"Forrest was against abortion under any circumstances. He was coming for her."

"But Apixza got there first," said Daphne sadly.

"As I said, I think he had probably been watching her movements. Stalking her."

"Forrest told Clip he was going to rescue Tamica, but not that Tamica had decided against an abortion. Why not tell him that?"

"He claims that he didn't think. He says, at that point, he didn't know what Amelia had told Clip. But-"

"But?"

"I think Forrest was unsure what Tamica was going do. If Apixza saw him, maybe he saw Apixza and had second thoughts. Else why did it take him so long to get there? He says he heard the first shot and ran towards her but there's no evidence of that. I think he saw Apixza coming towards her and that confused him. I think he climbed the tree to see what was going on. He held back until Apixza shot her. Then he jumped down and ran toward her but Clip fired before he could get to her."

"He had to have known she was dead and who shot her."

"Yes. He believes Clip's rage, suppressed all these years, exploded at just the wrong moment and he had the rifle in his hands. Tamica and Doreen merged in his brain."

"So Clip possibly killed his own grandchild?"

"Ironically, no. Pathologist said the first shot killed the unborn baby but would not have killed Tamica, had she gotten medical attention. And Apixza was right there."

"So if Clip had not killed Tamica, Apixza could've only been prosecuted for attempted murder at the most?"

"Probably just felonious assault. Or maybe nothing at all, if his story was accepted. People tend to believe doctors."

"How could Forrest just go home as if nothing happened?"

"Forrest Pointpar knew from the beginning who killed, really killed Tamica. But he was in shock and denial. He was hearing stories about blonde intruders. I suspect he did not understand it all completely until he talked to Amelia."

"Then he knew what a tragedy it really was."

"Yes. After Tamica's body was found, Amelia told Forrest what she believed at that time- that Tamica had been going to meet Apixza for an abortion. She told him what she had seen. She knew then that whoever had been on the tower had seen pretty much the same thing. She was not sure who was on the tower firing the shots. If it was Clip, she thought he had killed Tamica by mistake. But Forrest had known things Amelia did not know. He knew it was Clip on the tower. And he knew Clip was probably in the first stages of Alzheimer's. He realized then that the faulty connections in Clip's mind caused him to shoot Tamica. I think later, Amelia realized that also. That's why she ultimately concluded Clip was the killer."

"Forrest keeping silent is not a crime?"

"Yes and no. A gray area, it could be argued. Forrest considered Apixza the real murderer. I don't think he ever told the whole story to Clip. It was Amelia who told him when she finally understood what had happened."

"So then later, when Clip realized what he had done, Clip beat Apixza to death."

"Hmmm," said Plate. "Apixza was killed before Amelia saw Clip again."

Daphne sat up. "What do you mean by that? Clip did kill Apixza, didn't he?"

327

"An old frail man can fire a gun, but beat a man like Apixza to death?"

"Then who?"

"Self-defense," murmured Plate. "Whichever one it was."

"Whichever who?" Daphne practically shouted at him. "One of two people? WHO? WHICH TWO?"

Plate rubbed his ear. "Don't shatter my eardrum. I'm still recovering from the jazz music."

"Which two?" Daphne repeated in a low dangerous tone of voice.

Plate smiled at her.

"The only two with mutual unlikely alibis at the time Apixza was killed. They alibied each other. Ray Cathare and Forrest Pointpar."

Chapter 92

"So then was it really Clip who tried to shoot Corina and Stark Wynter?" Daphne concluded.

"Yes, he shot from the tower. In the confusion nobody understood exactly where the bullets were coming from. And, trying to protect Ken, Corina was making it even more confusing insisting no one else could have been on the grounds that night when she knew Ken had been there."

"Why shoot at Corina and Stark?"

"Well, with Corina, I'm not sure. Maybe Clip thought she saw him. She was not supposed to be out on the grounds. She trying to meet with Ken. But Clip had no way to know that. She was not his target, I don't think," Plate said.

"And Stark Wynter?"

"Best theory is this- Wynter told me he recognized Apixza at Tamica's funeral as the doctor that had tended to Doreen Darbell in Hollywood. He recalls a vague conversation with Clip after the funeral that probably led Clip to believe Wynter could connect him to Apixza."

"But Clip didn't kill Apixza. He shot at Wynter before Apixza was killed," said Daphne, confused.

"Maybe he knew about the plans for Apixza's fate. That would explain why he didn't go after Apixza himself. He didn't have to."

"But- that would make Apixza's death cold blooded murder. Okay, I think I see. Father and son covering for each other?"

"I'm just speculating. The Apixza murder case is closed. Powers-That-Be do not want it investigated further. So what can I do? Clip was not thinking straight, that's for sure. Who knows what was in his mind by then anyway? Would you read the completed report for me? Tell me if it makes sense."

Daphne took the papers from his hand and read it all silently until the last paragraph which she quoted out loud.

" 'At some point during all of this someone poured gasoline on some of the shrubbery. Possibly the burglar. But for whatever *reason no attempt was made to set the gasoline on fire, most of it evaporated and nothing came of it contaminating the ground except for the death of some landscaped bushes.*

It was undetermined how much later Edward York and his ex-wife Grace York arrived at the estate and discovered the death.'

"That's a bit weak. I'd cut that out and just end it with the death of Apixza."

"Okay. I thought as much myself. I'll do that."

Daphne could wait no longer.

"What about Grace York?" she asked.

"Nothing will happen to her. She's committed no crime."

"I mean about you and her."

"Oh, I don't know."

Daphne's cat picked that moment to emerge from hiding and jump on her lap.

"Listen, can I leave this with you?" Plate asked rapidly. "It's getting late. I'll come back tomorrow and finish it and you can help me edit it as you suggested."

"Um, well, okay," said Daphne, caught off guard at the prospect of his departure.

"I need to get a good night's sleep tonight. I'll call you before I come over. You are free tomorrow? No, you probably have an appointment."

"No, I don't have an appointment tomorrow," Daphne fibbed. "Of course, great, that'll be fine."

She jumped up as he rose from the sofa.

And he was out the door before she could say another word.

Chapter 93

Grace and Edward faced each other at the kitchen table. It was very early Wednesday morning, still very dark, the guests had long ago left, the servants had cleaned up and gone home. All security personnel had been sent away.

Grace and Edward were alone in the York mansion.

Emotionally they had both already reached the same conclusion some time ago. They would start again.

Neither was quite sure how to proceed.

"What would've been our tenth anniversary is coming up. I can contact Father Thomas and see if that date is available for a remarriage ceremony," Edward suggested. "Regina is getting a quickie divorce which I will not contest."

"And in the meantime?"

"It's just a few weeks. You stay here as you have been."

"That's the interim. What about afterwards? We can't just take up as we left off more than two years ago."

"It will only be the two of us. No one to come between us. I won't allow that ever happen again."

"Do we live here? What do we do with all of this empty space?"

"You know what I would like to do with it."

"Still?"

"I would still like to fill it with children. Our children."

"We need to be realistic."

"We know now you can get pregnant. If you have trouble as the pregnancy progresses, treatments have come a long way since we first married. Getting pregnant is half the battle, they now say. We can find a good infertility doctor, not one like Apixza."

"Even if I don't have any trouble getting pregnant again," said Grace, as the fear of what other doctors might do passed through her. "Look at my age. I don't have enough years left to fill the house the children. I don't want to go to doctors. I don't want to be experimented on."

"You know I won't force you. We'll take whatever God gives

331

us."

"And if there are none. If the child, that child, was the only one?"

"We could always adopt. We could adopt anyway. There's no end to the number of children that need a home."

"Adopt?" asked Grace skeptically.

"Think about it," said Edward, getting up from the table. "Meanwhile, there is just you and me. We have the whole mansion all to ourselves. In the eyes of the church we are still married. We don't have to wait for legalities." He held out his hand to her. "Where shall we go?"

"Oh, I don't know. My guestroom is so bare and plain. I hate it."

"There's the third floor?"

"No no. I couldn't- everywhere, it's like the place is going to be haunted."

"One of the cottages, then?"

"Yes, but-" Grace mentally pictured the recent activities in each of the cottages. "Okay, then it has to be the one the movie producer stayed in. I think that will have the least amount of ghosts."

"Let me go upstairs and get my coat. It's really cold outside. Do you need anything?"

Grace shook her head. "Uh, no, no I don't."

As Edward left the kitchen, Grace also rose from the table. She walked over to the kitchen counter and picked up a small decorative ceramic canister. All the years she had kept the small packet hidden there and, once she had moved back into the mansion, even though she had occupied the guestroom alone, she had picked up the old habit of using the canister as a hiding place. It was totally decorative and hard to get open and it sat on a high shelf so it was rarely even dusted.

When she had shared her bedroom with Edward, it had become a game in her mind that if the pills were ever found she would disavow them and never take them again. But they had never been found.

She forced open the canister and retrieved them.

She had not been sure this moment would ever come, but as a precaution, she had resumed taking them as soon as she had moved into the mansion.

She snapped a little pill out of its package and took it quickly. Then walked into the foyer to await Edward. She gazed at herself in the foyer mirror and pulled her coat tight around her waist as snug as it would go.

Adoption, she thought. *Maybe that is the answer.*

She tried to imagine herself the mother of adopted children, probably imperfect children. It would not be easy. But what had Edward said previously? They had plenty of money. They could afford all the help they needed. Any child with needs would have the best of care in the world.

Grace took off her coat. Again she pulled her clothing tight around her waist and ran her hand over her flat abdomen.

She recalled the moment of extreme grief and repentance that has sent her screaming to the floor. Oddly, she wanted to repeat the feelings of that moment. She wanted to not become detached from those emotions. But they had been slowly slipping away as time passed.

Edward had talked to her about speaking to the priest. But she was afraid to speak to any priest, afraid to confide what all she had experienced and felt in that moment.

Instead, without Edward's knowledge, she had made an appointment with her psychiatrist.

She was vacillating about that as well.

Maybe she would do nothing. See what else happened in the future. If anything.

The noise of the elevator indicated Edward was approaching. Grace quickly put her coat back on.

"I think we should look into adoption," were the words she greeted him with as he stepped into the small cubicle.

"That would be wonderful," he said, putting his arm around her and leading her towards the door. "When I contact Father Thomas I'll mention that as well. But first let's get to work on making our own children."

"Yes, of course," said Grace, clutching his hand as they went out onto the porch.

"One other thought," said Edward as the cold air hit them. Clouds broke and stars glittered in the night brightly, giving their best, preparing to give way to dawn. "What about that police officer? Do you need to say anything to him?"

"No, I spoke to him already," Grace lied.

"I'm sure he understood," said Edward.

They trotted across the yard to the cottage.

As Edward opened the cottage door, Grace fancied she saw the dawn's first light reflect off his silver hair just before he flipped on the electric light inside the entryway.

She felt a warm rush as he reached his arm beyond the doorway and drew her inside.

Chapter 94

It was actually the next Monday before Daphne heard from Plate again. He asked, if she did not have an evening appointment, if he could come over after work to finish the report he had started and left at her place.

"No, my evening appointment canceled today," she lied, and canceled it herself as soon as he got off the phone.

Since the day of the funeral and their last meeting, the headlines had been full of nothing but Forrest Pointpar and what he had done.

The entire country was debating his actions on the new 24-hour news network. He had declared himself a candidate in the May primary for Congressman Brown's seat.

Previously unopposed, Brown was furious that a twenty something college student would run against him. In his political response, Brown came close to openly accusing Forrest of being a suspect in Apixza's murder. Apixza's role in Tamica's murder had come out.

So had Tamica's rumored relationship with Forrest.

Plate showed up in Daphne's driveway in his patrol car, not taking time to go home before driving to her house. He was an hour later than he had told her. But he did come with pizza.

"What about the death of Apixza?" asked Daphne, opening the flat square box and spreading the food on dishes. "They had to reopen it didn't they? That's what you have been up to, right?"

"Why?" asked Plate, as he grabbed a plate and went to the couch. "It is still closed as far as I am concerned. We can't prove anything."

"Can't or don't want to? We could eat at the dining table, you know." She followed him to the couch with her piece.

"Suppose I accused Forrest of killing Apixza. First, he has an alibi. Second, it's the word of an upstanding Sand Waves citizen against any possible defense a long time criminal abortionist might have procured if he had been the victor in that fight, or even just a survivor. Take my word for it, the grand jury would not indict."

"There would have been a time when a black man killing a white doctor would have gotten Forrest an automatic conviction."

"That's true. With an automatic death sentence."

"Times have changed some," said Daphne. "I suppose it would have been Ray Cathare who disconnected Apixza's security? What do you think?"

"If you asked me Forrest Pointpar or Ray Cathare, whichever, did mankind a service," said Plate. "That's just if YOU asked me. I have no comment to anyone else."

Daphne reached over and kissed him. "So what have you been doing? Security for Forrest?"

He pushed her away.

"Sleep. I have been sleeping. I actually had a day off. Uh, I think it might have been Saturday. And just a minute. You haven't lived up to your part of the bargain. If I tell you everything, you have to tell me everything as well."

"What?"

"About what Corina Skrale may have told you while she was at your house. For example, who does she think her real father was?"

"What makes you think we discussed that?"

"Because I know you."

"All right. The topic did come up. Tamica never told Corina who her real father was. Corina believes Tamica herself did not really know. And Corina has decided that she does not want to know. If she knew, Tamica took that secret to her grave."

Chapter 95

"There's something else I want you to see." Plate dashed out to his car and came back with a folder, before Daphne, in the middle of a slice of pepperoni with black olives and sausage, could even react.

"What's that?" She managed to swallow the pizza, as he sat back down beside her.

"It belonged to Amelia. Don't ask how I got it. It looks like a set of instructions. I can see that it is numbered. But I don't know what it says. It's in Spanish. Do you know anyone who speaks Spanish you could trust?"

"I can read Spanish."

"You speak Spanish?" Plate was a little jealous.

"No you're not listening to me. I said I can read Spanish. I can't speak it. I can't get the dialogue down. But I had it in college and I can read it and write it. Let me see the paper."

"Okay, but handle it with care. It's very old. It may be evidence, even though all the– well, there probably won't be a trial. I need to find out what it says and apply the proper procedure."

"Okay, give me a minute and I will write out a translation for you. That will be easier than my trying to read it to you. As I said, I really can't speak the language. I have a dictionary if there is a word I cannot recognize."

"Okay."

"I'll just be a minute." She went into her office.

Plate fixed himself a cup of cocoa while he was waiting for Daphne to translate the Spanish document. He was sipping it as it cooled when she came back into the room, handed him the document back along with her written translation.

"I think it's pretty accurate," she said, sitting beside him. "It is pretty unusual. Profound and spooky at the same time. It's actually a brochure with some instructions."

"At the top it says- 'Death Medication, 250 pesos.' "

Plate took the paper and started to read silently-

Instructions for Use of the Potion for the Death. The secret of the medication is not within the blend of herbs it contains, but its strength depends upon the force of the hatred of the distributor. He must possess sufficient hatred to cause a black cloud of death to descend around the recipient, no more than one week after the medicine is consumed by the recipient.

For administration to the self- a desire sufficient for death must be present for the death medication to function properly. If this is not achieved after numerous doses, a method that is different for the death should be considered.

Disclaimer- if the hatred of the distributor is not sufficiently strong the death potion will not work and the recipient may suffer effects of mild illness but will recover completely. No immunity will be developed, so if the first attempt is a failure, please contact the magician for a second bottle and repeat dosage at the next opportunity.

Additional disclaimer- be the recipient protected by the Christ, dosages will continue to be without success.

If medication does not bring the results satisfactory, absolutely no refunds will be given under any circumstances.

"What a con," said Plate. "If you believe this nonsense and you give this to somebody and they happen to die, then you think you've killed them. If they don't die, well, you just did not have a hate that was strong enough or they were protected by their faith or something beyond any control. So either way you ultimately feel good about the product."

"So Amelia really thought she had killed both Frenel and Clip?"

"Who knows? Her written confession to Reverend Skrale was more about other things she felt guilty for. She just mentioned them in passing."

"Legally, what was she guilty of?"

"Well, just giving somebody a potion and wishing them dead is certainly not a crime. Probably conspiring with the doctor to falsify medical records could conjure up a charge or two. If she had not died when she did."

"You wouldn't charge a 94-year-old woman?"

"Certainly I would."

"You think because of all the loopholes, the potion was a scam from beginning to end, with no basis in truth?" asked Daphne.

"Obviously."

"Yes, you may be right," agreed Daphne. "There's no way after a couple of weeks you are still going to want to kill somebody, if you think you've tried to poison them and it didn't work."

"Why not?"

"Well, it would be like a failed execution. Like when they try to kill you on death row and it fails, it's an automatic stay of execution."

"That's in the movies. If they try the first time on death row and it fails, they keep trying until they succeed."

"Really?"

"Really. The death medication, whatever it was, had to have been a total swindle. Autopsies were conducted on everyone. Clip died from the fall. Frenel and Amelia died of natural causes."

"I don't know," said Daphne, facing the truth about death row with some dismay. "We don't know what the herbs were. 'Strength depends upon the force of hatred.' How do we know that doesn't work, that our evil thoughts towards one another don't somehow do both us, and those we target, physical harm in the long run? That is if we're not protected by Christ like it says."

"See the problem? Are all Christians immune or just those in good standing?"

"Maybe the mental state of the mind of the potential victim is as important as the state of mind as the poisoner."

"It wasn't poison!"

Plate paused, as Daphne narrowed her eyes at him. He changed his tone of voice and avoided her gaze as he asked the next question cautiously.

"How do you view the inner workings of the human mind?"

"What?" Daphne's eyes widened with confusion and mild alarm. Whenever Plate began such intellectual conversations, she felt at a disadvantage. She was beginning to think she was going to need to keep the transcript of her college grades in her purse so she could whip them out whenever she needed to prove her cognitive capacity.

"I see the inner workings of the mind as sort of a miniature computer," said Plate. "You know, memories are like files, you can call them up at various times when you need them. Then there are the commands. You give your brain commands just like you give a computer commands."

"Hmm. I can see your analogy. I don't think I quite see the human mind that way."

"Then how do you see the mind? How do you think it functions?"

"I think I see it in sections," said Daphne, as if she had given the matter great thought in the past. When she had actually never even considered it before.

"What kind of sections?"

Daphne thought rapidly.

"Well. Let's say there's a section for love. Maybe a section for business," she said, watching Plate closely for reaction to the opening of her new theory. He was just looking at her with interest, waiting for her to continue. "And I suppose a section for physical instincts, you know, eating and such. And maybe a section for appearance."

"Appearance?"

"Appearance. Correct." Daphne was calculating hard. She wanted her theory of the mind to sound just as sophisticated as Plate's did, even if she was making it up as she went along.

"So how are all the sections of the mind connected?" Plate asked, taking her theory seriously.

"Well," said Daphne. "Like they say. With neurotransmitters. And let's say one section feels a- a wave of some type of emotion- to all the sections, and the sections either accept or reject that emotion. Same with knowledge- facts. New information."

"I see," said Plate, trying to picture this. "How do you define the sections?"

"The sections are like different, the way colors are different."

"You mean they are different colors?"

"No no. You're making it too simplistic. Just like colors on a continuum. You know, red fades into pink, yellow transforms into orange and so forth. The mind being so complicated, there's millions of these transitions going on all the time."

"Oh," said Plate.

She's a deeper thinker than I thought she was, he thought silently. He automatically started trying to reconcile his computer mind theory with her section mind theory. His head began to swim a little bit.

"I don't know why I said Destiny that day in the York foyer when I saw you there. In my mind I was saying Daphne, but it came out Destiny." Plate suddenly offered this explanation although Daphne had never mentioned it. "It was not that I didn't remember your name, believe me. I do apologize."

"That's okay," said Daphne, with an air of unconcern. She thought, *you don't know it, but it was because instead of saying my name, you were reading my mind...*

Chapter 96

"So she drank from the witch's potion and wished herself dead and died that night," said Daphne dramatically.

"She was 94!"

Pizza temporarily abandoned on the coffee table, Plate had put his arm around Daphne and she had snuggled close to him. Her cat had joined them and they had all sat silently on the sofa for several minutes. During this interlude, Plate let his mind rest while Daphne allowed her imagination to explore.

The cat had been dozing but sprang up at Daphne's words.

"A deadly silent potion of herbs! Black magic from deep in the forests of East Texas! Recipes going back generations."

"My family's from East Texas. There's no such black magic. That's hogwash. Most people are good Baptists. Some other Christian denominations..."

"For generations the voodoo witches have roamed the swamps!" Sitting up, Daphne widened her eyes as much as possible and made a sweeping round gesture with her arm, palm facing upward.

"That's Louisiana. And it is hard to roam a swamp."

"No matter. They have brooms, remember? And you think witches respect state lines?" Daphne dropped her arm and returned to a normal posture.

"Will you shut up? That's enough nonsense." Plate reached for another slice of pizza.

"Okay, so the herb potion in the bottle was not poison?"

"Definitely not. Harmless stuff, you can buy it all in the grocery stores these days."

"However," Daphne said more seriously and shook her finger at him. "The instructions say it is the hatred and intention of the administrator of the potion that causes the potion to kill. There could be something to that. After all, we now know how detrimental stress can be."

"Yeah, I've heard. I don't care if it is supposedly scientific. That stress can kill is bull. Also sounds like black magic to me."

"Okay, so suppose for a moment, keep an open mind, that there is some truth in there somewhere. Our hatred, our hostile thoughts to one another somehow does some harm. And you said the ingredients for the potion could make you a little sick?"

"They might cause a little nausea, stomach upset, depending on how sensitive you are to various herbs and spices. An overdose of anything can harm you, but Amelia only used tiny drops of the stuff. She only had a tiny bottle," Plate said.

"Maybe it replenished itself like magic."

"Daphne!"

"Okay, okay, let's suppose, just suppose there is some type of combination that works in some way we don't understand."

"It still would be impossible to prove in a court of law. There might be some law against giving somebody some active medication without their knowledge. But even if, coincidentally, they died shortly after of natural causes, it would not be murder."

"I guess what's bothering me is that nothing explains why the Reverend Frenel died."

"I'm not following."

"Well, the death instructions say the potion only works when combined with sufficient evil intent. But apparently, Frenel drank the potion intended for Apixza or Wynter. You see?"

"I see the death instructions were a clever work of fiction, designed to fetch a high price for common ordinary herbs."

"When she prepared the dose Frenel took, Amelia's evil intent was actually directed at Clip or Stark, but it was Frenel who died. If it was not the hatred that was the deciding factor, doesn't that prove there might be something poisonous in the potion?"

"That proves that people die of natural causes. Frenel died of heart disease. The autopsy showed no contributing factors, herbs, drugs or otherwise," Plate reminded her.

"Nevertheless, I think there is some truth to the idea that our hostile thoughts directed against each other can cause harm."

"Yes, that's called a fight, conflict. Sometimes shots are fired. Wars started."

"No. No, I mean physical illness, at least stress induced. Even if we're unaware of the hostility or it's not overt. You know, bad vibes, we used to say. In the seventies. In high school."

"Nonsense," said Plate, running out of countering comments.

"And, likewise, the reverse is true," Daphne concluded, ignoring his comment. "Our good thoughts, loving thoughts, prayers, can protect us, can make us feel better. You don't think that's nonsense do you?"

Plate shook his head grudgingly. "No."

"You got the death potion in the cookies. And all it did was put you to sleep. Stark Wynter wasn't harmed either. But Reverend Frenel died by accident after eating Clip's cookies. And then after getting his dose, Clip jumped-"

"Reverend Frenel died of heart disease. Clip was unbalanced. You don't know that I got anything other than some harmless relaxing herbs."

"Maybe. Maybe God protected you."

"As a police officer, I petition God to protect me all the time."

"See. I'm right. I knew it. You do have some sense."

"Can we change the subject? I think your cat wants out." The kitty had jumped up on the back of the couch and was meowing loudly.

"No, she's just being a pest because I'm not giving her my undivided attention. Is there any of that potion left? A little might keep her quiet."

"What am I going to do about you?"

"Well, I like movies, going out to eat..."

"That's not what I mean."

"What do you mean?"

"Well for one thing, there is the possibility of prosecuting you for forgery."

"I don't have any idea what you're talking about." Daphne stood up, protectively grabbed the cat and hugged it tightly. It yelped in protest, jumped out of her arms, and ran down the hall.

"The authorization from Amelia Mattworks giving Corina French permission to reside with you was a total complete fabrication."

"I don't see how you could say that."

"She would never have used such a modern word. She would have written 'Miss'. That's where you messed up. And all that elaborate calligraphy. She printed her 'confession' in simple block letters. You wrote that note."

"It is a moot point. And she might have used 'Ms.' for all you know. Just because she was old, did not mean she did not keep up with the times in some ways."

"It was a crime," Plate insisted.

"No, it wasn't. You now know the note was completely unnecessary. It was just a subterfuge. Corina did not have a legal guardian under the law. She was married. It was necessary at the time for everybody to think she still needed a legal guardian. That note put your mind at ease. It saved you a lot of stress. You should thank me."

"Speaking of stress, I need sleep at night to avoid it better during the day. It is getting late. I need to go home."

"Your apartment complex is just a few moments away. It is still early."

"But I have to go back to the station and pick up my personal car. I cannot take the patrol car to the apartment complex."

"Police department rules?"

"No, Sand Waves Apartment Complex rules. No service vehicles of any kind in the parking lot or garage."

"I should have known. Anyone in this neighborhood who drives a service vehicle has to hide it in their garage, slip it in and out during the dark so they don't get reported," Daphne said.

"That's the rules here. Nobody is forced to live here."

"Yet Edward York had an abortionist in his back yard. He may have not known it, but someone had to look the other way. The postman if no one else…"

"That's behind the gates. That's a different world."

"All those limousine drivers. Bringing in the abortion patients weren't they? Edward York was blind."

"We don't know that. And no one says they are not blind behind the gates."

"Yet our wants and desires are much the same as the people

who live there. And we face the same dilemmas."

"All I can say is the case would have been very different if abortion was still illegal. Which, in my opinion, it should be."

"I've given the matter more thought," said Daphne. "I think it is a great irony. What you said about the science being clear."

"And?" Plate felt a little speck of pride that she should speak so seriously with him about something so complex. He delayed his plan to leave. "It is murder, right?"

"It is certainly killing. The irony is that for many years there were all these theories about when life began. I remember hearing as a kid it was when the baby kicked."

"I've heard that too, some religious teachings were- that was when the soul entered the baby's body. Or something like that."

"And for hundreds of years abortion was illegal and there was uncertainty. Now, as you said, the science is clear. But now it is legal."

"Legal murder. An inconvenience. Abortion is designed to get rid of inconvenient children. Forget their names and look at the motivations. One person considers an abortion because the child might have been fathered by a man she was leaving behind. Another wants a child to go away because it might trigger a revelation of a great secret. Someone wants to foster an abortion to protect a career. Someone does not want a sick child. Someone doesn't want child of a different race."

"You cannot put Doreen Darbell in the same category. She faced ruination in the 1950s," Daphne protested, feeling Plate was being a little preachy.

"This is the 1980s." Plate pointed out. "We have perspective."

"And I still have mixed feelings. You have the situations like Tamica and her lost adolescent love. Suppress love between teenagers and you risk their lives turning out like Tamica's. Encourage it and, well, suppose it is not true love?"

"And most of the time it is not. Short of abstaining from relations, there is always the danger of unwanted pregnancies."

"Don't be self-righteous. That's why I never have-" Daphne broke off unexpectedly, as if she had said too much.

"Never have what?"

"Never have been, uh,-." She stood up and looked down the hall. "You're right. It is getting late. I do need to feed my cat. Kitty! Kitty!"

Plate looked at her in surprise. *As lovely as she is, as at ease as she is with me alone with her in her house, could it be possible…?*

"I don't want to rush you off," Daphne was saying as she picked up his jacket and handed it to him.

"I thought insurance agents didn't get up early."

"No, I don't. But you have to, don't you? You just said-"

"Yes, I do."

Something uncomfortable had come between them. They both looked down at the floor.

"I'm to see you next month about insurance," he said.

"Insurance. Yes."

"That's just a few days away."

"Yes."

"Maybe, before then, we could, I don't know."

"Go to the movies?" Daphne raised her head at the same time he did. The awkwardness between them vanished.

The cat bounded back into the den and then appeared confused by Daphne's lack of response to its actions.

"Yes," he said. "I'll call you tomorrow."

He saw her visibly relax. She reached down and picked up the cat which had prostrated itself before her. After stroking it a moment, she deposited it gently on the couch. It danced in a small circle, than curled up, paws underneath.

I know what to do now, Plate thought as he watched the gymnastics of the feline. *I'll court her. Just as if we were closer to 20 than closer to 30. I'll court her as if we were both still very young…*

As they walked outside to his car, Plate took Daphne's hand. Before letting go to open his car door, he raised her fingers to his lips and bowed slightly as he kissed her hand. She laughed with delight.

"It'll be fun," he said.

Chapter 97

Alone later than night, back at his apartment, Plate picked up the science fiction novel that he still had not yet finished. Beside it was the VCR tape sent from the Hollywood police, containing a video inventory of Stark Wynter's chauffeur Burress' apartment. He hesitated a moment before choosing between the two. After all, the case was over. There was nothing more to be learned. There was nothing more to do.

Maybe this is something else I can show Daphne when I next see her, he thought.

He turned on the TV, put it on channel 3 and pushed the VCR tape into the machine.

There was no sound. He sat back on the couch and propped his feet on the coffee table. And started the tape with his remote control

He flipped open the science fiction book as the tape silently scanned the humble apartment of the driver. Dilapidated furnishings clashed with crisp uniforms hanging on door hooks and an exquisite collection of blown glass inside a curio case. The photographer had scanned the case slowly, apparently fascinated by the blown glass ornaments, pianos, ships, musical instruments. And the photographer also had slowed down when filming the objects on top of the curio.

Plate put the book back down, leaned forward and stared closely at the images on the TV.

A short wide curio with a big flat top, the piece of furniture was covered with framed photographs. Prominent was a photograph of Tamica French as a young girl in Hollywood in the 1970s. She was standing with Stark Wynter and several other movie stars, all dressed in formal gowns and tuxedos. It was a formal professional shot. Near it though smaller, a snapshot of Tamica and Stark with a third person, an obviously young and handsome Burress, wearing a chauffeur's uniform. It and most of the other photographs were faded, except for two.

One was an 8-by-10 enlargement of Corina standing in front of the mirror in the foyer at the York mansion on the day of Tamica's funeral. The reflection in the mirror showed the ill, frail Burress holding the camera a little to the side so his face, reflected, would show. Marred by the flash in the glass, the picture was nonetheless bright and crisp in the sections that had successfully processed. The last was a framed composite of two photographs spliced together. One was Corina, a cropped close-up taken from the same photograph in front of the mirror. The other was the driver as an even younger man, a boy almost, his face fair and his hair blonde. This picture was faded compared to the one beside it. But the two faces, side-by-side, were cropped to be comparatively the same size.

Plate put the science fiction book back down. The inventive technology of the VCR was that it allowed the viewer to pause the tape whenever they needed and take a good long look. Plate held the side-by-side composite in the pause mode for the longest time period it would stay.

The resemblance was unmistakable.

After viewing the tape, Plate pulled out a thin flat large hard cover book accompanied by a note that the Hollywood police had sent along with the VCR tape.

"There is some indication that this individual was somewhat obsessed with Ms. Mattworks' granddaughter," a member of the Hollywood force had written. "It appears from the notation and drawings inside this yearbook, that it was actually the property of Tamica French Cathare. We can only surmise the individual, who had been under investigation before his death, somehow swiped it or possibly purchased it at some resale shop if Mrs. Cathare voluntarily disposed of it. Since the provenance cannot be established, and the deceased had no claimants to his estate, with the permission of his employer, Mr. Stark Wynter, who claimed his body for burial, we are unofficially returning it to Texas in anticipation you will deliver it to Mrs. Cathare's daughter."

Plate flipped open the thin yearbook, from a private Catholic junior high school, thinking how proud he was there were honest police in the world. On one of the first pages, there was a full size photo of Tamica. 'Homecoming Queen, Tamica French', the caption read. Like the celebrity she almost was, she had scrawled her signature over her own photo in the book.

349

This would fetch quite a bit of money on the collectibles' market, right after these deaths, he thought, *with this much writing and sketching in Tamica's hand. They could have just slipped away with this and no one would ever have known.*

He flipped through the book to Tamica's regular school picture among all the other students' photos lined up in alphabetical order. In the middle, on the top row of little square black and white photographs, was a photo labeled with her name in line with all the other students on the page. Under the pictures were notations of activities and interests of each student. Under Tamica's were the words *'choir, jazz band, acting'*.

Plate stared at Tamica's exquisite adolescent features for a moment before looking at the other students surrounding her.

Immediately to the left of her photo was one of a blonde boy. He had longish hair and a sweet friendly smile. His activities list was identical to Tamica's. This boy had a heart drawn around him in the same hand, in the same ink in which Tamica had doodled and scribbled in the front of the book.

'Love U 4ever', she had written above his head.

Plate contemplated the name under the boy's photo with wonder.

'Burress Franch', it read.

Published by Ruskras Corner

By Deborah DR Kralich-
Historical Fiction-
The Mystery of the Missing Persons

Historical Mystery Fiction-
Murder as the Organist Plays
The Mystique Woven in Our Land
Interlude of Carelessness

Lt. Sinclair Plate Mystery Series- 1980s era
An Innovative Murder for the Season
The Ruler of the Toys
A Kaleidoscope of Masquerades
The Unknown Puppeteer
Poised Like a Knife

Poetry
I Lift Up My Heart

By Carl S Kralich

Young Adult Science Fiction
3748 A.D The Return of the Cat
Auction of Worlds